TOUGH
⫾⫾⫾⫾⫾JUSTICE

TOUGH JUSTICE

TEE O'FALLON

Entangled Publishing, LLC
10940 S Parker Road
Suite 327
Parker, CO 80134
Visit our website at www.entangledpublishing.com.

Amara is an imprint of Entangled Publishing, LLC.

Edited by Heather Howland
Cover design by LJ Anderson, Mayhem Cover Creations
Model photography by Wander Aguiar,
background art stokkete/Depositphotos and
mathias_berlin/Depositphotos
Interior design by Toni Kerr

Print ISBN 978-1-64937-143-0
ebook ISBN 978-1-64937-165-2

Manufactured in the United States of America

First Edition April 2022

AMARA

ALSO BY TEE O'FALLON

PROLOGUE

As if the day couldn't suck any worse. His parents were home. *Both* of them.

Tyler pushed open the front door and wrinkled his nose. The smell of fish stunk up the air. His mom didn't care how much he hated fish. *Brain food*, she called it. Yeah, that would really bring his grades up. It wasn't that he couldn't do the math or dissect a frog or whatever. He just didn't care.

He hefted the duffle over his shoulder, grimacing when the heavy bag scraped noisily against the door. If he didn't want to be interrogated about school or practice or whatever else they decided he'd done wrong now, he was going to have to make it upstairs undetected. He slipped past the living room where his dad sat in his favorite leather recliner, drinking a beer and watching the news, then headed up the stairs.

When he hit the top step, the floor creaked, and he cringed. Holding his breath, Tyler waited for his dad to bellow up the stairs. Sweat beaded on his upper lip. If his dad realized he was home, he'd insist on talking about how practice was going. And if he got Tyler talking, he'd know something was up. His mom might be clueless, but his dad always seemed to know *everything*.

He stood there, listening to the sounds of his mom banging around pots and pans in the kitchen, and felt… empty.

His chest, his entire body, felt hollowed out, like the pumpkins he and his dad carved when he was a kid. Every minute. Every hour. Every day of his life, and nothing helped. Not even the beer he'd been swiping from his dad's stash. Sure, he felt great for the first twenty minutes, but then the high wore off and left him feeling even worse.

Depression. Social anxiety. Chronic stress. Terms the shrink had used to describe what was happening in his head. He could still remember that crappy day. He'd broken down in front of Mrs. Finelli, the guidance counselor. Fuck, he'd even *cried*, and he just couldn't seem to stop. Talk about embarrassing. The high school quarterback shouldn't be crying. If Coach or any of his teammates ever found out… *Shit*.

Naturally, Mrs. Finelli had ratted him out to his parents, and he'd been forced to go to Dr. Vernon. That hadn't done any good. Dr. Vernon couldn't tell him why he felt empty all the time and had for as long as he could remember. Dr. Vernon prescribed an antidepressant, but the only thing it did was make his mouth dry. His brain was just wired differently. His parents didn't know it, but he'd stopped taking the pills only days after they'd been prescribed.

No one could help him, so he was going to help himself. Or at least try.

Seconds ticked by, and all he heard downstairs was the TV blaring out something about driving carefully because schools were back in session. He let a full minute go by, soaking in the sounds, hoping to feel *something*, before giving up and continuing down the hall.

When he made it to his bedroom, he locked the door and dropped his bag on the floor. A huge breath of relief gushed from his lungs.

Twenty bucks was all it had taken, snagged from his mother's purse when she wasn't looking. Now, the stuff was burning a hole in his pocket. It might not make him happy, but it was supposed to help him relax and forget about all the shit that was bugging him. Most importantly, it would make him not care.

He tugged the small plastic bag from his pocket, dropped it on his bedside table, and stared at it. Part of him was a little scared. Aside from a few hits of pot here and there, he'd never done any drugs before. The only thing pot ever did was give him the munchies, and if he started reeking of the stuff, everyone would know. His parents. His coach. Everyone.

Gray death had no smell. It was supposed to be strong and kick in fast. He'd been looking to buy heroin, but the guy he bought this from said it was better, like supercharged heroin. He couldn't wait to disappear into a world where no one would yell at him about how much his grades sucked, force him to eat fish, or make him cry in front of the school guidance counselor. And the stress. The stress was killing him.

He dragged a hand down his face. Being the high school hero should have been a dream come true. At first, maybe it was. Now, the pressure was unbearable. Win, win, win. If they won, it was on him. If they lost, that would be on him, too, only a thousand times more. If he couldn't find a way to escape, he'd go freaking nuts. He just wanted to be alone. To just...*be*.

Tyler sat on the edge of the bed and opened the side table drawer, pulling out the straw he'd stashed there earlier. He untied the baggie and dumped the contents on the table. It didn't look anything like what he'd expected. Gray powder, like cement before you add water. He frowned at how boring it looked. *This stuff had better be worth it.*

Using a razor blade he'd swiped from his dad's workshop, he separated out two thin lines of powder. Since he'd never done anything stronger than beer and pot, he didn't know if he was doing it right, but this was what the scary-looking guy who'd sold it to him said to do.

With slightly shaking fingers, he gripped the straw, leaned down, and snorted an entire line into his left nostril. He sniffed, wiping some of the residue with the back of his hand. Then he did the same with the other line and snorted it into his right nostril. Less than a minute later, warmth infused his body, as if someone had wrapped a thick, cushiony blanket around his very soul.

Weightlessness was the only way to describe what happened next. Like he was bobbing up and down in a sea of air. The world and all the stress, anxiety, and sadness began melting away. *This* was the euphoria he'd been promised. Totally worth it. Man, he should have tried gray death sooner.

His lips began to tingle, the same way they had the first time he'd kissed the head cheerleader, Melinda Burke, behind the bleachers after practice one day. He lay down on his bed and sighed, peacefully, for the first time in what seemed like years. Then he smiled and closed his eyes. Forever.

CHAPTER ONE

"MOS arriving now!" one of the nurses called out from the hospital's emergency room desk.

Dr. Tori Sampson stood just outside ER 2, waiting for the ambulance to roll in with a "member of service," either a police officer, firefighter, or EMS injured on duty.

Seconds later, a large man wearing black cargo pants, a black shirt, and a gun strapped to his thigh, along with Aiko, one of the nurses who'd been waiting curbside to assist, rushed a stretcher through the ER doors. A paramedic held a bag-valve mask over the patient's mouth and nose, squeezing the bag, while another paramedic administered walking chest compressions as he kept pace with the stretcher. More uniformed officers crowded in behind them.

"In here." Tori pointed to ER 2, inside of which two other nurses and a respiratory therapist were already waiting.

They'd gotten the call from the paramedics while they'd been en route to the hospital. All Tori knew at this point was that the officer had been exposed to something highly toxic and was in cardiac arrest.

"Suzie, I need you," she called to her friend. To the other nurse behind the desk, she ordered calmly, "Call Dr. Barnett."

"Move aside, please." Suzie pushed through the throng of walking, talking testosterone. "We'll take it from here."

At only five-three, Suzie somehow managed to take control of the situation and helped roll the stretcher the rest of the way into ER 2.

Knowing how tightknit cops were, Tori closed the door in the men's faces. If she didn't, they'd be hovering like a swarm of bees. *Armed* bees.

Between herself, the two paramedics, the cop who'd come with them, four nurses, and Ashanti, the respiratory therapist, the small room was packed.

"Get him on the bed," Tori ordered, standing back to give the paramedics room to work. "What do we have?" she asked.

The cop assisted the paramedics in transferring the patient to the ER stretcher. That's when she noticed the embroidered words on the cop's shirt: DEA K-9 Unit. *Wonderful.* It just *had* to be DEA agents. The bane of her family's existence.

"Patient is thirty-five years old, found down with suspected opioid exposure during a raid. He was in respiratory arrest when we arrived on scene. This guy," the paramedic said, nodding to the cop, "was giving him mouth to mouth. We tubed him." Again, he nodded to the cop. "He gave him eight milligrams intranasal Narcan. We gave him another two. He went into VTAC arrest during transport. We've been doing compressions, gave him two epis, three hundred milligrams of amiodarone, and three shocks. The last was two minutes ago. On our monitor, he's still in VTAC. Our last rhythm check was PEA."

Pulseless electrical activity. Damn. He still wasn't responding. "How long has he been in VTAC?" Tori asked.

"About eight minutes."

"Hook him up to our monitor, start another line, and get the auto-compressor on him." She watched the flurry of activity as Suzie quickly started another IV line, while the other nurses switched the heart leads to the ER's cardiac monitor and moved to position the chest compression system over the patient's chest. "Stand back," she ordered the cop. As if the room wasn't tight enough with all the hospital personnel, now she had to contend with this giant K-9 cop getting in her way. "Please, go to the waiting room."

Finally, he backed away but didn't leave the room. Right now, she didn't have time to deal with him.

While the auto-compressor was positioned and turned on, the respiratory therapist took over for the paramedic squeezing the bag-valve mask.

"Give him another milligram of epi." Tori moved over to give one of the nurses room to adjust the auto-compressor and bumped into something solid and unmoving. Correction, some*one* solid and unmoving. The damned cop. Hadn't she told him to get lost?

Since he was still here… "What exactly was he exposed to?" she asked him. Not that it made a difference in her treatment protocol, but she wanted to confirm her suspicions.

"I don't know *exactly*," the cop bit out. "Some kind of opioid."

"Opioids? Where are his clothes?" The patient was in his underwear, and she didn't want hospital staff exposed to any opioid residue.

"Bagged," the cop said.

"A bad batch of something's going around," one of the paramedics said. "We've been averaging eight ODs a day in our area alone this week. And those are just the ones we know about, let alone hung on long enough for us to get there. We're going through naloxone like it's water."

Tori held back a few choice expletives. This particular opioid concoction was killing people left and right. Apparently even the DEA wasn't immune. She suspected this agent had been exposed to the same thing. The detailed labs she'd been requesting on her OD patients would confirm it.

"His capnography just jumped," Ashanti said.

"Stop the compressor, and check the rhythm." Keeping her eyes fastened on the monitor, Tori checked for a pulse at the man's carotid.

C'mon. Beat, goddammit. Her own heart seemed to slow as she waited for a telltale blip.

The green line on the cardiac monitor jumped, and she felt a weak pulse beneath her fingers. "There you go. Hang in there."

A collective sigh came from everyone in the room, including her. "Sinus rhythm." Now to get him breathing on his own. "How much naloxone do we have in this room?"

"One vial." Suzie tore the wrapper off another syringe. She popped the cap and drew out the remaining naloxone.

"Push another point-five milligrams, then check Room 4 for more. Hit up the pharmacy if you have to." Because if this agent was exposed to the same opioid cocktail she suspected he was they'd need a lot more naloxone. "And page Dr. Barnett. Tell him we have another one, and I need his help." Her friend, Wil, had an inherent understanding of just what treatments worked best on OD patients, especially the bad ones. Like this one. With that much naloxone, he should have responded and been breathing on his own by now.

Suzie administered the next dose of naloxone then hustled from the room.

Tori touched the man's cheek. "Cold and clammy," she muttered then pushed up one of his eyelids. "Pinpoint pupils." All classic symptoms of an overdose. Still examining her patient, she asked the paramedics, "How long wasn't he breathing on his own?" When no one answered, she looked up to find them watching the K-9 cop, who was grinding his jaw so hard the muscles in his lean cheeks rippled and flexed.

"Do *you* have any idea how long he wasn't breathing?" she asked.

"No," he gritted out.

"No?" She glared at the agent—A. Decker, according to the tag on his shirt. In addition to him, there had to be a dozen other cops and DEA agents in the waiting room. "He's one of your own. How could you not *know*?"

"We got separated," he growled.

"Did he inhale it, or just touch it?" She'd read that a police officer in Pennsylvania had brushed some kind of opioid powder off his hand then passed out a few minutes later.

"I don't know." His brows lowered as he watched her with something akin to suspicion.

What he had to be suspicious of *her* for, she didn't know.

Suzie ran back in, holding a full box of vials. "Got it."

"Push another point-five milligrams," she ordered then watched Suzie inject it into the IV.

The man's pulse grew stronger, as did his blood pressure. His chest began rising and falling on its own. "Spontaneous ventilation."

Tori blew out a breath. Another overdose snatched from the clutches of the Grim Reaper himself.

She turned back to the agent. "He's stable, but since we don't know how long he wasn't breathing, we won't know for a while if there was any hypoxic brain damage. We'll monitor him until he wakes up. For now, you can go to the waiting room with your colleagues, and I'll be out later to give you an update."

Decker's glower darkened as he crossed powerfully muscled arms over his broad chest. "I'm not going anywhere."

Tori clamped her jaw together. "I really don't have time for this. What I need is for you to leave my ER." She turned back to her patient, expecting to hear the agent's size twelve shit-kicker boots clomping on the tile floor as he left the room. She didn't. What she *did* hear was the man's impatient exhale.

Slowly, she turned and parked her hands on her hips. "Agent Decker, I'm only going to say this one more time. Get. Out."

This time, *he* clamped *his* jaw. "Forget it, doc. I'm not leaving."

She eyed the man from head to toe. He was about six-two or more, seemingly made of solid muscle and probably weighed in at well over two hundred pounds. She, on the other hand, was five-four and around one hundred twenty-five pounds. Manhandling him out the door was a pipe dream. "Why the hell not?" she countered.

His nostrils flared as he crossed his arms. "It's protocol. We don't *ever* leave one of our own unconscious and unattended in a hospital."

"He's in the safest place he could possibly be. This is one of the best medical facilities in the state of Colorado. I assure you he's safe here."

His eyes narrowed. "Maybe he is. Maybe he isn't."

"What's that supposed to mean?" She fisted the hands already on her hips. For some reason, this guy didn't trust her. Not that she cared one bit whether anyone in the heavy-handed DEA did. *She* didn't trust *him*.

"You're a *doctor*, aren't you?" He spat out her profession as if it tasted badly rolling off his tongue. "Not all doctors know what they're doing."

"Newsflash, tough guy. *I* do. I took an oath to save people, and I'll do everything in my power to make sure your friend lives." Regardless of the fact that he worked for the DEA—the agency responsible for making her family's life a living hell. "Perhaps you'd care to explain what you're so concerned about."

"I don't trust doctors. I want to make sure you don't give him something he doesn't need."

"Doesn't *need*?" She shook her head in disbelief, still not understanding what this guy's problem was. "If he needs something, I'll give it to him. If he doesn't, I won't. Giving patients meds they don't need isn't something we do here."

Dark eyes narrowed farther, as if he were contemplating her words and not sure whether to believe her. "Okay," he said finally. "As long as you're the only doctor making that decision for him. Promise me."

Ah, the irony. If it weren't for the DEA, her life could

have been so different. Maybe her mother would still be alive today. "Fine, I promise," she capitulated with a discerned edge to her voice that she couldn't hold back.

Tori's friend and fellow ER doctor, Wil Barnett, strode through the doors, followed by David, the orderly whose assistance she'd needed an hour ago on another case. David stood off to the side, averting his gaze as if he was afraid to look at her.

Wil eyed Agent Decker curiously. He often joked that guys in law enforcement were all macho men who needed big guns to make up for having small genitalia. "Can I ask what you're doing here?"

"Standing guard," the agent said. Backing up his words, Agent Decker stood his ground, holding Wil's amused gaze without flinching. Not that she was surprised. In addition to the gun on the agent's belt, he probably had at least sixty pounds on her friend.

"Against what?" Wil asked, brushing past him.

"You wouldn't understand," Agent Decker said with a deadly glint in his eye as he followed Wil's every move like a tiger ready to attack.

"Probably not," Wil conceded with an arched brow.

Exhaustion settled over Tori like an angry storm cloud. She was mentally exhausted from treating overdose victims. The last few months had been like a revolving door in the ER, but this week was shaping up to be a whole new level of chaos.

The most recent victim, Tyler, was a seventeen-year-old boy on life support. That one had hit her the hardest. Unlike this DEA agent, Tyler's parents didn't find him until it was too late. He wasn't breathing, and hypoxic brain injury had already set in. Medically speaking, the boy's brain was dead. His parents were grappling with the traumatic decision to take their son off life support.

She checked her patient's vitals one more time. "He's doing well," she said, hoping to reassure Agent Decker sufficiently to get him out of the ER. "We'll know more when he wakes up."

Beneath his crossed arms, the agent's knuckles whitened.

Okay, so he wasn't going to take her hint to leave.

She had to crane her neck to look up at him. A pair of intense, dark brown eyes that held zero warmth stared down at her. If he thought for one second that his glowering cop-look would intimidate her, he was about to be sadly mistaken.

Controlling everything that happened in the ER was paramount. Lives depended on everyone doing things by the book and according to protocol. Having a cop the size of a linebacker taking up critical space in the room was unacceptable. "I gave you my word. I'll watch over him personally, but I want something from you in return."

"What?" he growled.

"I want you out of here. *Now*."

Agent Decker took another deep breath, and for a moment she didn't think he would obey. Finally, he surprised her by executing a military-precision about-face and heading for the door.

"Wait." A last-minute spurt of compassion took root, along with a sprinkling of guilt over her unprofessional bitchiness toward the man. DEA or not, he obviously cared for his friend, and she respected that. She deposited her gloves and mask in the biohazard bin then escorted him to the waiting room doors. "I can't make any guarantees, but your friend really is responding well to the naloxone."

When he turned and locked gazes with her, her mouth went just a teensy, weensy bit dry.

In the examining room, she'd been concentrating on her patient, then she'd been so annoyed with Agent Decker that she hadn't really *seen* him. There was no denying he brought out the fifty shades of animosity, but one thing was for certain: with his chiseled jawline, slightly cleft chin, and sexy as all-get-out five o'clock shadow, the man was about as handsome as it got. Hard not to admire his muscular physique, either. He must spend all his free time in a gym, lifting barbells and dumbbells and whatever other bells made a man's body that way.

He closed his eyes, as if reciting a mental prayer. "Thanks, Doc."

The last thing she wanted was gratitude from the DEA. The short-lived attempt to rein in her internal bitch flew out the window as the past came roaring back in a rush of emotion. Especially the distraught look on her dad's face that fateful day.

"Don't thank me," she bit out. "I'm just doing my job. Maybe if the great and powerful DEA did *its* job, drugs wouldn't be sold on every street corner in Denver, and Colorado's opioid crisis wouldn't be spiraling out of control. Your friend is the third opioid overdose I've treated today, and the tenth this week. Three of those patients died. And that's just on my shifts. I can't speak to what happens when I'm not here or how many are dying before they even get to the hospital." She blew out a breath and grappled for a calm she didn't feel. "Whatever just hit the streets could be the beginning of something really scary, and there's nothing I can do to stop it. But *you* can."

He opened his mouth to say something, but she cut him off. "And another thing." She jabbed a finger at him. "This is *my* castle, not the DEA's. If you ever come into my ER again, I'll have you thrown out on your muscled ass."

CHAPTER TWO

Deck and Thor strode through the hospital's main entrance door, grateful for the air conditioning. Being situated on an upland desert, the Denver climate was dry, but it didn't matter. Even in September, if you were out in the sun, it was damn hot.

All heads in the lobby turned to stare, some backing away. Deck was used to it. At nearly eighty pounds, his Belgian Malinois K-9, Thor, was big, even for a male, and commanded attention everywhere they went. Not even the DEA K-9 vest designed specifically for public events put people at ease. On both sides of the vest were emblazoned: DEA K-9. Next to that was an embroidered badge, identical to the one on Deck's polo shirt.

"Let's go, boy." He headed for the elevator bank, ignoring the skeptical looks from some of the hospital personnel. Thor was not only a federal agent but a trained therapy dog. After everything his friend had gone through yesterday, he figured Dan could use a little canine therapy.

Most overdose victims could leave the hospital within an hour after recovery. Due to the severity of Dan's OD and the looming possibility of hypoxic brain injury, he'd been kept overnight. This morning, they'd gotten word he'd be released soon. Guess that doctor had kept her word, after all, although for a moment there, he wasn't sure. The second she'd dumped him in the waiting room, he'd done a little checking on her.

Victoria Sampson had been at North Metro for four years. Her friends called her Tori. In other words, *he'd* never be calling her Tori.

Deck had done his best to keep his shit together, then his uber-mistrust of all things medical had reared its ugly head like a three-headed dragon, and he'd let Dr. Sampson have it with both barrels. He *didn't* trust doctors, and it couldn't have hurt to let her know it. It was his subtle-as-a-Sherman tank way of letting her know he'd be keeping an eye on his friend *and* what she prescribed for him. Deep down, he knew not all doctors were bad, just some. The problem was those that were bad could leave a trail of bodies in their wake. Like his sister.

The elevator door opened, although the couple inside hesitated. Courteously, he held Thor back so the couple could get out. Inside the elevator, he pushed the button for the third floor. Seconds later, he and Thor stood outside Dan's room. A child's high-pitched giggle came to his ears, and he hesitated before going in.

Dan had been seconds from dying, and his little boy had nearly lost his father. It never should've happened, but it had. Deck was ready to do whatever it took to make sure there were no repeats of last night.

"Deck, are you gonna stand out there all day, or get your ass in here and kiss my ugly mug?" Dan motioned him inside.

Lisa, Dan's wife, smacked her husband affectionately on the shoulder. "Dan, what did I say to you about cursing in front of Tommy?"

"Sorry, sweetie." Dan gave his wife's hand a squeeze, looking appropriately chastised. "Won't happen again. At least, not today."

Lisa shook her head, laughing.

"Thor!" Five-year-old Tommy Prince slid from the chair beside his father's bed, rushing over and wrapping his little arms around the dog's neck. Thor's tail whipped back and forth as he licked Tommy's ear. "Hi, Deck." Tommy giggled as Thor licked the boy's face.

"Hi, Tommy." Dan's little boy could always make Deck smile. The kid was a mini version of his father but with his mother's blond hair.

"Deck." Lisa rose from the side of the bed to give him a tight hug. "It's good to see you. It's been too long since we've had you over for dinner. As soon as Dan is well enough, we're going to have a big barbecue at our house."

"Can Thor come?" Tommy's big blue eyes widened as he looked hopefully at Deck then to his mother and father.

"Of course Thor can come." Lisa winked at Deck. "Let's go get something to eat while your daddy talks to Deck." Lisa grabbed her purse then practically had to drag little Tommy away from Thor.

When Lisa and Tommy had gone, Deck met Dan's eyes. For a long moment, neither of them said a word, then Dan gave him a sheepish look. "Yesterday sure sucked."

Deck's gut tightened as he recalled the moment he'd found Dan face down, unconscious. "Yeah, it did." In fact, it had more than sucked. It had been one of the worst days of Deck's life. Second only to the day Marianne died.

What should have been a routine warrant on a cocaine dealer had turned into a real shit show. Whatever the guy was dealing in, it wasn't coke.

Dan had gone inside the main house with the rest of the

entry team then headed out back to secure the fence line and passed out cold behind a pile of debris and discarded tires. By the time Deck got to him, he wasn't breathing. Even now, the DEA lab was doing a rush job on the baggies of gray powder they'd seized, along with Dan's clothes. There'd been no visible residue, meaning that whatever Dan had been exposed to was more potent and deadly than anything they'd encountered before in Colorado. As soon as those lab reports were in, he'd compare them to the DEA's database to see if there was a match anywhere else in the country. It might be the first time the DEA had encountered this particular opioid cocktail, but he had a feeling Dr. Sampson's rash of OD deaths was connected, and she was right. This could quickly become a deadly health crisis of mammoth proportions.

Dan tried smiling, but the sentiment didn't fully make it to his eyes. "How'd the rest of the warrant go? Did you get him?"

He nodded, falling heavily into a chair. Thor rested his head on the mattress for Dan to stroke his ears. "We got him, but he's not talking." Just like the last two heroin dealers they'd busted, no one would give up the name of the distributor. They were no closer to shutting down the flood of opioids today than they were yesterday. The only difference was that something new was on the streets, and his friend had nearly died from it.

Maybe that prickly ER doctor was right. Maybe it *was* the DEA's fault that opioid deaths were skyrocketing. He exhaled on a groan. Unusual for a K-9 agent, but Deck had taken point on the last two warrants. *Maybe what happened to Dan was* my *fault.*

"It's not your fault, Deck. Even with protective gear, shit happens."

He shook his head. "We weren't prepared for what happened yesterday, and we never will be. Some of us are trained EMTs, and we all carry small doses of naloxone, but that wasn't enough to get you breathing. You didn't respond until we got you to the hospital."

Voices and the clomp of heavy boots sounded in the corridor. Deck's soon-to-retire boss, Assistant Special Agent in Charge Santiago Rivera, came through the door first, followed by two of Deck's closest friends, ATF Special Agent Brett Tanner and FBI Special Agent Evan McGarry. Like Deck, both were K-9 agents on Denver's Special Ops Task Force.

ASAC Rivera carried a large vase of flowers and set it on the window ledge. "Compliments of Uncle Sam."

"And this," Brett said, balancing a large pizza box in one hand, "is compliments of us." He set the box down on the rolling tray and lifted the lid.

"Figured you'd want something besides Jell-O." Evan took a chair on the other side of the bed.

"You got that right." Dan leaned over, inhaling as he closed his eyes. "I think I love you."

"You should," Brett said. "You don't know what we had to do to smuggle that pizza in here. They've got a real Nurse Ratched sitting at the nurses' station."

Evan grimaced. "She's scarier than some of the guards at Sheridan."

Deck had to agree with Evan. That prison was a real crap hole. "Only one," he said, catching Dan slyly slip Thor a piece of pepperoni. "You're not the one who has to clean up after he eats spicy food."

Thor inhaled the thin circle of pepperoni, barely chewing it before swallowing and licking his lips as if he just ate a rare sirloin steak. All the agents on Denver's SOTF—Special Ops Task Force—loved Thor, but Dan had an especially soft spot for dogs.

"I hate to interrupt the party." ASAC Rivera sat in another chair. "Deck, I read your report, but I wanted to confirm a few things with all of you in person."

Not that his boss needed it, but Deck nodded his approval. He really was going to miss Rivera. The man was the best boss he'd ever worked for.

"We don't need to go over the logistics of the warrant," Rivera continued. "That was all textbook. What I want to talk about is Dan's exposure. Walk me through it in as much detail as possible. Special Agent in Charge Osaka wants changes made to our high-risk warrant protocol, and I want to get your input." Rivera looked around the room at all of them, stopping at Dan. "Dan?"

Dan cleared his throat. "Before I went outside, I did a sweep in the basement where they were bagging the stuff. I felt fine then. Right after I went outside, I took off my mask then started checking out the backyard. I noticed a few specks of what I thought was coke on my shirtsleeve, so I brushed it off. That's the last thing I remember before hitting the deck."

"We think when he brushed it off," Deck said, "he inhaled it. But it couldn't have been very much."

Rivera's brows lowered. "So, this stuff is that dangerous."

"Yup." Brett nodded.

"What about the dogs?" Rivera tipped his head to Thor,

who lay on the floor, gazing lovingly up at Dan in the hopes of another slice of pepperoni. "Do we need to take additional measures to protect the K-9s?"

Deck reached down to scratch his dog's ears. "The latest protocol includes facemasks, booties, and body coverings. A body suit would be too restricting. But we've added a full bath to the protocol after every warrant."

"Good." Rivera nodded. "Aside from keeping our masks on, what else can we do to prevent this from happening again?"

Needing more time before he blurted out what he was thinking, Deck stood and went to the windowsill, leaning back against it. Given his family's less-than-stellar track record with doctors, he couldn't believe what he was about to suggest. "The changes we've been talking about are all defensive moves, and they all makes sense. But I think we need to supplement that defense with a good offense."

"Go on." Rivera began stroking his goatee.

"To start with, we need more field training, and I'm not talking about tactics. The entire SOTF sat through a one-hour training session on treating opioid exposure in the field. We all carry naloxone nasal spray, but the ER doctor who treated Dan yesterday said she's seeing more ODs now than ever and that whatever this new cocktail is, it's not as responsive to naloxone. We need to start tipping the scales in our favor with everything we've got. I've been doing some research, and there are a few studies out there suggesting naloxone auto-injectors are more effective than the intranasal version. We need to get those and get trained on them ASAP."

"I'll shoot an urgent request to HQ." Rivera began

tapping on his phone. "We'll have to set up mandatory training for every DEA agent in the state and every SOTF officer working with us." Rivera kept tapping. "Since this involves needles now, not just spray, I'm telling SAC Osaka that we already have someone in the medical profession lined up as our instructor. In the meantime," he added, looking directly at Deck, "find me someone."

"Yes, sir," Deck replied. Immediately, Dr. Sampson's face flashed before his eyes. He would probably never completely trust doctors—*any* doctor—but in between glaring at him and reaming him a new one, she'd exhibited total command of the situation and knew exactly what was necessary to save Dan's life. She'd make a kick-ass instructor, *and* she had hands-on experience with opioids. If they went through regular channels, they'd wind up with a contractor who probably sat at a desk all day and hadn't seen an overdose in years, if ever.

"What else have you got?" Rivera asked.

"Whatever this stuff is, it's new to Denver," Deck continued. "Last night, I contacted every snitch we've got. A few of them said it's gray death but a whole lot stronger. No one knows who's distributing it or where it's coming from."

Rivera frowned. "Do we know what's in it?"

Deck shook his head. "Not specifically. We've seen it before in other parts of the country, but the formula varies from one batch to the next. As soon as we get the info from our lab, I'll compare it to what we already have in the agency database. Maybe we can narrow down the manufacturer. Remember that gray death case our office had in Pennsylvania? A lot of people died there, too. Maybe whoever was making it there is branching out. Could be a bad batch hit the street. Either way, I'll check the reports and reach out to the Philly case agent."

"That's a good start," Rivera agreed. "But we need to do more, and we need to do it fast. The press and the governor's office are breathing down our necks enough as it is about the opioid crisis. The uptick in cases will make the media see red and turn this into a mass feeding frenzy."

Rivera was right. The DEA was getting slammed and, as the good Dr. Tori Sampson had accused, rightfully so. People were dying at an alarming rate, and if Dan's experience was anything to go by, the situation had the potential to go sideways in a major way. Standard investigative methods weren't working, at least not fast enough. "We can keep putting money on the street, and eventually one of our snitches will come through. But in the interest of time, we should go at this from all sides. Find a new way to get to the source more directly."

"I gather you have something in mind," Rivera said. "And from the look on your face, I gather it's unconventional."

His boss knew him well. He really was gonna miss this guy when he left. "Maybe." Deck hesitated, still unsure if he could work that closely with a doctor. For the sake of every agent and cop on the task force, he had to put his personal feelings aside. For whatever the reason, Dr. Sampson had a bug up her butt for the DEA. Or maybe that bug was directed specifically at him. "I don't know if she'll do it."

Deck flipped his gaze to Dan, who nodded in agreement. They'd already discussed the plan over the phone that morning. "The ER doctor who treated Dan said there'd already been ten opioid ODs this week. The hospital has the labs on these people. I don't know how specific they are, but I want to see those reports and compare them to Dan's labs and what's in those baggies we seized."

"That's easy enough," Brett said. "We can get subpoenas for the labs and any autopsy reports. Dan can sign a release form for his own medical records."

"Already done." Dan reached for a piece of paper on the side table and handed it to Deck.

Rivera *hmphed* and started stroking his goatee again. "What else?"

Now for the unconventional part. "Last night, I also checked with half a dozen other hospitals in Denver and Aurora. They're all seeing a spike in ODs. I want to get that doctor to hook me up with any overdose victim who rolls into this hospital. If they live, that is." A very real complication.

"Then you'll need subpoenas for that, too," Rivera said. "Without them, you'll never get those patients' medical records. The hospital will scream HIPAA and tell you to pound sand."

"I've already thought of that," Deck said. "The Health Insurance Portability and Accountability Act protects patient information from being disclosed without the patient's consent or knowledge. But I don't *want* their medical records. What I *want* is the patients' source. Who did they buy gray death from, and where did they go to get it? I want this ER doctor to notify me anytime an OD patient rolls through the door and lives. I want her to ask them if they'll talk to me. The timing is tight, though. If they live, most overdoses are released within an hour."

"Make it happen." Rivera gave him a meaningful look then stood. "Do whatever it takes. Take her to lunch, buy her dinner... I have to get back to the office. Dan, glad you're doing okay."

"Me, too," Dan said. "Thanks, boss."

The second Rivera was out the door, they all dug into the pizza. Thor sat up and uttered a high-pitched whine, his nostrils flaring as he pulled in the multitude of scents the pizza gave off.

Deck caught Dan picking another piece of pepperoni from his slice. "Don't even think it, buddy."

"Okay, okay." Dan shoved the pepperoni into his mouth and swallowed. "Sorry, Thor."

"You really planning on hitting up that ER doc?" Evan asked between chews.

Brett reached for a slice. "I know one of the nurses who was on call last night. She said Dr. Sampson chewed you a new asshole."

"True," Deck had to admit. "I'll have to wow her with my subtle charm."

"You don't *have* any subtle charm," Brett kicked back drily.

True. Fortunately, charming her was the last thing on his mind. There'd be no wooing, no dinners, and no romance. Keeping things strictly professional was the plan, one he suspected she'd appreciate.

"I was there," Evan said. "Standing right on the other side of the door. What she actually said was, 'If you ever come into my ER again, I'll throw you out on your muscled ass.'"

"Well," Dan said. "She's got my vote."

"Pizza!" Little Tommy ran to the bed and grabbed a slice from the open box.

Dan's wife came into the room, carrying a tray of sandwiches. "How did you guys get a box of pizza past that crabby old nurse?"

"Charm." Brett winked. "Unlike Deck, I have some."

Lisa rolled her eyes. "Bachelors." Then she snuggled on the bed next to her husband and gave him a quick kiss on the cheek.

When Deck dropped a piece of crust into a nearby garbage can, Thor all but glared at him then twisted his neck in the direction of the garbage, his nostrils flaring hopefully. Tommy grabbed his father's free hand, holding onto it while he gobbled down a slice. The gesture was so natural and loving, an observation that left him... wondering.

His life was 24/7 all about the job and had been that way for fourteen years. Getting hooked up wasn't in the cards anytime soon, if ever. He'd seen firsthand how fragile families were, breaking apart and dying an ugly, painful death for all kinds of reasons. He'd read that the divorce rate for first marriages in this country was at a whopping 43 percent, and Deck had no intention of adding to that statistic. Guess Dan and his wife were in that lucky 57 percent still hanging in there.

No sooner did he finish the thought than he stowed it away, deep in a hole reserved for other distractions. Not only wouldn't he risk becoming a divorce statistic, but there were way too many dealers to take out, something he couldn't do if he was always worrying about a wife and kids.

"Gotta go," he said to Dan. "I'll stop in tomorrow."

"Heading back to the ER?" Dan asked.

"Yep." When he grabbed Thor's leash, his dog shot to his feet.

"Good luck." Evan reached for another slice. "You're gonna need it."

"Tell me about it," he mumbled. A round of snickers followed him and Thor out the door.

As they headed for the elevators, the decision he'd made sat no better than a burning lump of coal in his stomach. For what he was about to attempt, he'd need more than just luck.

He and Thor stepped into the empty elevator, and he pressed the down button. Christ, what had he been thinking when he'd come up with this half-assed idea?

Tori Sampson struck him as a strong-willed, by-the-book doctor who wouldn't break easily from protocol. Swaying her to what she would undoubtedly consider "the dark side" would be a challenge. Sure, he loved a good challenge and hadn't met one yet that he couldn't overcome, but there was more to it than just her reservations. There were *his* to consider.

Going through with this would test every ounce of his restraint. Doctors had failed him and his family before, and his sister had paid the price with her life. His trust in the medical community ranked deep into the negative numbers. Even if she agreed, working with Dr. Sampson would be about as comfortable as rubbing up against a cactus. Guess he'd have to suck it up and take one for the team.

CHAPTER THREE

Tori placed her hand on the door, readying to push it open, but stopped. This would be the hardest thing she'd ever done in her medical career.

"You did everything you could for him," Suzie said. "He was found too late, you know that."

She did know that. By the time Tyler Wojcik's parents found him unconscious in his bedroom, hypoxia had already set in. In all likelihood, the boy was probably brain dead before he'd even arrived at the hospital. That didn't make her feel any better.

Wil's hand came to rest on her shoulder. "Are you sure you don't want me to come in with you?"

She shook her head and took an unsteady breath that seemed to rattle her rib cage. "No, you've got patients to see, and this won't take long." It couldn't. Not with the organ donation Tyler's parents had agreed to.

"Okay, then." Wil's voice was gentle, understanding. As a senior doctor, he'd been through this many more times than Tori had, and she appreciated his unwavering support. "I'll find you afterward. We can go to the lounge, grab a coffee, talk if you need to... Anything."

"Thanks, Wil." She looked up into his brown gaze, grateful for the compassionate understanding she glimpsed there.

"Ready?" Suzie asked.

No. Not really. For what she was about to do, she'd

never be ready. She pressed her fingers to her eyes, willing herself not to lose it. Tyler's parents needed her to be strong for them. *They* were the ones entitled to cry, not her. Not now, anyway.

Tori pushed open the door to the private room. Tom Wojcik stood up from where he'd been seated beside his wife, Emma. Sitting next to Emma was the organ donor coordinator, a kind woman named Mrs. Joba who held one of Emma's hands.

Quietly, Suzie closed the door behind them. For a moment, the room was dead silent. Tori couldn't get her feet to move. Then one of the monitors beeped, calling her attention to the handsome teenager on the bed. Various tubes containing fluids and artificial nutrients led to the IV in his arm. Since Tyler was incapable of breathing on his own, a ventilator did the job for him. Once it was removed, his heart would continue to beat anywhere from minutes to up to an hour. For the Wojciks' sake, she hoped it was the former. Prolonging things would only make their decision to take Tyler off life support that much harder to live with.

With her heart squeezing as if someone had tied a noose around it, Tori went to the couple. "Hi, Tom. Emma."

"Dr. Sampson." Tom's eyes were red and puffy, his face haggard and looking as if he'd aged ten years in the few days she'd known him. Slowly, and with obvious reluctance, he nodded. "We're ready. We've made our peace with this and said our goodbyes."

A gut-wrenching, gurgling sob came from Emma's throat. "I still can't believe this is happening," she began, shaking her head. "This is just so…surreal."

Mrs. Joba hugged Emma's shoulders. "I know it's hard, but what you're doing is a very beautiful, very generous thing."

"I know." Tears ran freely down Emma's cheeks, her eyes as equally red and puffy as her husband's. "I know," she repeated, as if to reassure herself.

Tom took his wife's other hand then sat down again, his shoulders shaking as he began sobbing.

As an only child, Tyler was the center of their universe. Soon, he would be gone.

Tori rolled her lips inward and tilted her head back, hoping the tears backing up behind her eyes didn't start rolling. Once they did, they'd never stop. *Be strong. Be strong for Tom and Emma*. That's the only thing she could do for them now.

"Okay," she whispered to Suzie. To Tom and Emma, she said, "You can hold his hand, if you like." Miraculously, her voice hadn't shaken, and it gave her the strength she so desperately needed.

Through her tears, Emma managed a grateful smile. Tom helped her to stand then tucked her against his side as they followed Tori and Suzie to the bed. Mrs. Joba stood at a respectful distance, waiting to accompany the couple from the room before Tyler was taken to surgery to have his organs removed. Tori had already discussed the process with the Wojciks so they'd know what to expect.

Grimly, it occurred to Tori that the opioid epidemic sweeping the country had led to a great many more life-saving organ donations.

She stood on one side of the bed next to the Wojciks. Suzie stood on the other, awaiting Tori's signal. She gave a single head nod, then Suzie turned off the EEG and disconnected the leads. The ventilator would remain on to keep Tyler's organs oxygenated prior to surgery.

Emma leaned over and kissed her son on the mouth. "Oh, my sweet, sweet boy," she whispered, kissing him again on the cheek. "We love you. We will *always* love you."

Tom uttered a low moan then leaned down and kissed his son's forehead in a gesture that threatened to crack Tori's heart wide open. *Hold it together.*

Mrs. Joba stepped closer, resting her hands on the Wojciks' shoulders. "Tom, Emma, I have another private room for you to wait in. After the surgery, you can spend more time with him. I promise."

As Mrs. Joba accompanied the Wojciks from the room, Tom turned. "Thank you, Dr. Sampson."

Unable to move, unable to speak, Tori watched them go, staring numbly at the door. The Wojciks' grief remained, lingering in the room like a dark shroud and reminding her of another horrible day. The day her mother died of a broken heart. She was no stranger to grief herself, but she'd never had to make the decision to take a loved one off life support.

"You okay, Tor?" Suzie asked.

Tori opened her mouth to answer when the door reopened. An orderly came in to take Tyler's body to the surgical unit where his organs and some tissue would be extracted then whisked away to help some lucky souls. As the orderly covered Tyler with a sheet, the tears that had been backing up steadily stung her eyes like someone had thrown a vat of acid in her face.

"I'll be in the chapel," she managed then rushed from the room.

• • •

Before heading to the ER, Deck put Thor up in the air-conditioned SUV specially designed for K-9s. At the admissions desk, he asked for Dr. Sampson. Several minutes and several unanswered pages later, Deck badged his way past the desk and went in search of the prickly doctor.

Part of him still couldn't believe he was about to do this, but he'd already decided he wouldn't take no for an answer. A doctor who looked vaguely familiar walked past. Deck was almost positive it was the other doctor in the ER with Dr. Sampson. About five-eleven, fit, and with a thick shock of brown hair. "Excuse me," he said.

"Yes?" W. Barnett, according to his name tag, stopped and turned.

"You were in the ER helping my colleague last night." Deck held out his hand. "Thank you."

"You're welcome." The doctor shook Deck's hand. "But I didn't do anything. Dr. Sampson was in charge, and your friend was lucky to have her. I hear it was a close call."

"Yeah, it was." Something he hoped no other DEA agent had to go through again.

"Think you'll get this gray death, or whatever it's called, off the street anytime soon?" Dr. Barnett asked.

"We're doing our best." Which, lately, was piss-poor. "Actually, I'm looking for Dr. Sampson."

For a brief moment, Barnett's gaze shifted down the

corridor in the direction Deck had been heading. "She's tied up at the moment. I don't think she'll be able to meet with you today, but you could leave a message for her at the nurses' station." He indicated the opposite direction.

"Thanks." Deck pulled his phone from his thigh pocket, pretending to take a call as the doctor continued down the hall. As soon as Barnett was out of sight, he headed in the direction Barnett clearly hadn't wanted him to go. Along the way, he snagged an orderly whose nametag said D. Landry and that Deck thought had also been in the ER yesterday. "Have you seen Dr. Sampson?"

"Yeah." The man looked behind him. "Saw her go that way about ten minutes ago."

"Thanks." Deck continued on until he came to another intersection. He looked left then right. Both corridors were empty. He turned right, walking to the end of the hall that dead-ended at the hospital chapel. The doors were open. A lone figure sat in the first pew. He recognized her long, straight hair tied up in a high ponytail.

Dr. Victoria Sampson. With her deep auburn hair and bright green eyes, she was extremely pretty. Too bad all that *pretty* was covered by a steel glove capable of punching a man's testicles right up to his tonsils.

Her shoulders shook, the way someone's might if they were laughing. Or crying. Given the location, he'd go with the latter. Who would have thought that the thorny ice queen who'd threatened to throw him from the ER on his "muscled ass" had a heart after all? The woman was all irony. As he stood there, her muffled sobs ripped straight into his gut.

Deck turned to leave, giving one last look over his

shoulder to see her lower her head in her hands and make him wonder what had upset her to the point of tears. No matter how important his quest, he didn't have the heart to bother her right then and there.

Quietly, he pulled the chapel doors closed behind him then headed back the way he'd come. When he turned left, he nearly bumped into a nurse wearing blue scrubs. Nurse Torres, he definitely remembered from yesterday. He'd catalogued everyone who'd come into contact with Dan. Just in case things had gone to shit.

"I heard you were looking for Dr. Sampson," Nurse Torres said.

"I was, and I found her." He nodded toward the chapel.

"Oh, I was trying to stop you. This isn't a good time. She just lost a patient, a teenage boy, and it hit her very hard."

"I could see that. I actually didn't speak with her, but I think she could use a friend right about now." Deck was certain he didn't fall into Dr. Sampson's "friend" category.

Nurse Torres nodded sadly. "We all could. That boy makes the fourth OD death at North Metro in the last week from this new drug."

"Jesus."

"Exactly," the nurse agreed solemnly. "Excuse me."

Deck stared after Nurse Torres as she turned right toward the chapel. He wondered how old the kid was. Opioids were indiscriminate killers, not caring what age, race, or sex its victims were. Marianne had been only sixteen when she'd OD'd. Thinking about his baby sister had guilt twisting his insides. For a moment, he wondered if anyone would notice a big hole in the wall after he rammed his fist through the sheetrock.

He wasn't a fan of involving civilians in his cases and certainly not a doctor, of all people. But he was desperate, and Dr. Sampson could very well be the key he needed to smash this investigation wide open.

CHAPTER FOUR

"I need to get back to work." Tori plucked a tissue from the pack Suzie held out to her. The tiny diamond in Suzie's engagement ring sparkled in the sunlight streaming in through the chapel's one and only stained-glass window. Suzie couldn't wait to marry her fiancé, Hector, and have kids. Tori prayed her friend would never have to go through what the Wojciks had. Quickly, she dabbed at the tears wetting her face. "I'm fine now."

"Are you?" Suzie's eyes brimmed with sympathy.

"I have to be, or I won't be able to do my job." And her job was everything to her.

After what had happened to her father all those years ago, all the money he'd set aside for her and her sister's tuition…gone in the time it took for the judge to pound his gavel. As a result, she'd had to get a job. While all her friends were playing after school sports or shopping at the mall, she'd worked. During college, she'd worked nights and weekends. It had taken blood, sweat, and tears — literally — but she'd finally gotten into med school then graduated with honors. Allowing her emotions to interfere with her work was simply unacceptable.

Renewed sobs bubbled up from somewhere deep inside her anyway, and she let Suzie wrap her arms around her. "He was so young. He didn't deserve to die." None of them did, but this boy dying on her watch had taken a lot out of her. People died in hospitals all the time, but overdoses were so senseless, so avoidable.

Being an ER doctor, she was used to death, had even become somewhat immune. Watching Tyler Wojcik die today was the straw that had broken her emotional back.

Tori grabbed a fresh tissue to dry her face. "Thanks, Suze." She squeezed her friend's hand. "At least no one else caught me bawling like an infant."

Suzie grimaced. "Um, that's not exactly true."

"What do you mean?" She looked around the chapel, taking in the empty pews.

"Just before I came in, I ran into that DEA agent from yesterday. You know, the Double H?"

"Double H?"

"Come. On." She splayed a hand across her chest. "Hunky Hottie, the one with the gorgeous brown eyes?"

Oh, right. Double H. Suzie's elite group reserved for only the handsomest men on the planet. And of course she remembered him. Who wouldn't? Just because she had no love for the DEA didn't mean she was blind. Being dateless for the last year didn't mean all her girly parts had dried up. *Yet.* "What about him?"

"He was looking for you. I think he found you but figured out his timing sucked and left you alone."

Tori narrowed her eyes. "Did he say what he wanted?"

"Nope. But I think he's still skulking around here somewhere, waiting for you."

"Wonderful." Just what she needed, on top of everything else.

Together, they left the chapel, although her heart still felt as if it had been used as a punching bag. Coming toward them was David Landry, the orderly.

"Something's up with him lately," Suzie whispered quickly.

"You noticed that, too?" she whispered back.

Instead of passing them, David stopped in front of Tori. The orderly was a big, burly man, about six-foot-two. "Dr. Sampson? I wanted to apologize for not responding right away to your page the other day. I, uh, must have eaten something that didn't agree with me. I was in the men's room and missed the call."

"That's all right," Tori said, although it hadn't been then. "We managed."

"Thanks." David continued past them.

Tori started walking again when Suzie stopped her. "Wait. David wasn't in the men's room the day you asked for an orderly. I saw him standing outside the main doors talking to his brother, Pete. David introduced us once. He said Pete moved in with him about two months ago and that he's helping him get back on his feet."

Tori frowned, torn between being angry and just plain pissed. "Why would David lie about where he was?"

Suzie shrugged as they continued down the corridor. "I don't know."

"If David's odd behavior continues, I'll ask Wil to talk with him. For now, let's keep this to ourselves." As the head of North Metro's ER, handling personnel issues was part of Wil's responsibility.

In a corner behind the nurses' desk, Dr. Ethan Dexter, one of the hospital's residents, stood listening intently to Wil. The glum look on Ethan's face didn't match the cheery yellow-and-orange Hawaiian shirt under his white coat. Ethan had come to North Metro about two years ago, around the same time Wil had. Since then, Wil had taken the younger man under his wing.

They were still too far away to hear what Wil was saying, but Ethan looked perturbed. When Ethan shook his head, a long ponytail that could rival hers swished back and forth.

"It'll be okay," Wil said, patting Ethan's shoulder. "Go take a break."

Ethan's jaw clenched as he came around from behind the desk. He nodded to her and Suzie, then brushed past, striding toward the doctors' lounge.

"Wil," she whispered, "everything okay with Ethan?"

"He's fine. He just made a misdiagnosis." Wil made a face. "But I wish he wouldn't dress like a hippie straight out of Woodstock. Sometimes, I swear I can smell pot on his clothes. I don't care if it's legal. It's not appropriate for a doctor to show up smelling like weed." His expression softened. "Are you all right? How'd it go with Tyler?"

In addition to being an amazing ER doctor, Wil was also her friend and confidante, had been since he'd transferred to North Metro from out of state. Right now, she needed her friends around her and was grateful they didn't let her down. They were her sounding boards.

"About as well as anyone can expect." She swallowed down another lump of sadness and helplessness that had been building steadily since the Wojciks had watched their son's heart beat for the last time.

"I'm sorry. He was way too young to die," Wil said. "Want to grab lunch and talk?" He bumped shoulders with her. "I hear they're serving heart attack mac 'n' cheese, today. Less mac and more cheese."

She smiled, grateful for his attempt at humor and to

ease her pain. "As much as I'd like to, there's a DEA agent around here somewhere, looking for me."

"DEA?" Wil frowned. "Oh, right. There *was* one looking for you earlier. Sorry, I forgot to tell you. I think it was that gorilla from yesterday. Remember?"

Why did people keep asking that? How could she *not* remember?

"How about this?" Wil glanced at Suzie. "We'll wait for you to have lunch. Come find us when you're done with this guy."

"I will," she reassured them both.

"Dr. Barnett?" One of the other nurses nodded to a team of EMTs pushing a stretcher into ER 4.

"I've got this one," Wil said, following the stretcher.

"I think your next appointment just found you." Suzie looked over Tori's shoulder then winked and followed Wil.

"Dr. Sampson?"

The "hunkie hottie" leaned against the other side of the nurses' station desk, watching her, waiting. She'd hoped he'd have given up and gone away. *No such luck*. Dealing with the DEA *any* day of the week was rock bottom on her list of things-I-want-to-do, let alone today. Somehow, she had to scrounge up enough professionalism to get through it.

He pushed from the desk, his thick biceps flexing beneath the sleeve of the black polo shirt he wore, one that seemed to cling to every other muscle in the man's sculpted torso. Every nurse within range stopped to watch him come toward her.

"What can I do for you, Special Agent…" She'd already forgotten his name.

"Decker." He held out his hand, and for a moment she just stared at it. Eventually, she put her hand in his. The simple gesture should have been just that—simple, but it wasn't. The man's grip was strong and gentle at the same time, and warm. *So* warm. "Is there someplace we can speak privately?"

She glanced behind her. If Ethan wasn't in the doctors' lounge cooling his jets, she would've taken the agent there. "We can go to the cafeteria."

Decker frowned. "Is there someplace more private? What I have to say isn't for public consumption."

Moments later, they sat across from each other at a table in one of the vacant doctor's offices.

"First off," Decker began, "I want to thank you for what you did for my colleague, Dan Prince. If it weren't for your expertise, he would've died."

"Thank you, but again, I was only doing my job."

"And doing it well. That's why I'm here."

"I don't mean to be rude"—*Liar*—"but I have patients to get back to. What did you want to speak with me about?"

His mouth tightened. "I need your help. You're absolutely right. The DEA *should* be doing more to address the opioid epidemic, especially this new designer drug. We need to be proactive, get to the source as quickly as possible."

About time. Although it wouldn't help Tyler Wojcik. "I'm very glad to hear that. Now, what does this have to do with me?"

"You said there were three OD deaths at North Metro in the last week. I want to see—"

"Four," she bit out, her voice clogging with emotion. "As

of an hour ago, there have been four."

Decker's brown eyes softened, and frown lines burrowed into his forehead. "Right. A teenage boy. I heard. I'm sorry."

"You should be." Tori clasped her hands together tightly on top of the desk, sorely regretting taking this meeting so soon after taking Tyler off life support. Her emotions were still too raw.

The defensive retort she expected never came. Rather, her blunt declaration of blame was met by stony silence. Finally, Decker took a deep breath that tightened his shirt over his broad chest. "Yeah," was all he said. "Which is exactly why I need your help. I want to see the lab reports for those ODs, including Dan Prince, and compare them to the powder we seized yesterday."

"As for most of those reports, you'll need a subpoena, and you'll have to deal with our legal department."

"Consider it done."

"As for your friend, you can get him to sign a release form."

Decker pulled a folded piece of paper from his pocket, unfolded it, and handed it to her. A quick glance told her it was, indeed, a signed release form. She handed it back to him, but he didn't take it. "Again, you'll have to deal with the hospital's legal department."

"I don't have time for that. Don't you think this request will be processed faster if you hand-deliver it?"

Reluctantly, she set the request form on the desk. Expediting his request was a small thing she could do.

His eyes took on a suspicious glint. "You've already looked at the labs. Haven't you? I'm guessing you already know what's in this new drug."

In truth, she *had* looked at *all* the lab reports for the OD deaths, and she'd been astounded by what she'd discovered. And she knew precisely what Decker was getting at. "I can't divulge anything specifically connected to any patient by name."

"Of course not." He leaned forward, giving her a close-up view of just how richly brown his eyes were. "I wouldn't want you to violate HIPAA."

"Nor *would* I. *Ever*." Breaking any law or medical protocol wasn't now, nor would it ever be, part of her professional repertoire. "What I *can* tell you is that the blood samples contained various levels of heroin, fentanyl, carfentanil, or U-47700."

Decker leaned back in the chair. His brows lowered as he stared at a spot over her shoulder. He began tapping his fingers on the desk, as if he were deep in thought. Abruptly, his fingers stilled, and he refocused his sharp gaze on her. "I need fresh intel on where people are buying this drug. I'd like to speak with every overdose victim that comes into this hospital. I need *you* to make that happen."

Tori snorted, suppressing a full-blown laugh. "You expect me to betray patient confidentiality by calling you every time some poor soul overdoses? That's if they even live to talk about it."

"No." Decker's perfectly chiseled jaw hardened. "I'm asking you to *inquire* if they would be willing to speak with me. If they will, I want you to notify me right away. I'll come to the hospital and conduct a quick interview, and that's it."

Beneath the table, Tori curled one hand into a fist.

"You've got to be kidding."

"I'm not, and there's more." He held up his big hand. "What happened to Dan Prince could happen again. We're putting together a seminar to train our people on the use of naloxone auto-injectors and the specific dosages they might be looking at if they come across gray death. We need someone from the medical profession to give this training, preferably someone familiar with this drug and with current, hands-on experience treating overdoses from this particular drug. We need *you*, Dr. Sampson."

Shock spread through her system. When she'd agreed to speak with him, she'd had no idea what he wanted. Hooking him up with patients and training DEA agents were most definitely *not* possibilities she'd considered. "First of all, your request for me to hook you up with my patients is inappropriate."

"Is it?" he countered. "If they agree to speak with me voluntarily, it's not illegal."

"Perhaps not, but it's highly irregular." To say the least. "Secondly, you must have trained personnel in your agency who are perfectly capable of giving that kind of training. I have very little spare time as it is." More accurately, there was no way on earth she would ever help the DEA. Twenty years ago, they'd done nothing to help her father, just the opposite, so there was absolutely no chance she would help *them* now.

"*First* of all," Decker said, using the same words she had and annoying her further, "this is a one-time training, a few hours at most. *Secondly*," he added, again mocking her word choice, "there's a precedent for this. A few years back, a doctor from St. Anne's gave us first aid and CPR refresher training. The DEA worked something out with the hospital's administrators, and we can do the same for you."

Tori leaned forward slamming her palms on the table. "You must be out of your fu—freaking mind." She stood, appalled at her outburst. "I'm sorry you've wasted your time. Perhaps you can try another hospital and another doctor. Maybe the same doctor at St. Anne's wants another thrill."

"They wouldn't have your experience, and I want the best for our people." Decker remained seated, his handsome face a blank mask. "Dr. Sampson," he said in a low voice. "If we don't stop this, more people *will* die."

They locked gazes, his so intense and mesmerizing that she couldn't look away. "Clearly, you're passionate about your work, and I can appreciate that. But it doesn't change anything. I can't help you." Getting into bed with the DEA wasn't something she was prepared to do. Not after the callous, unconscionable way they'd treated her family. They'd ruined her father's life, altered the course of her and her sister's futures, and broken her mother's heart to the point it had actually given out. Some things could never be forgiven.

He straightened and inhaled deeply, exhaling through his nose. "I'm sorry you feel that way."

She headed to the door, placing her hand on the knob. Decker's hand appeared on the door over her head, preventing her from opening it. Warm breath washed over the top of her head. "I hope you'll reconsider my requests. I saw you in the chapel today after that boy died. I'm thinking you don't want the body count to rise any more than I do. If there was something you could do to prevent that from happening, wouldn't you want to do it?"

She squeezed her eyes shut, resisting the urge to slap Decker's face. This guy was good. He knew what strings to pull and just when to do it, but she refused to be manipulated into this crazy-ass agreement. The DEA was aces at that song and dance. When they'd come for her father, they'd manipulated him, too, made it seem like what he'd done was okay. Once he'd cooperated and they'd gotten what they'd wanted, they threw him in jail like a bag of trash.

A few more seconds of silence followed before he removed his hand. A business card appeared in front of her eyes. In the interest of getting out of there, she snatched it and stuffed it into her coat pocket. Without looking behind her, she opened the door and went back to the ER.

The man's concern about more people dying was legitimate. His mistake was in not doing his homework. If he knew about her family, he never would have approached her in the first place. Even if she didn't despise the DEA with every fiber of her being, Tori didn't take risks anymore. The very idea of stepping outside her safe little box to assist with his investigation was too frightening. Her father had stepped outside the box, risked everything for what he believed was right, and look where it had gotten him. Nope, that wasn't for her. Not anymore.

Walking briskly and refusing to check behind her to see if Decker was watching, she headed for the elevators, pulling out her cell phone to text Wil and Suzie to see if they were free for lunch. A text greeted her, saying they were already waiting for her in the cafeteria.

Two minutes later, she spied Suzie and Wil at a table with Max Maynard, North Metro's star neurosurgeon, and Neil Shibowsky, the hospital's equally famed cardiac surgeon. As she approached, she caught some of the conversation while the surgeons proudly showed Wil their Rolex watches.

She sat in the only empty chair and set her tray of mac 'n' cheese and a salad on the table.

"Hey, Tori," Max said then went back to flashing the gold watch closer for Wil to inspect. "As head of emergency medicine," he said to Wil, "you should get one of these."

"No, get a silver one." Neil tugged up his sleeve. "The gold one's gaudy. This one's classier."

Wil shook his head. "Too rich for my blood. Besides, I always carry my cell phone around, so who needs watches anymore, right?"

Some of Max's enthusiasm dimmed.

"How's it going, Tori?" Neil asked, shoving his watch hand into his pocket.

"Well," she said, picking up her fork, "you're not going to believe what I was just propositioned with."

"Do tell." Suzie bobbed her brows suggestively. "Does this have anything to do with the DEA agent?"

"That federal agent all the nurses were talking about?" Max asked.

Wil groaned. "So he has muscles instead of brains. Big deal."

"See?" Suzie smirked. "Even Wil thinks the guy is hot."

"I did *not* say that." He gave Suzie a pointed look. "I believe I referred to him as a gorilla."

"So, what was the proposition?" Suzie asked in a hopeful voice.

"Get your head out of the gutter." Tori gave Suzie's shoulder an affectionate smack. "He wants me to help with his investigation, specifically to notify him any time an OD comes into the ER so he can interrogate them about who they buy their drugs from. He also wants me to help train their people at a seminar he's arranging."

"As long as you can fit it into your schedule, the training shouldn't be a problem," Wil said. "But letting him grill patients could violate all kinds of protocol. It's risky, and you don't want to get sued. It might be a HIPAA violation."

"That's basically what I told him." Tori nodded emphatically, although she hadn't even considered the possibility of a lawsuit.

"I'd check with Herrmann before letting him talk to your patients," Max suggested.

Like her, Dolph Herrmann, the hospital's primary administrator, was a stickler for protocol. It was doubtful he'd agree to Decker's request.

"Hypothetically," Suzie said, "let's say the hospital did approve. It might be good for you. Training a room full of DEA agents could be fun." She leaned in to whisper, "Besides, you haven't had any excitement in your life since Mike left."

Tori groaned. "*Please*, don't go there." The last thing she needed were reminders of the other ER doctor she dated briefly last year. He'd all but been fired by Herrmann over something she thought was a totally trumped-up issue. In the end, he'd resigned and relocated to the West Coast. While Tori had commiserated with Mike over the circumstances of their parting, it had actually given her the out she'd needed. She'd been on the brink of breaking up with him but hadn't had the courage to do it yet. Mike was a great guy. His love of extreme sports—including skydiving—*not* so great.

As an ER doctor, she'd seen firsthand that people's lives were dangerous enough, and that was *without* extreme sports. Being with someone who got their yucks living on the edge was something she could never do.

• • •

Tori dropped her bag on the hallway chest. As always, the house was quiet. *Too quiet.* Maybe she could get a couple of cats or even a goldfish, something to take care of. What she really wanted was a dog, but that could never fit in with her hectic schedule. She was almost never at home, and it wouldn't be fair.

She went into the kitchen and poured a glass of Chardonnay, savoring the cool, buttery wine as it trickled down her throat. On the granite counter sat the teardrop terrarium she'd been working on. There'd been a time when her hobbies were more exciting and action-oriented, like hiking, camping, and snowshoeing. Those days were long gone. Now potting plants was about as exciting as things got.

She set down her glass then picked up one of the delicate, green-and-red Tillandsia air plants. Using a tiny spade, she wiggled the white pebbles aside, making a space for the plant. After placing it in the hole, she picked up another plant, this one a small plug of moss. With a sigh, she set the plant back down on the counter.

Normally, she worked on her terrariums every evening.

It was a labor of love, with the added benefit of stress relief. Not tonight, however. The grief and desperation she'd witnessed today had torn her guts wide open, and they were still bleeding.

Tyler Wojcik had his whole life ahead of him. Now, he had nothing. No life, and he'd never give or receive a minute of joy ever again. He was just…gone. And for what?

When Tyler's father had thanked her, she understood he was only expressing his gratitude for helping him and his wife through what had to be the most difficult day of their lives, but at the same time, she'd been flabbergasted. Because she hadn't done anything to deserve their thanks. But that was the thing—there hadn't been anything she *could* have done.

Then.

But what about now?

She picked up her glass, staring at it for a full minute. Tyler's lifeless face was all she could see. She set the glass down and stared at the other three empty bottles of wine on the counter. For her, alcohol was becoming a way to cope. A bad sign indeed.

She looked around her empty kitchen, empty living room, and equally vacant backyard. Her only companions were the plants in her terrariums. *Pathetic*. So maybe, just *maybe*, Suzie was right. For the last five years, she'd been an ER dynamo, but other than short relationships here and there, her life had gone more sterile than an operating room. Shaking things up a little bit might be just what the doctor ordered. But aligning herself with the DEA?

When she'd described Decker's proposition, she'd

completely agreed with Wil's assessment. It *was* risky, borderline inappropriate, and she'd be nuts to go along with it. Now, she wasn't so sure. Half the ambulances pulling into the ER were transporting an OD victim. Heaven forbid she say the words out loud, but helping the DEA would be an opportunity to do something proactive.

Could she really do this?

She shook her head but at the same time was already wondering how in the world she would ever explain it to her father and sister. She couldn't. It wasn't remotely possible. If she did this, it would have to be her little secret. *Big* secret, actually. Gargantuan, even. But she had to do *something*. Standing on the sidelines wasn't enough anymore.

Just do it. Make the call.

Pressing her lips together, she strode to the hallway and dug through her bag for the business card she'd tossed in there earlier. She called the number on the card. A deep voice answered.

She opened her mouth, but no words came.

"Hello?" he said again.

Tomorrow, she might very well regret the words she was about to say. Today, they seemed right.

She gripped the phone tighter. "This is Dr. Sampson. I changed my mind. I'm in."

CHAPTER FIVE

Deck stood outside the SOTF building just south of Aurora, waiting for Dr. Sampson to arrive so he could swipe her into the staff parking lot.

When he'd gotten her call two days ago, hers was the last voice he ever expected to hear. He'd only given her his business card as a Hail Mary, and he still wasn't sure getting mixed up with a doctor wouldn't fry every one of his nerve endings.

Thor sat calmly at his side, eying a dark red Subaru as it drove up to the gate. He already knew this was her vehicle. At Deck's request, Sammie Aikens, the task force's primary intel specialist, had run a criminal history and DMV query on Dr. Sampson. It wasn't a complete background check, but it would suffice. As expected, she had no criminal history, not even a parking ticket.

"Right on time, Thor." Hearing his name, Thor wagged his tail, ears upright and alert. Like him, his dog was always ready to work. In fact, Thor was probably the only other DEA agent in Colorado ready and willing to work more hours than Deck was.

The window lowered and clear green eyes set against a creamy complexion met his. As it had been every other time he'd seen her, her auburn hair was tied high in a ponytail. The thing was pulled back so tightly, he wondered if it gave her headaches. On the other hand, it showed off the tiny gold studs in her cute earlobes.

"Park over there." He indicated an empty spot in front of the door and waited while she pulled in.

The car door opened, and she grabbed a bag, slinging it over her shoulder before stepping onto the pavement. She wore slim black slacks and a light-green Henley shirt that hugged her body and made her eyes even more green. Thor's tail thumped faster against Deck's leg.

"Who is this?" She surprised him by reaching out her hand to Thor without hesitation. Most people were afraid of him.

Deck rested his hand on his dog's head. "Thor, meet Dr. Sampson. Dr. Sampson, this is my partner, Thor." When Thor lifted his paw for her to shake, she obliged him. "You seem comfortable with dogs."

"I had a dog when I was a little girl, but I haven't had one since." Her expression turned wistful.

"Why not? You're good with them."

"I'd like to get one again, but I don't have enough time to give a dog what it needs."

He indicated to the building's main entrance, holding open the heavy glass door. He followed her inside, inhaling her pretty, flowery scent.

Deck stopped at the desk to pick up a visitor's pass he'd already had made. He handed it to her, waiting while she clipped it to her shirt. "What made you change your mind?"

Her eyes softened, turning pensive. "If there's something I can do proactively to stop the rising body count, I want to do it." Absently, she stroked Thor's ears, allowing him to lean his head against her thigh. Deck suspected the change of heart had something to do with the dead teenager. "But let's be clear on something." Her pretty eyes glittered like shards of green ice. "You have your rules, and I have mine."

He and Thor led the way to the elevator. He glanced over his shoulder to make sure she was behind him. "Meaning?" Two seconds into their alliance, and he was already on the verge of regretting it.

"Meaning"—she stared up at him frostily—"you will not skulk around the ER, waiting or searching for overdose victims. You'll wait until I notify you that a patient is willing to speak with you."

"Skulk?" Deck held back a snort. Somebody woke up on the wrong side of the bed this morning. "DEA agents don't *skulk*."

She pursed her lips. "I beg to differ. History has shown otherwise."

He leaned his shoulder against the wall by the elevator bank, tensing. "*What* history?" He had no idea what she was talking about. Whatever it was, they really needed to clear the air fast or this partnership would sink faster than the *Titanic*.

"Never mind." She shook her head and looked away, as if she'd said something unintentional. "There is one other thing, however."

"*What* other thing?" Yeah, two minutes into it, and this arrangement was already fixing to be a cluster.

"If a patient changes their mind in the middle of your interrogation and no longer wishes to talk, you'll leave, no more questions asked."

"Fine." Between them, Thor swung his head back and forth, as if watching a tennis match. "And for the record, it's not an *interrogation*. It's an interview. Anything else?"

"Yes. You have to promise never to use a patient's name in any report."

Deck pushed from the wall, towering over her, but she stood her ground, craning her neck to look up at him. The elevator door opened, but he ignored it. "No dice, Doc. That's how I get my PC—probable cause. If an OD victim has information about the source of the opioids and can direct us to the location where they purchased it, I may need to put their name in an affidavit for search and arrest warrants."

She crossed her arms and jutted her chin up at him. "Then that part of the deal is off."

What had he gotten himself into? They'd made a deal over the phone, and she was already changing the rules. He should've known he couldn't trust her. Maybe he should find someone else. But they were here, and he didn't want to waste more time finding another doctor. "Let's compromise. I'll do everything in my power to leave names out, but you have to understand that sometimes that's what it takes to get a dealer off the street. If a judge allows me to refer to victims as 'confidential sources' instead of using their real names, then I'll do it. Deal?"

Before meeting his gaze, her lips compressed into a tight line, and he expected her to tell him to pound sand. "Deal."

"Good, and I have a condition of my own. Everything we do together, everything we discuss, is confidential. You need to be discrete about DEA operations."

"Understood," she said curtly. "And for the record, that seems obvious."

The door began to close, and he reached out his arm,

stopping it. "Is there anything else I should know?"

Her lips twitched. "If there is, I'll tell you."

"I'll bet you will." This woman was hardcore. Delicate and pretty on the outside. Inside, she was a drill sergeant, barking out orders like a seasoned federal agent. Like *him*. He'd bet she could hold her ground against some of the best defense attorneys he'd ever run into.

He outstretched his arm, letting her get into the elevator first. "Thor, heal."

Undeterred, Thor bolted into the elevator and sat next to Dr. Sampson, nuzzling her hand for attention. To Deck's further irritation, when she obliged and began stroking his ears, Thor had the traitorous audacity to groan happily and lean his head against her thigh again, as if they were best buds. When they got home tonight, they were having a serious talk.

The doors closed, and the elevator rose to the third floor. When they opened again, he outstretched his arm. "After you, Doc."

Loud voices from the large conference room drifted into the hallway. The place was packed. He recognized DEA agents from around the state, along with state drug agents and SOTF agents from the ATF and FBI, including Brett and Evan.

Dr. Sampson stood at the entrance to the room but didn't come in. Her eyes rounded as she took in the size of the audience. Maybe he should've warned her there'd be over two hundred people here.

Brett hitched his head as they approached. "Hey, Deck."

"Doc, this is ATF Special Agent Brett Tanner and FBI Special Agent Evan McGarry. They're also K-9 agents."

"Nice to meet you, Doc." Brett extended his hand first, followed by Evan. "Thanks for doing this. The second notification of your presentation hit the air waves, every slot filled up within two hours."

"Please, call me Tori." She licked her lips and swallowed, suddenly looking like a high school girl about to give her first oral report in front of the class. "I had no idea there'd be so many people."

Deck arched a brow. *Whatdya know. A chink in the woman's steely armor.* "Can I get you something to drink before we get started? Coffee or water?" he asked, amused and yet oddly protective at the subtle fear on her face. Despite his reservations, something about her made him want to ease her worry. "I promise," he said, tipping his head to the crowd, "they won't bite you."

Thor *woofed*.

"I'm not so sure about that," she murmured, again taking in the size of her audience. The silver charm bracelet on her wrist jingled as she gripped the strap of her bag tighter, turning her knuckles distinctly white. "But I will take some coffee."

Interesting. The woman was a powerhouse in the ER, but in a room filled to the gills with law enforcement agents, she looked as timid as a baby bunny. His protectiveness kicked in full force, and he placed his hand at the small of her back, using his body as a shield between her and the crowd, leading her to the refreshment table.

Along the way, many sets of male eyes turn to look at her. Not that Deck was surprised. She was more than just pretty. She was beautiful. He wondered if she let her hair down from the ponytail if it would soften her face. He also wondered if the permission she'd given his friends to call her *Tori* instead of Dr. Sampson extended to him.

He grabbed a cup and flipped the lever on the carafe, filling the cup but leaving some room. "Cream?" He handed her the coffee and pointed to the open containers of milk and half-and-half at the end of the table.

She took a sip and swallowed. "No, just black." He must have transmitted his surprise at her not wanting creamer, because her brows rose. "What?"

Stepped in it this time, Decker. How to respond without being labeled sexist? In his experience, most women and many men, for that matter, put some kind of creamer in their coffee. "Have you ever tried a cappuccino? Or a white chocolate mocha?" Two of his faves to amp up the caffeine and sugar when he needed it.

"Never."

"You don't know what you're missing."

Deck was rewarded with the reluctant upturn of her lips, the first hint of a real smile in his direction since they'd met. Only then did he notice the pale pink gloss on her lips. "I've always taken it black."

"You should try something new. You might surprise yourself and like it."

"I'm a creature of habit." The noise level in the room ratcheted up, and renewed apprehension fell over her face.

"Is it the large crowd or public speaking in general?"

She gave a self-deprecating smile. "I'm okay with public speaking, and I'm okay being in a large crowd. It's the combination of the two that makes me a little anxious. It's outside my comfort zone."

Thor insinuated his snout into her hand, as if sensing

she needed a little canine support.

"You'll do fine." He rested his hand on her shoulder. When she glanced at where he touched her, he let his hand drop.

"It's time." He led the way to the podium at the front of the room and could swear the sound he heard behind him was her audible gulp.

• • •

The leather strap of Tori's bag was damp where she'd been gripping it. This was like being in the devil's den—a federal building packed with drug agents. A few women dotted the crowd, but mostly her audience was comprised of men. *Huge* men, most over six feet tall and carrying guns, no doubt. She felt like a munchkin in a room full of giants.

She followed "Deck," as his friends called him, and Thor to the podium. Deck's powerful presence made her uneasy. His dog didn't. Having Thor nearby was comforting. Being around him reminded her of all the wonderful things she'd been missing by not having a dog in her life.

The closer they got to the podium more heads turned in their direction. *I should have worn a suit. Or a coat of armor.* Anything to hide behind so these federal agents wouldn't see how nervous she was.

She'd reached out to a local veterinarian and learned that the ideal placement for a naloxone injection was the same for humans and dogs, in the meaty part of the thigh. As requested, Deck had made sure there was a table up front, one she could use to demonstrate the proper technique. Thor would be her canine subject, while Deck would be her human guinea pig.

He faced the crowd. Talking turned to loud whispers then hushed silence. The man could certainly command an audience.

After she'd set her bag behind the podium, he handed her a small black box, attached to which was a wire and a small black microphone. She hooked the box to her belt then fumbled with trembling fingers to attach the mic to her shirt.

"May I?" he asked, indicating the microphone in her hand.

Tori let out a grateful breath. "Please." She handed him the mic, and as he expertly clipped it to the collar of her shirt, one of his fingertips grazed her collarbone, sending shivers across her skin.

A sea of unsmiling faces stared back at her, many with close-cropped hair, some with long hair and tattoos. *Undercover agents?* That was what they always looked like in the movies.

Deck grabbed a handheld microphone from the podium. "Thank you for coming. For those who don't know me, I'm Special Agent Adam Decker with the DEA's Denver office and the Special Ops Task Force. Many of you know my K-9, Thor." Thor barked, and half the audience laughed. "And this is the speaker you've all come to hear. Dr. Tori Sampson is a physician at the North Metro Hospital emergency room in Denver. She has extensive experience treating opioid overdose victims."

Without reading from any notes, Decker recited her medical credentials, including the fact that she did her residency in Boston and worked at Boston General before coming back home to Colorado four years ago. He *could* have dug up that information from the hospital website. Or he could have checked up on her. That's what Feds did, so apparently, he hadn't done a *thorough* check.

"Four days ago, Dr. Sampson was on duty at the ER when we brought Dan Prince in. Dan suffered an acute opioid overdose during a search warrant. We believe he was exposed to a cocktail of heroin and synthetic opioids known as 'gray death.'"

He clicked on the screen and flicked through a series of photos, each displaying a fine powder that reminded her of gray all-purpose flour or cement. "Gray death isn't a new drug on our streets. However, the formula currently making the rounds in Denver is extremely potent. A miniscule amount can lead to an overdose, so you can imagine what it's doing to folks who don't have a clue that what they just bought isn't run-of-the-mill heroin."

Concerned murmurs spread through the crowd, as well they should.

"It's impossible to predict what we're up against because opioid cocktails like gray death, by their very nature, are almost never the same formula. This makes raids particularly dangerous. An accidental exposure might give you a buzz one day and kill you the next."

"Remind me never to let Deck give an inspirational speech," an agent in the front row who reminded Tori of a young Danny Glover grumbled. Chuckles swept over the room.

"Sorry to disappoint you, Davis," Deck said with a grin that did funny things to Tori's insides. Luckily, it faded back to scary intensity almost immediately. "I've been looking at similar cases across the country," he continued. "It appears this current formula is similar to a drug that killed a dozen people in Pennsylvania about three years ago. Variations have also popped up in Ohio and throughout the Midwest and the South, though the numbers haven't been quite as bad."

He clicked to the next screen, showcasing a headline on the front page of the *Philadelphia Inquirer*: "Killer Cocktail Kills Five More." "The case in Pennsylvania is still open," Deck continued. "The source of that drug was never found, no arrests made. After seven more people died, it disappeared from circulation. We can't ignore the possibility that the same source moved out west and set up shop here. Or this could be a copycat drug made by someone else. Gray death is cheap and potent. A dealer's dream—if they can keep their clients alive long enough to buy more, which they will. Nothing else is strong enough to give them that kind of high."

Deck clicked to another screen showing a pile of clear plastic baggies filled with a gray, powdery-looking substance. "This is gray death we seized four days ago. The most commonly used opioids are heroin and prescription drugs, like hydrocodone, oxy, morphine, codeine, and fentanyl. Fentanyl is an end-of-life painkiller for cancer patients, but it's also the leading cause of overdose deaths. It's fifty times more potent than heroin and a hundred times stronger than morphine. Fentanyl is just *one* of the ingredients that could be present in gray death."

The next screen showed several small gray chunks that looked like clay. "Another ingredient is carfentanil, the most dangerous opioid on the planet. It's not even intended for human use. It's an animal tranquilizer used for anesthetizing elephants because it's ten thousand times stronger than morphine."

Tori had to admit Deck was extremely well-versed on opioid facts and statistics, far beyond that of even most doctors.

"Like the drugs seized in the Pennsylvania investigation," he continued, "DEA analysis of the baggies seized here in Denver indicates this version contains heroin, U-47700 aka 'Pink,' fentanyl, *and* carfentanil."

Someone let out a low whistle.

"Exactly," Deck said. "Fortunately, our gray death is slightly less toxic than the drugs seized in the Pennsylvania case, but it's still deadly. The problem for addicts *and* us is that reactions vary by the individual and dose. We think Dan was exposed after he took his mask off. All it took was a few aerosolized grains to take him to the ground. A lethal dose may not even be visible to the human eye."

"Shit," the agent in the first row muttered, shaking his head. Similar hushed expletives came from the audience as they absorbed the dire meaning of Deck's words.

Given Deck's determination, it shouldn't have surprised her that in the days since she'd seen him at the hospital, he'd been busy. Not only had he procured subpoenas for the other overdose patients' labs, he'd also managed to get North Metro's legal department working at light speed to turn over those reports as well. She already knew Dan Prince's lab reports had been turned over to the DEA almost immediately, in part due to her personally walking the request form to legal.

"Dr. Sampson has treated several of these patients

personally," Deck continued, "and she saved Dan's life. That could have been any of us lying on her table, and we all owe her a debt of gratitude for saving one of our own."

Decker faced her and began clapping. Everyone else in the room stood and also began clapping, the sound becoming so loud Tori could barely hear herself think. This was the last thing she ever expected. Hundreds of law enforcement officers—DEA agents, no less—giving her a standing ovation. A lump formed in her throat, and no matter how hard she tried, she couldn't dislodge it. It seemed like five minutes before the crowd quieted and sat, although in reality, it had probably been no more than twenty seconds.

"Take it away, Doc." Deck set the microphone back on the podium then walked to one side of the room and leaned against the window ledge. He snapped his fingers. Thor ran to his side and sat.

Too bad. It was childish, but she considered the dog her buffer. Having him close gave her courage. "Thank you." The shock at hearing her voice coming from what seemed like every inch of wall and ceiling space was enough to momentarily destroy what little remaining composure she had.

Get a professional grip on yourself. These men and women put their lives on the line every day to keep the public safe. The least she could do was to give them some information that might one day save their lives.

"I understand that many of you have already gone through field training on how to treat an inadvertent overdose. My job today is to build on that. I'll go over early onset symptoms of an overdose, then we'll discuss using the auto-injectable naloxone."

Deck had informed her that most, if not all, officers carried the nasal spray but would soon be given auto-injectors. Some people were squeamish where needles were concerned.

"Symptoms to look for," she began, counting off on her fingers, "include nausea or vomiting, dizziness, lethargy, cold or clammy skin, slow breathing, or no breathing at all. Other classic signs are very small or pinpoint pupils, slow heartbeats, extreme drowsiness. If your partner falls asleep on you for no reason at all during a warrant, you should assume there's been an exposure. Administer naloxone right away, then watch for signs of improvement. You may have to administer additional doses. If they stop breathing, you'll have to breathe for them. If their heart stops beating, you'll have to administer CPR until the paramedics can take over and get your partner to a hospital."

"Above all else," Deck interjected from where he still leaned against the window ledge, "on these high-risk warrants, work in pairs. Don't get separated. Dan nearly died because we—*I*—lost track of him. He passed out before we discovered he was missing."

From his stiff body posture and his use of the word *I*, only now did she realize how much of the blame he shouldered for what had happened to Dan.

Tori cleared her throat. "Agent Decker initiated rescue breathing until the paramedics arrived. Before he arrived at the hospital, Dan went into cardiac arrest. And this was a case of *very* minimal exposure," she added for emphasis to the crowd, whose expressions were sobering more by the second. "The effects of this particular formula of gray death are unlike anything we've seen in the ER. It works fast, so if you think you or one of the officers you're with have been exposed, don't take any chances. Naloxone is key to counteracting the effects of opioids. It blocks or reverses the effects. How many of you are authorized to carry naloxone with you in the field?"

Nearly everyone in the room raised their hands. "How much do you carry?" she asked the agent in the first row.

"Two nasal spray bottles, two milligrams each."

She moved down the aisle, pointing to a woman in the fifth row she'd seen with her hand in the air. "The same."

"And you?" Tori indicated another man several rows down.

"The same."

She stopped in the middle of the room. "Even if you all carried as much as these three officers combined, statistics at North Metro show that it might not be enough to reverse the effects of gray death. After we got Dan's heart beating again, we had to push a total of eleven milligrams of naloxone into him before he started breathing again on his own." The faces staring back at her were appropriately disturbed. "So, if you only have a few milligrams and one of you is exposed far away from mobile emergency services or a hospital…you could die."

While she paused to let that unsettling statistic sink in, murmurs went around the room.

Decker and Thor rejoined her at the podium. "The DEA is working with other agencies in Colorado to equip you with naloxone auto-injectors and specialized PPE," he said. "A few of you have the injectable kind already, but most of you don't. That's about to change. What we're going to do now is instruct you on how to use it."

As they'd planned in advance, Deck sat on the table. It was impossible not to notice the muscles in his forearms flexing as he lay down on his back. The muscles in his abdomen were so well-defined their outline was easily visible beneath his black polo.

As much as she hated to admit it, Suzie's assessment was spot on. Tori still found him infuriating, but he was definitely Double H material.

Thor leaped onto the table and licked Deck's face. A few snickers came from the front row.

"Atta boy, Thor," commented Brett Tanner, Deck's ATF friend.

"Before you touch the individual, assess the scene," she began. "If there's any contaminant on the victim's clothes, you should, at a minimum, wear gloves. Most ODs won't be transdermal. Inhalation is more likely, so wear a mask if you have one. An N95 works, but if you've got an air purifying respirator, use it. If able, put the clothes in a bag or cover the victim in a sheet. It'll go against your instincts, but your priorities should be to protect yourself, then get the naloxone into the victim. Understand?"

There were nods and a rumble of agreements.

"Good. So, where to give the injection? Assuming you don't have an IV set up, the best place to administer the injection is in the outer thigh." She approached the table, gently placing her hand on Decker's thigh. For a moment, their gazes met and held, and his strong, thick muscle twitched beneath her fingers. Was it her touch or was he just not a fan of needles?

Tori yanked her hand away. "In an emergency, which

you should consider any opioid exposure to be, don't waste time. Give the injection right through the person's clothing. For an adult, the usual dose is between point-four and two milligrams. If you have the spray, the typical dosage is two milligrams. Use it. If the person remains unresponsive after the first injection, keep administering another dose every two to three minutes, and transport them immediately to the nearest emergency room."

"What if we run out of naloxone before the person starts breathing again?" Agent McGarry asked.

Then your colleague will most likely die long before they get to the ER. "Aside from getting appropriate quantities of naloxone to have with you in the field at all times, my advice is to bone up on your CPR and mouth-to-mouth resuscitation skills, because you may need them in order to keep the victim alive until paramedics arrive and they make it to the hospital."

Deck sat up. "Thor, stand," he ordered.

"For K-9 officers," Tori continued, "one dose likewise may or may not be sufficient if your dog has been exposed to gray death. As with human victims, be prepared to administer repeated doses." She placed her hand on the dog's back and pointed. "Similarly, the most effective injection site on a dog is the rear thigh."

Buzzing came to her ears. Deck sat up and checked his phone. He slid off the table, catching Brett and Evan's eyes first then hers. "We have to go."

"What is it?" she asked. From the way he clenched his jaw and seriousness of his face, the presentation was over.

"A judge just signed off on another search warrant."

CHAPTER SIX

An hour later, Deck had printed out his ops plan, gotten it signed by ASAC Rivera, and handed out copies to the twenty or so agents he'd personally selected to participate in the warrant. The PC indicated it was a dealer's house, and the product would be going mobile shortly. If they didn't haul ass, all they'd find was an empty house.

In the parking lot adjacent to the SOTF building, Deck outfitted Thor with booties to protect his feet. On either side of him, other officers were busy strapping on tactical and safety gear.

Tori had finished the rest of the training without him. Now, she stood by her car in the parking lot, preparing to leave. Instead of getting into her car, she headed his way. From her determined stride, she had something on her mind.

"I want to go with you," she said as she began rubbing the backs of Thor's ears. The tip of his tail thumped against the Interceptor's rear bumper.

Deck grabbed an extra loaded magazine and stuffed it into a pocket on the front of his vest. "Go with me *where*?" He reached into the back of the Interceptor, searching for his baton.

"On the warrant."

His fingers froze around the baton, then he slowly turned to find her watching him, arms crossed, the same determination he'd glimpsed in her stride now gleaming in her bright green eyes. "And do what? Kick the door in?"

"Yes." Her gaze dipped to his boots. "Do you have a pair of door-kicking boots that will fit me?"

He shoved the baton into another pouch on his vest. Mimicking her stance, he leaned against the bumper and crossed his arms. "No, I don't." Though he was sure she was kidding about the door thing. "Even if I did, there's no way you could accompany us for a ride-along on a high-risk warrant. That takes reams of paper and weeks to get approved. Why do you want to go with us, anyway?"

"Training is one thing, but…I need to do something more proactive." She uncrossed her arms and stepped closer, so close he could see the gold flecks in her irises that he hadn't noticed before. "Let me go with you in case something happens to another one of your officers."

"No." Rivera would have his head, his arms, *and* his legs on a platter.

"What could it hurt?" she insisted, advancing even closer.

He uncrossed his arms, straightening abruptly and forcing her to take a step back. "You. *You* could get hurt."

"And so could *you*." She parked her hands on her trim waist and glared up at him. "I always keep a fully stocked medical bag in my car. My father was a—" She broke off and cleared her throat. "He taught me to be prepared for anything, so I am. Consider this a free house call. I won't even charge you my usual rate. Hopefully, no one will be exposed like Dan Prince was, but if they are, I'll be there."

With more force than was necessary, he yanked down the Velcro strap over his baton. During the seminar, he'd made a comment indicating he blamed himself for what happened to Dan. Clearly she remembered, and now she was using it to try and get her way, something he suspected she was accustomed to. Annoyingly, he conceded she had a point.

Denver paramedics were aces at what they did, but their skills couldn't compare to that of an experienced ER doctor's. But he questioned her motives. For someone who'd initially been about as eager as a gazelle was to cuddle up with a lion, now she wanted to be an active part of his team?

Then it hit him—the image of her in the chapel after the teenager had died. Her grief had been about as real as it got. That boy and others like him were the reason she was doing this. *That* he could relate to.

Normally, he'd need a half-dozen layers of approval, but there wasn't time. "I'll agree to this on one condition, and it's *not* negotiable." He paused to ram home just *how* not negotiable his condition was. "You stay in the truck. You don't get out of the vehicle for *any* reason, unless I tell you to."

She pursed her lips, glaring at him and telling him what he already knew. Dr. Victoria Sampson didn't like taking orders, especially not from him. "Fine," she bit out.

"Then let's get you geared up." He tugged out a spare body armor vest from the back of the Interceptor. She'd be swimming in it, but it was better than nothing.

"Is this really necessary?" She eyed the black vest like it was a viper ready to strike. "I thought you said I was staying in the car."

"It is, and you are. I'm not taking any chances with your safety." He pulled open the Velcro straps on the vest and held it out to her. "Put this over your head."

She managed to get the vest over her head but not without snagging her ponytail on one of the Velcro straps. "Ouch."

"Let me help." Working swiftly but gently, he freed several strands of silky-smooth hair, all while breathing in her scent and wondering if it was from her shampoo or perfume. Either way, he liked it.

He adjusted the shoulder straps, trying not to look at the graceful curve of her neck or the rapidly beating pulse just below her ear. Big green eyes pinned him, freezing him in place for a second. *Pretty eyes, too*. "Good?"

She nodded then licked her lips, sucking her full lower lip between her teeth.

Next, Deck adjusted one of the side straps at her waist. Her incredibly *tiny* waist. He managed to secure one side, but as he tightened down the other, his hand inadvertently brushed the side of her breast. "Uh, sorry." He cleared his throat.

"No problem." A faint blush crept up her neck just above the vest. "I'll get my bag."

He watched her return to her car then unlock the trunk and lean over. The movement tugged up her shirt, exposing several inches of smooth, bare lower back. She pulled out a classic, black doctor's bag then slammed the trunk closed and walked back over.

Deck kneeled on the pavement to finish strapping on Thor's booties. "I didn't know they actually made those old-fashioned bags anymore."

"They do." She patted the bag affectionately. "Most doctors prefer something trendier, but my dad gave me this when I graduated from medical school. I've been using it ever since. In case of emergencies, I keep it fully stocked at all times." To prove her point, she set the bag down just inside the Interceptor's bed and unclipped the metal lock. "Including naloxone."

Deck counted at least four boxes of naloxone auto-injectors. He had to give her credit. "Failure to prepare is preparing to fail."

"That it is." She held out her hand to Thor, who raised his paw. As she inspected the protective bootie, Thor nuzzled her cheek then licked it. A smile lit her face, one bright enough to make him jealous. His dog had a major crush on Tori Sampson.

Deck took in the rest of the meds filling Tori's medical bag, many of which were pain meds. Like the ones his sister got addicted to. "Tell me something, Doc." He still wasn't completely convinced she'd appreciate it if he called her Tori. "You seem pretty passionate about helping to stop opioid overdoses. Why do you give people opioids in the first place?"

She snapped the bag shut. "Because they don't *always* lead to addiction. Opioids have a valuable place in medicine. Pain management being the first. Have you ever been in such incredible pain that you would have done anything to end it?"

"No," he said flatly, doing his damnedest not to launch into an all-out war with her again. "And that's *exactly* how some people get addicted in the first place." Marianne had. His sister was just a kid. She hadn't deserved to die, nor did anyone just because they were led down the one-way road to addiction.

"I—" she began.

"You guys all set?" Evan strolled over with Blue, his German shepherd K-9.

"Just about," Deck said, grateful for the interruption although curious what Tori had been about to say.

Thor and Blue began sniffing, snorting, then strutting around each other with their tails high in the air.

"He's beautiful," she said as she watched Thor and Blue perform their habitual greeting. She peered closer at Evan's dog. "Are his eyes *blue*? How unusual."

"It's a genetic variation," Evan said. "If it weren't for his eyes, he would have been a show dog, but it's considered a disqualifying trait. Sit, Blue. Shake hands with the lady."

Blue obediently sat then held up his paw. Thor did the same, trying to horn in on Blue's attention.

Without missing a beat, Tori took both dogs' paws, one in each hand, shaking them. "Nice to meet you, Blue," she said to Evan's dog, and to Thor, "Always a pleasure."

The dogs' tails wagged enthusiastically, whipping back and forth on the pavement. People tended to say dogs were good judges of character, when in reality, Blue and Thor were probably only responding to her subtle gestures and the tone of her voice. Still, the message to the dogs was clear: she liked them.

"You should have been a veterinarian," Evan observed.

"I almost was. For a while there, it was fifty-fifty which way my medical career would go, *homo sapiens* or critters. Humans won out by a very small margin." She stood and looked around the parking lot. "Is your friend, Brett, coming with us on this warrant?"

At her use of the word *us*, Evan caught Deck's eye, his

brows hitting his hairline.

"No." Although Deck sure wished he was. Blaze was a Chesapeake Bay Retriever and arson dog, but he was also one of the hardest hitting takedown K-9s Deck had ever seen. "He had to drive to Colorado Springs to look into all those fires popping up down there."

"Said he'd be back in time for foosball at Mick's later in the week," Evan said.

"Sounds good. Let's roll." Deck whistled then punched his arm in the air, making a twisting motion with his finger, indicating the wagon train was leaving the station. He opened the passenger door for her then went around to Thor's door. His dog leaped in with ease, his big body quivering with excitement. Thor knew the drill. Work time was a heartbeat away.

As one, nearly a dozen state and federal vehicles followed Deck from the parking lot en route to the Five Points section of Denver.

At the first traffic light, he hit the strobes and slowed at the intersection. The last thing he wanted was to get rammed broadside on the way to a warrant. The rest of the cavalry hit their strobes so they could stay with him.

"Can Thor really breathe in this?" Tori reached for the K-9 mask he'd placed on the console. Hearing his name, Thor stuck his head through the opening over their shoulders. As Tori examined the mask, she sifted her fingers through the fur on Thor's neck.

"Wouldn't use it if he couldn't. We'll stop a mile from the location to put on all our protective gear, including Thor's mask." When she returned the mask to the dashboard, her hand shook slightly. "Nervous?"

"I am," she admitted. "It's my first search warrant, and I never even went to cop school or wherever you guys get trained to kick in doors and take no prisoners."

Deck laughed. "A doctor with a sense of humor. I like that." He did, actually. She was turning out not to be quite as tight-assed as he'd expected. "Everything will be fine. I promise. When we hit the house, you stay—"

"I know, I know." She waved her hand in the air, cutting him off. "Stay in the truck. I got it. Trust me, I have no intention of stepping outside unless someone is overdosing."

"That's not the way this works." He pulled a small portable radio from a cupholder and handed it to her. "If I need you, I'll call you on this. It's already turned on and set to the frequency we'll be using. To talk, just push the button on the left side but wait about one second before speaking. Unless you specifically hear me request your assistance, you don't leave the truck. Got it, Doc?"

"Okay. And I'd appreciate it if you'd stop calling me 'Doc.' I have a name. It's Tori."

Ookay. Now it was official. Although he didn't harbor any illusions that this elevated him to "friend" status. "In that case, you can call me 'Deck.'"

"Why not Adam? That is your name, isn't it? It's on your business card."

"People have been calling me Deck ever since the Academy. Guess I'm just used to it at this point."

"Is that what your mother calls you?"

"No. She calls me Adam. She's the *only* person I let call me Adam."

They drove the remainder of the way in silence. A mile from the target, he pulled over and strapped on Thor's mask, then he donned tactical gloves specially fitted over the long-sleeve shirt he wore. Last, he pulled on a snug-fitting hoodie and his own mask.

As they drove past Cheesman Park and turned onto Colfax Avenue, it was as if someone had flipped a realtor light switch. Large, grand houses morphed into dirty little row houses with unkempt yards. Vehicles parked in driveways were no longer Mercedes and BMWs, but beat-up, rusty cars and trucks.

Thor pranced back and forth on the bench seat behind them, his excited snorts escaping through the mask's ventilation cups.

Deck parked just past the one-story house they were hitting and flung open the door. "I'll leave the engine running so you'll have AC, but no joy rides."

"Funny."

When she gave him a sarcastic smile, he hid a quick grin behind his mask then popped open Thor's door with the key fob on his belt. As it always did during a warrant, his pulse jacked up. His breathing sounded raspy through the mask. He hooked on Thor's leash, and as a team, they rushed to the front door. Half the group stayed with him, while the other half continued on to the backyard to cover the rear entrance and windows.

He pointed to the vehicle in the driveway—a battered Chevy Camaro. One of his team ran to the car, sidearm out as he searched through the open windows. The blue minivan Deck had expected to find in the driveway wasn't there.

Six of them crowded onto the tiny porch. Deck unclipped Thor's leash, tucking it into his belt before pounding on the front door. With his head down and his tail erect, Thor's body language told Deck everything he needed to know. There were illegal drugs in the house.

He signaled to a burly state agent carrying a battering ram. The big cop sent the heavy iron ram crashing against the door, ripping it off both hinges and sending it flying backward inside the house.

Deck, Thor, and the other agents went inside, weapons out and shouting.

"Police, don't move!"

Two men wearing white T-shirts and white paper masks covering their mouths and noses flung their hands in the air. In front of them was a table covered with plastic baggies and a small scale. Even with the masks, based on stature alone, Deck could already identify the men as *not* being the main dealer they were looking for. Alonzo Jones.

Also perched on the table was a larger bag containing gray powder. These guys were in the middle of portioning out smaller baggies for distribution, and no way was Deck taking off his mask. "Where's Jones?" With his mask on, he had to shout to be heard. Both men shrugged.

"I ain't telling you anything, cop," one of the men said.

"Me, either." The other guy pulled aside his mask and spat on the table.

Whatever. If they wanted to play hardball, so could he. Getting locked up tended to loosen lips.

"Cuff 'em," he ordered the other agents.

"We got a runner!"

"Thor!" Deck shouted, pointing into the room the voice had come from.

Thor took off, bounding out of sight. Deck barely caught up with his dog in time to see another man—this one carrying a gun—hurling himself out an open bedroom window. Deck started to call his dog back, but Thor was already leaping through the broken screen.

CHAPTER SEVEN

Tori picked up the radio then put it back in the cupholder. She'd been impressed with the professional way Deck had handled the large crowd during the training. She'd also appreciated his efforts to ease her anxiety. He'd been kind to her, and she hadn't deserved it. Not after being such a pissy bee-otch to him at the hospital.

The warrant team had been inside for several minutes now. She'd watched in total awe as they'd "hit the house," smashing through the front door as if it were no thicker than a piece of cardboard then rushing inside. Despite all the initial movie-like action, the radio Deck had given her remained eerily silent.

How long does it take to execute a high-risk drug warrant? She had no idea and couldn't begin to speculate. One thing for certain was Deck's dedication to his job. Back in the parking lot, she sensed that part of his passion for shutting down the opioid network stemmed from something personal. It had been on the tip of her tongue to ask him about it when they'd been interrupted. It was just as well that she hadn't. His personal life was none of her business.

Tori dug her fingers between the body armor vest and her rib cage. Talk about uncomfortable. She felt sorry for all the cops who had to wear one of these things every day.

She let out an impatient breath. Being here—at a federal search warrant—was so far outside her box, it was ridiculous. She slumped lower in the seat and crossed her arms, or rather *tried* crossing her arms. The darned vest made it impossible.

Tori sat up in time to see Thor hurtling through the air at a man running along the side of the house. The dog took the man to the ground, latching onto his wrist. Even with the SUV's windows closed and the engine still running, she heard the man's screams.

Deck charged out the front door—correction, where the front door *used* to be—and bolted to where Thor hunched on the grass, his tail in the air and his head low where he still gripped the man's wrist.

She leaned forward, trying to get a better view of the action. Deck drew his gun and aimed it at the man's head, clearly being careful to keep the muzzle's line of fire away from his dog. Two other agents raced over to assist Deck. Tori cracked the passenger window, straining to hear what Deck was shouting.

A blue minivan sped past and screeched to a stop in the middle of the road. A man bolted from the driver's seat then hurled open the passenger door. The two agents on the lawn charged the man, weapons out, shouting at him to get on the ground.

Ignoring the agents' commands, he lifted a small child about five years old from the minivan's rear seat, cradling the limp body and yelling for help. The child's head lolled back at an awkward angle. Even from this distance, Tori could see the girl's red skin and the hives breaking out.

Completely against Deck's orders, she grabbed her medical bag from the floor at her feet and shoved open the door. She ran to where the man had set the girl down on the sidewalk.

"Help her! Somebody, please help her!" the man shouted as agents grabbed his arms and flung him to the ground. Seconds later, he was cuffed and lying face down on his belly.

Deck grabbed a radio from his belt, and she could just make out him calling for an ambulance.

The girl's lips and face were swollen, and her chest rose rapidly with shallow, wheezing breaths. Tori opened the girl's mouth. Her tongue was enlarged, and her lower lip seemed bigger than it had been ten seconds ago. Whatever the issue was, the girl was in anaphylactic shock.

Tori dug into her bag, pulling out a hard-sided leather case. She unzipped it, grabbed an EpiPen, and stuck it in the girl's thigh, pushing the plunger.

Deck crouched at her side. "Can I help?"

"No." She dug into her bag again, pulled out a stethoscope, then placed the tips in her ears and the diaphragm on the child's chest. Between the man's incessant crying and all the agents shouting back and forth, she couldn't hear a thing.

"Quiet! I can't hear anything!" she yelled, and everyone within earshot clammed up. Tori picked up a weak, rapid heartbeat. The child's wheezing had already lessened.

"Hand me the blood pressure cuff in my bag." When Deck handed it to her, she wrapped it around the girl's upper arm and pumped up the bulb. "Bring that man over here." She indicated the handcuffed prisoner. "I need to talk to him."

The agents guarding the man hesitated until Deck ordered, "Do it!"

"Is she allergic to anything?" She looked up at the man whose arms were gripped firmly by an agent on either side of him.

"Not that I know of," he said as tears streamed down his face. "Please, help her. I just picked her up at her mother's and she couldn't breathe."

She looked at him over the girl's body and was moved by the genuine concern in his eyes. A moment later, the girl's eyelids fluttered, and her breathing began shifting back to normal. "What's her name?" she asked the father.

"Amy. It's Amy."

"Amy." Tori tapped the girl's cheeks. "Can you hear me?"

"Y-yes. I feel funny. My lips feel fat." With her swollen lips and tongue, the words had come out somewhat garbled and slurred.

"You're going to be fine." A siren wailed in the distance, quickly becoming louder. To Deck, she said, "Let's get her up so she can breathe easier."

Deck lifted the girl upright, cradling her against his chest. "Hey, there," he said, softly and with such tenderness that Tori felt a twinge of…something. "Feeling better?"

"Uh-huh." She nodded.

"Atta girl."

Amy raised her hand, pointing to where Thor sat twenty feet away on the grass. "Whose dog is that?"

"Mine." Deck canted his head in Thor's direction. "Thor." The dog trotted over and sat. "Amy, meet Thor. Thor, shake."

Thor lifted his paw in the air, holding it up until Amy reached out and shook it, revealing a slightly raised red welt near her armpit.

"He's pretty," Amy said.

"Amy?" Tori asked. "Were you stung by a bee or a wasp?" She touched her finger to the welt.

Amy pouted. "Uh-huh."

"Have you been stung by one before?"

"Uh-huh. It hurt."

"I know it did." She looked up as an ambulance pulled to a stop. "They'll make it feel better at the hospital. I promise."

When the paramedics parked and pulled out a stretcher from the back of the ambulance, Deck carefully picked Amy up and laid her gently on the stretcher.

Tori quickly explained to the paramedics what had happened then unstrapped her BP cuff from Amy's arm.

"Is my daddy coming with me?" Amy's eyes teared up, sending a jolt of sympathy through Tori.

"Sorry, kiddo." Deck squeezed Amy's hand. "Your daddy and I need to have a little talk first. Where's your mommy?" He glanced at his prisoner.

"I'll give you her number," the father said, breathing easier now that his daughter was conscious and talking. "We're divorced. She lives two blocks away."

Deck dialed the number the man gave him then quickly explained what had happened. "She's on her way."

Before putting Amy in the ambulance, the EMTs did a quick workup while Tori described the girl's symptoms and the dosage of the EpiPen.

Less than two minutes later, another car came screeching to a stop on the opposite side of the road, and a young woman jumped out and rushed over. "My baby! My baby!" She stroked Amy's cheek. "Are you all right?"

"Yes, Mommy." Amy nodded then pointed to Deck, who stood on the sidewalk, talking into his phone again. "That nice man let me play with his dog. Can I have a dog?"

Tori couldn't hold back her smile. Children's priorities were entirely different from that of adults. Amy could have died, but the most important thing that happened to her today was meeting Thor and Deck.

The woman took in all the uniforms standing on the front lawn then glared at Amy's father. "We *will* talk about this later." She walked next to the stretcher as the EMTs rolled it to the ambulance then climbed inside to go with her daughter to the hospital.

Moments later, the ambulance drove slowly down the road.

Tori shook her head. Ironically, the man in handcuffs was dealing in drugs that killed people, but his quick actions had just saved his daughter's life. *This* was why she'd become a doctor. She turned to find Deck scowling at her.

"You did good, Doc. I mean, Tori." His scowl deepened. "Aside from leaving the truck against my orders."

She pressed her lips together. "If I hadn't, that little girl could have died."

"Yeah, I know," he relented, the irritation on his face easing. A bit, anyway. He pointed a finger at her. "But get back in the truck. We're not done inside."

Blood began simmering in her veins. She jabbed a finger right back at him. "Listen, you bossy, arrogant jerk. I am *not* a child." Chastising her like she was, let alone in front of his colleagues, was beyond inappropriate.

Without waiting for a response, she collected her bag

and got back into the SUV, slamming the door shut none-too-gently. She clenched her fists in her lap. "Ooh, that… that…*man*."

That *man* began speaking to his prisoner. With the window still cracked, she could almost make out the conversation but not quite. Amy's father nodded in her direction, and Deck turned to stare at her. They talked for a few more minutes before Deck put him in the backseat of one of the other vehicles.

With her anger mellowed enough that she could think straight without wanting to strangle Deck, she made a mental note to check up on Amy later and make sure the family stocked up on EpiPens. She also reluctantly acknowledged that Deck had been really good with the little girl, and shoot…she and Deck made a great team. When they weren't at each other's throats.

Instead of going to the driver's side door of the SUV, Deck came to her door and opened it. Thor maneuvered his head onto her lap, urging her to pet him.

"Have you come to apologize for yelling at me?" Tori pursed her lips. She doubted the man had an apologetic bone in his body. That was the DEA way. She knew that firsthand.

"No. I came to thank you."

Huh? Shock must have shown on her face.

"Yep. That's Alonzo Jones." He jerked his finger to Amy's father. "The main guy we were looking for. Seems Jones didn't plan on talking to me. Until you saved his daughter's life. Turns out he's grateful and wants to repay the favor. Because of you."

"Really?" She couldn't contain the excitement bursting

inside her and grabbed Deck's arm. "What did he say? Did he tell you who his supplier is?" If her actions had not only saved a life but gotten Deck something useful for his investigation that would get another dealer off the street, that was heady stuff, indeed.

He glanced to where her hand encircled his forearm. Well, half his forearm. It was too thickly muscled for her fingers to get completely around it. She released him, tucking her hand against her chest.

"He doesn't know the supplier's name, but he gave me a description. Said they meet in public places to make the money exchange. Even gave me some locations."

"So that's good, right?"

"Wait, there's more." When he grinned, Tori had to blink. That grin brightened up his usually serious, scowling face, making him even more attractive. "During one of the money exchanges, another guy was with the supplier, a guy Jones *thinks* is the source."

"Does he know where this source is making it?" Tori asked hopefully.

"No, but he overheard something about the guy coming from up north."

"Up north? What does that mean? Northern Colorado, or north of Colorado? Canada?"

"My questions exactly. It's more than we had before, so I'd say this warrant was a success."

"A success?" His definition of a success was different from hers. "You still don't know who the distributor is."

"True, but Jones gave me a description of that guy, too."

"What does he look like?"

"Late thirties, about five-eleven, with brown hair and

wears a ball cap. And he drives a fancy black sports car."

"That's it?" She couldn't contain the disappointment in her voice.

"It's more than we had before. Sooner or later, someone will spill his guts and give us a name. Until then, we'll keep busting these dealers." He gave Thor a gentle pat. "We'll be a little longer inside."

As she watched Deck stride toward the house, she settled back in the seat to wait, giving a mental fist-pump. For the first time since she'd agreed to this pact with the devil, she began to feel good about it. Maybe, despite all her reservations, this partnership could actually work. It had been a wild and crazy ride, and this was only the first day. God only knew what would happen next.

CHAPTER EIGHT

In Deck's opinion, the only thing Thor did better than sniffing out drugs was climbing ladders. He clicked the timer button on his watch. "Thor, up."

Methodically and confidently, his dog pawed his way up rung after rung until he was at the top of the twenty-foot ladder. With athletic grace, he vaulted onto the observation tower set in the middle of the Rocky Mountain K-9 Training Center. He circled the tower, looking over the edge at all of them and sporting an undeniable canine smirk that said: *That's right. I'm bad.*

Deck stopped the timer. "Eight seconds. That's an unofficial course record." He looked up at his dog. "Nice going, buddy."

Thor threw back his head and *woofed*.

"Your boy's amazing," Brett said. "He climbs ladders faster than any house painter or roofer I've ever seen. Blaze is way too big and clumsy. He'd faceplant in the dirt after two rungs. You have other talents, don't you, boy?" He leaned down to scrub the ears of an enormous golden-brown Chesapeake Bay Retriever. The big dog leaned against Brett's leg, groaning his pleasure.

"Even Blue never mastered the ladder thing." Evan knelt at his shepherd's side and wrapped an arm around the dog's back. "But you can find a body—dead *or* alive—faster than any K-9 this side of the Rockies." Blue snorted and licked Evan's face. "Yeah, I know. Flattery will get me everywhere."

Blaze stuck his snout in the air and sniffed.

"What's he got?" Deck looked in the same direction the retriever was looking. South.

"Who knows?" Brett likewise looked to the south. "Gasoline, any accelerant picked up on the wind. Could be there's enough smoke blowing up here from the fires down in the Springs."

Above them, Thor remained watching with nothing short of cocky, canine satisfaction gleaming from his eyes. Deck could swear his dog's chest was puffed up with pride. "Thor, down."

With as much speed and agility as he'd displayed going head first up the ladder, he showed off coming down backward. Thor ran to Deck's side and sat.

"You think you deserve something special after that?" Thor bobbed his head up and down. "You know where to find it."

Thor ran to the scarecrow Deck had erected in the center of the field then stood on his hind legs and dug one of his paws into the scarecrow's pants pockets. Less than five seconds later, he pulled out a small dog treat Deck had hidden there earlier.

"I swear, that dog might as well have fingers," Brett said.

When Thor loped back to him, Deck leashed his dog, giving him a sound patting on his back. "We still on for beers and foosball at Mick's Saturday?"

"Absolutely." Evan unleashed Blue to sniff out a scent rag he'd hidden in a tree.

As he watched Evan and Brett put their dogs through their paces, Deck wondered if Tori was on duty today. It had been three days since the warrant, and he hadn't spoken to her since. His innate skepticism had him doubting she'd actually call him if an overdose patient was willing to talk. Could be she was still pissed at him for reprimanding her at the warrant. It *had* been kind of a dick move, but he'd only been concerned for her safety.

"I heard what happened at the warrant," Brett said as they both watched Evan work Blue around the field until he sat at the base of the tree and looked up. "Sorry I missed all the action. Heard your girlfriend saved the day in more ways than one."

"Funny," Deck muttered under his breath. Although she *had* kicked ass. Without her interference, even if it was against his direct orders, he never would've gotten those descriptions from Jones.

"What'd I miss?" Evan and Blue rejoined them.

"Not much," Deck said. "The descriptions we got from Alonzo Jones on his supplier and the distributor were helpful, but we still don't have names or a location where this new cocktail is being made."

"He couldn't pick these guys out of a mugshot array?" Evan asked.

Deck shook his head. "I think Jones knows the name of his supplier, and he's afraid of him. The distributor, I'm not so sure about. Whoever the supplier is would have to be someone known to the drug world, probably someone with a record. We also can't discount the possibility that the source doesn't have a mugshot. Yet, anyway."

"Why do you say that?" Brett asked.

"It's only a theory," he began. "Based on the lab reports from that DEA case in Pennsylvania, the drug we're dealing with is very similar but not quite as potent. It's as if someone's been tweaking the drug, trying to make it less deadly but still addictive to the point where users need something that strong to get the high they want."

Brett hooked a leash onto Blaze's collar. "You said that case was never solved. What happened with that case?"

"It's still open. It was only when people started dying that we opened that case in the first place. The Philadelphia SAC office thought they were getting close." That's when the trail went cold. "What if whoever was making that drug in Pennsylvania decided things were too hot, closed up shop, then moved here with a new recipe? What if it's the same guy?"

"Or gal," Evan suggested. "Let's not be sexist here. Remember Thelma Wright?"

"Who's Thelma Wright?" Brett asked.

Every DEA newbie learned about Wright in training. "Back in the 1990s, she was the drug queen of Philadelphia, transporting enormous quantities of cocaine and heroin between that city and L.A."

"Speaking of women," Brett said to Evan, canting his head toward Deck, "we were discussing Deck and Thor's hot new doctor partner."

"Is she married?" Evan asked. "A lot of tongues were wagging at the seminar the other day."

"Not that I know of."

"Wonder why," Brett said.

Deck had wondered that, too. *Not my business*. So he hadn't asked.

Evan stooped to give Blue his reward—a rolled-up towel. "Well, I can't imagine that lasting long. Seems like a catch."

"Heard she saved a little girl." Brett uncapped a bottle of water for Blaze and poured it into a bowl. "Sorry I missed that."

Deck shook his head, still amazed at how she'd taken charge of the situation like a quarterback yelling at his team. "You should've seen her. The kid was lucky she was there."

Brett and Evan stared at him, both with smirks on their faces.

"What?" Deck asked.

"Nothing." Brett held up his hands.

"We're just surprised," Evan said. "Knowing how you feel about doctors and all, we never figured you'd partner with one, let alone *praise* her."

Brett snickered. "But she *is* pretty. And smart."

"It's a temporary business arrangement." Deck glared at his friends. "Nothing more."

The vibration of his cell phone saved him from more adolescent insinuations. "Decker."

For the next five minutes, he listened while ASAC Rivera filled him in. By the time his boss was done, Deck's head pounded with the mother of all headaches.

"Bad news?" Brett asked.

"You could say that," he said as they all headed back to the parking lot. "Three more suspected ODs, all in Fort Collins. Two of them DOA."

"The third?" Evan opened the side door of his SUV while Blue hopped in.

"Alive but in a coma." After Thor jumped into the kennel, Deck closed the door. "It's the governor's son." His friends' eyes widened. "For the last hour, the governor's been on the phone with the DEA administrator in Washington, demanding to know what's being done to shut down opioid trafficking."

Brett stood by the side of his SUV with Blaze. "No pressure, huh?"

Right. No pressure at all. Christ, he needed to nail down the source of this shit, and he needed him—or *her*—yesterday.

His cell phone buzzed again, and he ripped it from his belt. *What now?* But it wasn't his ASAC again, as he'd expected. *Tori.* He'd added her to his contacts earlier in the week. "This is Deck." As he listened, his pulse thumped faster.

The break he needed might have just fallen into his lap.

CHAPTER NINE

"I'm sorry to interrupt," Tori said, joining Wil and Ethan at the nurses' station. "Wil, can I speak with you for a minute? It's about your overdose patient."

The woman had come in an hour ago. Luckily, the hits she'd taken hadn't been that big and she'd come around after only two doses of naloxone. The second she was alert and talking, Tori had spoken with her privately about meeting with Deck. Now, the coffee she'd just drank gurgled in her stomach. Wil wouldn't like what she was about to say.

Better to beg for forgiveness than to ask for permission.

"Leslie Batista?"

"Yes. Let's talk in the lounge." Without waiting for a response, she started walking to the lounge. Over her shoulder, she caught Ethan's gaze following them and looking none-to-happy. The upbeat demeanor he'd arrived here with two years ago after graduating from Temple University's med school in Philadelphia seemed to have vanished. North Metro had already taken a toll on the young man. Not for the first time, she considered speaking with Wil about Ethan, but one issue at a time.

Once inside the lounge with the door closed, Wil raised a brow. "Why the cloak and dagger?"

"I need to discuss something with you privately."

"Okay." He leaned back against the kitchenette counter. "Something tells me I'm not going to like it."

"Probably not." Her stomach lurched again. "I spoke with your patient."

"What about?"

"I asked her if she would be willing to speak to the DEA about where she bought her drugs."

Wil's forehead creased. "You shouldn't have done that and certainly not without consulting me. It's unethical. I thought we were a team."

Tori shook her head. "Technically, it's not unethical. But I agree, since she's your patient and you and I are friends, I should have spoken with you before I did it." She'd known Wil wouldn't approve, but from his expression, he was royally ticked. More than she'd expected.

"Then why did you?"

"I already told you that DEA agent, Deck—Special Agent Decker—wanted me to notify him anytime an opioid OD, particularly a gray death OD, came into the ER so that he could speak with them about where they bought the drugs."

"And you agreed to this?"

"I did. The hospital administration approved my request. He'll be here any minute."

Wil pursed his lips. "Why didn't you just ask me first? This isn't like you, at all, and I'm shocked that you'd do this behind my back."

"No more shocked than I was," she admitted. Partnering with Deck dug up all kinds of guilt.

The distraught look on her mother's face the day DEA agents had taken her dad away in handcuffs flashed front and center, and that was only the beginning. Six months in a federal prison had left a lasting mark on her father's soul.

Her mother's, too. After the fine had been paid and the lawyers siphoned off their share, her dad was forced to shut down his business. By court order. Financial hardship had nearly destroyed her family.

But helping the DEA wasn't why she'd partnered with Deck. She'd done it to help *save* people.

"I'm worried about you," Wil said. "I know you're still upset about that boy who died. Just promise me you'll be careful working with the DEA."

He probably wouldn't want to hear that she'd gone with Deck on a search warrant. She hadn't told anyone at the hospital about that. Not even Suzie. "I regret not asking you before speaking with your patient. I promise I won't do it again." Not if it meant destroying her friendship with Wil. Nothing would be worth that.

Wil seemed to relax. "At least, let me be there with you when this agent speaks with my patient. Maybe I can help."

"Thank you," she said, knowing how good Wil was with patients. "That would be great."

Wil tapped his watch, an old leather wristwatch his father had given him. "We'd better go."

As they left the lounge and headed back to the ER, relief swept over her. She never should have doubted Wil's support in the first place.

"Dr. Barnett?" Suzie pointed to ER 4, meaning a new case had come in and Wil was next up on rotation.

Wil groaned. "I'll be right there," he said to Suzie. "Fill me in later?" he said over his shoulder then headed into the examining room.

"I will," she called after him, then went to meet Deck.

At the admin desk, three nurses stood with their heads

together, whispering like teenage girls as they stared at something down the hall.

"What's going on?" Tori asked, joining them.

"Him," one of them said, pointing. "*He's* what's going on."

Just inside the ER doors, a boy about nine years old and wearing a Rockies baseball cap sat on a stretcher. In one hand, he clutched a mitt to his chest. His other arm was in a sling. The kid was adorable, but that wasn't what had caught the nurses' undivided attention. On one side of the stretcher stood a woman Tori presumed was the boy's mother and on the other side were Deck and Thor.

Dressed in what she now knew was typical for him — black tactical pants and matching polo shirt with the DEA badge and K-9 Unit insignia — Deck was a formidable sight. The ever-present handgun strapped to his right side completed the fearsome image. The man really was handsome with a capital H. No wonder the nurses were staring. Now that Tori had seen him, even she couldn't tear her gaze away.

Deck leaned in to talk to the boy, whose eyes were red, and his shoulders shook as he strived valiantly not to cry.

"Tori." Deck waved her over.

The moment Thor caught sight of her, his tail began whipping back and forth.

"Hello, Thor." The dog wore a vest around his body with a DEA badge on both sides. She leaned down to scratch his ears and let him lick her chin. "It's always nice to see your happy, furry face, although I'm not sure you should be in the emergency room." The reprimand was, of course, meant for Deck.

"Morning," he said, ignoring the hint, and when he smiled, her belly fluttered. Worse, he smelled good. All citrusy and fresh. *Please, not me, too.* Did all federal agents smell this good? "This is Dylan and his mom, Andrea," he said. "This is Dr. Sampson."

"Hello, Dr. Sampson," the boy's mother said, smiling grimly.

"H-hi." A tear rolled down Dylan's cheek, and it was all Tori could do not to wipe it away herself and give him a big hug.

"Dylan's a big baseball fan, aren't you?" The boy nodded. "He fell from his bike on the way to practice, and it sounds like he may have broken his arm. Now he's worried that he won't be able to play ball for a while."

Again, Dylan nodded, and when his lower lip started trembling, Deck rested his hand on the boy's shoulder. "I broke my arm when I was kid, too. It hurt a lot, but it healed up just fine and I was back to playing ball in no time. Dylan's being very brave about all this."

"I can see that," Tori agreed. She could also see the positive effect Deck was having on the boy. As if someone had flipped a switch, Dylan's shoulders stopped shaking and his lip stopped trembling.

Deck pulled something that looked like a deck of cards from his pocket.

"Are those baseball cards?" Dylan set the mitt in his lap and pointed.

"Kind of." Deck handed one of the cards to the boy, returning the rest of the stack to his pocket. "It's a K-9 trading card. It has a picture of Thor, and it tells you all about him. What kind of breed he is, what his specialty is, and what he likes to do for fun."

Dylan looked at the card, turning it over to read what was on the back. "Does he do tricks for fun?"

"He sure does." Deck looked at Thor. "Thor, up." To Tori's astonishment, Thor rose on his hind legs in front of the stretcher, standing straight up and hovering there. "Spin." Deck twirled his finger, and Thor began turning in circles.

Dylan laughed. Beside him, his mother looked on, sending Deck a grateful smile.

"Wow," Dylan said, reaching out to touch Thor's outstretched paws.

"Cool, huh?" Deck said.

"Really cool." Dylan grinned.

"Down, boy." Thor lowered his front paws to the floor then uttered a low snort. "Tell you what." Deck pulled something else from one of his thigh pockets, handing them to Dylan. "These are four tickets to Family Night at Coors Field. You can go see the Rockies in person."

"*Wowww*. For me?" Deck nodded, and the boy's eyes practically popped from his head. "Thanks, Deck."

"Thank you." His mother blinked rapidly. "You didn't have to do that."

"It was my pleasure," Deck said. "Every kid should see the Rockies play in person at least once."

Behind them, someone cleared their throat, and Tori turned to see Ethan looking on with an amused expression. Ethan must have been assigned the boy's case and was waiting to examine him.

"I think someone's waiting to take a look at that arm," she said to Dylan. "You're going to be playing ball again in no time."

"Stay brave, my man." Deck held up his fist, and when Dylan fist-bumped him back, Tori couldn't stop smiling at the gesture and Deck's kindness to the boy.

Deck and Thor fell in step beside her as she led the way to Leslie Batista's room. "That was very sweet what you did back there." And very much like what he'd done with Amy on the raid. She began to suspect that beneath all that body armor and muscles lay a heart of gold.

"We saw Dylan and his mom coming in. The kid looked so upset we thought he needed a little cheering up. And don't be mad with me for sneaking Thor into the ER. In addition to being the best drug dog in the state, he's also a certified therapy dog."

"I didn't know that." Along with not knowing what a soft spot Deck obviously had for kids.

"There's a lot you don't know about me." The corner of his mouth lifted, and her belly did that same annoying fluttering thing.

"Um." She had to shake her head to clear it. Any of her body parts fluttering over this guy was *so* not good. "We're here." She led the way into Leslie Batista's room, momentarily hesitating. Neil Shibowsky, the hospital's cardiac surgeon, sat at the foot of the bed. Leslie was laughing at something Neil had said.

"Dr. Shibowsky?" Tori shot Neil a questioning look. "I didn't know Dr. Barnett had called for a cardiac consult."

"Leslie and I were just chatting." Neil took his sweet time getting off the bed. "I'll come back and check on you later." He winked at Leslie before leaving the room.

"Good morning," Deck said, taking immediate charge. "Thank you for speaking with me." He held out his hand to Leslie.

Leslie was barely nineteen and had come in with a moderate overdose. Color was already back in her cheeks, and the prognosis was good. Catching sight of Deck, Leslie flipped back her thick blond curls and managed to sit up straighter. Her gaze drifted down then up Deck's tall, muscular form.

"Good morning to you, too." Leslie smiled appreciatively, taking Deck's hand and holding it, in Tori's opinion, far longer than necessary. Tori had already discovered that, when not under the influence of opioids, Ms. Batista was not only quite pretty but no shy flower. "I'm happy to help any way I can."

"Great." As Deck extricated his hand, Tori was reminded of the moment when he'd been helping her put on the body armor vest. His fingers had inadvertently grazed the side of her breast, sending chills up and down her spine and heat to her face. *Get real, girl.* He was so far outside her comfort zone, the only thing she should be thinking about where he was concerned was their business relationship. Anything else was preposterous.

"I know you want to get out of here, so let's get started." Deck took out a small pad and pen from his thigh pocket. "Where did you buy the drugs that you OD'd on?"

"Up north. I met a guy in a supermarket parking lot."

"And what did you go there to buy?"

"Heroin. But the guy said this was better. He said it was *supercharged* heroin and that it was such good stuff I'd be back for more."

"You said 'up north,'" he repeated. "*Where* up north exactly?"

"Loveland. At that new shopping center off Garfield Avenue. Behind the big bakery."

"I know it." He nodded. "How did you know where to go?"

"Everyone knows this guy's there on Friday nights after nine o'clock, as soon as it's dark out."

"What's his name?"

"I think his name is Jack. I don't know for sure, and I didn't really care at the time."

"What did he look like?"

Leslie gave a sketchy description that didn't match the ones Alonzo Jones had given Deck. Maybe it was an independent dealer. Either way, Tori wondered if this would be enough to get another warrant.

"What kind of vehicle does Jack drive?"

"A pickup."

"What color?"

Leslie shrugged. "I don't know. Like I said, it was dark out."

"Was there anyone else with Jack?"

"Yeah. A couple other guys collecting the money."

"Can you describe them?"

Again, Deck took notes as Leslie gave descriptions of two men who sounded like they could be anyone walking on the streets of Denver.

"All right, then," he said after a few more minutes of Q&A. "One last question. Are you planning on going to rehab?"

Leslie's eyes filled quickly. Tears spilled down her cheeks. "I want to, but I tried it before, and it didn't work."

Deck took the young woman's hand. "You do have

what it takes to get through rehab. You have to want it badly enough."

"I know. That's what they told me." Her shoulders began shaking. "But I don't think I can do it, and I have no one to help me."

Deck sat on the side of the bed and took Leslie in his arms, rocking her gently while she cried.

Wow. First Amy, then Dylan, and now…big tough federal agent going all soft and mushy. *This guy is amazing.*

Leslie curled her fingers into Deck's shirt, clutching him tightly before he pulled away. He grabbed a tissue from the table next to the bed, dabbing it at the tears still rolling down her cheeks.

The way he held Leslie had Tori wondering what it would be like to be held by this man. *Really* held, with his big arms wrapped tightly around her.

Oh, for heaven's sake. She blinked and gave herself a mental smack. *What am I doing?* Her cranium was going bonkers today.

On the rare occasions that she actually did date, the men she went out with were accountants or doctors or investment bankers. They all had safe, unexciting jobs, and that was the way she wanted it. Going out with a wild, thrill-seeking DEA agent…not gonna happen. The only thing going on between them—now or *ever*—was that he needed her help, and something inside her *wanted* to help him. Well, not him, precisely.

He stood and tugged two business cards from his thigh pocket, handing them to Leslie. "Here's my business card and a card for the best rehab center I know. They specialize in people your age, and they're good at it. Trust me."

"Thanks." She sniffled then took the cards.

"Thank *you*," Deck said, taking her hand in his. "You've got this, Leslie. Be strong. Okay?" She nodded. "Good. The most important thing you can do is to let people help you. Family. Friends. Don't shut them out. Let them know exactly what's been going on with you, and as soon as the rehab center allows you to have visitors, invite them to your sessions. It makes all the difference."

Tori watched Deck closely, curious about the look on his face—intense and yet…sad was the word that popped into her head. There was something deeply meaningful rooted in the advice he'd given Leslie. Was someone close to him an addict? Did they die? It wasn't any of her business, but she couldn't help wondering about his personal life. She didn't even know if he was married or had a girlfriend or kids of his own. Not that it was any of her business.

Wil rushed into the room. "Turned out that case wasn't all that urgent. What did I miss?"

"Not much." Deck shoved the pad and pen back into his pocket. "We're all done here."

"Shall we?" Tori extended her arm toward the door, indicating she and Deck should leave. Being the conscientious physician that he was, Wil took his follow-up care very seriously.

Deck followed her from the room. "Thanks for setting that up."

"You're welcome." She continued with him to the ER exit. "Do you think you can get another warrant with that information?"

"I'll have to do surveillance up in Loveland. But yeah. I do."

She grabbed his arm, forcing him to stop walking. "I want to go with you."

"Not a chance."

"Why not? I accompanied you on the last warrant."

He began shaking his head. "That was a one-time thing."

"Then how about making it a two-time thing?"

"Why?" He quickened his pace, forcing her to hurry to keep up with his long stride.

When he beelined for the door, she knew the only way she'd get him to agree was if she did a lot of sweet-talking, and fast. "Because you need me." Ironically, it was probably more that *she* needed *him*, at the moment. To give her the continuing chance to make a difference out there.

"We have agents cross-trained as EMTs, so no offense, but we *don't* need you." He pushed through the ER exit door into the waiting area. "If that's not enough, paramedics are either on standby or a quick call away."

She followed him through the door. "*Or* you could have *me* right there with you on standby. We already established that there's no one more qualified, and there's precedent for it. With the nationwide rise in mental illness, some police departments have started taking psychiatrists with them on mental health calls because they're better trained to handle those situations."

"Those are shrinks, Tori." He turned and kept walking.

Was that the first time he'd called her by her nickname?

"Psychiatrists are physicians, too," she countered, following him.

He turned so abruptly she nearly slammed into his chest. "Why do you really want to do this?"

Because of Tyler. But she didn't want to discuss him. His eyes softened as he gazed down at her, eyes so deep brown she could easily see herself getting lost in their warm, chocolaty depths. "Please," she said, latching onto his forearm and squeezing it. "I *have* to do this. I have to do something *more*."

CHAPTER TEN

What does *a girl wear to a federal warrant?*

Tori stared at the blouses hanging in her closet. Last time, she'd been totally unprepared and had to go with what she'd been wearing at the training presentation. Now, she had time to make just the right selection.

She glanced at the clock on her bedside table. Six p.m. Deck would be here in an hour to pick her up. Unable to make a decision about a shirt, she dug into her bureau and pulled out a pair of black jeans. *Perfect*. Deck wore black all the time, so that seemed like the right choice.

Tori put on the jeans then went back to her closet. The shirt shouldn't matter that much, since he'd make her wear that awful, itchy body armor vest again. *So why am I fussing so much about my wardrobe?* It was an arrest warrant, not a beauty pageant. Deck couldn't care less what she was wearing.

Pride. She was a doctor, after all, with a reputation to uphold. *Oh, bull*. There was that bonky brain of hers again, forcing her to acknowledge the truth. She wanted to look good for him. A stupid, stupid thought, but there it was. *Shit, shit, shit!* That was the last place she should go.

She grabbed the least sexy, least attractive shirt in the entire closet—a slightly too big, rumpled, short-sleeve, scoop-neck, cerulean-blue shirt that she never wore because it made her look frumpy and screamed boring. The plan had been to donate it to Goodwill. She just hadn't gotten around to it yet.

Tori slipped it off the hanger and put it on. The mirror affixed to the inside of the closet door confirmed it. "Frumpy with a capital *F*." No man would give her a second look in this awful shirt. "It's perfect."

Her cell phone blared from the top of the bureau. She put the call on speaker then set the phone back on the bureau while she searched for shoes. "Hi, Wil." The second she said his name, she clapped a hand over her eyes. She'd completely forgotten about their dinner plans.

"I'm leaving now," he said. "Should be at your place in twenty minutes."

"You're going to kill me." She grimaced at the mirror. "I'm going on one of those DEA warrants tonight up in Loveland. Can I take a raincheck?"

A moment of silence, then, "You're going on a *warrant*? Seriously?" *Oh, boy*. She never should have mentioned it. On the other end of the phone, there was no mistaking Wil's grumbling censure. "This is exactly what I was worried about—that you'd get roped into something that could land you in hot water. You really need to rethink this, Tor."

"I'm going. This is probably the last time."

"The *last* time? When was the *first* time?"

Whoops. "Uh, a few days ago."

"You should have told me."

"It was last minute. It wasn't planned or anything. Besides, I actually saved a little girl who'd just gone into anaphylactic shock. I can totally understand the excitement of being a paramedic." Helping people in the ER was more of a controlled environment. Saving people in the field had really gotten her juices flowing in ways she'd never imagined.

"Okay, okay," Wil relented. "And hey, we never got around to talking about how it went with Leslie Batista yesterday. Did that DEA agent get anything useful?"

"Well, he got a warrant, so I guess so." She frowned, sticking her finger through a hole at the hem of the shirt. Rumbling from a powerful engine came from outside. "Can't be," she mumbled, going to the window.

"Can't be *what*?" Wil asked.

Deck's black SUV sat in her driveway. He was an hour early. *Crap*. She shoved her feet into a pair of rubber-soled shoes. "Wil, I'm sorry. I really have to go."

"I'll catch up with you next shift. Just be careful, and if the bullets start flying…duck."

"Oh, you're hilarious."

After ending the call, she speed-walked to the bathroom and grabbed the first brush she could get her hands on. Once brushed, she quickly tied her hair up in its usual ponytail. One more mirror-check and—

Groaning at the ridiculousness of her vanity, she plucked the cap off a stick of black eyeliner and did her eyes. A swipe of mascara and she was ready.

Ready for what? A prom date?

Tori reached for the box of tissues to wipe off her makeup when the doorbell rang. "Oh, forget it."

She hustled down the stairs and unlocked the door, opening it. Deck stood there, holding two large paper cups of coffee from her favorite café down the street. Thor sat beside him, his tail swishing back and forth.

No fair. Why did men always look so good with no

makeup at all and hair still wet from a shower? A bead of water trickled down his temple—or was it sweat? Either way, the man looked good.

Hissing and a deep growling *meow* came from the bushes separating hers and her neighbor's driveways. Thor's head swiveled, and he took off for the bushes. To her surprise, Deck didn't seem to pick up on the fact that a war was about to begin.

"Uh-oh. That's the neighbor's cat." Tori rushed past Deck, warning over her shoulder, "You should call Thor back. For a cat, Tigger's meaner than a junkyard dog."

"He'll be fine. Trust me."

There it was again. The trust thing. But Deck didn't know Tigger. Tori did. She still bore a scar on her ankle from where Tigger had gotten in a savage little bite the same day she'd moved in. Some welcome wagon that had been.

An orange paw swiped through a break in the bushes. She expected Thor to start barking, as most dogs did when confronted by the neighborhood's feline general. To her amazement, Thor lay down in front of the spot where Tigger was hiding and made the oddest sound she'd ever heard a dog make. He was *cooing* like an owl.

Thor craned his neck toward the hedgerow, his lips forming a perfect *O* as he softly *cooed* at the cat. Tigger stopped hissing. An orange, striped face appeared, then Tori's jaw dropped as Tigger strutted to Thor with his tail in the air and—

No way. Tigger touched noses with Thor's nose. No biting. No hissing. No clawing.

"Told you to trust me," Deck said smugly from behind

her. "Thor has many talents. Sniffing out drugs. Climbing ladders. Making friends with cats. He's a cat-whispering dog. I'm told they're rare."

"I'll bet." Her jaw dropped farther when Thor rolled onto his back and Tigger nuzzled the dog's belly and—*oh my god*. Was that deep rumbly sound coming from Tigger's throat *actually* purring? *Can't be.* But it was.

"I have never seen anything like that in my entire life." She couldn't stop shaking her head in astonishment. "That cat is a menace to anything else that breathes. Including me. I was sure a canine-feline battle of epic proportions was about to kick off and we'd have to call in the National Guard to break it up. We should notify *Animal Planet* stat!"

Thor whined softly, kicking his legs in the air but gently, so as not to hurt the cat. "All right, Thor," Deck said. "Let's go. Say goodbye to your new friend."

With obvious reluctance, Thor slowly got to his feet. Tigger *meowed*, touching his nose one last time to Thor's.

"Unbelievable."

"Brought you coffee," Deck said just before they went inside. He handed her one of the cups, and there was that darned grin.

"Thank you. That was—" She'd been about to say thoughtful, when she got a whiff of the coffee. Tori didn't take the cup. She stared at it as if it held poison. It smelled different. "What is this?" It definitely wasn't a large black coffee, her caffeinated beverage of choice, and he knew it.

"White mocha with an extra shot of espresso."

She grimaced. "Sorry, but no can do."

"Try it."

"No, thanks. But come in, anyway. I want to say hi to

Thor." She stepped aside for them to enter then knelt to give Thor a sound scratching behind the ears. In return, he gave her a sound licking.

Deck nudged the door shut with his shoulder. "So, the only reason you're inviting me in is to see my dog?"

"Pretty much." She crooned to Thor, "Aren't you just the most handsome boy?" Thor bobbed his head up and down. "Yes, you are." To irk him all the more, Tori made an intentional show of hamming up how glad she was to see the dog.

"Try the coffee," he insisted.

"Not a chance."

"Chicken."

She looked up to see an adorable I-dare-you look on his face. *Don't fall for it.*

"I am *not* chicken." She stood and jutted her chin out. "I just don't have your sweet tooth."

"It's not that sweet. You'll like it. Trust me." Again, he held out the cup.

Trust. There it was again. A tiny little word that held so much meaning. For her, trust didn't come easily. Trusting a DEA agent was ten—*no, make that a hundred*—times harder.

Tori flicked her gaze to the cup then back to Deck's face. She couldn't decide if his eyes were more chocolate- or coffee-colored. Whichever they were, they glimmered with amusement, daring her.

"Fine." She accepted the cup, lifted off the lid, and took a sip. Before she'd even swallowed, she scrunched up her nose. Then the hot, creamy liquid hit her tongue. She blinked then took another sip. A not-too-sweet white chocolate essence cloaked strong espresso in a blanket of yumminess, making her taste buds stand up and cheer. Her eyes widened as she looked at Deck over the brim of the cup.

A smug grin transformed all the ruggedness of his face. "Told you."

Childishly, she rolled her eyes. "Okay, you were right."

"See? Stepping outside your comfort zone can be fun." He looked around her living room then made himself at home and walked to her fireplace.

Thor nudged her leg. Absently, she gave him another quick pat on the head, but her focus was on Deck, who was examining the photos on her mantel. Annoying though it was to admit, since meeting him, she'd done more things outside her box than in her entire life, and she was, dare she say, enjoying it. Why *was* that?

"Do *you* ever step outside your comfort zone?" she asked as he stopped in front of a framed photo of her and her family.

"I don't *have* a comfort zone. If I want or need to do something, I just do it." He picked up the photo. "Is this your mom, dad, and sister?"

That was a quick change of subject. Hiding something much?

She took the photo and sighed. It was taken at the last Christmas they'd had together as a family. "Yes. It was taken a long time ago."

"Does your family live here in Colorado?"

"My dad and my sister's family do. My mother died ten years ago." Tori's throat knotted. She still missed her mother as if she'd left them only yesterday. It had taken her family a long time to find their way out of the dark hole they'd fallen into after her funeral.

"I'm sorry," he said, sounding as if he truly meant it. "Does your dad still work?"

"No. He's retired." *To an extent, courtesy of the DEA.* The knot in her throat tightened, this time with a hefty dose of guilt added to the sorrow. Not for the first time, she questioned the wisdom of helping Deck. It seemed like a betrayal of everything her family held dear. She set the photo back on the ledge.

Deck's focus shifted to the dozen or so hanging terrariums by the sliding glass door to her little backyard. He went to the kitchen counter, set down his cup, then picked up the terrarium she was still working on. Cupped in his big hand, the tiny pyramidal glass looked so delicate. "My mom loves these things. But you're taking them to a whole new level. You could sell these, they're so good."

"Thanks. It's my stress reliever. I do a little bit every day after work."

"How'd you get into making them?"

"I started with regular houseplants, but they always died because I'd forget to water them. Then I switched to cactus and other succulents that can survive long periods of drought, like aloe plants." She pointed to the gray-green plants on her window sill with thick, fleshy leaves and spiny edges. "Did you know that aloe has a multitude of medical benefits? Some say it's effective at treating burns and reducing scars."

Tori looked away. She was babbling. Something about him being in her house made her nervous. His questions about her family brought back all the pain and grief she could never forget, yet there was no denying the growing attraction to him that she couldn't push aside no matter how much she wanted to. When she looked back at him, the corners of his mouth lifted slightly.

"Sorry." She gave a self-deprecating laugh. "Didn't mean to lecture."

His mouth lifted more. "I like it. You were saying something about how you got into terrariums."

Right. Terrariums. "They're my favorite way to garden. Semi-enclosed, they're like mini ecosystems, so water doesn't evaporate. During the day, moisture accumulates on the inside of the glass, then at night it drips down and waters the plants."

"That really produces enough water to keep them alive?" He looked skeptical.

She nodded, picking up a green-and-pink Tillandsia. "I use air plants. They're epiphytic, meaning that in nature they grow on top of other plants, even on tree branches. The water produced inside a terrarium is enough that I never have to water. That's why I absolutely love them. Did you know that orchids are air plants?" He shook his head. "I love those, too. The colors are amazing. Do *you* have any hobbies?"

He laughed—the first time she'd heard him do it—and a jolt of awareness shot through her. "My job *is* my hobby. I pretty much do it 24/7."

"Sounds lonely." If anyone knew lonely, she did. Being a doctor made people think her life was perfect. It never occurred to them that she was still a woman with any woman's problems. And fears. "No girlfriend?" she pried.

"Not really." *Not really?* What did *that* mean? As if

reading her mind, he added quickly, "I don't really have time to socialize, let alone get involved."

Odd. He had such a natural way with people and not just kids. Women must flock to him.

"Are you working tomorrow?" He picked up the Tillandsia, twirling it between his big thumb and forefinger.

She shook her head. "No. Why?"

"Once a month, Thor and I volunteer at a rehab center, the one I told Leslie Batista about. We talk to the kids, try to keep them on track so they'll stay in the program."

"And?" She narrowed her eyes, sensing there was a big ask coming.

"And I thought you could come with me, add your medical perspective."

"I knew it!" She snapped her fingers. "That's the *real* reason you brought me a white chocolate mocha. You were buttering me up so I'd give up my day off."

He shrugged. "Did it work?"

It was for a worthy cause and yet another thing she'd never done before. Whatever it was about this guy, he was constantly taking her to new places. "Yeah. It did."

They both laughed, the first true moment of joy she'd shared with him since the start of their odd little partnership.

CHAPTER ELEVEN

Deck pulled out of the King Soopers parking lot on Eagle Drive, several miles from where "Jack" the dealer set up shop as soon as it was dark out. For the last two nights, Deck and Thor had surveilled the area, confirming the information Leslie Batista had given him.

Both nights, after the sun went down, a pickup truck had pulled into the lot behind the bakery off Garfield Avenue, parking in the shadows just beyond the light posts. After that, the shop was open until three a.m., with vehicles pulling up and money exchanging hands for small baggies. The tag on the truck hadn't come back to anyone named Jack or John, but everything else fit with Leslie's intel.

The rest of the warrant team followed closely behind. They had a five-minute drive to Jack's location. Right before an op, Deck would normally be 100 percent focused on the takedown. Tonight, his mind was full of weird thoughts, including the fact that he'd lied to Tori.

Unlike what he'd said, he *did* have a comfort zone, but only about one thing. Getting married was *way* outside his zone. After what happened to Marianne, his parents' marriage hadn't survived. It was devastating for them and about killed Deck to watch their relationship unravel. Married life seemed to work for a select few, but it wasn't a risk Deck was willing to take.

Strangely, he thought of Tori. Considering how she'd wept for that dead teenager, he'd bet she'd faced loss before. Personal loss.

On top of that, as an ER doctor, she saw the end game up close and personal. Death. Her passionate plea to do more had struck home, and he admired her for stepping outside what had to be her normally by-the-book comfort zone. So he'd convinced ASAC Rivera to let her tag along. To his surprise, Rivera had approved, couching it as a safety precaution. No one wanted a repeat of what happened to Dan. Deck had conveniently neglected to inform his boss that he'd already taken Tori on a warrant, *without* authorization. She had more grit and determination than any woman he'd ever met. Except maybe his mom.

Thor paced back and forth on the bench seat, snorting beneath his mask. His dog was itching for action. Even Tori seemed amped up. When she'd put on her body armor, he'd caught her hands trembling. There was definitely another side to her—an adventurous side—that she worked hard at keeping in check. She really needed to cut loose once in a while.

Just before she'd tugged the vest over her head, he'd gotten a look at her shirt. It had seen better days and was probably a size too big, but it did nothing to hide what looked like a perfect set of breasts. Yeah, he'd looked. And those black jeans made her waist look even smaller. He could easily span most of her waist with his hands.

"Here we go." He pulled on his mask then turned into the parking lot where he'd been surveilling Jack and his two goon helpers.

When he was thirty feet from the pickup, he and the rest of the DEA vehicles hit the strobes and spotlights, lighting up the area like a Broadway stage.

"Be careful," Tori said, freezing him in his seat for half a second. He could swear there was genuine concern in her voice, and he liked it.

"Always." He grabbed his rifle and was out the door, hitting the fob button to release Thor.

As a unit, a dozen armed agents rushed the group of five men clustered around the pickup truck, shouting, "Police! On the ground!"

Two of the men—customers—flung their hands in the air then dropped like rocks to their knees.

Thor stood his ground, barking at the other three men who were less compliant. Evan and another agent dragged two of them to the pavement. The one remaining guy stupidly yanked open the driver's side door of the pickup, got in, then slammed it shut.

"Thor!" Deck shouted.

His dog leaped partly through the open window, his hind legs dangling as he latched onto Jack's forearm, shaking it back and forth with a throaty growl. Jack would be going to jail with a set of incisor marks on his arm.

"Get him off, get him off!" Jack screamed.

Deck whipped off his mask. "Don't move," he ordered the whimpering dealer, carefully aiming the muzzle of his rifle at the man through the front windshield but avoiding Thor's body.

Another agent had run to the other side of the truck and opened the door, also aiming a rifle at Jack.

The dealer's head disappeared for a second.

"Show me your hands!" Deck shouted. "Show me your hands!" Nothing good ever came from a drug dealer reaching under the seat.

Thor continued growling, shaking his head back and forth as Jack resisted more and more. Something black appeared in Jack's right hand.

"Gun!" Deck shouted.

"Thor, release! Down!" The last thing he wanted was his dog caught in the crossfire.

Thor unclamped his jaw from Jack's arm and dropped to the pavement.

Stupidly, Jack began raising his arm. He still held the gun in his hand. *Don't do it.* But Jack did.

The muzzle of the gun rose above the level of the dashboard. Deck fired two rounds through the windshield, but not before Jack got off a round. The agent at the passenger door fired another shot.

"Stay aimed in," Deck ordered. Keeping his rifle aimed at the driver, he opened the door. The dealer lay slumped in the seat, eyes open and sightless. In his lap was a Glock 9mm. Deck yanked off one of his gloves then reached inside the truck and touched two fingers to the man's carotid, waiting to feel even the hint of a pulse, but got nothing.

"You okay?" Evan yelled from the rear of the pickup.

He verified Thor was lying safely on the ground then let out an uneasy breath. "Yeah." Except that he'd really wanted to interrogate this guy. "I'll call it in."

After making sure the rest of the team had things under control and the scene was secure, he grabbed his phone and queued up ASAC Rivera's number. There'd be red tape to file for any shooting. Agency policy dictated he notify his boss ASAP.

"That was quick. How'd it go?" Rivera asked without preamble.

"Jack pulled a gun. He's—" Deck had been about to say *dead*, when he got a closer look at the guy. It wasn't Jack. At least, not if Leslie Batista's description was accurate. This guy had red hair and a beard, not brown hair and relatively clean shaven. "Stand by," he said to Rivera.

He dug into the man's back pocket and pulled out a wallet. Inside was a thin wad of cash and a driver's license. Chuck White. The DL photo looked enough like the dead man that Deck was reasonably certain of the ID. Given that this guy probably had a record, autopsy fingerprints would confirm it.

Deck quickly described everything that had gone down, being careful not to say too much. He'd write it all up in a report that would be reviewed by his bosses and a shooting review board. It was a good shoot, if there really was such a thing, but the process would take him out of the field for a while. Right in the middle of a major investigation.

His ASAC's frustration was audible through the phone. "There's something else you should know. The governor's son is still in a coma. One of his friend's confirmed he got it from a guy named Jack 'up north.' In Loveland, to be exact."

Could Leslie have been wrong about the location? Deck didn't think so.

He retrieved his mask and glove from the pavement. "We were in the right place. We just got the wrong dealer." As Deck gave Rivera the dealer's name, he couldn't shake the feeling that something didn't fit. Not only had Leslie been definitive about this parking lot, but drug dealers were notoriously protective of their turf. Sharing wasn't in their nature, and neither was letting another dealer horn in on their customer base.

"I'll notify the governor. He may give you a medal."

Deck grunted. Getting another dealer off the street had been the plan, but not this way.

"Send your report in within the next forty-eight hours. Have everyone on your team do the same."

"Will do." Deck stuffed the phone back into his pocket. *Now for the fun part.*

"Thor, search." He clipped a lead onto Thor's vest then ran his dog in and around the pickup. Within minutes, Thor's highly trained nose hit on three hidden compartments filled with cash and plastic baggies containing white powder. *Not gray.* The agents assigned to evidence collection began photographing and carefully placing them in evidence bags.

Deck glanced at the four men on the ground, two of whom worked for the dead guy in the pickup.

"Separate them," he said to one of the state agents guarding the men. "Start your interviews. Leave this one here." Deck pointed to the guy closest to him then waited while the others were taken to the other side of the truck out of earshot.

"Evan, you're with me." If this guy said anything useful, he wanted a witness.

"You got it." Evan and Blue rounded the truck.

"Good boy, Thor. Sit." As a reward for a job well done, he pulled a short piece of twisted rope from his vest and gave it to his dog to chew on. Then he read the remaining guy his rights. He wanted to make damn sure any statements made wouldn't be thrown out.

"Where does White get his product?"

The man sneered. "Why should I talk to you?"

"Because White is dead, so you and your buddy will take the full hit for this."

"No way." He shook his head emphatically. "This is all Chuck's deal. We're just here to protect the money."

"Well, then." Deck made a *tsk*ing sound, feigning disappointment. This guy's ass was in a sling. He just didn't know it yet. "I guess there's nothing I can do for you. You're looking at five to ten in federal lockup." He turned, as if to leave.

"Hey, wait."

Gotcha. Deck turned back.

"If I talk," the guy said, "what's in it for me?"

"Brownie points."

"Yeah? How *many* brownie points?"

"Depends how good your information is," Deck replied truthfully. In reality, he didn't have the authority to make specific promises of leniency. That decision would be up to a prosecutor and a judge. But if this guy gave up the name Deck was after, he'd put in a good word with the Assistant U.S. Attorney and give the guy a whole *tray* of brownies. "But don't bullshit me. I'll know it if you do."

The goon glanced at the truck where White's lifeless body still sat slumped in the driver's seat. One thing the guy *didn't* have to sweat was retribution. He hung his head and exhaled. "Chuck gets his stash from a guy who gets it from *another* guy up north."

That fit with what Alonzo Jones had told them. There was a distributor *and* a source. "I need names."

"I don't know their names. Chuck never took us with him."

"Then you've got nothing to bargain with." And all they'd get from tonight was a dead body. Again, Deck turned to start interrogating the other prisoner now proned-out on the pavement behind the tailgate.

"Hey, wait a minute. I'm trying to give you information."

"You're wasting my time," Deck snapped. He was sure the guy had something more to say. Apparently, he needed more motivation. "I'll see if your friend wants any of my brownies."

"Wait, I remembered something else." His eyes lit with eagerness. "One night, Chuck canceled on us. He said the Big D had to make a new batch and it wasn't ready."

Deck mentally ran through everything he knew about all the players in this investigation and came up empty. "What do you mean, 'the Big D'?"

The man shrugged. "That's what he called him."

"What does the D stand for?" Deck asked.

"I don't know."

"What else *do* you know?" He leaned down, getting in the guy's face.

"Nothing, I swear it. Except Chuck said the Big D drives a fancy black sports car and has a thing for watches."

"Watches?"

"Yeah, you know. Rolexes, Tags. Stuff like that."

Now, we're getting somewhere.

Deck and Evan repeated the process with the other prisoner, who pretty much confirmed the same information.

Chuck's two customers were put in the backseats of a patrol vehicle. When they were driven away, Deck and Evan exchanged looks.

"You heard of the Big D?" Evan asked. Deck shook his

head. "Think they're lying?"

"Doubt it." Separating suspects during questioning usually weeded out the crap. Usually. "I'll have Sammie run that nickname through all the databases. Maybe we'll get lucky and get a hit." If anyone could find the Big D, it would be Sammie.

"At least she stayed in the truck this time." Evan nodded to Deck's SUV.

"*This* time." Although it was hard not to admire how she'd sprung into action at the first warrant he'd taken her on. The woman took her Hippocratic oath seriously, even at the risk of her own personal safety. "I'd better check in with her before she gets antsy."

"Smart man." Evan chuckled under his breath as Deck and Thor walked over to the passenger side of Deck's SUV.

One of the patrol car's spotlights reflected off the window, so he couldn't quite see Tori inside. He reached for the door handle and froze. Fear—the likes of which he'd never experienced—exploded up his spine.

Just above the handle where the window met the door, a bullet hole pierced the metal.

CHAPTER TWELVE

Deck ripped open the passenger door. He'd removed his head covering and mask, and his dark hair was completely askew in different directions. "*Tori!* Are you okay?"

His eyes radiated an odd mix of fear, shock, and anger as it traveled from her face down her body. Thor stood by his side, his body quivering.

"I'm fine. Why wouldn't I be?" Despite hearing several loud pops that she swore could have been gunshots.

"You're sure?"

"Yes, I—"

He hauled her from the truck, cupping her face with both hands, then massaging her neck, which felt rather nice, but it wasn't really a massage. His movements were jerky, frantic, even.

He ran his hands down the sides of her vest then knelt, sliding his hands next along the outside of her legs.

"What are you *doing*?" Again, not that him touching her was a bad thing. Pleasant goose bumps shot across her skin as his hands continued stroking her body over her clothes. "Deck?"

He straightened then stripped off her vest, lifting the hem of her shirt and exposing her midriff.

She swatted his hands away. "Stop it!"

Ignoring her, he spun her so that her back was facing him then tugged up the hem of her shirt again, skimming his hands over her bare skin. Why, she had no clue.

"Are you going to tell me what in the *world* you're doing?" she asked over her shoulder. This was ridiculous, and their conversation was attracting attention. Evan and his blue-eyed German shepherd were striding over. Others on Deck's team were staring in their direction.

He closed the SUV's door then clicked on his flashlight, shining it on the door. "Look." The tone of his voice was filled with tension.

At first, she didn't understand what she was looking at—a hole about the size of a dime in the metal just above the door handle. *Oh my god.* "Oh my god!" Those pops she'd heard… They *were* gunshots. "I could have been killed," she whispered, still not fully comprehending what had nearly just happened.

She turned to find him watching her intently again, brows lowered, lips compressed into a tight line. "Fuck, I'm sorry."

I could have been killed.

"This never should have happened. I'm definitely not taking you on another warrant. It's too dangerous."

I could have been killed.

A wave of dizziness hit her, and she reached out blindly. Deck's hands gripped her shoulders. She wrapped her arms around her stomach to ward off the sudden chill. Her body began shaking. For a doctor, she should have recognized the signs for what they were. *Shock. I'm going into shock.*

Deck pulled her against his chest, holding her tightly. "Jesus, I'm sorry." Then he uttered a string of expletives, snugging her more into his warm embrace, and wow, did it feel good.

Tori melted against him, wrapping her arms around his

back and wishing he wasn't wearing his vest, so she could dig her fingers into his bare skin and absorb his heat into her chilled body.

"You guys okay?" Evan asked.

Without turning around, Deck answered, "Yeah, we're good."

Was his voice trembling?

She breathed in his fresh, citrusy scent and tried not to think too deeply about the fact that she could have been shot. The metal and inside of the doorframe must have stopped the bullet. A few inches higher, and it would have shattered the window and embedded itself in her chest or her skull.

Tori shuddered, and Deck adjusted his hands, slipping one of them to her nape, and she could swear she felt his lips on the top of her head.

She'd really gone and done it. She'd stepped outside her comfort zone and look what it had almost gotten her. *Dead*. Something Deck did every day of his life, ramming home just how incredibly dangerous his job really was. She couldn't imagine being his girlfriend or wife and living with the fear every day that he wouldn't come home.

Tori took another shaky breath, resting her cheek against the chest portion of Deck's vest.

Ironically, as she stood there wrapped in his arms, she'd never felt warmer, safer, or more comfortable in her entire life.

• • •

Deck took the keys from Tori's shaking fingers and opened her front door. She went inside, continuing into the kitchen then turning on the tap and splashing cold water on her face.

After Thor scooted past, Deck closed the door. She was still in shock, and it was his damned fault. *Christ, she could have been killed.* This was exactly why he shouldn't have let her talk him into going on another warrant.

He'd gone on more high-risk drug warrants than he could count. Faced down some of the most dangerous criminals in the state. But when he'd seen that hole in the Interceptor's side panel, he'd never been more scared in his entire life.

Thor sat in the middle of the kitchen, watching Tori with a sympathetic expression on his furry face. Even Thor understood that something bad had happened.

Deck shoved his hands into his pockets. He couldn't think of anything to say. What *could* he say? *Sorry I almost got you killed?*

Thor whined then held up his paw to Tori, keeping it in the air until she knelt and took it in her hands. Thor nuzzled her face, and she wrapped her arms around his dog.

"You're not coming in the field with me again," he said in an emotionless voice, although inside, his guts were still churning with fear. "Ever."

Tori jerked her head up. "Why not?"

He shook his head in total disbelief. "*What* about nearly getting shot don't you understand? It's too dangerous."

Where only moments ago, she'd been trembling and unsteady, she shot to her feet, steady as a rock. "I *need* to be out there with you. It's given me purpose. Instead of waiting on the sidelines for another DOA, I finally feel like I'm being proactive, doing something out there to help you."

"Help me?" He pulled his hands from his pockets. "How does it *help* me if you get killed?" Not for the first time, the thought of her with a bullet hole in her head gutted him. He stared into her clear green eyes, thinking how incredibly beautiful they were when it struck him. "The answer is *no*."

"Don't you think *I* should have a say in this? Maybe we can figure something out." Ignoring his slowly shaking head, she continued, "I can take my own car. I can park down the street. I can still be in the vicinity if anything goes wrong. I can—"

"No," he repeated, crossing his arms. She must be out of her mind. No way would he risk losing her again. "You can still feed me information if another OD comes into the hospital and wants to talk, but that's it."

"There must be some kind of workaround we can come up with."

"There isn't."

When she stomped her foot, it was so adorable he wanted to take her in his arms. When she pressed her lips together, all he wanted was to kiss the annoyance off of them. That urge to kiss her rose steadily until he could barely concentrate on anything else.

"What's really the issue here?"

The issue? The issue was he couldn't take it if anything happened to her. The issue was that he wanted to keep her safe. The issue, dammit, was—

He took another step toward her, invading her personal space and giving in to the craving obliterating all rational thought. "This is." Gently, he cupped her face. Her eyes rounded with shock as he leaned in…and kissed her.

"Deck," she said against his lips.

"Don't talk," he whispered then angled her head to cover her mouth with his, slipping his tongue inside and uttering a throaty groan.

Kissing her hadn't been in the ops plan, yet something about it seemed…right. She ran her hands up his chest. When she reached his neck, she touched one finger to the part of his neck that was thumping wildly.

The taste of her was like nectar on his tongue, and it was all he could do not to lap her up like a honey bee and beg for more. But she was more than a quickie on the counter, and he didn't have time for relationships. Nor did he want one. If only she didn't feel so good in his arms, all soft and curvy, so incredibly warm and sexy.

He dragged himself away from her lips. How could he be so attracted to someone he argued with so much? She drove him straight up the wall, but he'd rather fight with her than make small talk with anyone else.

Her lips glistened from his kiss, and it took every ounce of strength not to do a one-eighty and dive right back in there. He rested his forehead against hers. "Don't you get it?" he asked hoarsely. "I care about what happens to you. I couldn't take it if anything did."

Gently, he kissed her one last time on the forehead then backed away. The expression on her face mimicked the way he felt. Shell shocked.

"Thor." Drawing on every ounce of strength left in his body, he headed for the door. "You can still go with me to the rehab center," he said over his shoulder, adding, "I'll pick you up at noon." Then he opened the door and walked out.

At the Interceptor, he opened the door for Thor, waiting for him to jump into the kennel. He slid onto the passenger seat and started the engine. Silently, he swore.

He'd nearly lost it, given in to his physical urges like some out-of-control teenager. That's all they were. Urges. She'd taken him completely off guard. No, he'd taken *himself* completely off guard and come a heartbeat from giving in to his dick.

Getting involved with Tori was too complicated. First, she was a doctor, one whose help he needed at the hospital, *not* in his bed. Maintaining a clear head and keeping their temporary truce going had to be his priority. This investigation was too important to fuck up.

He put the gearshift in drive. What had just happened between them was the result of latent adrenaline from the warrant.

But as he headed onto the main road, he knew it was more than that. The problem was that he couldn't risk exploring exactly whatever *it* was.

CHAPTER THIRTEEN

"Shoot." Tori dug through her bag for something to tie her hair up with. She could swear she'd left her usual stash of black elastic ties in the tiny zippered compartment.

"Something wrong?" Deck asked, keeping his eyes on the road.

"No, not really." Other than the fact that since the moment he and Thor had picked her up at her house, there'd been no mention of their kiss the night before.

After he and Thor had left, her legs had turned to limp noodles, and she'd all but fallen right on her ass. Her lips had tingled, and the skin around her mouth still stung from Deck's five o'clock shadow. It was just as well that he'd left without taking things further.

How could she kiss a *DEA agent*? A man who worked for the very organization that destroyed her family? He wasn't for her in any way, shape, or form. The man was like a lightning bolt, illuminating her sky for one brief moment, then disappearing just as quickly. Which was exactly what would happen the moment he caught the distributor they were after and no longer needed her.

If only his kiss didn't send her craving for another one into unstoppable overdrive.

Stop it. Just stop it. Focus on something else. Anything *else.* Take his wardrobe, for instance.

Like her, he'd worn jeans. Unlike hers, his were soft and worn, showcasing every cut muscle in his thighs and butt.

The shirt he'd worn was a dark brown polo that matched the color of his eyes. Okay, that *so* didn't help her refocus.

"Can we stop at a convenience store or a drug store?" She scanned the road ahead for a strip mall.

"What do you need?"

"Something I can put my hair up into a ponytail with." She kept digging through her bag, getting antsier by the second. She never went out without her hair up. Having it down this way left her feeling undone. It was part of her every day, neat and tidy wardrobe. Everything in her life, including her hair, had to be under control. Nothing left to chance. "Hey, stop!" She pointed to a drug store, but he kept right on going. "Why didn't you stop?"

He glanced at her. "You should leave it down."

"I don't *want* to leave it down." She uttered an exasperated huff and crossed her arms, feeling exactly the same way she always had when her mother had told her she couldn't have ice cream until she'd finished all her green beans.

"Try something new." He turned off the road into the parking lot for the Bear Creek Teen Center.

Seemed like that was all she'd *been* doing lately, trying new things.

Thor uttered a low bark as Deck parked in front of the main doors.

"Is Thor coming in, too?" She turned to give him a scratch under his chin and was rewarded with a lick to her hand.

"Yep." He grabbed a leash from inside the console. "He's more popular here than I am, especially with the girls."

"That's hard to believe." The second the snark left her lips, Tori groaned inwardly.

"C'mon. We're gonna be late."

As she followed Deck and Thor into the Center, a woman with short blond hair and wearing a navy-blue sleeveless blouse greeted them from behind the visitor's desk. "Good morning, Deck." Thor barked. "Good morning to you, too, Thor." The dog gave an appreciative wag of his tail.

"Pam, this is my friend, Dr. Tori Sampson. She's an ER doctor who's treated a lot of overdose patients." Deck touched the small of her back, sending a stream of tingles up her spine.

As a doctor, she would have attributed tingly sensations to a possible injury involving the nervous system. In her case, however, there was no denying it was the direct result of attraction. Pure, animal attraction.

"Tori?"

"Huh?" Deck's brows rose slightly as he flicked his gaze to the other woman. And her outstretched hand. "I'm sorry. I was thinking about a patient." Heat flooded her face as the lie rolled off her tongue, and she shook Pam's hand.

"Very nice to meet you, Dr. Sampson, and thank you for coming." Pam's greeting was warm and welcoming. "They're all inside waiting for you, Deck. It's a rowdy bunch this week."

"What's the breakdown?" he asked.

"Most are in their sixth week, the same crew as last time. Only one newbie. You'll know him when you meet him." Pam lowered her voice and leaned forward, whispering, "He's got a rough road ahead of him. See if you can work your magic."

He smiled. "I'll do my best."

"I know you will," Pam said. "The kids enjoy your sessions more than the ones given by *our* people."

Deck led the way down a short hallway, at the end of which were two open doors. Thor's nails clicked on the tile, his tongue hanging out and his tail wagging as if he knew he was about to have fun.

When they walked in, twenty pairs of eyes turned their way. A mixture of girls and boys between the ages of fifteen and nineteen sat on chairs arranged in a big circle.

"Thor!" One of the girls jumped up and ran over. Thor's big body wriggled and his tail whipped back and forth, thumping against Deck's leg. "Can I take him first?"

"Sure." He handed over the leash. "But no hogging him like last time. You have to share him. Walk him around the room so the other kids can say hi, too."

"Okay, okay." She led Thor back to the group and inside the circle to greet the others.

"That's Rhianna," Deck said. "She and Thor have a love-fest going on."

"Apparently so." Tori watched Rhianna lead Thor around the group where he sat and lifted his paw to every one of the kids, allowing them to shake hands and pet him thoroughly.

"Hi, Deck," several of the older girls said in unison.

"Hi, Mia, Carmen, Hannah," he answered. "How's it going?" he said to everyone else.

"Hey, Deck," one of the bigger boys said.

Deck indicated she should sit in one of the two vacant chairs. "So, how's it *going*?" he repeated with more emphasis after they sat.

"Good."

"Fine."

"Another day in paradise."

Tori watched and listened while Deck made eye contact with every single kid in the room, never failing to elicit an optimistic greeting. Except for one kid, who practically spat out that his name was Aidan. The boy was around seventeen, probably the one Pam warned them about. He sat with his legs outstretched, arms crossed, and pursing his lips with an expression that screamed how much he didn't want to be there.

Aidan aside, she still thought Deck had a way with kids, and she wondered where that came from. When they'd been discussing her family, he hadn't said anything about having brothers or sisters, and he wasn't married. She assumed if he had kids of his own, he would have said so.

"Is *she* your girlfriend?" a pretty blond-haired girl asked, flicking her gaze to Tori.

A chorus of *ooohs* and whistles went around the room.

Deck held up his hand. "All right, everyone. Settle down, especially you, Mia." He pointed to the blond girl, who giggled. The room finally quieted. "This is my friend, Dr. Tori Sampson. She works in the emergency room at North Metro Hospital. She's here to talk to you about what she's seen there and some of the long-term effects of opioids on the body."

Friend? Did he kiss *all* his friends the way he'd kissed her?

Tori gave a quick wave of her hand. "Hi."

"If you're not dating him, can *I* have him?" This from the

girl sitting next to Mia.

Another round of snickers and whistles, this one lasting longer.

"Are you done, ladies?" One side of Deck's mouth lifted. He sure seemed to take all this ribbing in stride, as if he'd been through it before. "Rhianna, give Thor to Aidan."

As Rhianna held Thor's leash out, Thor sat in front of the boy with his paw in the air, waiting patiently. Aidan refused to take the leash. "Tight ass," Rhianna grumbled as she handed Thor off to somebody else.

"Since almost all of you were here the last time I spoke to the group, I won't piss you off by repeating myself. But I do want to ask a few questions. How many of you got addicted to opioids because of stress, or you felt pressured by your friends, or because you just wanted to fit in?" About two-thirds of the kids raised their hands. "How many got addicted after being prescribed opioids by a doctor for an injury?" The other third of the group raised their hands.

Deck sent her a meaningful look, and she couldn't help squirming in her seat just a bit.

"I'm guessing you've had it rammed down your throat," he continued, "that group therapy is an important part of your treatment." Every head nodded. "It's a place to get positive support from other kids who've gone through what you're going through, and it's something you can continue to do for the rest of your lives. Even after you leave here, you can come back anytime, and you can bring anyone with you. Your brother or sister. Your parents. After you get married, your spouse. Helping your family to understand your addiction could save your life."

The only sound in the room came from Thor's occasional pant. These kids were listening, really listening.

"I never had that opportunity," Deck said quietly. "More than anything, I wish I had."

What? Tori's eyes went wide. Deck was an addict?

He cleared his throat. "My sister, Marianne, was sixteen when she started sneaking out of the house at night to hang with her friends. I knew she was doing it, but I didn't say a word. I thought that's what all teenage girls did, being rebellious and going out to have fun. There's not one day that goes by that I don't regret not saying something."

Thor whimpered, straining at his leash so hard the boy holding him was forced to let him go. The dog went to Deck, resting his snout on Deck's thigh.

"One night, there was a car crash. They'd all been drinking. The driver—Marianne's best friend—was pronounced dead at the scene. The steering wheel was embedded in her chest. She had twice the legal limit of alcohol in her blood. My sister's two other friends got out of the car with barely a scratch. Not my sister. She was badly hurt and was prescribed opioids to deal with the pain. She got addicted."

"Why did they do that?" Mia asked. "I mean, didn't the doctor see what was happening before she got addicted?"

"Good questions." He nodded solemnly. "I think it's easier to prescribe a strong pain med than to deal with a patient's emotional state. An average of one hundred thirty people in the U.S. die every single day from an opioid overdose. That's over forty thousand people annually, and half those deaths involved a *prescription* opioid."

He glanced at Tori again, sending her a not-so-silent

message. A doctor had played a role in his sister becoming addicted, and he wanted her to know it. In addition to his scrutiny, she felt the eyes of every kid in the room on her. It was all she could do not to squirm even more.

"Whatever drove my sister to go out partying and drinking was still there after the accident. Opioids just gave her another way to retreat from what was really bothering her."

"What was bothering her?" Rhianna asked.

Deck sifted his fingers through Thor's thick ruff. "Me."

Huh? Tori couldn't imagine what was coming next. Whatever it was, she could already sense his grief from the tightening of his shoulders and the way his throat worked.

"I never figured on being a DEA agent. I was the high school senior they make movies about. Valedictorian. Star athlete with baseball scholarships to any Division 1 school I wanted. I excelled at everything. I was the proverbial 'golden child,'" he said bitterly. "Everything came easily to me. Not for Marianne. She struggled, trying to live up to her big brother. Then she gave up trying."

Deck stared at the ceiling, clearly reliving some part of his and his sister's lives. "I was so self-absorbed, so focused on my own success and popularity that I didn't see it before it was too late. Neither did my parents. My sister felt like she was living her life in my shadow. She even found out that some of her friends weren't really her friends at all. Some only pretended to be so they could get a date with me."

"What happened to her?" one of the boys asked.

"Eventually, her doctor cut her off from the drugs, and she resorted to stealing money from all our wallets, including mine, to buy whatever she could off the street.

One day, she never came home." Tori swallowed the lump in her throat. Like everyone else in the room, she understood what Deck would say next. "The police found her body in an alley. Dead at sixteen." His last words came out choked, as if he rarely talked about it and still had difficulty dealing with it.

"Um, Deck?" Rhianna asked. "You said you and your parents didn't know what was happening with her. Since she died and you couldn't ask her, how did you know what she was thinking?"

"We found her diary. She wrote everything down." He took a deep breath and let it out. "As I read it, it hit me. Hard. I *did* see it coming, but I was in denial. What happened to her was at least partly my fault. I didn't want to see what was happening to her because it would have interfered with *my* life." He jabbed a finger at his chest. "I'm telling you this for a reason. I'm still selfish. You may think I come here on my days off out of the goodness of my heart just to help you guys. True, that's how it started, but I also come here for *me*. *Your* group therapy is *my* group therapy. Back then, I wish I'd had the support of other people my own age, so don't ever hesitate to bring your loved ones here. Maybe if Marianne had gotten the help she needed in time and if the people who loved her had seen it coming and admitted what was happening, *maybe* she'd still be here. Married, living in a house with a white picket fence, two-point-three kids, and a dog."

The room was deathly silent, then Deck rested his hand on Thor's head. "At least I've got the dog."

Thor craned his neck to lick Deck's chin.

Gentle laughter went around the circle, lightening the

mood some but not much. That had been his intention.

"Thanks for listening, guys," he said.

To her amazement, every kid in the room clapped, except one. Aidan.

Tori joined in, clapping and blinking back the tears. Now, she understood so much. Like why Deck had become a DEA agent and was a walking, talking library of opioid factoids. But she'd also learned something more about the man.

There was no doubting he was a tough-as-nails federal agent. He was also a human being with a big heart that he'd just shared with a room full of teenagers. He would do everything within his power to keep each and every one of these kids from becoming a statistic, like his sister.

He might be a badge-carrying, gun-toting agent, but he was only one man, not the DEA as a whole. And like her, he'd suffered great loss.

Shockingly, she found her resentment toward Deck slipping away more and more every day.

• • •

As Tori gave her presentation, Deck couldn't stop watching her lips which, naturally, made him remember kissing her last night and how much more he wanted than that one kiss he'd allowed himself.

He'd barely gotten a straight hour of sleep last night without waking up with the sheets twisted around his legs. Each time he'd woken up, he'd reminded himself why he'd done the right thing by leaving. Professional reasons aside, with his baggage, she deserved more than he was capable of giving.

A bitter taste rose in the back of his throat. The taste of sheer, raw jealousy. Whatever Tori Sampson needed, he didn't want anyone else being the one to give it to her.

"The bottom line is," she continued, tucking strands of auburn hair behind her ears and reconfirming how much he preferred it down, "there are many long-term effects from using illegal drugs. Infection for one." The way her hair shimmered in the light, cradling and softening her face... And that green blouse really set off her eyes. "Shared needles can give you all kinds of communicable diseases, including HIV, hepatitis B and C, and those are just for starters. Drug abuse can also cause irreversible heart damage. Your heart can become inflamed and have to work harder to make up for the damage."

"Can it explode?" one of the boys asked, looking up from petting Thor.

When Tori smiled, Deck's gaze was drawn to her mouth again. Man, he needed to quit fixating on her lips.

"Hearts can't really explode," Hannah said. "Can they?"

"No, it really happened," another kid said. "I saw it in a movie. I swear it."

"That's a movie even *I'd* like to see," Tori said, eliciting laughter from most of the kids.

Deck was impressed. She had an easy, natural way with kids. He didn't think she had any children of her own. There was no sign of them at her house and no pictures of any on her fireplace mantle.

A shot of sadness hit him in the chest. At the rate he was going, there'd be no children of his own, and with Marianne gone, there'd be no nieces or nephews in his life.

Today was the first time he'd spoken about her at any of the Center's therapy sessions. Deck hadn't lied to the kids. It *had* been therapeutic to vent, but he'd done it today of all days because Tori was there. Because he'd wanted her to know.

"I don't want to see an exploding heart." Carmen scrunched up her nose. "That's gross."

"It *is* gross," Tori agreed. "But that's essentially what happens. And it can happen to anyone, even a teenager with a young, robust heart. One of the last overdose patients I treated was about your age." She pointed her finger in an arc around the circle. "He was only seventeen. High school quarterback, good looking, popular with all the kids at school. His name was Tyler. He died from an overdose." Her expression turned somber.

Tyler. The teenager she'd lost the day Deck had found her in the chapel. Until now, he hadn't known the boy's name.

"As much as I've enjoyed your company," she said, "I hope I never see you again. In the emergency room, anyway."

"Let's thank Dr. Sampson for being here today." Deck began clapping, and all the other kids joined in. The only one who didn't was Aidan.

The boy still sat low in his chair with his arms crossed, legs outstretched. Figuratively, he was halfway out the door. Deck was sure the Center knew it, but he worried Aidan would become just another number in the country's teen recidivism statistics. He guessed Aidan was no stranger to the criminal justice system and probably lacked healthy peer support and constructive parental guidance. Fear of the unknown without that essential support would drive him out the door and back on the street. If someone didn't intervene and soon...

I need to talk to him before it's too late.

As he and Tori exchanged a few more words with some of the kids about exploding hearts and brains, Thor remained lying on his side, eyes bright, tail wagging, the ecstatic recipient of Rhianna's belly rubs.

Aidan went to the table at the far side of the room and grabbed a bottle of water. Not a good sign. He might as well have the word "loner" stamped on his forehead.

"I want to talk to this kid," Deck whispered to Tori. "Come with me."

"Are you sure? I have more than a strong suspicion he'd rather be alone."

He shook his head. "That's exactly what he *doesn't* need right now. He just doesn't know it yet."

"Lead the way."

Deck grabbed Thor's leash. At their approach, Aidan's lips pursed and his eyes narrowed. "Hey, Aidan."

The kid took a long drink from the bottle, swallowed, then deliberately burped. "What do you want, cop?"

Yeah, he's definitely been through the system. He'd be a tough nut to crack.

"To see you *not* end up like my sister." Miserable then dead. "Here." He handed the kid his business card, not sure he'd take it.

Surprisingly, Aidan took the card then stared at it for a moment before shoving it into his pants pocket. "That was a real sob story. Got me all teary. That bullshit might work on *them*," he said, tipping his heads to the other kids, "but it won't work on me. It's probably not even a true story."

The dig had Deck gripping Thor's leash tighter. *Don't let him get to you. He's angry, threatened, and scared.*

"I get it," Deck said. "A judge gave you a choice. Jail or the Center. Why not give this place a chance?"

"Are you fucking kidding?" Aidan raised his voice, getting in Deck's face. "It was a cop just like you who arrested me. The last thing I'd do now is take some lame-ass advice from one. I'm outta here." He threw his open water bottle against the wall and stalked to the door.

"Thor, sit," he said to his dog then dropped the leash on the floor. He'd blown it, but he wasn't giving up. "Aidan, wait," he called out.

"Deck." Tori touched his arm. "Maybe you should let him cool off."

He clenched his jaw. If that kid walked out the door, he'd never come back. He caught up to Aidan, gently grabbing his arm. "Wait," he repeated.

"Get off me, cop!" The kid spun and shoved at Deck's chest.

A brown blur flew through the air as Thor took Aidan to the floor, teeth bared and growling as he stood over the kid.

"What the fuck?" Aidan raised his arms to cover his face.

"Release!" Deck shouted, grabbing Thor's leash. "Stay."

His dog sat, although the hair along his spine remained as stiff as spikes.

"Sorry. He thought you were attacking me." He extended his hand, but the boy didn't take it. His eyes blazed with enough fury to singe Deck's hair.

Running feet told him the other kids had rushed over to

check out the action. Aidan crab-walked backward, the expression on his face turning to one of horror.

Great. On top of everything else, I thoroughly embarrassed him.

"Take my hand," Deck said, trying to get through to him and knowing that he wasn't.

"I wouldn't take shit from you." Aidan scrambled to his feet and pushed open the door.

Deck shoved a hand through his hair. "This is my fault."

"It's *not* your fault," Tori said. "I may not be an expert in this area, but even I can see that he would've left anyway."

He knew she was right. Maybe not today or tomorrow but eventually, he would have. Aidan had only been waiting for the right moment to leave, for something to set him off. Deck and Thor were the convenient trigger. Still, he couldn't stop thinking that he'd blown it. He'd come here to do some good, and he'd done exactly the opposite.

His chest tightened as the inevitable image formed in his mind. Aidan would wind up in an alley one day, soon. Dead. And there was nothing Deck could do to prevent it.

CHAPTER FOURTEEN

"Are you ever going to tell me where we're going?" Tori asked after they'd dropped Thor off at Deck's house. "If I haven't mentioned it, bungee jumping is on my to-*don't* list, not my to-*do* list."

"Noted." He massaged his forehead again, something he'd been doing off and on since they'd left the Center. "We're meeting Brett and Evan at Mick's."

"Who's Mick?"

"Mick's is a bar."

She'd never heard of the place. "Do you want any aspirin? You seem like you have a headache, and I have some in my bag." She opened her purse and fished around for the bottle of pills.

"I don't take any of that. But thanks."

"It's just aspirin. It's not—"

"Opioids?"

"I wasn't going to say that." After hearing what happened to his sister, she understood his no-tolerance policy, although she did think he was taking his absolutely-no-drugs policy too far. "I hate to see anyone in pain when I can help."

He shook his head. "I don't take any of that stuff, even over-the-counter meds."

"Okay, okay." She dropped the bottle back into the bag, looking up in time to see him check his rearview mirror for what must be the tenth time. "Why do you keep looking behind us?" Now that she mentioned it, he *always* did that. She'd just never realized it until now.

"It's a habit. See that beat-up blue Honda two cars back? It's been behind us since I pulled out of my neighborhood. It's probably nothing, but drug agents tend to make a lot of enemies."

She looked in the sideview mirror. "Isn't that a little paranoid?"

"Maybe." He shrugged. "Maybe not. Last year, Thor and I helped seize hundreds of pounds of illegal drugs and nearly a million dollars in cash. Bad guys remember little things like that."

"I see your point." A very *scary* point.

A minute later, he pulled into a small strip mall and parked.

"Mick's *Foosball* Bar?" She couldn't contain the incredulity in her voice. "Seriously?"

He shut off the engine. "Don't look so shocked. It's the same as shooting pool or throwing darts. Only with foosball, you need precision hands *and* speed. Don't knock it 'til you've tried it."

Reluctance trickled through her head. Between cramming for tough bio and organic chemistry exams, followed by long residency hours, she'd never had time for the bar scene during college. Arcade games weren't even on her radar now as an adult.

Skepticism must have shown on her face because Deck squeezed her hand then quickly removed it, as if he hadn't intended to touch her. "C'mon. I need to blow off some steam." Tiny lines fanned the corners of his eyes. Eyes dark with latent grief.

Between talking about his sister then the altercation with the belligerent teen, today had sucked the life out of him. She figured it was misplaced disappointment in himself that was the real culprit. "Is that the first time you talked about your sister at one of these sessions?"

He hesitated before answering. "Yeah."

"You said you volunteer at the Center regularly. Why did you wait until today to talk about Marianne?"

"Dunno." A small sliver of light returned to his eyes. "Let's go in."

She understood the message. *Topic closed.*

The moment they pushed through the door to Mick's, Tori was hit with music, laughter, bells, and whistles—literally—because Mick's was one big funhouse.

Abba's "Dancing Queen" pumped from so many speakers on the walls and ceiling she practically cringed from the noise. A huge square bar packed with customers took center stage. Pinball machines lined one wall, while the other had a long shuffleboard table at which people slid round metal disks to each end. A sharp clack rent the air from one of two pool tables. Deck led her deeper into the bar, all the way to the back where every inch of space was crammed with foosball tables.

"Yo, Deck." Brett Tanner waved them over. Deck's other K-9 friend, Evan, stood opposite Brett at one of the foosball tables.

The standing crowd thickened, and Deck stepped aside so she could go first. Brett went wide-eyed, turning to look at Evan, whose brows rose.

"Good to see you, Doc." Brett extended his hand.

"You, too, Brett." His long fingers closed over hers, the

muscles in his forearms flexing beneath a vicious raised red patch of skin. She tried not to stare, but being a doctor, it was impossible not to. That had to have been a third-degree burn. What the swirling black marks were, she couldn't be sure. *A dragon tattoo?* The scars looked like flames shooting from the dragon's mouth.

She dragged her gaze away from Brett's arm and reached across the table. "Hi, Evan."

"Glad you could join us, Doc," Evan said as his equally large hand clasped hers.

"Guys, call me Tori. Remember?"

Brett nodded. "Doc Tori, then. Wasn't that an old TV show?"

Deck waved over a red-haired waitress. "That was *Daktari*. It was about a vet in Africa. What'll you have?" he asked her when the waitress wiggled her way through the masses of people.

"Chardonnay."

"You got it, hon. Deck, the usual?"

"Yep. Thanks, Ginger."

Ginger sent a definitively suggestive look. "Have fun now." The waitress disappeared through the crowd, heading for the bar.

Clearly, Deck and his friends were no strangers to Mick's. Then again, Tori was in a bar with three of the handsomest men she'd ever met. Brett's sandy blond hair and blue eyes made him look like a classic California surfer hunk. Evan's dark brown, nearly black hair made his gorgeous slate-gray eyes stand out like diamonds. All three men were built like warriors—tall, all muscle, and probably not an ounce of body fat amongst them.

Evan took a sip of the beer he'd had resting on the edge of the table. "Did the shooting review board clear you yet?"

Deck shook his head. "Too soon. I'm on the beach until they do."

"Heard it was a good shoot." Brett rubbed his forearm, telling Tori it either itched or hurt. Which also meant it had to be fairly recent.

"What does that that mean, 'on the beach' and 'a good shoot'?"

"Here you go." Ginger handed Tori her Chardonnay and Deck his beer. She rested her hand on Deck's thick biceps. "Flag me over when you're ready for a refill." As she sashayed away, Ginger looked back over her shoulder. The woman's gaze practically stroked Deck's body. If Deck were a sailor, he could have a woman in every port. *Make that a harem.*

"So, what did that mean?" She nudged Deck with her shoulder, catching Brett and Evan exchanging looks again. *Yikes*. Okay, then. No touching in public.

Deck took a swig from the beer bottle. "Whenever a federal agent discharges a firearm, let alone shoots someone, a board of inquiry convenes to review the facts. When someone dies, the scrutiny is worse. A shooting is considered 'good' when it's legally justified. Until then, I'm on the beach, meaning I'm relegated to admin duty."

"You killed someone? When?" How had she missed that?

"In Loveland," he answered matter-of-factly.

"The same night that—" She'd nearly been shot through the door of his SUV. She'd been so completely freaked out, she hadn't even known someone had died. "I'm sorry. I didn't know."

Deck shrugged. "Forget it." He guided her to the foosball table. "I'll teach you how to play."

Deck's friends stood shoulder to shoulder on one side of the table, while she and Deck took positions opposite them.

"You'll be offense. You're responsible for these two players." He indicated to the two handles near the center of the table. "I'll be defense." He gripped the handles closest to one of the goals at the end of the table. "The ball is dropped in the center. You can push, pull, or turn the handle to make the man kick the ball into your opponent's goal."

"Got it." She closed her fingers around the handles, turning her wrist awkwardly, trying to get a feel for how to manipulate the plastic men attached to each rod. "How many goals wins the game?"

"Five. But let me show you a better way to hold the handles. It'll help you to move the men easier."

He stood behind her then placed his hands atop hers and adjusted her grip. His chest pressed against her upper back, his thighs against her ass. With his arms around her shoulders, she was completely cocooned by warm, solid muscle. Goose bumps paraded straight up her arms to her neck, and her entire body heated.

"That's it." He helped her turn her wrists in each direction. "Better?"

"Um, yeah." *Aside from the solar flares flaming my face.*

Brett pursed his lips. "You guys gonna get a room, or are you gonna play ball?"

That did it. *Can anyone say "up in flames"?*

"Wise ass." Deck released her hands and took up

position to her left. "Drop it in," he ordered. "Losers buy next round."

Evan dropped the ball in the center of the table. Tori flicked her wrist, shooting the ball straight into the goal.

"Whatdya know?" Brett scratched his chin. "We've got a ringer, here."

Deck puffed up his chest. "Maybe I'm just a great teacher."

"I swear, this is my first time I ever played foosball."

"Uh-huh." Evan nodded. "Sure it is."

Twenty minutes later, she and Deck were up three games to one.

"We're getting crushed," Evan said. "How about we take a break and get another round? C'mon, Brett. I'll buy this one." The two men headed for the bar, leaving her and Deck alone.

"You were right," she said. "This *is* a great way to blow off steam. But I would've figured you more for going to the gym and pumping iron instead."

Deck pulled out a chair for her at the hightop. "We do that, too," he admitted. "When I'm lifting weights, all I think about is work. When I play foosball, I'm watching the balls, thinking about strategy, estimating the angles. It's a quick game, so there's no time to think about anything else. Like work." He pinched the bridge of his nose.

Like Aidan. The boy he couldn't help. The incident still bothered him, and his headache apparently hadn't gone away. He should have taken the aspirin she'd offered.

Deck pulled his phone from his belt, staring for a moment at the screen. "Sorry, I have to take this." He went to the nearest door, pushing it open and stepping outside.

Tori looked around the bar. This certainly wasn't how she'd expected to be spending the evening. Playing foosball, of all things, and thoroughly enjoying herself with a DEA agent and his federal friends. She never saw *that* coming. *Or kissing him and kind of hoping it will happen again.*

"Here you go." Brett slid another Chardonnay in front of her, giving her a closer look at the burn on his forearm. The black swirly things were definitely part of a tattoo.

Evan plunked baskets of curly fries, nachos, and loaded potato skins on the table. The heavenly smells of melted cheese and more carbs than she'd seen in months wafted to her nose.

"So, Doc Tori," Evan said. "Outstanding foosball skills. Did they teach you that in medical school?"

"Hardly. I never went out much during med school. There was never any time." She took a sip, enjoying the relaxing effect of the alcohol.

"Where's Deck?" Brett looked around, not seeing him.

"He stepped outside to take a call."

Brett shook his head. "Leave it to Deck to abandon his date alone in a bar."

She nearly choked on her wine. "I'm not his date."

"Oh, really," Evan said in a disbelieving tone.

"Really." She plunked her glass down too hard. Some of the wine sloshed over the side, and she busied her nervous hands mopping it up with a napkin. One kiss didn't automatically make her his date. "We went to the rehab center today. It was probably more convenient to bring me with him rather than go out of his way to drop me at home first."

Brett scratched the burn on his arm. "Come to think of it, he's never brought a date here before."

"You know"—Evan turned slowly to face Brett, his mouth sporting the beginnings of a grin that made him achingly handsome—"you're right. He hasn't."

"I am *not* his date," she insisted again. "We have a professional relationship, that's all." Albeit, one involving super-hot kissing. A change of subject would do nicely here. "Forgive me if I'm overstepping." She pointed at Brett's forearm. "Have you tried aloe on that burn? It might ease the itching and facilitate healing. If you like, I can give you an aloe vera plant. You break off a leaf then squeeze the oil directly onto the burn, massaging it in. I think it's more effective than the processed gel version pharmacies sell."

Brett stared at her, and for a moment, she worried she really had overstepped. His forehead creased. Blue eyes turned hard as ice then clouded, as if something deep and dark were brooding inside his head. Or he was angry at her for bringing up a painful memory. However he'd gotten burned, it must have been painful.

"I'm sorry," she said quickly, grabbing a curly fry and popping it into her mouth, chewing. "It's a doctor thing. I see someone in pain, and I want to help."

Evan watched them silently, his expression revealing nothing.

Brett looked at her a moment longer. "Thanks. I'll take you up on that aloe plant."

They all turned as Deck stepped back inside the bar. His expression was dark. As if a silent message had been relayed, Brett and Evan set their beers on the table and joined him by the door.

• • •

"Let's talk outside." Deck pushed open the door, and they stepped into the parking lot behind Mick's. He searched the lot to verify no one was within earshot. "Just got off the phone with Rivera. The stash we just grabbed…it was dirty cocaine. Not a speck of gray death or any other opioid."

Evan grunted. "You're the drug expert, but I've always heard that dealers are possessive about their turf."

Deck nodded. "That's true. They're like the mafia that way. And there's more. In the last twenty-four hours, there've been twelve more ODs brought in. All of them concentrated in hospitals north of Denver." *Up north*. Again.

Brett's phone buzzed, and he looked at it.

"Need to get that?" Deck asked.

"Nah." He clipped the phone back on his belt. "It's an FYI. There's another fire in the Springs. They're getting closer to the Air Force Academy. It's drier than a desert down there and with no rain in sight."

"How many does that make in the last few months?" Evan asked.

"In the Springs," Brett said, "four. All suspicious."

"You think it's the same arsonist?" Deck asked.

"I don't know, but Karen's about to dump my ass. Running off to the Springs and working all that overtime is pissing her off. Speaking of dating," Brett added, "what's up with you and the doc? You guys dating?"

"No," he snapped then muttered, "Shit." The three of them had been through a lot together. Being a dick to his friends was, well, being a dick. He didn't want to admit it, but kidding himself was stupid. He was beginning to have real feelings for Tori. "I just…like her." He *more* than liked her. *Christ.*

"We get it," Evan said. "She's a doctor. After what you and your family went through, trusting one doesn't come easily."

"Yeah." But working with Tori was changing his perspective. The doctor who'd cavalierly prescribed opioids to his sister was bad enough. What really kickstarted Deck's mistrust of the medical profession was that after Marianne died, every single doctor who treated her had rallied and covered for each other. Tori wasn't like that. He was beginning to trust her, and she'd already proven she was an asset to the SOTF.

"Guess we've all got ghosts in our closets," Evan said.

Given the parking lot's dim light, neither he nor Brett could see Evan's expression clearly, but the pain in his voice said it all. None of them needed to say it to know they were all thinking the same thing. Marianne was never coming back, but at least Deck had closure. The McGarry family never had a body to bury. Evan's sister was just plain gone.

His phone buzzed again, this time with a text. Deck stared at the screen and his stomach went rock hard. This was the absolute last thing a federal agent ever wanted to hear.

"What's up?" Evan asked.

"Just got a text from an old informant, one I haven't used much in the last few years. He's always been reliable." He hoped this was one instance where his snitch was wrong. Deck held up his phone for his friends to read the message.

Jack didn't show because he knew you were coming.

You've got a leak.

From what little he could see of his friends' faces, they were as grim as his own. He shoved the phone back onto his belt. "There were at least a dozen agents at that warrant, and I handpicked them myself."

Brett looked at the door to Mick's. "Hey, you don't think—"

"No. I don't," Deck said with conviction.

"She *is* the only outlier here," Evan countered.

Deck turned on his friend. "You're suggesting that a doctor I *also* handpicked to work with us leaked logistics about a federal search warrant to a drug dealer?"

Evan held up his hands. "You're right. Forget I said it."

"Forget I *thought* it," Brett added.

Deck headed to the door, intending to go back inside, but stopped before opening it. Somebody had dimed them out, the consequences of which could have been deadly. *Were* deadly.

Whoever the leak was, they'd just made themselves a prime target of his investigation, and before they executed another warrant, he'd find out who the rat was.

CHAPTER FIFTEEN

"Is anything wrong?" Tori asked, breaking the silence.

"Just thinking about the case." A partial lie. They'd been driving for five minutes, and Deck couldn't think of anything to say that wouldn't sound forced.

His gut told him there was no way Tori was the leak. If there even was one. Regardless of how reliable his informant was, a cryptic text like the one he'd received was still unsubstantiated. Concerning, but still unsubstantiated. His brain, on the other hand, told him not to make decisions with his dick. What he needed was a little distance from her. To get a grip on his professionalism.

He turned onto Alameda, taking the curved road at the base of Green Mountain. For the next quarter mile, a few houses dotted the hillside before giving way to trees and rock, with steep ravines on either side. He hit the brights to light up the road in case a deer or an elk jumped in front of him. A big rack could do a lot of damage to a vehicle.

"Why did you take me to Mick's?"

That was a question he hadn't expected. A few seconds went by before he answered. "I don't know." Yeah, he did. He'd taken her there because he'd just plain wanted to spend more time with her. And he figured if his friends were there, he wouldn't do something stupid. Like kiss her again. "I thought you'd enjoy it." The flash of headlights behind them had Deck looking in his rearview mirror.

She laughed. "I have to admit, I did."

"Told ya." He checked his rearview mirror again. The headlights were gone. Deck squinted, looking in the sideview mirror this time, still not seeing anything. He knew this road like the back of his hand. They hadn't passed any other roads or turnoffs, so where had the other vehicle gone?

That's when he saw it—the shadowy outline of a car keeping pace twenty feet behind them. They'd turned off the lights. Maybe he hadn't been imagining a beat-up blue Honda following them the last few blocks before they'd turned into the Center that morning. In the darkness, he couldn't verify it was the same car.

But it could be.

He pressed his foot on the gas to see if the other vehicle kept pace. It did.

"Deck? Please tell me you're just doing that checking-the-rearview-mirror-for-bad-guys thing out of habit."

"I'm not." The car crept closer. "We're being followed." Another mile, and they'd be back in civilization. If these guys were going to make their move, it would have to be soon, and Deck didn't plan to wait around for that to happen.

He gunned the Interceptor. Three loud pops came from behind them. The rearview window shattered, then the windshield cracked as one of the bullets went straight through the SUV.

"Get down!" He grabbed Tori's shoulder, pushing her upper body below the level of the dashboard. Automatically, he reached to his right hip and closed his hand around...nothing. "Christ," he gritted out. He was still on the rubber gun squad until the shooting board cleared him next week.

More gunshots, louder this time. Leaning down as much as possible, he veered into the center of the road, trying to block the car from coming alongside them. If they managed that, he and Tori were dead meat.

"They're shooting at us!" she shouted.

"Yeah. Stay down!" The road curved sharply to the right. He slammed his foot on the accelerator. If he punched it too hard, they'd career on two wheels and fly over the guardrail into the ravine. If the goons with the guns didn't kill them, the crash would.

More gunshots blasted, some taking out the left side windows, more pinging against the quarter panel.

Tori screamed. Shards of glass flew at his face, stinging like tiny ice picks. Deck's pulse hammered as he continued into the *S* curves. The Interceptor's center of gravity was higher than the car chasing him. He could already feel the SUV tipping. If he didn't slow down, they'd never make it. If he *did* slow down, they'd get caught in a hailstorm of flying lead.

At the next turn, the car pulled alongside. Up ahead, lights from the C-470 interchange glowed brightly. Tall streetlights marking the entrance to a new development lit the road. It wouldn't matter to him and Tori if they were dead, but he knew for a fact there were city cameras strategically placed at the C-470 on-ramps. If they made it that far, they should be able to get a tag reading off the vehicle. If there *was* a tag.

An arm stretched out of the car's window. Something glinted in his hand—a gun. Deck swerved to his left, slamming into the side of the car. The guy pulled back inside, barely avoiding getting his arm crushed.

They hit the straightaway at the entrance to the development. Headlights came at them, another car in the other lane. Again, Deck slammed his foot down on the accelerator, gunning onto the straightaway. The tire warning light lit and dinged. The SUV began tilting and veering sharply to the left. The tires were hit and deflating fast.

He glanced at the vehicle gaining ground and moving alongside again. The goon in the passenger seat aimed the gun at him. The driver leaned over, shouting something just as headlights from oncoming traffic fell across the guy's face. A face Deck knew.

A face he could *identify*.

The car shot past them, barely missing a head-on collision with a tractor trailer on the opposite side of the road. The car fishtailed as it hit the entrance ramp to the highway then slammed on the brakes and began doing a quick one-eighty. They were turning around for another pass.

With at least two tires shot out, the Interceptor was barely drivable. He was practically on the rims as it was. There'd be no way he could punch it.

Just as the shooter's car turned the wrong way on the one-way ramp, two other cars coming from the opposite direction on Alameda turned into the narrow highway entrance. With the headlights off, the first car slammed into the shooter's vehicle. The second car slammed into the first, careening off to the side and effectively blocking the ramp completely. Somehow, the shooter managed to back up, spin around, and take off up the ramp and disappear.

Deck slowed the shuddering SUV and pulled onto the shoulder. He blew out a heavy breath to try and calm his racing heart. "You okay?" Tori was hunched over with her hands covering the back of her head. When he touched her shoulder, he felt her entire body trembling. "Hey, hey. It's all right now."

Slowly, she sat up, staring at him with fear-filled eyes. "Are they gone?" He nodded. "What just happened?"

"Someone tried to kill us." A fact that stabbed him in the chest like a red-hot poker. She'd almost been hurt again because of him.

"Tell me something," she said in a shaky voice. "How many gunfights do you get into every week?"

"Normally, none." Breaking his own rule, he cupped her face, needing to feel her warm skin against his rough fingers. "This week has been an exception."

His thumb touched something wet and sticky, and he flipped on the overhead light. Blood trickled from several scratches on her left cheek. She must have caught some of the flying glass from the window as it shattered with enough force to send shards into her face. The left side of his own face still stung from the impact of tiny bits of glass, but his only thoughts were for her. She could have been blinded. She could have been—

Killed.

He squeezed his eyes shut, clamping his jaw together tightly. If his window wasn't already shattered, he would have punched it out with his fist. He reached over her and pulled clean napkins from the glove compartment then dabbed one gently at her cheek. He clenched his jaw tighter as bloody splotches soaked the napkin.

She stared blindly through the windshield. "Where did they go?"

"They got away." He reached for his cell and dialed 911.

"Do you think the police will catch them?" she asked after he'd made his report to the dispatcher.

"No. The car was probably stolen. They'll ditch it somewhere. Most likely, they'll burn it to get rid of prints. But it doesn't matter." He opened the door. "Stay here. I need to check on those other drivers."

"Wait!" She reached over the console to grab his arm. "Someone just tried to murder us, so why the *hell* doesn't it matter?"

Murder *him*, not *her*.

He looked at her lovely face, the scratches and blood on her cheek, the fear in her rounded green eyes. Because of him, she'd nearly become another statistic in the war against illegal drugs.

All-out rage had him so wired he was practically vibrating with it. One way or the other, he'd find the POS who'd put those scratches on Tori's skin then adorn the guy's face with the imprints of his knuckles.

"Because," he said as he stepped out of the SUV, "I can identify the driver. I don't know his name, but I've seen him before." Somewhere.

The question was *where*.

CHAPTER SIXTEEN

Tori picked at one of the ham-and-cheese sandwiches Detective Ruiz had procured for her and Deck. Something about getting shot at—*again*—took her appetite away. *Go figure.*

Only a few minutes had passed after he'd called 911 before they were surrounded by police cars. Then a tow truck came to drag off Deck's SUV. What was left of it anyway. Both left side tires had been shot out, along with all the windows on the left side. Bits of glass littered the interior, including Thor's kennel. *Thank God he wasn't with us.* He most certainly would have been hit by one of the flying bullets. It was a miracle she and Deck hadn't been hit. Aside from minor scratches, they were both okay. At least she'd finally stopped shaking.

They'd been at the police station for two hours now. Deck's boss, ASAC Santiago Rivera, and another DEA agent had shown up shortly after they'd arrived. Lakewood PD Detectives Mark Ruiz and Joe Schwartz had been assigned to the case.

After they'd all listened to Deck describe what had happened, Detective Ruiz indicated to his partner, "Joe, set Deck up over there with that mugshot database."

Deck walked over to her. "Sorry this is taking so long. Someone from my office should be here soon to drop off a spare K-9 unit. If you don't want to wait that long, I can get a patrol car to take you home."

She shook her head. "I'll wait for you to finish."

He touched two fingers to her chin, tilting her head as he took in the tiny red scratches. She hadn't even known they were there, hadn't felt any pain. Adrenaline would do that to a girl. "Okay." Then he opened his mouth to say something else.

"Deck, you're all set." Detective Schwartz waited for him behind a desk with two computer monitors.

"Sit tight. I'll be back." He went to the desk, sat, then began tapping away on the keyboard.

Tori took a sip of water then leaned back in the quasi-comfortable chair. Somewhere in that database was a picture of the man who'd tried to kill them. It didn't matter that Deck thought he was the target, not her. This was the second time she'd nearly been shot in two weeks. She so was not cut out for this line of work. Was anyone, really?

He is. Deck stared at the monitors and kept pecking away at the keyboard with his big hands.

Wil would have a field day when he found out what happened. She could hear his groan and admonishment already.

She bit her lip. Maybe she wouldn't tell him.

She had no intention whatsoever of telling her dad or sister about this. *Any* of it. Worrying them wouldn't help matters any and after what her dad had gone through, he'd probably file a lawsuit against the DEA on her behalf.

"Tori." Evan had arrived, along with his blue-eyed German shepherd. The dog was even bigger than she remembered. "You okay? Deck texted us what happened."

"I'm fine. We're *both* fine," she reassured him. As fine as two people can be after nearly getting drilled by over a dozen bullets. That was just an estimate, based on the number of holes in the side of the truck. Who knew how many times they'd missed?

"Deck said he'll be here a while going through mugshots. Do you want me to give you a ride home?"

Disappointment flooded her bloodstream. Was he trying to get rid of her? "Did he ask you to take me home?"

"No. Just thought I'd offer."

Relief replaced disappointment. Still, since they'd left Mick's, she'd detected a slight chill from Deck, as if he wanted a little distance. The only break in that chill had been when he'd dabbed her bleeding face with a napkin.

"Gotcha!" Deck fisted his hand. "Timothy Lomax, aka T-Lo." He hit a button on the keyboard, and a printer on the desk began spitting out pages. He grabbed the stack and passed out pages to the detectives and ASAC Rivera. "Possession with intent to distribute, conspiracy to distribute, unlawful possession of a firearm, assault on a PO. A tiger never loses its stripes."

Ruiz held up the page he was reading. "This is the guy who shot at you?" Deck nodded.

"You're sure?" ASAC Rivera asked. "His lawyer will say it was dark out."

Deck snorted. "His lawyer will say a lot of things, but it won't matter. That's him."

"Okay. That's enough for a warrant." Ruiz returned to his desk and picked up the phone.

Deck came around the desk, sat on the corner, and crossed his arms. The movement hiked up his shirtsleeves, revealing thick, bunching biceps. "I knew I'd seen that guy before."

"Did you arrest him?" Tori went to the desk, leaning her hip against it. "Is that what this is about, revenge?"

He shook his head. "I never arrested this guy. Lakewood PD did, more than five years ago. I remember reading about it in a bulletin. It was big news. He got busted for dealing heroin and cocaine. Sentenced to five years in Sheridan. But we never crossed paths."

She frowned. "Then why did he try to kill us?" *You?* None of this made sense.

Deck nodded. "That's the $64,000 question. One only T-Lo knows the answer to."

"And he's still out there." He could try to kill Deck again.

"He doesn't know I just ID'd him. Once that warrant is issued, every police officer in the state will be looking for him. As soon as I take Tori home," he said to Rivera, "I'll get a team together and start looking for this guy."

"Aside from taking Dr. Sampson home, you'll do nothing." ASAC Rivera folded the sheet of paper in his hand and stuffed it into his back pocket. "You're the only agent—let alone one on the rubber gun squad—who ever managed to get involved in two shootings within five days."

"Yes, sir." Deck scrunched up his face, looking so much like a little boy whose father had just lit into him. How such a big, tough man could look adorable she didn't know. *But he does.*

"Get your ass in the office first thing tomorrow morning," his boss ordered. "I know you want to go and kick in some doors, but rest assured, we *will* put together a team to find this guy. You, however, won't be on it."

Deck ground his jaw so hard, she could swear his teeth squeaked.

"We just got this in." Detective Ruiz handed a sheet of paper to Deck. "Arvada FD is putting out a car fire as we speak. Vehicle fits the general description of the one you gave us. It was reported stolen a week ago."

Deck looked up from the document. "Any chance of pulling prints?"

"Doubtful. By the time the FD got there, it was fully engulfed."

"What do you think the connection is between you and T-Lo?" Evan asked.

"Dunno," Deck answered, frowning. "You know as well as I do that K-9 units usually supplement an investigation, not take point on one. The only case I've been working lately involves gray death. That's gotta be the connection. T-Lo's got a history that fits. If he's the one supplying the drug to all these dealers, we'll get him."

"You and Thor have been on just about every opioid warrant since this case started," Rivera pointed out. "Everyone remembers the K-9s. Could be you made yourself a target."

He shrugged, as if this kind of thing happened every day. "Comes with the territory."

"The territory?" She slid off the desk. "*Seriously?* How can you be so cavalier? Someone just tried to kill you."

Three weeks ago, it wouldn't have bothered her to know how difficult and dangerous his job was. Then she'd only viewed him as someone who'd destroyed her and her family's lives. Now that she saw him as a caring person who was just trying to do good in the world, the idea of waking up to hear that he'd been shot dead in the middle of the night was too much. She blinked back the tears then spun and stalked into the hallway.

Heavy footsteps followed, and she knew without looking behind her it was Deck.

"Tori, wait." He caught her arm, forcing her to turn and look at him.

"What?" she snapped, feeling as if her emotions were about to bubble out the top of her head.

Gently, he gripped her shoulders, his gaze dipping to her mouth as he leaned in. Her heart ticked faster, totally erratic now. Would he really kiss her in the middle of a police station?

Voices drifted down the hallway. He released her shoulders, straightening then nodding to several uniformed police officers as they walked past them, continuing down the corridor before exiting out a door.

Oh, lord. What did she want him to do? Hold her? Kiss her? Tell her that it was okay to have feelings for a man who lived an incredibly dangerous life?

She closed her eyes and let her head fall forward. *Yes. That was exactly what she wanted. All of it.*

The admission scared her to death.

CHAPTER SEVENTEEN

Tori set the terrarium in the bay window, turning it first one way then the other to make sure the plants were properly seated. This one had taken her an entire week's worth of evenings, and she was thankful for the distraction. It had given her something else to think about besides Deck.

She hadn't heard from him since last Saturday night when he'd taken her home. Not that she had a reason to expect him to, exactly. *Oh, bull*. She'd stupidly thought he'd at least say something about staying in touch. He'd merely walked her to the door and said good night. He'd seemed even more aloof than ever. Then again, he was number one on a drug-dealing hitman's list, so maybe she was being too hard on him.

She was no longer accompanying him on warrants, so their only possible interaction would be if another OD victim came into the ER. Chances were high that would happen again, and soon. Miraculously, over the last week, it hadn't. Possibly because of the raids. Maybe all the dealers were laying low until things cooled off. Hopefully, things would never cool off.

Tori tied her hair up in a ponytail then grabbed the pink sweater that matched her skirt. She headed outside to her car—the Subaru she'd bought the week after she finally made attending physician.

It was just as well that Deck had cut off ties with her.

Being around him gave her too many bizarre thoughts. Like convincing herself—for one fleeting moment—that she could see herself with a guy like him. What she needed right now was a quiet evening with her father and sister's family. Being around them always cleared her head, refreshing her perspective on things.

A Lakewood police car drove past her house. It sure seemed as if they were stepping up patrols in her neighborhood lately. Tori could swear she'd seen one driving on her road every time she went outside. Was this because of the car chase, or was this Deck's doing?

She got into her car and turned the key. *Click, click, click.* Again, she turned the key, and again the engine responded with a less than resounding series of clicks, followed by…nothing. "Nooo." She rested her forehead on the steering wheel.

A mechanic she wasn't, but even she understood the battery was dead. DOA, never to be resuscitated. The garage she'd last taken it to for an oil change had said it was old and on its last leg, but she'd gotten so absorbed in work and this DEA thing she'd forgotten about it. Another reason why ending her association with Deck was for the best. The man was too distracting than was good for her.

She fished out her cell and began searching for a car lift company when a blue SUV pulled up next to her. *Deck's SUV.* The one he'd been given as a replacement for his bullet-riddled K-9 unit.

Tori frowned. Why was he here and at the very moment she had car trouble?

Thor's massive head stuck out the window, his tongue lolling to one side as he panted. The bushes next to the driveway rustled as Tigger poked his head through then strolled casually to the front of the SUV and jumped on the hood. Thor began that odd *cooing* sound he'd made the last time he and Tigger had crossed paths. Again, Tigger astounded her by loudly purring his furry little heart out.

Deck strolled around the hood of her car. The scratches on his face from the broken window had healed nicely and were nearly invisible. She'd been putting coverup on hers so no one would ask how she'd gotten them.

He wore jeans and another polo shirt, this one blue. The only things his off-duty wardrobe seemed to consist of were jeans and polo shirts, and somehow, he always managed to look hot, as Suzie so succinctly kept putting it. Tori, on the other hand, always struggled to find just the right thing to wear. *Not. Fair.*

Reluctantly, she got out of the car. Thor stretched his head out of the SUV, and she scratched him behind one ear, unable to contain her smile when he leaned his head into her hand. "Good morning to you, too, Thor." A deep, contented rumble came from the dog's throat, followed by an equally discontented whine when she removed her hand.

"As nice as it is to see Thor, why are you here?" she asked. After what had happened to her family, she preferred her life and the people in it be up front, on time, no surprises, and totally predictable. Deck played by a different set of rules.

He watched her for a moment, his expression unreadable. "I wanted to check on you."

She narrowed her eyes. "Why?"

"To make sure you're okay."

"You could have just called."

"T-Lo's still out there."

"I thought you said he was after *you*, not *me*. Besides, the police must be staking out someone in my neighborhood. They drive down my street almost every hour."

"They *are* staking out someone on your street. *You*."

"Me? But I haven't done—" The meaning of his words hit her like a ton of bricks. "Did *you* arrange for police cars to drive by my house?"

"Just a precaution."

"Against what?" She parked one hand on her hip. "What aren't you telling me?"

Deck began stroking his jaw. At first, his silence annoyed her, as did him arranging for police protection behind her back. But then she felt a flash of...warmth. She'd jumped straight to assuming he was being overbearing. What if it was Deck being thoughtful?

"Coming or going?" he asked, completely changing the subject.

"Going." Trying to. "I think my battery's dead."

"Pop the hood." He moved to the front of her car. "I'll jump you."

"What?" She blinked then blinked again. *Oh, right*. Jump the *battery*. Not *her*. A tiny seed of disappointment nestled somewhere deep inside her belly. *Do I want to be jumped?*

Of course not. She didn't have to be a doctor to understand that the problem was that her basic biological needs were manifesting themselves. For the last two years, she'd essentially been a virgin. She was horny, that's all it was. That *had* to be all it was because there was no way in her orderly world that she'd ever have sex with Deck. Not that he'd offered or anything.

Tori reached inside her car and found the lever beneath the dashboard, popping the hood. She joined Deck and peered at the engine. Considering she could identify every part of the human body, one would think she could find the battery. *Wrong.*

"See that?" He pointed to a dirty black box, on top of which were thick wires connected to two metal thingies, one encrusted with bluish-green crud and the other with yellowish-white powder.

"What is all that gunk?"

"It happens when the sulfate in the battery reacts with the lead in the terminal posts."

"Can you dumb that down for me, please?"

"It means your battery is probably kaput. How old is it?"

"Five, maybe six years old."

"You need a new one. I can clean the terminals for you, but you really need a new battery."

"How can you clean all that crud off?"

"Simple." He touched the tips of his index finger and thumb together, forming a circle, then he inserted his other index finger through the hole. "I shove a wire brush through the terminal clamps and clean out the crud."

Tori gulped. Who knew auto repair could be so sexual? "Um, how long will that take? I have to be somewhere."

"Start to finish, maybe an hour."

She looked at her watch. "That won't work. I'm late as it is. I'll call an Uber. They can be here in ten minutes."

"Where do you need to go?" he asked.

"Westminster. My father's house for dinner."

"Stand back." He pulled down the hood of her car and locked it back into place. "I'll drive you."

Without waiting for a response, he placed his hand at the small of her back, urging her to the passenger door of his SUV. That touch—that one little touch—sent a shiver zigzagging up and down then back and forth across her spine, just like it had before.

Taking his charity didn't work for her. "You don't have to do this. I can easily get a car. I'll have to get one for the ride home anyway."

"Then I'll save you"—his eyes dipped then he cleared his throat—"half the trip."

Oh no. Her physiology was betraying her. Her nipples stood at full attention, thanks to his sexually charged battery-cleaning demo. Quickly, she draped her sweater over her shoulders, allowing the long sleeves to conceal her now-pert nipples.

"You're wasting time." He opened the passenger door, waiting for her to get in.

"Fine. Just give me a minute." She took her medical bag from the backseat, locked up her car, then stowed the bag in the trunk for safekeeping.

Thirty minutes later, they turned onto her father's street. During the drive, Deck had checked his rear and sideview mirrors no less than twenty times, a grim reminder of last week's near-fatal confrontation. According to Deck, T-Lo was proving elusive.

Her sister's car sat in the driveway. She shoved open the door, intending to make a quick escape, but stopped. "Thank you for the ride and for having the police watch over me. You didn't have to do that."

"I did." His eyes darkened as he leaned over the console and touched his fingers to her cheek. It was the barest of touches, but she felt it straight to her toes. He leaned closer, and his lips parted. Her heart pounded and her breath came in quick little gasps. Their mouths were only inches apart.

Thor snorted, blowing warm air against the side of her face and effectively separating them as he shoved his head through the connecting window. Tori jerked back then gasped loudly. Her father and sister stood not five feet away on the front steps, an amused look on their faces.

Heat flamed her face. Suddenly, she was a teenager again, caught by her parents kissing a boy on the top step in front of their house. Getting caught nearly kissing a man shouldn't have been a big deal. Getting caught kissing a *DEA agent* was a betrayal of her family. Could she be any more callous, especially to her father?

I'm a terrible daughter.

More to her annoyance, the corner of Deck's mouth lifted, and he opened his door.

"Wait!" She grabbed his arm. "Where are you going?"

"To open your door. A man doesn't bring a woman home in front of her father without executing proper etiquette."

Proper etiquette? She couldn't believe this was really happening. "Wait!" she repeated with more urgency. "Don't tell them what you do for a living, and don't say a word to them about the shooting." Correction, *shootings*, as in two of them. "I don't want to worry them. Okay?"

"Okay." He sobered then stepped out and came around to her side. "But if they ask about my job, I won't lie."

The second he opened the door, Tori bolted up the stairs to give her father a tight hug then did the same to her sister.

"Who's the hunk?" Margo whispered.

"A colleague." The quasi-lie rattled off her tongue easily enough, but reality was about to smack her in the face. The truth was bound to come out. What had she been thinking, letting him drive her here?

Margo made a snicker that sounded more like she was choking. "Do you kiss all your colleagues?"

Tori pulled from her sister's embrace. "We *weren't* kissing."

Margo smirked. "Only because we interrupted you."

To Tori's horror, her dad was already down the steps. "Nice to meet you, son. I'm Craig Sampson, Tori's father."

Deck shook her dad's hand. "Nice to meet you, too, sir. I'm Adam Decker. Everyone calls me Deck."

Tori flew down the steps with Margo right behind her. If she didn't derail this warm and fuzzy party, she knew exactly what her father would do.

"I hope you're hungry," her dad said to Deck.

Too late.

Deck cast her a questioning look but didn't wait for her answer. "Actually, I am." Thor barked, and Tori could hear his tail thumping against the inside of his kennel. "But I brought my partner, Thor."

"Your partner?" Her dad peered into the SUV. "Are you a K-9 officer?"

Tori's stomach lurched. *This is* not *going to be good.*

"What department do you work for?" her dad pressed.

Deck caught her eye, sending her a silent message that

made her stomach somersault. *The jig is up.*

"I'm a DEA K-9 agent," Deck replied.

Tori nearly stopped breathing. She flicked her gaze back and forth from her dad to Deck, not really certain what would happen next.

For one infinitesimal moment, her dad froze like a statue, the already-deep lines in his forehead deepening. Deck narrowed his gaze, a sign that he'd detected the simmering undercurrent.

"You're dating a DEA agent?" her sister whispered incredulously. "And you brought him *here*? You must be out of your mind."

No kidding. "We're *not* dating," she mumbled, reaching out for her sister's arm to steady herself for the onslaught. "I told you, we're colleagues. We're working on an important project together. One that could save lives," she added, scrambling to justify why she'd even *consider* sharing the same air with Deck.

At six-foot-one, her dad was a big man, but still shorter than Deck and slimmer in build. Silently, her dad cocked his head. She couldn't miss the chill in his eyes. "Girls, why don't you set another plate at the table? And get out bowls for Thor."

Tori smacked a hand to her forehead and groaned. *Can this possibly get any worse?* She and her sister were about to become spectators while the world as she knew it imploded around them.

As her father rounded the hood and went to Thor's window, the thumping inside the kennel intensified.

Deck opened the door and Thor leaped out, sitting in front of her dad. "Thor, this is Mr. Sampson." Thor raised his paw for her dad to shake.

Tori's dad grunted. "At least *he's* a very well-mannered DEA employee." Over his shoulder, he sent Tori a look only her and her sister would understand.

"You really stepped in it this time," Margo said in a hushed tone then held out her hand. "Hi," she said to Deck. "I'm Margo, the sister Tori so rudely forgot to introduce."

Yup. She really had stepped in it. *It* was up to her neck, and she was sinking fast.

"Nice to meet you." Deck shook hands with her sister then opened the rear door of the SUV, taking out a bag of kibble. "For emergencies," he said.

After glaring for several seconds at Deck's back, her father led the way inside, letting Thor gallop ahead of them. Just before going in, Deck whispered in her ear, "Something I should know?"

Warm breath tickled her neck and she shivered. "Uh…" *Too late now, Mr. Special Agent.* She'd tried to save his ass. Looked like her dad would spill the beans in his own sweet time.

She'd never wanted to tell Deck about her family. Given the fact that she hadn't heard from him for over a week, she assumed she'd never have to. Part of her wanted to protect him from her father, which was silly. Deck was a grown man—a *huge* man, actually—and a federal agent perfectly capable of standing up to her father, if and when it became necessary.

"After you." In a gesture becoming familiar to her, he put his hand at the small of her back just as her father turned around to catch the subtle gesture and arched a questioning brow.

Her face heated. Deck was the first man she'd brought to a family dinner, colleague or otherwise. No wonder her family was making assumptions. She'd have to end those thoughts *stat*.

When they were all in the kitchen, she grabbed a large bowl from the cupboard, filling it with water and setting it on the floor. Thor happily lapped up half the contents, licking his snout then expressing his thanks with a wet nuzzle to her hand.

"You're welcome, boy." She stroked his velvety-soft ears, appreciating the soothing nature dogs had on people. It couldn't have come at a better time.

Tori reached for another bowl on the higher shelf but couldn't reach it.

"I've got this." Deck stretched a long arm over her head, plucking the bowl from the top shelf and grazing his arm against her bare shoulder. Her skin prickled with goose bumps, and she crossed her arms to ward off anything else on her body getting prickly again.

"Thanks." She stepped aside for him to fill the other bowl with kibble.

Her dad watched on intently yet silently. The only sign of the turmoil Tori knew without a doubt was seething inside him was the muscle twitching in his cheek.

"Dinner's about ready." Margo piled up thick slices of ham surrounded by root vegetables on a large platter.

To her shock, her dad opened the refrigerator and pulled out two beers, handing one to Deck. "Beer?"

Am I in another dimension?

"Thank you." Deck accepted the beer and twisted off the cap.

For a fleeting moment, Tori had the ridiculous thought that her dad might've slipped something into his drink. Hopefully, Deck wouldn't drop dead on the spot.

"Tori?" Her dad held out another beer, her usual microbrew.

"Uh, no." She shook her head. "I think I'll fix something else." Like vodka, straight up.

"So tell me, Deck," her father said. "What made you want to work for the DEA?"

"I wanted to help people by getting illegal drugs off the street," Deck answered without flinching.

"And how long have you been...*helping* people?"

Oh, boy. Here it comes.

"Fourteen years."

Her dad took a sip of his beer then swallowed. "How do you feel about working for an agency that imposes excessive rules on small business, say mom-and-pop pharmacies, but allows pharmaceutical companies to essentially skirt the same laws and do whatever they please to line their pockets?"

Again, Deck didn't hesitate. "Given that pharmaceutical companies are responsible for supplying drug stores with their products, they should be held to even higher standards. Unfortunately, in Washington, money talks. Big Pharma has a lot of lobbying power, and that's way above my pay grade."

Her dad pursed his lips then narrowed his eyes on Deck.

"Anything else you'd like to ask?" Deck offered.

Her dad shook his head. "That'll do. For now," he tacked on half under his breath.

The corners of Deck's mouth lifted slightly, telling Tori

he'd heard every word.

"Well." Margo put on a bright smile. "Dad, Deck, you might as well go in and sit down."

Tori's eyes widened on her sister. *Alone? Together?*

Before she could stop him, her father motioned for Deck to follow him into the dining room.

The only sound in the kitchen came from Thor licking his now-empty bowl.

"Here." Margo handed her the martini glass she'd been drinking from. "You look like you could use something stronger than beer."

"You *know* I do." She took the glass and tilted half the contents of the rosemary-grapefruit martini down her throat, swallowing then sighing. "Where are Zach and the kids?" Margo's husband and kids usually joined them for family dinner.

"Zach took them to a Rockies game. They actually made it into the playoffs this year. Can you believe it?" Margo began mixing herself another drink.

"Too bad," Tori whispered. "Tonight, of all nights, it would have been nice to have them here." Anything to minimize the awkwardness.

"Yup, it sure would." Over the martini pitcher, her sister's eyes shimmered with censure.

Tori poured gravy into a gravy bowl and added a spoon, glancing into the dining room to make sure her dad hadn't beheaded Deck.

Margo poured herself another martini from the pitcher. "I keep waiting for the explosion."

"You and me both." She clinked glasses with her sister, grateful for the support. They'd always been close, and after Tori had moved back to Colorado, more so.

"Is he really *just* your colleague?" Margo asked. "I find it incredibly bizarre for you to bring home a DEA agent, of all people. Important life-saving project aside, of course." She pursed her lips, clearly not buying the story Tori had given her.

Again, Tori peered into the dining room where her dad and Deck talked about something she couldn't hear. "Yes, he *is* just a colleague." This lying thing was getting far too easy, but from the skeptical expression on Margo's face, her sister still wasn't buying it.

Margo took a sip and swallowed. "I call bull. You *are* seeing him, aren't you?"

"No. I just…"

"Just what?" Margo prodded.

Tori rolled her eyes. Might as well spill it. She never could hide anything from Margo, anyway. "I started thinking that maybe something between us was changing. Then he disappeared on me for a week, and I thought whatever was happening was over before it even began. Today, he showed up again."

"What did you *think* was happening?" Margo waggled her eyebrows.

"I don't know." Funny how she'd never experienced confusion when she'd been dating Mike last year. Somehow, she knew their relationship was fleeting.

Thor perked his head up then trotted into the dining room to join Deck and her father.

"The DEA thing aside for a minute, what do you *want* to happen between you?"

"I don't know," Tori admitted. "He's so…so…"

"So not like you?" Margo supplied.

"Exactly." She set down her now-empty glass, intending to switch to water. Then again… *I'm not driving, so what the heck?* She topped off her martini.

"He seems to like you. But you're asking for trouble." Margo handed her the mashed potatoes. "At least Dad hasn't shoved a pitchfork into his back yet, so that's a good sign."

"I suppose so." Something was up with her dad. Only time would tell what. "I'll put out another setting." Tori went into the dining room and set the bowl and her drink on the table, keeping one eye and ear on the men as they chatted, surprisingly amicably. She opened up the hutch and took out plates, silver, and another napkin, while Margo brought in the rest of the food.

"Let's eat." Her father took his usual place at one end, while Margo sat at the single place setting on one side of the table.

Tori reached for her chair when Deck stopped her, pulling it out then waiting for her to sit. "Thank you," she said, looking up in time to see the surprised expression on her father's face.

Her dad took a thick slice of ham from the plate then passed the plate to Deck. "How did you two meet?" He looked alternately from Deck to her.

"In the ER," Deck answered. "A colleague of mine was exposed to opioid powder and nearly died. Tori saved his life." He sent her a grateful look. "You should have seen her in action. You would have been proud of her, sir."

"I *am* proud of her." He smiled. "I'm proud of *both* my daughters. I never doubted they would be successful in any endeavor they pursued. So, you obviously stayed in touch?"

Deck nodded. "Tori's been helping me on a case."

"Helping you?" Margo stared at her. "How?"

Tori opened her mouth, but Deck interrupted. "We can't discuss the details, but she's gotten me useful information, and she's been a huge asset in the field. I wish we had more doctors like her willing to help us out."

Beneath the table, he squeezed her hand and didn't let go. When he began stroking his thumb over her fingers, her mind went utterly blank. When he looked at her with his big, dark, chocolate-brown eyes going all soft, the rest of her cranium shut down as if someone had flicked off the switch to every single neuron.

"Tori?"

Wow. She had no idea he valued her that much. Hearing it left her entire body bathed in the warm glow of his praise and appreciation.

"*Tori*?" Margo repeated, hooking her fingers into quotation marks. "What exactly are you doing 'in the field'?"

"I, um." She glanced at Deck, not certain how much she could divulge. When he nodded, she continued, "I went on a couple of warrants with him."

"How very James Bond of you," Margo said.

Her father frowned. "Isn't that dangerous?"

"Hardly." She waved a dismissive hand, hoping what remained of the scratches on her face really weren't visible beneath the makeup she'd applied. "Deck was the one doing all that special agent stuff. I just sat in the car in case someone needed medical assistance." Not exactly true, but they didn't need to know that.

Her dad scratched his chin. "Hmm." The sound had

come out more of a growl.

Thus far, he'd done an admirable job keeping most of his issues with the DEA to himself. Whether he could keep the rest of it in check for the duration of dinner and dessert remained to be seen. Tori understood that her family was shocked by what she'd told them. Her entire association with Deck was so *not* her, how could they *not* be in shock?

Just when she thought she'd escape more awkwardness, her father set down his napkin. In a clipped voice, he said to Deck, "You'll have to excuse me, *Special Agent* Decker. I'm going outside for some air." He strode swiftly from the room, and a moment later, the front door opened then slammed shut.

Tori rested her elbow on the table, covering her face with her hand. The explosion she'd been waiting for and hoping wouldn't happen was about to.

CHAPTER EIGHTEEN

Deck looked from one sister to the other. For lack of a better word, Tori looked anguished. Gutted, even. Margo didn't look much better.

The moment he'd told Tori's father he worked for the DEA, Deck had easily detected a discernible frostiness from the man. During dinner, he'd sensed more bad vibes barely held in check. He didn't know why, but Tori's father was a keg of dynamite, and somehow his fuse had been lit.

"Excuse me." Tori pushed from the table and left the room. Presumably to go after her father.

"Your dad doesn't like me much. Does he?" he tacked on when Margo didn't respond right away.

"It's not that he doesn't like *you*." She gave a heavy sigh. "He doesn't like the DEA." Her voice was sympathetic, but it did nothing to ease his concerns.

"Why not?" Craig Sampson didn't strike him as a drug dealer, so he could only imagine.

Margo held out her hands in a placating gesture. "It's not my story to tell."

Raised voices came from outside. Tori's *and* her dad's. She'd been reluctant to let him drive her here in the first place. Then she'd practically panicked, begging him not to say who he worked for. When Craig had invited him to stay for dinner, he'd jumped at the chance like a lovesick puppy because he'd stupidly wanted Tori's father to like him. Now he knew that would never be possible. He stood and pushed his chair back.

"Don't go out there," Margo warned.

"I have to." He left Tori's sister alone in the dining room, looking as forlorn as a lost child. Whatever was going on, he couldn't stand by and let Tori take the brunt of her father's rage which, apparently, Deck's presence had created.

Thor followed him to the front door, sitting by his side and looking up at him with big, questioning eyes. Through the screen, Craig Sampson's voice carried loudly. He gestured, pointing his finger at Tori.

"I tried, Tori. For you, I really tried. But how could you bring him here? Do you have any idea how hurtful that is?" Craig dragged a hand down his face, suddenly looking twenty years older.

"I'm sorry, Dad. I didn't mean for this to happen." Tori clapped a hand over her mouth. Her shoulders shook, and she looked as if she was about to lose it.

"I spent six months in jail because of the DEA. Our savings, our livelihood, your mother…gone because of guys like him." He jerked his head in the direction of the house but hadn't caught sight of Deck standing just inside the door.

Six months? Tori had said her mother died ten years ago. Based on Craig's words, her death was somehow connected to all this.

"Daddy, please." Tori's sobs cut straight to Deck's heart. "I'm sorry. I shouldn't have brought him here."

He pushed open the door, Thor following him as he walked up behind Tori to rest a protective hand on her shoulder.

Craig stiffened, his eyes fueled with rage and bitterness. "This is between me and my daughter."

Sensing the man's animosity, Thor lowered his head and exhaled a low growl, forcing Deck to reach down and rest his hand on his dog's head, reassuring him there was no threat he needed to worry about.

"Apparently," Deck countered, "it involves me, too, and I have no idea why. Whatever it is, don't even think about taking it out on her."

"Deck, don't." Tori clutched at his arm, looking up at him with anguished eyes that tore into his very soul and made him want to protect her that much more from whatever was playing out here. "Please, just go. I'll get a ride home."

"I'm *not* leaving you." When she began urging him to his SUV, he resisted. "Not like this."

"Tori!" Her dad's stone-cold tone had the effect of a slap on her face. She whipped her head around to stare at her father. A calm seemed to settle around the man as he gentled his voice. "Sweetheart, if he's going to be part of your life—*any* part of your life—he needs to hear the truth. I want you to go back inside, so Deck and I can have a little talk."

"*What*? No!" She gaped at her father then craned her neck to look up at Deck. "I'm not leaving you."

Despite the drama unfolding and the obvious anguish her entire family was experiencing, Deck nearly laughed. She actually thought she needed to protect him. Sure, Tori's dad was no small man, but still. Under the circumstances, it was sweet, and in his line of work, not many people exhibited sweetness toward him. "Tori, I'll be okay," he said, caressing her cheek before glancing at Craig to catch the older man's eyes tracking the gesture.

The screen door slammed, and Margo joined them on the front lawn. She hooked her hand around her sister's arm. "Tori, let's go have another martini, shall we?"

Tori didn't budge. She swept a worried gaze back and forth between him and her father. Reluctantly, she went back inside with Margo.

"Walk with me," Craig said the second the door had closed.

Deck and Thor fell in step with him as they began walking the property. The sun was on the verge of setting, casting the sky in a dim orange hue beyond the rail post fencing surrounding the property. The first words out of Craig's mouth weren't what Deck had been expecting.

"My girls had a dog of their own when they were little. After Tori moved to Boston, she always wanted another one." Still walking, he held out his hand for Thor to sniff. "Unfortunately, my daughter has never felt she had the time for another pet. Or anything that might force her to enjoy herself."

She *had* always struck Deck as being reserved and, at times, downright uptight. "Why's that?"

Tori's father stopped and rested his hands on the top rail post, staring off into the distance at the sunset. "I've always thought she had an adventurous side, but she was always overly cautious."

Again, why? Deck stroked Thor's ears, still wondering where all this was going and what it had to do with him and the DEA.

Craig's green eyes, so like Tori's, bore into him. "Her

single-minded focus on her job feeds her need to be cautious all the time."

Deck was tempted to shoot from the hip and ask why Craig was telling him—a man he'd known for less than two hours—such personal details about Tori. Particularly since Craig had something else on his mind. Deck suspected he'd get around to it when he was good and ready.

"As much as I don't want to see it, I do," he continued. "How much you care for my daughter, and how much she cares about you."

"I *do* care about her." In fact, he cared so much that he'd called in some favors from the local PD and they'd stepped up over the last week with regular drive-bys of Tori's house. He didn't think T-Lo knew who she was, but it gave him enough peace of mind that he'd finally been able to sleep at night. He'd even driven by her house several times himself over the last few days but hadn't stopped. When he'd seen her sitting in her car this morning, he'd folded like a cheap suit and had to see her. So much for keeping his distance.

"Has she told you about her box?"

"Her box?"

"More like a comfort zone, really."

"Ah, that," Deck said, knowing full well what Craig was alluding to.

"Yes, that," he agreed. "Some years ago, I ran into a little trouble that affected my whole family. Since then, everything in Tori's life has to fit safely into her comfort zone. Nothing risky, adventurous, or *un*safe gets inside. Except you." His deep green eyes locked on to Deck's. "You are most definitely outside that zone, and you're about to find out just *how* far."

Craig rested his forearms on the post rail. Beside him, Deck did the same, and beside Deck, Thor rose and rested his paws on the same rail. Together, the three of them remained silent as they watched the sun begin to dip lower behind the Rockies.

"I was a pharmacist for over thirty years," he said finally. "Before the DEA revoked my license."

Every muscle in Deck's body froze. That certainly explained the weird vibes he'd been getting and the way Tori and her sister had been walking on eggshells since the moment he'd arrived. No wonder Tori had hated him on sight. He was the bad guy. The DEA.

"What happened?" While the DEA was the primary agency that enforced pharmacy regulations, pulling a pharmacist's license was rare.

"At first, I was handing out pain meds to people who couldn't afford them. People without insurance, some folks without so much as a roof over their heads. Big Pharma has been jacking up drug prices to the point that only the wealthy can afford some of them."

"So your motives were altruistic, not for personal gain." Something the government tended not to take into consideration at times.

Craig clasped his hands together and gave a heavy sigh. "If that was my only transgression, the DEA might have looked the other way. The problem was that I graduated to administering death drugs to terminal patients who wanted to die."

Holy crap didn't begin to cover this. Try *mountains* of crap. The Feds didn't tolerate Doctor Death scenarios, no matter how well intentioned the motives. Deck hoped the shock didn't show on his face. "I take it that was before the passage of Proposition 106." He'd read up on Colorado's End of Life Options Act passed in 2016, permitting terminally ill patients over the age of eighteen to have physician-assisted suicide.

Craig nodded. "There are only eight states that currently permit physician-assisted suicide, along with Washington, D.C.—home to headquarters of the DEA and every other federal agency. Ironic, isn't it?"

Yeah. It was. "Did you ever try getting your revocation overturned? Under the circumstances and since the change in law, they might consider it."

"Bah." He waved his hand in the air. "It was incredibly painful to lose my license, but I knew what I was doing was illegal, and I accepted the risks. Perhaps I shouldn't have been so forthcoming with the DEA about all that I'd done. My lawyer warned me not to answer their questions, but I did anyway and told the truth. I got what I deserved, but I was selfish in taking those risks. I lost my business, and my family lost its income. My wife was devastated, and it took quite a physical and emotional toll on her. Her heart gave out. Tori believes it was the strain that killed her."

This was getting worse by the second. It was a wonder Tori hadn't kicked him in the balls that night in the ER. *When you step in it, Decker, you* plunge *into it, headfirst.*

"Financially, it was hard on all of us, especially Tori. The money I'd planned to give her for med school went straight into my lawyer's pocket to keep me out of jail, which didn't work, and to pay a big, fat fine. Without my pharmacy's income, Tori had to find jobs and worked every free minute she had. I don't regret helping all those people. That, I'm at peace with. But I do regret how it impacted my family. It sucked the life out of my wife, literally, and left a lasting impression on my daughters."

Now, Deck understood even more. "Tori's comfort zone."

"Now you're getting it, kid." Unexpectedly, Craig clapped him on the shoulder. "I came to grips with what I did a long time ago, and to an extent, so has Margo. But Tori hasn't. Since then, she's lived her life by the book so that nothing shakes her world apart again. You shake her world, in more ways than one. For her to bring you here tells me exactly how much she cares for you."

Did she? Care that much for him? It wasn't as if she'd actually invited him to dinner, and whatever their relationship was, they hadn't gotten to the point of talking about it. He'd only kissed her once, and he hadn't even taken her on a real date yet. There'd been way too many things going on for him to even consider going further.

Thor rested his head between his paws on the rail, flicking his amber gaze to Deck.

"I just want my daughters to be happy." Craig turned from the rail, indicating they should head back to the house. Deck and Thor fell in step again. "After the devastation I unleashed on this family to follow my own conscious, I owe them that and so much more. Margo is happy. Tori is still searching. If you're who and what she's been searching for, I'll accept that. For her sake."

He liked the old man and respected him for watching out for his daughters. Part of him even respected the guy for what he'd done all those years ago to help people. "You sure you didn't poison my food?"

Craig chuckled. "I might have been tempted there for a few minutes."

Well. Good thing he hadn't, because if Deck got his way, he very much wanted to be alive so he could court Tori properly.

CHAPTER NINETEEN

Tori angled to face Deck, making no pretense whatsoever that she was staring at him. He ignored her, keeping his hands firmly on the wheel as he maneuvered the SUV along the dark twists and turns of Route 285. Behind them, Thor snored happily in his kennel.

"Are you *ever* going to tell me what you two talked about?"

Right before leaving the house, she'd been floored when her dad had shaken hands with Deck. For the last twenty-five minutes, she'd been interrogating him, employing every last weapon in her social skills arsenal to squeeze him for specifics about what he and her dad had discussed out in the yard. Each time, Deck skillfully avoided giving her any relevant information. All he'd said was that they'd "come to an understanding." Must be another thing they taught in federal agent-school. How to be tight-lipped.

Instead of answering her, he grabbed her hand and laced their fingers together.

"You can't distract me that easily," Tori said.

His grin said otherwise, and he was right. *Damn him.*

Much as she tried to ignore them, tiny tendrils of steamy-hot awareness seeped from his hand to hers. She tried unlacing their fingers, but he only tugged her hand to his mouth. One by one, he began kissing her fingers, slowly, and with a tiny bit of tongue, as if each one of her fingers was a tasty chocolate morsel.

Oh, he was good at this duck-and-evade thing. Finally, she yanked her hand from his only to hear him chuckling in the darkness.

"You're like a defense attorney," he said, "but no matter how many different ways you ask me the same question, my answer won't change." He exited the highway and turned onto her road. "All you need to know is that your dad and I came to an understanding."

"You already said that." And she ought to be grateful for it. She'd actually expected there to be bloodshed. The call-911 kind of bloodshed. "But an understanding about *what*? What were you talking about the whole time?"

A few seconds later, he pulled into her driveway, cranked the gearshift in park, then turned to face her. "Mostly, we talked about *you*."

"Me?" What could they have possibly discussed about *her* for that long?

"Yes, you. The rest of the time he explained what happened ten years ago." He shoved a rough hand through his hair, leaving some of the strands askew. "You should have told me. It would have explained why you hated me on sight."

"I didn't hate you on sight." He gave her a *duh* look, telling her he knew she was lying. "Okay, maybe I did."

But she hadn't, not really. What she hated was what had happened to her dad, her mom, and how it had impacted their entire family. She'd never actually hated Deck and now realized she never could because she cared about him too much. Somehow, her father had seen that. *Somehow*, he'd managed to call a truce with Deck, and he'd done it for her. Because he loved her. If her dad could set aside some of his animosity, maybe she should, too.

Deck traced her jawline with the pad of his thumb. "I'm sorry for what happened to your dad. To you, your family. Don't say anything yet, but I'm going to look into getting your dad's license restored."

"You don't have to do that." Although it was an awfully kind offer.

"I want to," he insisted. "I can't change the past, but I can help now."

He would help, she realized, because that was who he was. Beneath all his drug-warrior toughness, he was a kind, compassionate man who'd sat through an uncomfortable meal, knowing something was off, then tolerated her dad's rant enough to listen and wind up with a handshake at the end of the night.

"I'm sorry," she said, feeling about as low as a girl could get. "I owe you as much of an apology as I owe my dad."

"The only part of your apology I'll accept is that you didn't tell me yourself. For the rest, you don't owe anyone an apology." He continued tracing her jaw, his touch gentle and tender. "Then again, there is one thing you could do to make it up to me."

"Anything," she answered, meaning it.

He leaned in closer, his breath warm on her face. "Put your money where your mouth is." Then he kissed her, his lips gliding softly over hers.

Before she could blink, he'd unbuckled their seat belts and hauled her onto his lap. He kissed her again, his tongue invading her mouth with the same swift assuredness that he used to break in doors at search warrants.

His hard chest pressed against her breasts while his

tongue swept her mouth, seeking and tasting. Demanding yet gentle. She ran her hands up his muscled arms to link them around his neck. If she'd been hooked up to a heart monitor, that green line would be jumping all over the screen.

Deck's erection pushed hard against her bottom where she sat on his lap. Just when she was about to slip her hands beneath his shirt and tear it over his head, he ended the kiss, pulling away and breathing as heavily as she was.

"I should walk you to your door." He landed another kiss on her lips, this one quick, as he shut off the engine.

Walk me to my door? Really? After lighting a fuse that was still sizzling and sparking like a live wire?

He eased from beneath her, getting out of the SUV then holding out his hand for her as she shimmied off the seat and exited out the driver's side. He opened Thor's door, waiting for his dog to jump out and do his business on a nearby tree.

Pine boughs rustled in the breeze as Deck and Thor walked Tori to her front door. With her nerve endings still sparking with need, she managed to insert the key into the lock. Waves of warmth emanated from Deck's big body only inches behind her, washing over her bare arms and neck. She pushed open the door, hesitating a moment.

All it would take was one simple invitation. To a man she'd fully intended to keep a safe emotional distance from. But after the last few hours, her entire belief system had been turned upside down. If her father could at least *try* to accept Deck being in her life, maybe that was one roadblock she no longer had to brake for.

Her next thought was both shocking *and* frightening.

Maybe it was time to ease up on the death grip she had on the past.

"Um, do you want to come in?" She held her breath, waiting to see if he'd finish what he started so she could drag him inside and ravish him. Yes, that's exactly what she wanted to do.

"Sure," was all he said, but enough moonlight filtered through the trees for her to glimpse the unmistakable hunger smoldering in the hooded darkness of his eyes.

Tori stepped inside and flipped on the lights. The leap she was about to take was huge. As she set her keys and bag on the hall table, Deck closed the door. Her belly vibrated with nervous energy she hadn't experienced in a very long time. She wasn't a virgin, but right now she felt like one.

Needing something to do with her hands, she went into the kitchen and filled a bowl with water. The moment she set it on the floor, Thor drank his fill then padded into the living room and lay down.

Taking a deep breath, she turned to find Deck leaning against the kitchen doorway, watching her. No, make that *tracking* her, like he was ready to pounce and eat her up. *Oh. Yeah.* As she moved toward him, the pulse at the side of his neck ticked faster. *Not faster than mine.* That imaginary cardiac monitor she was hooked up to had to be beeping like crazy.

Her mouth went drier than a piece of litmus paper. He was so handsome, so raw and virile. Where this relationship was destined to go was still a mystery. Right now, the only direction she wanted to take it was down the hall and straight into her bedroom.

"Are you hungry?" she asked. *What a stupid question*. Then again, none of them had eaten much after the confrontation with her dad, and Deck was a big man.

A muscle in his jaw flexed. "Yeah," he answered, his voice low and husky. "But not for food." Still, he remained motionless. This was her party. He was waiting for her to make the first move.

So make it.

As if in a dream, Tori watched her hands as she reached for him.

• • •

The second her hands contacted his chest, he moved, crashing his mouth down on hers and banding his arms around her back.

He tangled his tongue with hers, sweeping inside her mouth, trying to absorb her sweet scent and taste into his body.

She clung to him, their bodies pressed together from toe to head, and still, it wasn't enough. He skimmed his hands up the side of her rib cage, grazing her beautiful breasts. A soft moan escaped her lips, the vibrations of which traveled straight to his groin. They were like two halves of a combustion engine, and he was about to explode.

She tugged his shirt from his jeans, running her hands up and down his bare back, scoring his skin with her nails, and damned if he wasn't shaking.

Reluctantly, he tore his mouth from hers, dropping kisses along her jawline. "Bedroom," he heard himself growl, only that wasn't his voice. It was the voice of a barely contained animal.

"Um," she sighed, dropping her head back and giving him better access to the soft, creamy skin of her neck. "Down the...hall."

That was all the direction he needed.

He clasped her bottom, hauling her against him and feeling just how smooth the backs of her thighs were beneath that sexy little pink skirt.

She wrapped her legs tightly around his waist, putting his aching erection right where he wanted to be. He made it four strides when his mind blanked out and he spun, pressing her back against the wall and kissing her with everything he had as he ground himself against her.

"Ah, Tori," he muttered then hiked her skirt up to her waist. When he slipped his hands beneath her wet panties, his fingers found the hot, silky wetness of her folds.

"Deck." Her chest heaved, mounding her breasts beneath the thin pink fabric. "Touch me," she moaned. *"Please. More."*

He pushed two fingers into her and groaned from how wet she was. He'd bet she tasted just as sweet down there, too. As he pumped his fingers in and out, she undulated her hips, driving herself harder and harder against his hand until her breaths came in short gasps.

"That's it, baby. Come for me. I want to feel you come around my fingers. Do it, baby. Do it *now*."

She uttered a sharp cry, the back of her head banging against the wall as her body bucked and shuddered around him.

He caught her mouth again in a deep kiss, trying to

extend her orgasm as much as possible. Watching her like this…he was about to come in his pants.

Breathing hard, she fumbled between them and unsnapped the button on his jeans and pulled down the zipper. When she slipped her hand beneath the snug cotton of his briefs, he threw back his head, gritting his teeth as his body tightened. Then she cupped him, squeezing gently.

Holy sh—

If she didn't ease up and fast, he'd lose it in his jockey shorts. He backed away enough to lower her feet to the floor, but she only cupped him harder, moving her hand up and down as much as his jeans would allow.

"Tori, don't! *Stop!*" He smacked his hands on the wall on either side of her shoulders, throwing his head back as his body shook with the Herculean effort it took not to come.

"No," she whispered, pushing the waistband of his jeans and briefs lower and taking his cock in her hand.

Oh, man.

Sanity returned enough for him to grab his creds wallet from the rear pocket of his pants and whip out a condom that was old but not too old. He shoved the wallet back in his pocket and tore off the wrapper. With Tori still stroking him, his balls and cock tightened more than he thought possible. His fingers were clumsy, but somehow, he managed to roll the condom over his raging erection.

"Hurry," she said in a throaty voice, digging her fingers into his scalp. "Hurry!"

Yes, ma'am.

He reached under her skirt and grabbed the edges of her panties, yanking them down then deciding for the more expeditious route and ripped the thing in half, tearing the fabric from her legs.

As he clasped the backs of her thighs, she hiked up her skirt again, practically jumping into his arms. In one long, smooth stroke, he entered her, pushing until he was balls-deep inside her hot, wet channel.

The sound he heard next was the two of them groaning in unison. Her arms came around his back, and he began pumping, slowly at first, but her tiny cries of arousal were quickly driving him to the edge. He wanted her to come first, but... *Can't. Hold. Out. Much longer*.

He clasped her bare buttocks, driving into her faster, gritting his teeth with every thrust.

Deck fastened his mouth on the side of Tori's neck, sucking gently as he inhaled the sweet scent of her perfume and sex that was spiraling upward from their joined bodies. She stiffened in his arms, her fingers clawing at his scalp. Her breaths came faster, louder, and he knew she was on the edge, ready to explode as violently as he was.

"That's it. Let it go," he gritted out, pumping furiously as her walls squeezed his cock. When she screamed his name, he lost it and shot his release so hard into the condom, he worried it might break.

As he rode the powerful waves, he shuddered, pressing his forehead to hers. Beneath him, she gasped for air, repeating the words. "Oh. Oh. *Ohhh*."

Deck had to agree, it was *oh*. The kind of amazing, mind-blowing, earth-shattering *oh*.

They remained where they were, as intimately as two people could possibly be. Except for the clothes. He wanted to do this all over again but with nothing between them.

He kissed her forehead then pulled away to look down at her. Her lips were parted, her breathing slowed some. "You okay?" he asked hesitantly, because he'd taken her like a wild animal. When she'd touched his chest, he thought he'd lost control, but that had been nothing compared to when she'd palmed his raging hard-on. Holy hell, the woman knew how to drive him crazy in more ways than one.

When she tilted her head back, he tensed. Normally, her face was an open book. Now, it wasn't, and he couldn't tell if she was about to kiss him or smack him. Slowly, she blinked, as if in a mental fog.

"Tori, you okay?" he repeated, fear wedging its way in deeper when she still didn't answer.

A slow grin curved her lips as she clasped the sides of his face and kissed him thoroughly, hotly, leaving no doubt whatsoever that she was more than okay. Especially when she drew back just enough to whisper, "The bedroom's that way."

CHAPTER TWENTY

He carried her down the hall and into the bedroom, flipping on the lights with his elbow. "Tell me something," he murmured against her ear, sending tingles parading across her breasts. "Am I really outside your comfort zone?"

Rather than answer him because, well, all rational thought had abandoned her, Tori closed her eyes, reveling in the feel of his lips feasting on her sensitive skin.

He began dropping hot, wet kisses along the side of her neck just below her ear. "Am I?"

"Yesss," she breathed. His taste was on her tongue. His citrusy pine scent was in her lungs. Every inch of her body was completely tuned in and totally turned on by the feel of him pressed against her. Still inside her.

In a smooth motion, he pulled out of her, setting her on her feet. He skimmed his hand up her rib cage, grazing her breast, which did absolutely nothing to help her brain function any better. All it did was spark her nipples to full, upright attention.

"Maybe if we did this again," he murmured, his lips continuing their devastating onslaught against her collarbone, "a little slower this time, you'd be more comfortable with it."

"Uh-huh." She leaned into his hands, urging him to cup her breasts, which he did. The image of his mouth and teeth on her nipples was an erotic movie fast forwarding in her head.

He rubbed his thumbs over her nipples in slow, teasing circles. "Be right back." He went into the bathroom and closed the door.

Tori wavered on her feet, staring after him. She still couldn't believe what had just happened. She'd made love with Deck. *Up against a wall.* Except for her panties, all her clothes were still on yet this was by far, hands down, the hottest sex she'd ever had. And Wil's theory about law enforcement guys carrying guns to make up for small genitalia?

Totally debunked.

She sank to the mattress and winced. Deck's powerful thrusts had left a lasting mark on the most private parts of her body. She might not be able to sit down without wincing for a week. She grinned, anticipation rolling over her as she watched the bathroom door open.

Deck's hair stuck up in different directions, courtesy of her fingers as she'd dug them into his hair in the throes of uncontrolled lust.

His eyes locked on to hers. He knelt, pushing up her skirt again and tugging her to the edge of the mattress. He'd zipped up his jeans, leaving the top button undone. Beneath the denim, the unmistakable bulge told her how much he wanted her again.

He leaned in to take her mouth in a deep kiss. With each sweep of their tongues, he rocked his hips against her and groaned into her mouth. She tightened her thighs around his hips, craving more contact.

"I want to get inside you," he growled.

She could practically feel her inner walls weeping as her core muscles contracted.

He began stripping away her clothes, piece by piece, until the only garment she wore was her bra. Reaching around her back, he made quick work of the clasp when a soft *huff* came from the doorway. *Thor.*

"Sorry, buddy. Can you give us a little privacy?" He closed the door on Thor's clearly disappointed face. "Now, where were we?"

"About to come?"

"Yeah," he agreed, grinning. "Right about there." He urged her back on the mattress until she was lying down. His hands rested on either side of her head as he braced himself over her. For a long moment, he didn't move, didn't speak, just looked down at her as if he were absorbing every facet of her face. He stroked her ponytail, rubbing the strands between his fingers. Gently, he pulled out the elastic tie, freeing her hair. "Much better."

Impatience had her pulling him down on top of her.

"I don't want to crush you." The expression of concern on his face tugged at something that hadn't been tugged on in quite a while—her heart.

"You won't." She raised up to plant a kiss on his mouth. "I like the feel of you on me. *In* me."

Her breaths came quicker as his gaze shifted to her breasts. He kissed the soft mounds, sending a delicious arrow of sensation directly to her core. In excruciatingly small increments, he began sliding her bra straps off her shoulders and down her arms. Finally, her breasts lay bare to him, her nipples jutting out sharply. He flicked his gaze from one breast to the other and swallowed.

The waiting was too much, and she made it known by surging her hips upward until her bare mound contacted his denim-covered erection.

"I can't wait to taste these."

Then do it. Please, *just do it!*

He lowered his mouth and sucked, flicking her nipple with his tongue until it was impossibly harder. Waves of pleasure shot to her core as he pushed her breast deeper into his mouth. He shifted to her other breast while plucking at the nipple he'd just laved so lovingly with his tongue. "So, so sexy," he murmured.

Tori pulled his head tighter to her, sifting her fingers through his thick hair. She wrapped her legs around the backs of his thighs, desperately grinding herself against him. She'd never felt so wanton and carefree. "Deck," she moaned.

"Yeah. I'm right there with you, baby." He stood and whipped off his polo shirt then pulled up one of his pants legs and unstrapped something from his ankle. A holster. Apparently he was no longer on the rubber gun squad.

He set the holstered weapon on her side table then deftly shucked the rest of his clothes. After she'd gotten over the shock of not realizing he'd had a gun on him this whole time, Tori could swear she stopped breathing. All she could do was stare.

A smattering of dark hair arrowed from his muscled chest, down his ridged abs, and from there, to his thick length and long, powerful thighs and calves. Deck's body was a work of art. Or science, or physiology, or…whatever. For a man, he was beautiful.

"Please tell me you've got another condom somewhere in this house," Deck said.

"Um. Yeah." She licked her lips. *Condom. Get your brain*

back online.

Tori leaned over and yanked open the bedside table drawer. It had been a while since she'd had sex in her bedroom—or anywhere else, for that matter—but there should be one or two tucked away in there.

She rummaged around in the drawer, mercifully finding a condom. Deck held out his hand, but she tore open the wrapper herself. "Come here," she ordered.

Deck chuckled as he stepped closer. "Yes, ma'am."

He groaned as she rolled on the condom then pushed her back down to the mattress. His fingers were warm as he ran them up her thighs. "Your skin is so soft. I could lick every inch."

That would be nice. Her belly quivered as his fingers sifted through the thatch of curls between her legs. *Yes.* That was exactly where she wanted him next. His fingers were replaced by his long, thick erection. Then, he was there, pushing inside and stretching her slick walls.

She grasped his ass, pulling him in deeper as their hips met again and again, faster and faster until she cried out, letting her head fall back as the orgasm exploded inside her.

"God, baby." He pumped faster, then thrust once more, throwing back his head and groaning. For several moments longer, he held himself that way above her before lowering his forehead to hers, his body still shuddering. Eventually, he rolled off her, draping his arm about her waist and tucking her against him.

Tori smiled against his chest, completely taken by surprise at how wonderfully sated she felt, how…happy she was. It had been a long time since she'd experienced this kind of caring intimacy. Being a doctor, she believed in physical chemistry. She and Deck had it in spades from the moment they'd met, she realized, but somewhere along the line, it had become so much more. At least, *she* thought it was more.

Deck was exciting, exhilarating, pushing her boundaries in ways she could never have imagined and never would have done on her own. He was intelligent and funny. On the outside, he was tough, kicking in doors and taking prisoners. Beneath that rough exterior was a fiery passion that could make her body scream for his touch. But there was another part of him that she'd only just now gotten a glimpse of. The part that could make love to her as if she were the most beautiful thing in the world to him.

Despite everything between them, she cared for Deck, more deeply than she ever would have thought possible.

Whatever this was between them, she didn't want it to end.

• • •

Deck nuzzled his chin against the top of Tori's head, smiling as her hair tickled his lips.

Without realizing it until now, it struck him that she'd become the first thing he thought of when he woke in the morning and the last thing on his mind when he hit the sack. Those kinds of thoughts didn't normally enter the picture for him. Not because he hadn't cared about the women he'd been with. It was because his job always came first.

He skimmed the backs of his knuckles down her cheek.

"Feel good?" Cause *damn*. He sure did.

"Mm-hmm." She tipped her head to look at him, her eyes sleepy. "I was just thinking that you're not like any man I've ever—" She dipped her head down, averting her gaze.

Clearly, she was hiding something. He tipped up her chin. "Ever what? Made love with?"

"Er, that, too," she said, giving him a shy smile. "I was going to say *dated*, but we're not really dating, so…" A pretty blush the shade of bubble gum blossomed on her cheeks.

"What kind of men *have* you been dating?" As long as they weren't in her life now, that was the only thing that really mattered.

She held up her hand, counting. "Aside from the doctor, a financial advisor, a mortgage broker, and a data entry manager… But none of those relationships lasted very long."

"Why not?"

"They were…" She frowned.

"Boring?" he supplied.

Tori laughed, nodding. "Yes."

"Am *I* boring?" He'd never been told that, but who knew?

"Not even *close*." She rolled her eyes. "You're my walk on the wild side."

"Yeah?" He grinned, liking the idea of being her *wild* side. "You know, if every part of your life is filled with caution, you might miss out on the good stuff."

She drew a finger down his cheek. "You might be right."

"So we're dating, now?" he asked.

Her eyes shot wider. "No! I mean, not really. Oh, lord. I didn't mean that, I—" She covered her face with her hands, and the charm bracelet she wore jingled as it slipped down her forearm. "I sound like an idiot. I think I'll shut up now. God, this is embarrassing."

He pulled her hands from her face, taking in every inch of smooth, creamy skin, supple arms and thighs, and the most beautiful set of breasts he'd ever seen. "Trust me, you've got nothing to be embarrassed about."

She let out an exasperated breath. "That's not what I meant."

"No?" He smiled, thoroughly enjoying their conversation. "What *did* you mean?"

"I only meant that having the letters MD after my name makes everyone think I've automatically got every single facet of my life under control."

"Don't you?" From what he'd seen, she *did* like being in control, directing everything like a commando on a raid, and she was good at it.

"Hardly." She uttered a short laugh. "It's ironic how you never realize you're a control freak until things are *out* of control and you freak."

"And you're freaking out why, exactly?" When she hesitated, he knew. Despite the tentative truce with her dad, her family's history would always be with her. "Because I'm the DEA monster that yanked your dad's license. That was a pretty big secret you were keeping."

"It's not the kind of thing a girl just blurts out, but I am sorry. I saw those letters on your vest in the ER, and it was like a hammer of awful memories coming down on my head. I took all those feelings and dumped them on you."

He wrapped a lock of her hair around his finger and leaned down to kiss her, grinning and whispering against her lips, "I forgive you."

A loud crack came from outside the bedroom window. Thor barked. Through the closed door, he heard his dog's feet scrambling.

"Stay here." Deck bolted from the bed then shoved his feet into his jeans and grabbed his gun from the holster.

Stepping quietly, he moved through the house into the kitchen. Thor stood at the glass door to the backyard. Hair along his spine rose as he loosed a deep, throaty growl. His dog wouldn't do that if it were just an animal in the backyard.

Someone was out there.

Deck cracked open the door, then he and Thor padded silently to the edge of the yard. "Thor, seek."

His dog traced the edges of the property, sniffing the ground to pick up a scent trail. Somewhere in the darkness, branches crunched.

Thor set off at a dead run, and Deck followed. Rocks and broken branches gouged his bare feet, but he kept going. The road was barely a hundred feet away.

Over the sound of his own breathing, he heard a car start. By the time he got to the road, the car had driven off.

"Damn." He leaned over, resting his hands on his thighs as he sucked in air. Thor watched him, waiting for the signal to keep giving chase. "Not today, buddy."

Despite his precautionary driving, had T-Lo tracked him to Tori's house? Doubtful, but how could he be sure?

Wincing as he stepped on more rocks and twigs, he and Thor made their way back to the house. Deck slid open the door to the kitchen to find Tori knotting the belt of a robe around her waist. When he flipped on the lights, her gaze dropped to the gun in his hand. Her expression was pinched, the look in her eyes so frightened it sent a wave of fury rolling over his head.

He cared about her too much to risk bringing a killer to her doorstep. T-Lo didn't know who she was, and Deck intended to keep it that way.

His chest tightened more because the only way to accomplish that was to stay away from her. At least until he could nail the bastard and lock him up for good.

CHAPTER TWENTY-ONE

"There you go, Jimmy. Good as new." Tori finished wrapping the little boy's leg in a gauze bandage then smiled wistfully. Not for the first time, she wondered if she'd ever have a child of her own to coddle after he or she had fallen and needed stitches.

"Thank you, Dr. Sampson." The boy's mother smiled gratefully.

"You're welcome." She patted Jimmy's head of unruly red hair. "Take it easy on that bike from now on. Okay?"

Jimmy nodded. "Okay."

"Nurse Torres will get you checked out." She and Suzie exchanged knowing looks. These cases they didn't mind so much.

As Tori entered something in the boy's chart, Suzie strapped a BP cuff around the boy's arm, and as she did, the diamond engagement ring on her left hand sparkled and twinkled more than Tori remembered it did. She looked at it more closely, realizing it wasn't the same ring, not even close. The rock on *this* ring had to be three times the size of the one Suzie had shown her two months ago when Hector had proposed.

Suzie finished taking the boy's blood pressure, which was normal, then followed Tori from the room.

She turned to her friend, pointing. "Is that a *new* engagement ring?"

Suzie nodded, smiling as she held up her hand for Tori

to have a closer look. "What do you think?"

With all the wedding and honeymoon plans, Suzie had bemoaned how she and her fiancé were on a tight budget. The ring had to be crazy expensive. "It's gorgeous. Not that your first ring wasn't, but this one is just…wow!"

"The first ring was pretty," Suzie agreed, still gazing at the giant, glittering rock, "but I always wanted something bigger, and this one is *awesome*. Hector's been working a second job at night, and I fell into a little extra cash, so we bought a bigger diamond. I'll probably have the other one reset for a necklace, although it is kind of small."

Ohh-kay. Tori wasn't a gemstone expert by any stretch, but Hector's night job must pay *really* well, and whatever cash Suzie had fallen into must be pretty deep. As long as her friend was happy, that was all that mattered.

"It looks good on you." It did, but she was a bit worried Suzie was stretching herself too thin, what with all the impending wedding expenses. "I'm meeting Wil for dinner. Do you want to join us?"

Suzie shook her head. "You go ahead. I'll finish up this chart."

Tori headed to the elevators. Given that they'd both been working different shifts lately, she hadn't seen Wil in at least a week and was looking forward to it.

As she got into the elevator, her cell phone vibrated with an incoming text. She hoped it was Deck, but it wasn't. Just thinking about him sent a shiver through her body. After making love up against the wall and then in her bedroom… All her previous sexual experiences had been tame, in comparison. She hadn't seen or heard from Deck in the last week, and maybe that was okay. As great—no, make that as *awesome* — as it was being with him, she needed time to think.

When he and Thor had returned from chasing down the noise outside her bedroom window, all he said was that whoever had been out there had gotten away. But there *had* been someone out there. He'd been sure of it, which had only served to hack out a solid chunk from what was already her reluctant optimism.

Deck had one of the most dangerous jobs in the world. Danger seemed to follow him everywhere. Since he'd left her house that night, he'd called her only once, saying he was working around the clock to track down the man who'd tried to kill him and who might have been the same person outside her house. But every day that she didn't hear from him worried her more. What if Deck never caught T-Lo? Would he have a bullseye on his back for the rest of his life? Was she capable of withstanding the emotional torture of knowing that every time he went to work, he might never come home?

The issues looming between them could span the Grand Canyon. Losing someone she loved again would crush her.

Tori swallowed then gripped the phone tighter as she looked at the text from her sister, unable to focus on the words. She'd already started falling for Deck, and the consequences were frightening.

The elevator doors opened, and she headed down the hall. The cafeteria was filling up quickly with a mix of nurses, families of patients, and a few doctors, including Neil Shibowsky and Max Maynard at one table, and Wil at another. He'd already grabbed his food and was digging into a bowl of soup. She went through the line, ordered chicken marsala over egg noodles, then met Wil at the table.

"Did you see this?" He set down his spoon and plopped a copy of the *Denver Post* on the table beside her tray. "Your boyfriend arrested another drug dealer."

Tori glanced at the paper. *DEA Busts Opioid Dealer.* Next to the article was a small photo of Deck putting a handcuffed man into the backseat of a patrol car. Thor stood by his side, looking like a cop himself, tail straight in the air and ears alert as he guarded Deck.

Wil chuckled as he picked up his sandwich and bit off a hunk.

"What?" Tori asked.

He chewed then swallowed. "You didn't deny he was your boyfriend."

"He's not. Not really. We just…just…" She couldn't say the words, and in truth, she still didn't know *what* they were.

Wil's brows shot up, and he put down his sandwich. "I was only kidding. I didn't know you really *were* seeing each other." Without looking him directly in the eye, she nodded. "You slept with him, didn't you?"

She sighed. With some people, she'd be uncomfortable talking about her sexual partners, but not Wil. Since he'd moved to Colorado from the East Coast, their friendship had pretty much covered everything, including talking about their significant others. Given that he was good looking and had a prestigious job, she'd always been surprised that he'd never had anything more than short-lived relationships, and he'd never hit on her, not even once. "It might have been a mistake." All it had done was make her care about Deck more.

"Who says? Him or you?"

"Me, I guess." She cut off and ate a piece of chicken, trying in vain to savor the rich sauce and tender meat.

"Why, because of your family history with the DEA?" Wil asked, his tone sympathetic.

"That's part of it." It was still unclear if her dad could ever really accept Deck into her life. Into *their* lives.

"Look, even if he's not the right guy for you in the end, if it feels good now, why not go with it? You haven't dated since Mike left. Enjoy this while it lasts."

She appreciated Wil's encouragement, was even a little surprised by it. He'd never particularly approved of her dating Mike, and she'd never really understood why. "There are still too many impediments to count. We're just so different."

"In what ways?" Wil picked up his sandwich again and took a bite.

Where to start? "When we first met, he told me how his job is 24/7, and he doesn't have time for anything else in his life. It could never work."

"If you like him, I think you should go for it." Wil dipped the rest of his sandwich into the soup and shoveled it into his mouth. "How'd the warrant go the other day?" he asked between chews.

"Good, I guess." Aside from nearly getting shot.

"Any arrests?"

"Yes, just not the person Deck was looking for."

"Who was he looking for?"

Tori stabbed another piece of chicken with her fork. "Oh, just someone higher up in the food chain." As much as she trusted Wil, she'd assured Deck of her discretion.

Wil's forehead creased. "How did you get those scratches?"

The abrasions were nearly gone, so she'd stopped wearing makeup. Quickly, she recapped what had happened. When she was finished, Wil was frowning so hard his eyebrows practically met. "Christ, Tori. You could have been killed."

"I know, but I wasn't. Deck thinks they were after him, not me, and that I just happened to be in the wrong place at the wrong time." With him. Would being with Deck be dangerous to *her*?

"Are you going on anymore warrants with him?" Wil asked, nodding at Max and Neil, who'd stood up and were preparing to leave.

"No, he won't let me." Much to her chagrin. "He said it's too dangerous."

Wil grunted. "It probably is. But you can still help him by hooking him up with OD victims, right?" he said encouragingly.

She nodded. "Yes, I'll continue to do that." Although it wouldn't be nearly as hands-on and definitely not as exciting.

"Stick to that. I don't want to see you get hurt again, but I think this guy could be good for you."

Tori opened her mouth to ask why, when Max and Neil sauntered over.

Max gripped the back of one of the empty chairs. "Hey, Wil. Tori."

Beside him, Neil crossed his arms, revealing his pricey-looking silver watch. She couldn't stop from glancing at

Wil's watch with its simple leather strap and being a little annoyed with the surgeons. As an ER doctor, Wil made a good amount, but sometimes, the surgeons seemed to flaunt the differences in their salaries. Wil always took it in stride.

"I hear you got another Ferrari," Wil said to Max. "What color?"

"Black." Max smiled broadly. "Come for a spin. Once you get behind the wheel, you'll be buying one before you know it."

Wil laughed, shaking his head. "Not a chance. I like my Nissan, and I prefer to spend my money on vacations. I'll be sure to wave to you in your little Ferraris next time I'm racing down the runway in my private jet." Everyone laughed. Wil's European and Caribbean vacations were legendary. "But I'll take you up on that drive."

"Any time. Just say the word."

• • •

The sky was dark as Tori pulled into her driveway. She should have been home hours ago but wound up staying late to help with some tough cases that came into the ER at the end of her shift.

As she locked her Subaru, her entire body seemed to sag, but not just from sheer exhaustion. Her mind was frayed at the edges like an old rug. She still didn't know what to do about Deck. Starting a new relationship with this much doubt couldn't be healthy. Perhaps she'd been thinking too much with her libido and not enough with her brain or common sense.

She recalled her last conversation with Mike right before he relocated. He'd wanted them to try the long-distance thing. Somehow, she knew not to pursue it. The second he was gone from her life, she'd never given him another romantic thought. She'd spent only a fraction of the time with Deck that she had with Mike, but Deck was the one who remained in her thoughts.

Tori unlocked the door and flipped on the lights. As usual, the house was quiet. Coming home to someone again would have been nice. Coming home to Deck would have been *nicer*. But she had to consider the possibility that he'd already figured out how incompatible they were and that was the real reason he'd stayed away for the last week.

Or worse, now that he'd slept with her, maybe that was enough to satisfy him, and she'd never hear from him again.

The only sound in the house came from the refrigerator humming and gurgling as it made ice. When the last cube had fallen, an eerie silence settled once again around her. The loneliness, however, was deafening.

"Maybe I *should* get a dog," she muttered, thinking of Thor as she filled a glass with water and took a sip. She could always pay one of the local kids to walk it when she was at work. It would be a better fate than spending a life behind bars at the local rescue shelter. Coming home to a smiling, furry face and a wagging tail would be nice. And how great would it be to take him or her outside after a long shift and unwind together?

Tori set her glass on the counter then went to the kitchen doors that looked out over the yard. Fencing would be a must. She flicked on the backyard light and froze. Her muscles went bowstring taut and her heart slammed against her ribs.

A man stood in the shadow of her yard—a *big* man.

She gasped, stumbling backward and slamming into her dining room table before her ass hit the floor. *Call 911. Find a weapon. Do something!*

The man turned and ran to the door. Deck was wrong.

Someone was after her, too.

CHAPTER TWENTY-TWO

"Tori!" Deck bolted up the steps to the back door. He couldn't miss the fear in her eyes as she stumbled and nearly fell.

Being away from her for a week had driven him so crazy he had to come see her. So no one would see his Interceptor, he'd parked way down the street, then he and Thor had waited in the dark on her back porch for nearly two hours.

Sensing the urgency in his voice, Thor bounded onto the deck beside him. All he could do was watch helplessly through the glass slider as Tori scrambled backward on the floor, her eyes still wide with shock and fear, her chest heaving. "Tori!" he repeated. "It's Deck!" One of the neighbor's lights came on in the adjacent lawn. That's all he needed. Local police responding with guns blazing. His dog snorted. "Easy, Thor." He rested a hand on his dog's head to calm him down before he tried crashing through the door.

Deck knew the instant Tori recognized him. Her eyes squeezed shut and she put a hand to her chest. Slowly, she made it to her feet and unlocked the slider. Thor's tail thumped wildly, and he nuzzled her hand.

"I'm sorry. I didn't mean to scare you." As much as he wanted to pull her into his arms, it was obvious from the pulse pounding at her throat that she needed more time before he touched her.

"I thought you were—" She let out an unsteady breath. "Never mind."

"Are you okay over there?" a voice from the neighboring lawn yelled.

"I'm fine, Stew." To add credibility to her words, she waved.

"Can I come in?" Before the entire neighborhood went to DEFCON 1.

Tori stepped aside for him to enter. After closing the door, she knelt beside Thor and wrapped her arms around his wriggling, tail-wagging body.

"Who exactly did you think I was?" Then again, after the other night, maybe she thought he was T-Lo. "Tori?" he asked when she didn't answer.

Thor twisted his neck to land a lick on her cheek. His dog was a cop, through and through, but he was, first and foremost, a dog with a canine's inherent sense of knowing when someone needed comfort. Only problem was Deck wanted to be the one to comfort her.

He knelt beside Tori, gently lifting her by her arms and pulling out a chair for her to sit. "Did you think I was T-Lo?"

She nodded. "You were standing in the shadow, and I couldn't see you and—" Thor rested his head on her lap, and she sifted her fingers through his fur.

Deck clenched his hand so hard his knuckles cracked. When he caught up to T-Lo, he fully planned on ramming his fist down the guy's throat. "I'm sorry," he repeated, sounding stupid even to himself, since *he* was the cause of this whole mess. He and his job. For the last week, he'd been busy tracking down leads, but he also understood the wisdom of giving Tori a little space from the craziness of his job. If she couldn't take it, they had a problem.

Her fingers stilled on Thor's head. "Are *you* okay?"

"Me?" Amazing. Only minutes ago, she'd thought she was about to be attacked, and here she was asking *him* if he was okay. "I'm fine."

"I haven't heard from you in a while, so…"

"We nailed another dealer yesterday." Totally *not* the reason he'd swung by her house.

"I saw that in the paper. You didn't have to come by to tell me that."

"I know, but I couldn't stay away." It was a risk being here, but he was selfish.

"You couldn't?"

His gaze dipped to her lips. "Nope." Because she was compassionate and selfless. Intelligent and fun to be with. And sexy as hell. In his book, the total package. "Are you okay with that?"

When she nodded, his relief was overwhelming. He still had a shot with her. *If I don't fuck it up.* Kicking off a relationship with so many known problems already out there might not be the smartest move, but he didn't care. The only thing Deck knew was that he didn't want to let her go.

He leaned in and kissed her, gliding his lips across hers in a feather-soft kiss, waiting for her to kiss him back. "Do you want me to leave?"

Gentle fingers caressed his cheek, and she sighed into his mouth, parting her lips and gradually kissing him back with a heated fervor he recognized in himself. Without breaking contact, she slid off her chair onto his lap.

Deck hadn't been to church since the day they laid his sister to rest, but... *Thank God.*

Tori wriggled closer, straddling his thighs and seating herself firmly on top of him. She angled her head, deepening the kiss until his body zinged with so much need he thought his zipper would bust. "Honey, do you want to take this into your bedroom?" Or up against the wall again?

"Nuh-uh," she whispered against his mouth. "I want you right here."

Well, alrighty, then.

"Thor." He pointed to the living room. "Go lie down."

With a disappointed *huff*, Thor slunk into the living room, circled twice, then lay down in the middle of the rug.

Deck reached over to the wall and turned off the lights, bathing them in what little ambient moonlight filtered into the kitchen. No sense giving the neighbors anything else to gossip about. Beneath her shirt, he slid his hands up her back and flicked open the catch on her bra. He tugged the shirt and bra over her head and dropped it on the table.

Her breasts were about at eye level, her nipples calling to him like a beacon. He pulled her closer and sucked one into his mouth. She arched her neck, and a throaty, sexy purring sound came from the back of her throat.

When she grabbed the hem of his shirt, he lifted his arms so she could pull it off. Next, she undid his belt and popped open the button on his jeans. She stood and eased down his zipper. Her hand was hot as she freed him then closed her fingers around his stiff length.

Oh, Jesus. Blood shot to his balls faster than a bullet leaving the chamber. Now it was *his* turn to throw back his head and groan. With steady motions, she stroked him, up then down. Faster and faster until—

He grabbed her hand. "Baby, stop. We've been through this before." Around her, he had next to no control. His cock did whatever it pleased.

When her tongue darted out to lick her lower lip, his cock jerked to attention. "Please, tell me you have a condom," she said, repeating his exact words from the last time they'd been together.

"Yes, ma'am." In record speed, he whipped one from his pocket and began rolling it on. As he did, his attention was torn between the job at hand and watching her shimmy out of her slacks and panties. When she leaned down to take off her shoes, her gorgeous breasts hung low and her pretty ass caught the moonlight streaming through the glass door.

"Come here," he said in a gravelly voice. "Spread your legs." He helped her by sliding his hands up the inside of her thighs, positioning her legs on either side of his.

She rested one hand on his shoulder, cupping the back of his head with the other and urging his mouth to her breast. "Deck. Taste me."

He did as she commanded, sucking her nipple into his mouth, rolling it around with his tongue before nipping gently with his teeth. She moved over him, intending to mount him, but he wasn't done playing. He wanted to set her body on fire the way she was doing to him.

Still sucking on her nipple, he slipped two fingers into her wet heat, pumping in and out as the pad of his thumb circled and teased her sweet spot. She began rocking to his rhythm, driving his fingers deeper inside her body. Wetness engulfed his fingers. She was ready for him.

He slipped the holster off his belt and set it on the table. Even in the near darkness, there was no doubting how stiff and hard he was for her. He gripped her ass then with tortured slowness eased himself in, drawing out the exquisite torture of feeling her tight walls take all of him.

She gasped, sitting fully on his lap, his cock completely sheathed inside her. It was all he could do not to explode like the space shuttle launching off the pad. When she wriggled her hips, he had to grit his teeth to keep from growling like a dog.

Deck lifted her until he was almost out then slid her back down. He pressed his lips to her neck, sucking gently on the skin but not so much as to leave a mark. He increased their pace until blood pounded in his ears and they were both panting. For both their sakes, he wanted this to last but doubted he could make that happen.

"I'm going to come," she said in a breathy whisper. "Oh, Deck, I'm—" She cried out, shattering in his arms. He held her tightly against him, wanting to feel every bit of her orgasm. Only when she'd stopped shuddering did he let himself go. "Tori," he growled as he came hard, wave after wave pummeling him, leaving him so weak in the knees that if he wasn't already sitting down, he'd melt to the floor in a heap of totally and completely sated man.

When their breathing went back to normal, he carried her limp body to the bedroom then pulled down the comforter and laid her on the bed. After shucking his clothes, he disposed of the condom in the bathroom then slipped in next to her. He skimmed his hand over the gentle curve of her hip.

Deck couldn't delude himself any longer. He was getting closer and closer to the edge, that fine line between liking a woman and falling in love. But what if she couldn't take it when something bad happened again? Because in his world, something bad *always* happened.

The silver charm bracelet jingled as she touched the scar on his shoulder. "How did you get that?"

"A knife." He'd been helping out on an arrest, and the arresting officer didn't search his prisoner well enough.

"Judging by the length, I'd guess you got about a dozen stitches." The tip of her finger continued tracing the raised ridge.

"Twelve exactly. You know your knife wounds." When she frowned, he guessed this hadn't been the right moment to joke. A tactical error on his part. He waited, knowing there was more to her line of questioning than how many times an ER doctor had punched a needle through his skin.

"So you get shot at a lot *and* you get into knife fights? I thought braving traffic on I-70 was dangerous enough." Worry clouded her features, and he had a sinking feeling that she was actually *looking* for reasons to break it off with him. Like there weren't enough already.

"My job can be dangerous," he admitted. "You've seen that. But it's not usually filled with gunfights and knife fights." Although things *had* been heating up since he and Thor had been working the gray death case. In fact, the next time he came to see Tori at her house, he'd consider bringing another vehicle, one whose registration didn't come back "not on file," which was code for U.S. Government.

"I know, but it could happen. Again, I mean." The uncertainty in her eyes put a major hurt on his heart.

"I wish I could tell you it won't." He really did wish it, more than anything. With Tori, he felt a rare connection, one he worried was slipping from his grasp at light speed. "But I can't."

A single tear spilled from the corner of one eye, and she wiped it away. "It scares me to care about someone and know they might get hurt—or worse."

His throat went dry. Despite the spark of hope he felt knowing she cared about him, Deck knew where this conversation was headed, and he didn't like it. *He* might be the one with the dangerous job, but the thought of losing her scared the shit out of him. As much as he wanted to lie to her, he couldn't, even if it meant going their separate ways.

Trust and honesty were the only things that could possibly get them through this. So he'd tell her how he felt about her. "Tori, I want you to know how cra—"

. . .

Something vibrated, and Deck looked over his shoulder. He leaned over the edge of the mattress, snagging his jeans and pulling out his cell phone. When he looked at the screen, his body went as rigid as a scalpel. "Hello?" he said then ten seconds later, "Stay calm. Where are you?"

Tori sat up and tugged the sheet to her breasts. As much as she wanted to know what Deck had been about to say, now her stomach churned with apprehension. She strained to hear what the caller was saying but couldn't make out any words.

"Stay where you are. I'm calling 911. I'll be there in—" His eyes narrowed as he listened intently. "Okay, but don't move, and don't hang up. Aidan, are you there? Aidan!" He looked at the screen.

Over his shoulder, Tori also stared at the phone. *No Caller ID*.

He punched in 911 and recited an address along with a description of the boy she'd met at the rehab center. Then he dropped a quick kiss on her forehead. "Gotta go."

"What's going on?"

He swung his legs over the mattress, grabbing his jeans again. "You remember that kid from the rehab center, Aidan?"

"Of course." How could she forget? "Is he okay?"

Deck shoved his legs into his jeans. "He said he took too much of something and feels like he's OD-ing."

"Then I'm coming with you." She flung back the covers and started for her bureau for another shirt and jeans.

"No, you're not." He sat on the mattress and began putting on his boots. "We've already discussed this. You're not coming in the field with me again."

"This is different." Ignoring his edict, she opened the top drawer and pulled out white panties and a bra. "This is a *medical* emergency, one *I'm* better suited to respond to than you are. I still have all that naloxone in my bag, and it sounds as if Aidan needs it." When Deck stood and began shaking his head, she ran her hand up his bare chest. "You know I'm right. Besides, you're not serving a warrant this time. No one will be shooting at us. You said you wanted to help this kid, so let's go help him."

His jaw clenched, and he exhaled tightly through his nose. "Okay. But you do *exactly* as I say." He spun and charged from the room. "Thor," he shouted. "Let's go!"

CHAPTER TWENTY-THREE

Deck pushed the Interceptor down the twisting lanes of Route 285. They were still a solid twenty minutes from Denver's Union Station where Aidan said he'd wait.

"Dammit." He pounded the wheel with his fist. "If he hadn't hung up on me, we'd stand a better chance of finding him."

He turned up the radio, listening in on Denver's universal police frequency. Several patrol cars were already speeding toward Union Station.

"Deck." Tori rested her hand on his shoulder. "No matter what happens, you tried. That's all we can ever do. You called 911, so maybe they'll find him before we get there."

He gripped the wheel tighter, taking the ramp to C470 faster than he should. Luckily, at this time of night, the roads were relatively empty. A deep *woof* had him looking over his shoulder. Thor leaned into the turn, as he'd learned to do during high-speed pursuits. "I hope so."

"Why do you think he called you?" she asked. "I mean, you and he didn't exactly hit it off."

"I don't know." The same thought had occurred to him, but he'd given the kid his business card. "When someone gets in a jam, sometimes they reach out to the last person they ever expect to."

He hit the accelerator, glancing at the radio as a Denver PD unit called in.

"We just searched Union Station. Negative on the boy."

Aidan had begged him not to call 911. The kid already had two strikes against him, including one conviction involving enough cocaine to be charged with intent to distribute. Only a sympathetic judge had stood between Aidan and doing hard time. This could be three strikes, but the kid's life trumped any promises. So Deck had called in the troops anyway.

He took another ramp then slammed his foot down on the accelerator, speeding east on Route 6. Less than ten minutes later, they entered the LoDo section of Denver and pulled up next to a patrol car parked in front of Union Station.

Deck rolled down his window and held up his badge. "Did you find him?"

"Negative. Station's got a few people in the restaurants. Aside from that, the place is pretty empty. Nobody fitting the description."

"He's gotta be here somewhere. We'll check the surrounding streets." Without waiting for a response, Deck eased back onto the road, driving slowly as he turned onto another street.

"He could be anywhere," Tori murmured, lowering her window and peering into the darkness.

"If he'd just call me again." He glanced at the phone that he'd set in a dashboard cradle. The screen remained dark. "He could be right behind any of these doors, and we'd never know it."

His cell phone rang, the screen lighting up the SUV's dark interior. *No Caller ID*. Deck answered, putting the call on speaker. "Aidan, is that you?"

Heavy breathing, then, "Yeah."

"Are you still at Union Station?" He slowed the SUV, ready to hang a one-eighty back to the station.

"No, I *told* you not to call the cops. You know what they'll do to me." Unidentifiable, muffled sounds came from the phone, as if Aidan had covered up the speaker. "I'm at that park near the river, the one a few blocks behind the station."

Deck turned right, heading toward the South Platte River. "Commons Park?" The park was about three long blocks from the station.

"I-I think so. Can you hurry? I don't feel so good."

Deck narrowed his eyes. In the time it had taken he and Tori to get into town, Aidan *could* have made it to the park. *Hopped up on drugs?* Maybe. Or not. Could be the kid was fucking with him, but he couldn't take the chance that he wasn't. "Stay with me, this time. Don't hang up. I'll be there in a few minutes."

"O-okay."

"Are you going to—" Tori began, but he interrupted her.

"Wait." He muted the phone. "Go ahead."

"Are you going to call the police?" she asked.

He shook his head. "If I spook him, he'll run again."

"For someone overdosing, he sounds pretty lucid. Maybe he's already coming down from the high."

"Yeah, maybe." He couldn't shake the feeling that this was some kind of a setup.

He slowed as they came alongside a tree-lined promenade bordering the south side of the park's twelve acres. During the day, the place would be packed with people on their lunch breaks and joggers using the paved trails lining the river banks. At night, the park was deserted.

Deck lowered his window, trying to catch a glimpse of Aidan. The park was dark, the only light coming from restaurants and bars across the street. He parked at the entrance and took his phone off mute. "Aidan, I'm outside the main entrance. Where exactly are you?"

"On the grass…somewhere," came the kid's breathy response. "Hurry, please. I-I'm getting sleepy, and I can't breathe." Gasping sounds came through the phone.

"Deck, we have to get to him." Tori grabbed her medical bag and opened her door.

"Wait." He muted the phone again then clicked the mic on his radio. "The kid's in Commons Park. Send backup and an ambulance."

"Ten-four," said the dispatcher.

Again, he unmuted his cell. "Aidan, we're on our way." He set the phone down on the dashboard then grabbed the hand radio and clipped the microphone to his shirt collar. Before picking up the phone, he unslung the tactical flashlight hanging from the rearview mirror. "Tori, stay close to me." When she nodded, he got out and opened Thor's door. His dog bounded from the SUV. "Let's go."

With the phone to his ear, they moved deeper inside the park. Deck swung the flashlight's beam ahead of them and to either side. Other than the flashlight, darkness surrounded them.

After they'd walked for several minutes, he held his arm out in front of Tori. "Stop." The only sound came from Thor panting. "Aidan, talk to me." Nothing. "Aidan?" The hackles on the back of his neck stood at full attention. A crumpled form lay on the ground twenty feet ahead.

Lowering his head, Thor let loose with a throaty growl.

"There he is," Tori whispered. "Let's go."

"Wait." Alarm bells pinged in his head. Something felt off about this. He clicked the mic. "Dispatch, any word on that backup?"

"Two units are on the way. ETA three minutes."

"C'mon, hurry." Tori clutched his arm. "We have to go to him. Seconds count. You *know* that."

His warning radar was pinging louder, but he couldn't take the chance that Aidan was really lying on the ground twenty feet away, moments from dying. "Let's go. Slowly."

They started walking. Five feet. Ten feet. Deck swung the flashlight's beam in an arc ahead of them, searching for anyone hiding in the shadows. Fifteen feet. Engines roared behind them, getting louder. Deck figured that was the patrol cars jumping the curb onto the grass.

Thor reached Aidan first, sniffing and circling, only it wasn't his dog's typical behavior at approaching a person. The engines roared louder, closer. Deck spun. *No headlights. No strobes. Not* patrol units.

"Tori, move! Thor, come!" He grabbed her arm, pulling her away from what he now suspected wasn't a body lying on the ground. He dragged her from the path of the oncoming vehicles, racing toward a thicket of trees.

The vehicles were almost on top of them. He looked over his shoulder. The moon peeked from behind the clouds enough for him to catch sight of a pickup truck. Headlights flashed, blinding him, and he stumbled. "Keep going!" he shouted over the roar of the engine.

One of the vehicles peeled off to follow Tori. *No.* He took off again, running at top speed, catching up to her and shoving her out of the path of the oncoming pickup.

Something slammed into his right side, sending him flying to the ground. He felt a distinct pop, then intense pain knifing into his body like an ice pick.

Tori screamed, sending another kind of pain through his body, this one out of fear that she'd been run down, too. He had to get to her. And where was Thor?

Extreme pain stabbed at his shoulder and ribs. Vaguely, he heard the pickup and another vehicle slow as they turned and headed back around. *To finish the job*.

"Deck! Deck!" Tori screamed.

He rolled to his side, trying to push upright. Another shaft of pain, the likes of which he'd never experienced in his life, sent him to the ground again. He hissed in air through gritted teeth, which only worsened the pain. Breathing was becoming difficult. He tried pulling his gun from the holster, but his right hand wouldn't cooperate. More pain. His vision clouded, and he felt lightheaded.

"Get to the trees!" he shouted, and god*damn* did it hurt to yell. "Take Thor with you."

"I'm not leaving you." Tori fell to his side, trying to haul him to his feet. "Get up!" she demanded, taking his good arm and helping him stand.

As she got him to his feet, he nearly doubled over and passed out.

Thor barked, circling them, uncertain what to do.

Headlights bore down on them again, engines roaring. The copse of trees was barely ten feet away. They weren't going to make it. With Tori's help, he half walked, half stumbled. Every step was sheer torture, sending more pain directly to his shoulder and torso.

They made it to the trees just before the pickup caught up to them. Both vehicles braked. Car doors opened.

"They're in the trees!" someone shouted.

"I got 'em," a different voice said.

Unable to take another step, Deck fell to his knees, sucking in shallow breaths. Every inhalation sent a blast of fire to his ribs. Beside him, Thor whimpered, licking his face. "Leave me," he said to Tori. "Run, dammit!"

Crunching of boots on the dry leaves told him there were at least three men approaching. With his good hand, he ripped the hand radio from his belt. "Officer down. Commons Park, in the trees. Need help fast!" He let the radio fall to the ground then reached around and pulled his gun with his left hand, aiming it at the oncoming assailants.

Thor growled then leaped from Deck's vision.

A man screamed. "Get him off me! Shoot the dog!"

More growling.

Sirens wailed in the distance. Blue and red strobes flashed, reflecting off the trees.

"Let's get out of here!" one of the men shouted.

"Don't leave me, motherfucker!"

Car doors slammed. Headlights shut off as the pickup and the other vehicle sped from the park.

Deck began slumping to the ground. He tried blinking away the white stars clouding his vision.

"I've got you." Tori's arms came around him, preventing him from whacking his injured shoulder even harder. He was too heavy for her. His back hit the ground, and he grunted.

Gentle hands examined his body, which had begun to

shake. His forehead and upper lip beaded with sweat, and he felt like vomiting. Buzzing took up shop in his ears. Screaming sirens cut through the haze settling over him.

Shouts of "Police!" were followed closely by, "How do we get the dog off?"

Thor. He couldn't see his dog but understood Thor had his jaws wrapped around someone's body parts. "Thor," he mumbled. "Release. *Release*." The effort to speak sent another wave of pain crashing through his ribs. He had to get up, had to call Thor off before he killed someone.

Deck tried pushing to a sitting position, but Tori held him down.

"Deck," came Tori's worried voice. "Try not to move around."

More growling. More screaming.

He shoved at her hands, trying to twist on the ground to see what was happening. More stabbing pain stopped him. It hurt just to breathe.

"Deck!" Tori shouted. "Stop fighting me! I think you have a cracked rib and maybe a punctured lung. Moving around will only make it worse."

Thor's growling intensified, and again Deck fought to get up. His teeth chattered, and sweat rolled down his temples. The moaning sound he heard next was his own, as he struggled to breathe. The pain was so intense, he thought he was dying.

"We need help here!" Tori shouted. "I'm a doctor. Get my medical bag. I dropped it in the grass. And someone get a blanket. He's going into shock."

Deck could barely focus but understood one thing as clearly as if it were written on his forehead. *I'm in deep shit*.

The growling stopped.

"Cuff 'em!" he heard one of the officers shout.

A moment later, a warm body snuggled against Deck's left side. *Thor*. His dog knew something was wrong. Deck hadn't been injured since he and Thor had become partners, and his K-9 didn't understand what was happening.

"Shine that light down here," Tori ordered.

He cracked his eyes open to see a cop plunk down her black medical bag. She opened it and pulled out a small bottle before tearing the wrapper off something else. *A syringe*. "No," he muttered, rolling his head from side to side. Whatever was in that bottle, he didn't want it.

She tipped the bottle upside down, stuck the needle into it, drawing liquid into the syringe.

"What is that?"

"Fentanyl." She pushed up his sleeve.

"No, dammit!" He reached across his chest with his good arm and grabbed her wrist. "No. Opioids."

"Deck." Through the murky haze whittling away at his senses, her voice held a scary-ass sense of urgency and fear. "You need to trust me. You *have* to stop moving around. This is the right treatment. *Please*."

Something wet fell on his cheek. Her tears.

• • •

"No." He squeezed her wrist so tightly, pain shot up her arm. "Do *not* put that in me," he said through gritted teeth. Sweat glistened on his forehead. His chest rose and fell rapidly with shallow breaths as he struggled to breathe.

She knew his aversion to taking *any* meds, let alone his

zero-tolerance against opioids. This was different. She palpitated one side of his chest. When he grimaced in pain, she was almost certain he'd suffered a punctured lung. Assuming she was right, with every second that passed, air was accumulating in the pleural cavity, putting more pressure on his lung. If they didn't decompress his chest soon, he could die. She didn't have the appropriate setup to do it herself. He needed an ambulance, *stat*.

Her hands began to shake. Now, she had a firsthand understanding of why doctors shouldn't treat their own family or anyone else they cared about. Because the panic she was experiencing threatened to obliterate her ability to think clearly.

"I can't stand seeing you in this much pain," she managed. "I can't sit by and do *nothing*."

His jaw clenched, his face contorting with every breath. "Then leave!"

Tori gasped. He might as well have slapped her. "Where's that ambulance?" she shouted over her shoulder to no one in particular, trying not to dwell on how much his words had hurt.

When he began writhing with the pain, she set aside her fear and focused on him. "Somebody, help me hold him still." If he didn't stop moving around, bone fragments could further lacerate the lung and make it worse.

As two officers moved in to assist, Thor leaped to his feet, growling and barking, snapping his jaws. The two men jumped back.

Oh no. Thor thought the officers were attacking Deck, and she didn't know how to call him off. "Thor, don't. Let them help him." But the dog ignored her, his amber eyes gleaming as he bared his incisors at the other men, his growls getting louder.

Panic and a miserably helpless feeling bubbled up inside her. It had been the same way watching her mother weaken before her eyes then die.

I love him.

Her heart raced with fear. The admission only made her feel more panicked, more hopeless.

"Lady, we can't go near him," one cop said. "That dog will tear us apart. We might have to shoot him."

"Thor!" someone else shouted. *Evan.* "Release."

Evan and Brett appeared, stepping into the light. With everything happening around them, she hadn't heard them drive up.

"Release," Evan repeated, inching closer to Thor, whose body quivered.

"Careful," Brett warned.

"Yeah, I know." Evan held out his hand, and Thor curled his lip back. "Easy, Thor," he said in a low, soothing tone. "I know you think you're protecting him, but you have to work with us here. Okay, pal?" Thor's lip fell back into place. "That's it. Easy does it."

Tori held her breath, glancing from Thor to Deck. His neck and torso twisted as he endured the pain. "Please, Evan. Hurry."

"Good boy." Slowly, Evan reached for Thor's head, resting his hand between the dog's ears. "That's it. Release. Release."

The moment Thor backed off and sat, Brett snapped a leash on Thor's collar and drew the dog away from Deck, wrapping the leash twice around a nearby tree trunk.

Getting him to a hospital was becoming more essential by the second. She was about to order one of the patrol units to transport Deck when an ambulance pulled onto the grass near the copse of trees.

"He has a dislocated shoulder and a punctured lung," she informed the paramedics as soon as they were within earshot. "He's refusing pain meds." Beside her, Deck jolted. "You may have to strap him down," she said in a shaky voice.

"Are you a doctor?" one of the medics asked, placing an oxygen mask over Deck's face.

"Yes. ER."

The medic nodded, and her panic diminished fractionally as she observed the pair expertly hustling through standard field protocol. One readied the needle they'd use en route to the hospital to release the air collecting in Deck's pleural cavity.

When it was time to load Deck into the ambulance, Brett came up beside her. "Do you want to go with him?" he asked when she didn't automatically follow the stretcher.

Did she? For her, Brett's question was loaded with so much more meaning than just accompanying Deck to the hospital. Being with him and potentially getting that horrible call again... She didn't know her heart could hurt so much and still be beating at the same time.

"Tori?" Evan said.

At first, she didn't realize what she was doing. Shaking her head.

As the ambulance doors began to close, she took a step then stopped.

The paramedics were more than competent. They didn't need her.

And in the depths of her soul, she knew Deck was right. She *should* just leave. Leave his life.

Slowly, the ambulance rolled away. She continued staring as it turned onto the road and drove off. Only then did she collapse onto the grass, shaking as tears rolled unchecked down her face.

Deck was the wildcard in her orderly, protocol-based life. She loved him with everything that she had, but being with him, knowing she could lose him any day of the week, was too far outside her comfort zone. Even in his pain-fueled state, Deck knew that. He understood and gave her an out.

Emptiness yawned inside of her. She'd follow up on his medical condition, but anything beyond that would be more than she could endure.

It was over between them.

CHAPTER TWENTY-FOUR

"What's the prognosis?"

"Fractured rib, punctured lung, dislocated shoulder. The rib should heal on its own. Traction to reset his shoulder... complications. Some of the fibrous tissue...severely stretched. There may be nerve damage."

"Whatever they gave him, he's really out of it."

Words blurred together, but Deck easily identified the voices. Brett, Evan, and his boss, ASAC Rivera.

He tried opening his eyes, but they stuck together as if someone had glued them shut.

He managed to squint. Images wavered then slowly took shape. His friends sat in chairs on one side of the bed, his boss in one on the other.

"There he is," Brett said. "Sleeping Beauty awakes, and we didn't even have to kiss him."

"Sleeping Beauty, my ass." Evan elbowed Brett's shoulder. "He might have been pretty once. Now, he looks like shit."

"I can hear you." Deck grimaced as he shifted on the mattress, anticipating lightning bolts of pain. All he felt was a dull throbbing in his torso.

He looked at the IV line taped to his hand. He had no idea what was dripping into his veins. Back in the park, he'd been in excruciating pain. It killed him to admit it now, but he wasn't really in *any* pain now.

A block of ice lodged solidly in the pit of his stomach.

Tori had been about to give him fentanyl. Not just an opioid, but one of the ingredients in the very drug they were trying to track down. He didn't remember all the details of what had gone down, but he remembered *that* as if they'd just had that conversation seconds ago.

That block of ice wedged more firmly in his gut. She would always give meds because that's what she believed in, and he'd never be okay with that.

"Is Tori okay?" he asked. More details came to him in pieces. Getting slammed by the truck. Denver PD swarming in. Thor growling—

Numbers on the monitor by his bed soared. "Where's Thor?" He snapped his gaze from Brett to Evan then to his boss.

"Relax." Brett rested a calming hand on his good shoulder. "He's fine."

"In fact," Evan added, "he was in rare form and spitting mad. He practically attacked the PD when they tried to get near you."

"Where is he?"

ASAC Rivera cleared his throat. "He's staying with Evan until you're discharged and well enough to take care of him."

"Thanks." Thor was more than his partner. He was family.

Evan gave a curt nod. "You'd do the same for me. For *any* of us."

He would. If necessary, he'd take a bullet for his friends, and they'd do the same.

Brett yawned, covering his mouth with his fist.

"What time is it?" Deck asked then realized the

ridiculousness of his question. He was so doped up, he didn't even know what *day* it was or how long he'd been out.

"Two in the morning." Brett yawned again.

"Thought you went down to the Springs." Deck noted the dark circles under his friend's eyes. After the last big case Brett worked—the one in which he'd been badly burned—nightmares kept his friend up, preventing him from getting any real sleep.

"I did. When Evan called and told me what happened, I hauled ass back up here."

"You didn't have to. But thanks." Something lodged in Deck's throat, and he blinked rapidly. *Great*. Besides dopiness, tears were a side effect of opioids. "What hospital am I in?"

"North Metro," Rivera said.

Tori's hospital. Hearing footsteps and voices outside his room, he glanced at the open door. If she was here, she hadn't made an appearance. Then again, until a few minutes ago, a herd of buffalo could have stampeded through the room without him knowing it.

Following his train of thought, Evan said, "She stopped by earlier to check on you."

Deck closed his eyes. Part of him wanted to see her. Part of him didn't. At least, not right now. He remembered the fear in her eyes, in her voice, and the words they'd said to each other. True, he'd been angry when she'd been ready to stick him with that needle. But when she'd said she couldn't take seeing him in pain, he'd had to give her the out she needed.

As a DEA agent, he could be hurt or killed. That was

the job. He accepted the risks, but she'd never signed up for that. Daring to hope she could put up with the dangers of his job when her world was dedicated to saving others was too big of an ask. So he'd let her go.

"Think you're up for discussing a little business?" Rivera asked.

"Always." Even laid up in a hospital, he was still all about the job. He was good at stowing away his personal crap. For now, anyway.

Rivera tipped his head to Evan, indicating he should close the door.

"Evan and Brett interviewed Dr. Sampson," Rivera began. "We also have preliminary reports from the responding Denver units. They didn't see the whole thing but were able to corroborate most of what Dr. Sampson said. I'd like to hear *your* perspective on what went down."

An unsettling feeling came over Deck as he recounted what details he could remember, beginning with the call from Aidan and ending with him blacking out. "Any sign of the kid?"

Evan shook his head. "The PD searched the entire park and a surrounding ten-block radius."

All but confirming Deck's original suspicion. "I was set up."

"Looks that way," Rivera agreed. "We put a BOLO out for him."

Deck dragged his hand down his face. There'd come a point where he'd known he was getting played, but his need to help addicted teens had overruled his common sense. Maybe Tori was right. No matter how hard he tried and no matter how much he wished otherwise, he couldn't save everyone. Some people didn't *want* to be saved.

He could still remember the cop who'd come to his house the day they'd found Marianne's body in that alley. Had she really spiraled so far down there'd been nothing any of them could do for her? Maybe all the guilt he'd carried around with him had been a waste. He would never know for certain.

"Did you tell him?" Rivera looked from Brett to Evan.

Brett shook his head. "While you were napping, the PD talked to the guy Thor took down in the park. That dealer in Loveland was tipped off by someone called 'the doc.'"

Deck's brows shot up. *The doc?* "As in, a *real* doctor?" What the dealer's hired muscle had said at the Loveland warrant came back to him. "The Big D," he murmured, locking gazes with Evan. "Sammie didn't find anything in the databases on the Big D, but maybe the D stands for 'doctor.'"

"Yeah, and something else." Brett frowned, telling Deck whatever was coming next would suck. "This 'doc' ordered the hit on you. Word on the street is that the doc set you up because you're taking down too many of their dealers."

"You and Thor took a major bite out of their business," Evan added.

"Did you get any specifics?" Deck asked. "Like where this doctor works?"

His boss exchanged a quick look with Brett and Evan before focusing on Deck. "You said you got a text from an informant about a leak in our operation, and that was how Jack knew about the warrant in Loveland before you hit the place. You've been working closely with Dr. Sampson. Is there any possibility that she's involved? She has no criminal history, but that doesn't mean—"

"I *know* what it means." He couldn't wrap his brain around the possibility that she'd tipped off a drug dealer. But he was personally involved. Back at her house—in bed—he'd practically blurted out how crazy he was about her, so how could he possibly remain impartial? "I don't think she'd tell anyone."

"You need to be sure about this," Rivera said. "It's important."

"Don't you think I *know* how important it is?" he shouted, instantly regretting it as the dull throbbing in his shoulder and ribs worsened.

"Could Dr. Sampson have tipped them off?" Rivera asked quietly.

Could she? Yes. *Did she?*

Deck had witnessed for himself how strong her desire was to help people. If she were the leak, what would have been her motivation?

"Deck?" Rivera asked again.

He shook his head, more to himself than anyone else in the room. Was it possible her hatred of the DEA was so bad that she'd done it out of revenge? He'd thought they'd gotten past that. Maybe he was wrong.

God, his head hurt.

Deck squeezed his eyes shut, knowing his boss and his friends were watching him closely, waiting for the response he had to give and didn't want to.

"I don't know," he answered truthfully.

• • •

With her heart in her hands, Tori took the last steps to Deck's room.

Would he even remember what happened or the things they'd said to each other?

It was possible that the extreme pain he'd been experiencing might have impacted his memory. Not that it mattered. She'd been given a ringside seat to what being part of his life would entail, and she was too much of a coward, even to hold on to something she so desperately wanted. *Him*.

All she wanted was to see with her own eyes that he was really okay, then she'd leave. Thinking he might be sleeping, she began pushing the door open as quietly as possible but stopped when she heard Brett and Evan discussing someone called "the doc." With the door cracked, she listened a moment longer. Apparently, someone had tipped off that drug dealer, Jack, about the Loveland warrant. Another man, one who's voice she didn't recognize, asked Deck if *she* could have tipped Jack off.

Tori held her breath, waiting for his answer.

"I don't know."

Her jaw dropped, and she let the door fall back into place. It wasn't possible. *I must have misunderstood*.

Her first inclination was to kick the door open the rest of the way and vehemently deny the allegation. But if Deck thought so little of her, *cared* so little about her that he could possibly think such a thing, then she had no intention of wasting her time defending herself.

Smacking the palm of her hand on the door, she shoved it open so forcefully that it banged into the wall.

Immediately, all conversation ceased. Four sets of eyes focused on her, but the only one she cared about was Deck's. Things were over between them, but damn him for thinking she could have ratted him out.

His color was back, so that was good. An ACE bandage encircled his rib cage, and the shoulder he'd dislocated was wrapped snugly in white bandages with his right arm immobilized against his bare chest. A drainage tube was taped to the other side of his chest.

For a moment, his expression was utterly blank. Then his eyes became guarded. Was it because he thought she'd tipped off a drug dealer or because she'd tried administering opioids to him? *Or both?* Either way, the heart she'd held in her hands dropped to the floor with an audible *splat.*

"Good morning," she said, looking at all of them and recognizing the other man in the room as Deck's supervisor, ASAC Rivera. Nobody answered. She went to the rolling computer to re-read Deck's chart. His friends, men she'd thought liked and respected her, tracked her every move.

As if I'm a criminal.

Reading his chart wasn't necessary. She knew every word that was in it and every dose of medication that had been administered. Since the moment he'd been brought into the ER, she'd personally supervised everything that was done to him. He just didn't know it.

It took every ounce of strength not to go to him, to hold him and kiss him. "How are you feeling?"

"All things considered, fine."

Tori shoved her hands in her coat pocket, fisting them

tightly. She couldn't take his reticence a moment longer. She hadn't planned on it, but after what she'd overheard, they needed to talk. "Gentleman, could you give us a few minutes?"

The atmosphere in the room went ice cold. Except for a quick glance at Deck, Brett and Evan didn't budge, and neither did Deck's boss.

"It's okay." Deck hitched his head to the door.

Deck's friends threw her a cautionary glance then started for the door. ASAC Rivera went with them.

"We'll be in the hall if you need us." Evan threw her a look that said it all. They no longer trusted her.

They hadn't said a word about their suspicion, but it was there just the same, hovering in the air like a thundercloud ready to cut loose with a barrage of rain, hail, and lightning.

She gripped the bedrail with both hands. "I didn't tell anyone about the warrant. I would never betray your—"

"Trust?" His lips twisted as he spat out the word. "You were about to."

"No, I—" But he wasn't referring to the warrant. She drew in a calming breath. "Giving you fentanyl would have been the right call. You were thrashing about so much you could have worsened your condition."

"That was *my* decision to make."

"I know. That's why I didn't give it to you. But that doesn't mean it wasn't the right call." She took a step toward the side of the bed, stopping as she caught sight of Evan and Brett in the corridor. Both shot her warning looks. "You're so obsessed over what happened to your sister and with saving the world from opioids you can't even think straight. I wasn't trying to give you something to hurt you. I tried to do it because I—"

Quickly, she looked away. She hadn't realized what she'd been about to say until she'd almost blurted it out.

"You what?" Deck asked quietly.

Love you. Saying it wouldn't change a thing. It would only make this more difficult. "Because I couldn't stand by and see you in so much pain when there was something I could do to stop it."

If her heart weren't already lying on the floor in a pile of mush, she would swear it was breaking. "Even if you didn't suspect me of providing information to a drug dealer, I can't take wondering if one day you'll leave for work and never come back," she said, swallowing hard and doing her best not to shed a single tear. "It was a mistake to think this could have possibly worked between us."

She waited for Deck to say or do something, to at least tell her she wasn't a suspect in his mind. Instead, he remained maddeningly silent.

"I agree," he said finally.

Sorrow nearly took her to her knees. It really was over. After today, she'd never see him again. "Well then. I'll leave you to get some rest. Good luck with…everything."

She went to the door, nearly bumping into Brett and Evan on the way out. Keeping her back straight and her head held high, she brushed past Deck's friends. "And for the record," she threw over her shoulder loudly enough for all of them, including Deck, to hear, "I *don't* have any drug dealers on speed dial. I would never betray you—*any* of you."

She made it to the doctors' lounge just before the

floodgates opened. Wil stood at the coffeemaker, mug in one hand, carafe in the other.

"Tori?" He set the mug down and returned the carafe to the hot plate. "What's wrong?"

She covered her face with her hands. Wil's arms came around her, and she clung to him, sobbing silently.

"Shh," he whispered, stroking her hair. "Whatever it is, it'll be okay."

As much as she wished his words were true, they weren't. It would *never* be okay.

CHAPTER TWENTY-FIVE

"Are you boys *still* lifting weights?" Deck's mother stood in the doorway of the gym Deck had converted the basement of his house into. Despite it being a random Thursday afternoon, she was dressed in her favorite purple outfit and glittery jewelry, and her makeup and salt-and-pepper hair were done up really nicely. "I still don't know how I ever gave birth to someone who grew to be your size."

Brett and Evan chuckled, but his mother had a point. She was only five-foot-one, and he'd sprouted to six-three and weighed in at two-thirty.

From his bed in the corner, Thor whined. She went to Thor and gave him a quick pat on the head. "Do you want me to make you all some sandwiches before I leave?"

"No, thanks, Mom." Deck sat up on the bench and grabbed a towel, wiping the sweat from his face. In the eight weeks since he'd been injured, his rib and lung had healed, but his shoulder was still achy and tight. He was probably working out more than he should, but he was going stir crazy. "But I appreciate the offer."

The moment she'd been notified that he was in the hospital, she'd rushed over and taken charge, bullying the nurses until they were afraid to come into his room. When he'd been discharged, she'd set up shop in the vacant bedroom and plied him with so much food he felt as if his stomach was about to explode.

"Brett, Evan, sandwiches?"

"No thank you, Ms. Albright." Evan grabbed a set of fifty-pound weights.

"No, thanks, Ms. A." Brett sat up. "We're taking Deck out for lunch as soon as we're done."

After Deck's parents got divorced, his mother had wanted a clean break and had gone back to using her maiden name, Albright. Years later, it still sounded strange not hearing his mom referred to as Mrs. Decker.

She glanced at her watch. "Good, because I'm late."

Deck had been in mid-reach for a bottle of water. "Late for what?"

"First, I'm going to my music class, then I have a date. Enjoy your lunch." She turned to leave.

"A *date*?" Deck shot to his feet. "You didn't tell me you met someone. When did this happen? Who is he, and where are you going for lunch?" Okay, so he was a little overprotective.

She walked to him and stood on her tiptoes to pat his cheek. "There, there, dear. No need to worry and no need to run a criminal history on every man I date. But it's such a sweet thought." She turned to leave.

"Wait! What do you mean *every* man you date? Exactly how many have there been?" Did he really want to know? Probably not.

She began counting on her fingers. "In the last few months, three. But this one, I really like."

"*Three*?" Since the divorce, his mom hadn't been with anyone. That had been almost twenty years ago.

Again, she patted his cheek, reminding him of when he'd been ten and lost his first baseball game. "Sweetie, I know your shoulder still hurts, but you have to stop being so cranky. You've been this way since you got out of the hospital. Maybe a nice lunch out with your friends will do you some good."

"Mom, you're missing the point." He shook his head, uttering a huff of major disbelief. "Where are you meeting all these guys? You're not—" The thought was mind boggling.

"Online dating?" She batted her eyelashes. "Yes, I am."

His jaw dropped. *My sixty-four-year-old mother is online dating?* The world as he knew it had just spun totally out of control.

"You should, too, dear. You aren't getting any younger, either. If it makes you feel better, the man I'm seeing today I met in music class, not online." His mother turned and went out the door. A minute later, the front door opened then closed.

Deck sat back on the bench. For a moment, he felt lightheaded. Thor whined then stood and went to the rack, grabbed a ten-pound barbell in his jaws, and presented it to Deck. Absently, he took the weight and set it on the bench. "Talk about a bombshell," he muttered.

Brett and Evan began laughing their asses off.

Evan positioned himself on a mat and began doing sit-ups. "You should have seen your face when she said 'online dating.'"

Brett grabbed his water bottle. "Wish I'd taken a photo."

Still shellshocked, Deck didn't know what bothered him more, that his mom was online dating after all this time or that she'd suggested he do it, too.

Or maybe it was because the comment made him think of Tori.

They hadn't spoken since that night in the hospital. She

hadn't come to his room again, and he hadn't made any effort to reach out to her. He'd made sure to keep busy, going to the doctor's office for checkups, plowing through PT, then rehabbing at home. When he wasn't working out, he'd been catching up on the police reports about the attempt on his life. The *second* attempt. But he couldn't deny there was a gaping hole in his heart.

"Your mom's right," Evan said between crunches. "You really *have* been cranky."

Deck shot his friend a *duh* look. "Nearly getting assassinated will do that to a guy."

"You sure that's all it is?" Brett stood and returned his weights to the rack.

No. "Yeah." He gave Thor a quick pat then stood and grabbed the bottle of over-the-counter meds sitting on the table. It was a compromise, of sorts. He popped two, washing them down with a swig of water.

Compromise. Not for the first time, he considered one of Tori's parting shots. Was he really too hung up on the past?

"Have you talked to her?" Brett asked. There was no need to specify who *her* was, and they all knew it.

"No." But he missed her more than he thought possible. In fact, he missed everything about her. Her quick wit, her laughter when he'd taught her how to play foosball. And making love to her. The connection they had was off the charts, physically *and* emotionally. "It's better this way. She can't handle my job, and I'm not about to leave the DEA." Then there was that other issue still hovering in the air. She still hadn't been cleared of diming out their operation to a drug dealer.

"Maybe you don't have to," Brett suggested. "Didn't you say Rivera was retiring? You've got enough time on the job to put in for ASAC."

Deck shook his head. "I'm not a desk guy. I'd go nuts pushing paper for the rest of my career. Besides, I can't imagine not working with Thor."

Hearing his name, Thor went to Deck's side and sat, looking up at him.

"Is it really just about the job?" Evan asked. "Only Rivera actually thinks she may have ratted out the Loveland op. Brett and I were talking. We don't believe it."

Deck didn't believe it, either. He never really had.

"As for being pissed she wanted to give you pain meds, what did you expect her to do?" Brett added. "Watch you writhe around and punch another hole in your lungs? We were there." He looked at Evan. "You were in bad shape, man. If the decision were left up to me, I might have done it anyway, to hell with what you wanted."

Evan's brow furrowed. "I'd do *anything* to save someone I loved." He didn't have to say who he was referring to. His missing sister.

Deck was reminded of the last Christmas before Marianne died. Like typical teenage siblings, they'd fought over something stupid that morning, but he loved her anyway. He would have done anything to save her. *Anything.* In fact, hadn't he?

Only weeks before she died, he and his parents had essentially kidnapped her and forced her to go to rehab. *Against her will.*

He grabbed a towel from the table and slung it around his neck. Tori was all the more trustworthy because she'd listened to his wishes, even when it clearly broke her heart. Could he say the same thing? No.

Another image came to mind, him tracking Tori down and begging for forgiveness. But to what end? He would always be a DEA agent. They'd already had that conversation. Like their relationship, it was dead and buried.

Deck felt sick to his stomach. *I fucked up.* "Tori and me…not in the cards. But the least I can do is get her off Rivera's radar."

Evan's brows rose. "How?"

"Did you guys read the interview report of the guy Thor took down in the park?" His friends nodded. "What did you think?"

"It sucked," Evan said.

Brett nodded. "Piss poor. Totally superficial."

Exactly what Deck had thought. "Up for a detour before lunch?"

• • •

The cell gate clanged shut behind them. A uniformed guard led Deck, Brett, and Evan to one of the prisoner interview rooms. They'd had to pull some strings, but since Ricky Beauchamp didn't have a pot to piss in, he hadn't made bail. For some stupid reason, Beauchamp was representing himself, so Deck hadn't needed authorization from defense counsel to talk to the guy. Beauchamp could still tell him to pound sand, but Deck wanted a go at him anyway.

Another guard led Beauchamp into the room. Wearing

shackles, he shuffled in before sitting at the table opposite Deck. The guard ran a chain through his cuffs, securing it to the table. Something about those orange jumpsuits always seemed to suck the life out of a prisoner, and Beauchamp was no different. Deck already knew the guy was only thirty-one, but the bags under his eyes and the deeply etched lines fanning his tight lips made him look fifty.

Beauchamp's gaze flicked to Deck, then he warily eyed Brett and Evan leaning against the wall. He jutted his chin at Deck. "You the fed from the park?"

Deck took a few seconds to answer, wanting time to dig into the guy's head, make him antsy. It worked. Beauchamp shifted in the chair. "We didn't come here to answer *your* questions. Do you want to answer ours?"

He shrugged. "Depends. What's in it for me?"

"You're wasting my time." For effect, Deck stood as if he were about to leave. By virtue of consenting to the meeting, he already knew the guy wanted to talk.

"Look, man." Beauchamp leaned forward, and the chain running through his cuffs rattled. "Nobody gave me a deal. I already talked to the cops, told them everything I know. I *want* a deal."

Deck stared him down. This fucker and his friends tried to kill him. It took every ounce of willpower not to pound the guy's face into the table. "You haven't talked to *me* yet, and I have more questions. Are you willing to answer them?"

"Are you gonna give me a deal?"

Like Beauchamp had done, Deck shrugged. "Depends on your answers. No deal without cooperation." Beauchamp had been arrested half a dozen times on drug charges and petty larceny. He knew the drill. "Talk to me, and I'll tell the prosecutor you cooperated. Hold anything back or lie to me, and you'll be an old man when you get out of jail."

Beauchamp averted his eyes, but Deck wasn't there yet. He smacked his good hand on the table, wincing as a shaft of pain traveled up his arm and across his chest, directly to his almost-healed shoulder. "You're representing yourself, so I don't think you fully understand the charges you're facing. You could get life for attempting to murder a federal agent."

Beauchamp wiped the sweat from his brow and lip. His shoulders sagged. *Almost there.*

"Your buddies took off and left you to hang for it," Deck continued. "You've been through the system—talking is the only way to help yourself, and you know it."

The man hung his head. "What do you want to know?"

"Read this and sign it." He pulled out a waiver of rights form and a pen from his pants pocket and dropped them on the table. Without a signed waiver, anything the guy said would be inadmissible.

A minute later, Beauchamp signed the form, with Deck and Evan as witnesses.

Deck took the chair opposite Beauchamp. His plan was to start with the easy stuff then work his way up to attempted murder. "Do you know a dealer named Jack?"

"Yeah. I used to run with him, guard the cash while he did business."

"Was Loveland his turf?"

Beauchamp nodded. "Until he got a tip that the feds were looking to bust up his operation."

"Who tipped him off?" When Beauchamp didn't answer right away, Deck began tapping his fingers impatiently on the table. "Who was it?"

"A guy called him that night. Said not to show up, so Jack offered up his turf to a coke dealer."

A guy. Deck exchanged looks with Brett and Evan. "How do you know it was a guy and not a woman?"

"Cause I was there when Jack got the call. He put it on speakerphone."

"You *sure* it couldn't have been a woman?" Just because the caller Beauchamp had overhead was a man didn't mean that guy hadn't gotten tipped off by a woman.

"Yeah, man." Beauchamp frowned. "There's no chicks working this ring. If there were, I'd know it."

Deck held back an audible sigh of relief. This was probably enough to get Tori off the hook. Now for the hard stuff. "You told the cops 'the doc' ordered the hit. What do you know about this person?"

"Nothing." He shrugged. "I already told the cops I never met the doc. We were paid to do a job, that's all."

"What's the going rate for murdering a federal agent?" Deck asked.

"Five grand. A piece."

"Who else was there with you?"

Beauchamp began shaking his head. Sweat dripped down his temples. "I can't tell you that."

"Why not?" Deck prodded, clenching his jaw. "You already told us the doc ordered the hit, so why not give us everyone else's name? If you don't, you'll spend most of your life locked up in a maximum-security federal penitentiary. That's hardcore. They don't even have the

Disney Channel."

"I can't. I got a family. Three kids. The guys I was with *know* this. I know I'm going to prison, but I need to know they're safe while I'm inside. I don't give a rat's ass about the doc. I don't even know who he is."

"How is T-Lo involved in this?" he prodded, knowing full well T-Lo was the doc's hit man.

"I didn't say he *was*. I *didn't*."

He was afraid of the doc's distributor, and with good reason. T-Lo wouldn't hesitate to reach out into the prison system and pay someone on the sly to knife Beauchamp in the back.

"All I'm saying is that *someone* told us where to find you and when you'd be there," the man said. "The place kept changing because all of a sudden the cops were everywhere."

Union Station. Aidan had begged Deck not to notify the police, but he'd done it anyway. If T-Lo was feeding information to Beauchamp and the others, then Aidan was taking orders from T-Lo, who changed the location to the park. Deck had checked in twice with Denver PD and the rehab center, but no one had seen or heard from Aidan since that night. "Ever hear of a kid named Aidan?"

"No." Beauchamp shook his head.

"Where does the doc operate out of?"

"Beats me," Beauchamp answered.

"What kind of car does he drive?"

"How should I know? But"—he paused—"I heard he's into sports cars."

"One more question." Deck thought he already had the answer but needed to confirm it. "Are the doc and the Big

D the same person?"

"Yeah, man. Same dude."

Twenty minutes later, they left the prison and headed to Mick's for lunch. Beauchamp hadn't given them anything else Deck could use to ID the doc aka Big D, but vindicating Tori had made the trip worth it. He owed her that much.

He grabbed his cell phone to call Rivera and give him an update on Beauchamp, but it was already ringing. *ASAC Rivera.*

"Decker."

"Deck, I've got some bad news."

Several minutes later, Deck ended the call. His limbs felt heavy.

"Problem?" Brett asked over his shoulder from the front passenger seat.

You could say that. "State Police found Aidan's body."

"The same kid who set up the ambush?" Evan asked. "I know you tried to help him."

A lot of good that had done. Like Tori said, no matter how hard he tried, he couldn't help someone who didn't want to be helped.

"Overdose?" Brett asked.

"No." He gripped the phone tighter. "Gunshot to the face. They found him in an oil field outside Fort Collins. ME says he's been dead around eight weeks."

"Eight weeks?" Evan turned into Mick's parking lot. "That can't be a coincidence. What do you think happened?"

"Can't say for sure." Deck tried massaging his aching shoulder, but that only made it worse. "He probably mouthed off to someone about our confrontation at the rehab center. Word could have gotten back to T-Lo, who used Aidan to lure me and Thor into a trap. Helping to set up a federal agent would be worth bragging rights. T-Lo probably killed him before he could shoot his mouth off again. The kid was just an angry addict. He didn't deserve this."

Deck shoved a hand through his hair. *Good intentions, my ass.* All his good intentions had accomplished was to get the boy killed. He didn't think the day could get any worse but knew better than to verbalize the thought.

CHAPTER TWENTY-SIX

Late afternoon sun peeked through the blinds, painting the bedroom wall with horizontal shadows. Tori glanced at her watch. It was almost time to leave for the p.m. shift.

She stuffed the last of her things into her overnight bag and zipped it closed. For the last two nights, she'd stayed at her father's house, enjoying a couple of much-needed days off. Talking to her dad about what was going on in her life had been the plan, but when the moment had presented itself, she'd chickened out. Instead, they'd talked about the past and cleared away a lot of ugly cobwebs.

After meeting Deck, it seemed that some of his latent anger toward the DEA had lessened. He'd seen how much Deck cared for her, respected him for it, and couldn't remain angry at one man for what an entire agency had done to him and their family over ten years ago.

Although her dad knew there was something else on her mind, in his typically patient way, he'd said nothing and given her space.

The rich smell of coffee plied her out of her misery. She carried her bag downstairs to find her dad pouring them each a cup and adding milk to a small creamer.

"Thought we both could use a little late-day jolt." He set the mugs and creamer on the kitchen table.

"Thanks, Dad." She put her bag by the door then pulled out a chair.

"I'm teaching a class today, and you have to get to work,

soon, so…" He paused to pour cream into his mug. "I know you like spending time here with me, but I'm guessing you also came here for a specific reason."

She picked up the creamer, adding it to her coffee and looking up to find him watching with a puzzled expression. She followed the direction of his gaze to the tiny pitcher in her hand. *Creamer*.

He knew she always took her coffee black, but ever since Deck had strong-armed her into trying that white chocolate mocha, she'd been enjoying her coffee with a bit of cream. She rolled her lips inward as unexpected tears backed up behind her lids.

"Did something happen between you and Deck?" When she nodded, he gave her forearm a gentle squeeze. "Tell me."

So she did, starting with Deck's sister, followed by a running chronology about everything that had happened between them. Well, almost everything. A father doesn't really want to hear about his little girl having sex or being nearly killed.

"Hmm." He pursed his lips. "So *he* feels you betrayed his personal *and* professional trust, and *you* don't want to be with someone who has such a dangerous job."

When she sniffled, he plucked a tissue from a pack he always carried in his breast pocket and handed it to her.

She took it and dabbed at her eyes. "That about covers it."

"You know, I always wanted more exciting opportunities for you." He leaned in, resting his forearms on the table. "It killed me not to be able to pay for your college tuition, but I couldn't have been prouder of you for working so hard to make that happen anyway. But from that moment on, you always played things safe, never taking a single chance at doing something that might not turn out exactly the way you planned it or thought it should. You were…content."

"What's wrong with being content?"

"Nothing. But that's not how it always was with you." He sat back. "Before I lost my license, you used to try all kinds of new and exciting things. You went on overnight hikes into the mountains. You snowshoed across town during a blizzard just to see if you could. Do you remember?"

She nodded. He was right. "But why didn't you ever say anything?"

"Because it's your life to live as you choose. If you want to stay home in front of the fire every night and read a book, then that's what you should do. But if you want to go cliff diving or bungee jumping, then that's also what you should do."

Tori let her dad's metaphor hang there in the air. Funny how she'd said something to Deck about how she wasn't into bungee jumping. In fact, *all* the decisions she'd made until now had been safe. Her dad had taken risks, and it had cost them everything. Not that she blamed him, he'd been following his heart, doing what he strongly believed in. Until now, *she'd* never had the guts to do that. She'd been so careful not to make the same mistakes or take any risks that she'd been living her life with her head down, not held high. Deck had forced her to look up.

"One day, he'll realize he's been living in his past. Despite what agency he works for, I must admit that he has character. Trust me, he'll figure out soon enough that he's a horse's ass and that he never should have let you go."

Perhaps, but she'd never be capable of ignoring someone in pain when there was something she could do to help them. Deck having a problem with that because of what happened with his sister wasn't fair to her. "Even if he does, I'm not sure *I'm* ready to take that kind of leap."

Her father leaned back in his chair and smiled. "Only *you* can answer that question. As for Deck, while I wasn't exactly happy about it at first, I saw the way he looks at you. It's the way a man looks at something—or *someone*— he wants really badly. Fathers are always right, so take my advice and noodle on this for a while."

• • •

Tori sat at the traffic light, waiting for the light to change before turning into the hospital. Her little Subaru purred like a kitten, thanks to the new battery she'd had installed.

Thinking about the battery made her think of Deck. Actually, *everything* made her think of him.

The light changed, and she pulled into the lot, parking next to Wil's blue Nissan. She'd taken her dad's advice, noodling during the entire drive to work but was nowhere near being happy about the direction it had taken her. Her head hurt. More importantly, her heart still hurt. *How can I be in love with someone I'm so completely incompatible with?* Or who didn't trust her enough to know she'd never risk hurting him, Thor, or his friends?

The painful, hollowed-out feeling was worsening by the second. She shut off the engine and sat there, wondering if there were anything she would have done differently and coming up blank. She'd get past this. Everyone who's ever been jilted always does. Right then and there, it didn't seem like she would.

She grabbed her purse and was about to go inside but stopped. Max Maynard pulled in, driving a brand-new silver car just like out of the movie *Back to the Future*, the one with doors that opened up like wings. A DeLorean. And just last week, Neil Shibowsky had driven up in his new black Ferrari, the one he'd bragged to Wil about. That was an awful lot of cash to drop on a car. Then again, they *were* surgeons.

Surgeons having flashy cars was nothing new, but it was an unwelcome reminder that her trusty Subaru and Wil's practical Nissan labeled both of them as being something less-than in the doctor world.

As she stepped onto the curb, she noticed David Landry, the orderly, leaning on the open window of a blood-red sports car, the make and model of which she couldn't identify from this distance. Maybe that was his brother, Pete. Judging by the car, it looked like Pete had gotten back on his feet pretty quickly.

Honestly. The ER parking lot was turning into a veritable whose-dick-is-bigger showroom.

Tori stared at the car. During the first search warrant she'd gone on, Deck had mentioned that the distributor they were looking for drove a fancy black sports car. These weren't black, but perhaps the distributor had a collection. There had to be hundreds of fancy cars on the road in Denver at any given moment, let alone the entire state. The distributor could be anyone.

Reluctantly, she pushed through the door and went inside. It was barely four o'clock, and the front desk lounge was already crammed with patients' relatives trying to find out how their loved ones were doing. She swiped into the ER, hoping to be so busy there wouldn't be time to think about anything else but work.

Wil stood at the nurses' station, reviewing a form. "How were your days off?" he asked, handing the form to one of the admins.

"Good." *Not*. "Just…quiet."

Wil's brows rose. "Did you spend them with your DEA agent?"

"No." In the last eight weeks, she and Wil hadn't been on a single shift together. He probably didn't even know that Deck had been badly injured. "We're not working together anymore, and we're no longer seeing each other, either."

Wil's lips pressed tightly into a grimace. "I'm sorry. I know you liked him. I'm here for you if you want to talk."

"I know that. Thanks."

"Dr. Barnett," a nurse called out. "There's a patient waiting for you in ER 4."

"Coffee later?" Wil asked over his shoulder, already heading down the hall.

"Sounds good." Anything to occupy her mind would be a welcome relief.

• • •

Six hours into her shift and Tori's feet were killing her. A ten-car pileup on I-25 had kept the ER hopping nonstop. Finally, most of the cases had either been treated and released or sent to other floors for X-rays, MRIs, or surgery. Except for one.

Tori had examined an unconscious young woman who she suspected had neurological damage. Since Max Maynard was the neurosurgeon on call tonight, she'd requested him for a consult.

"Good thing you called me in on this," Max said, having just completed his examination. "She needs surgery to release the pressure on her brain." He glanced at his watch. "I'll get her on the schedule right away." Without another word, he left the room.

Tori entered a few notes into the patient's computerized chart then headed to the doctors' lounge to splash cold water on her face. Along the way, she heard a raised voice coming from ER 4. She poked her head in to see Wil and Ethan standing beside the examining table.

"Don't you fucking touch me." A man of about forty, with a blood-soaked towel wrapped around his wrist, hopped off the bed, his face twisted in anger. "You nearly killed me with the shit you gave me in Sheridan. I should report your ass."

He pointed at one of the men, but she couldn't tell whether it was Wil or Ethan. The movement had tugged up his shirt sleeve, exposing what looked like tattoos—two rings of barbed wire around his biceps. "Get me another doctor. *Anyone* but *you*."

"Relax." Wil moved his hands in a calming gesture. "You came to the ER for help, and that's what we're trying to do. Help you."

Tori cleared her throat. "Dr. Barnett. Dr. Dexter. Can I assist you?"

Wil spun, his eyes widening at the sight of her standing in the doorway. "No. Thank you, Dr. Sampson. We've got this." With a move so subtle she barely caught it, he stuffed something—*a syringe?*—into the right side pocket of his coat. It happened so fast she couldn't be sure. Normally, nurses administered injections in the ER, not doctors.

"Would you like me to get Nurse Torres?" They both knew Suzie had a natural way with people and was good at handling difficult patients. Like this one obviously was.

"No," he practically spat out.

"Hey, wait." The man pointed to her. "Is *she* a doctor? I'll take her instead."

Wil gave a subtle yet dismissive nod, the message of which was clear: *Do not undermine me.*

"Okay." Reluctantly, she left the room. It wasn't like Wil to be so curt, especially with her.

"Tori," Suzie called out, pointing to another room. "You've got a customer."

For the next ten minutes, Tori attended to a young patient who'd broken his arm on a trampoline. "We'll send you upstairs for an X-ray then get you set up with a cast."

Raised voices came from the corridor. Suzie and another nurse rushed past with a crash cart. As much as she wanted to run down the hall and help, she had her own patient who was counting on her. Tori patted the boy's shoulder, giving his mother a meaningful look. "You'll be fine, I promise. No more trampoline for a while." If she ever had children, there'd *never* be a trampoline in their yard. Kids loved them, but they were responsible for an outrageous number of broken bones.

After finishing with her patient, she followed the direction of the crash cart and found ER 4 crammed with medical personnel. Ethan was no longer there, but Wil was.

The man who'd been shouting lay on the table, unmoving. Leads from his chest led to a cardiac monitor. The flat green line indicated his heart had stopped.

Suzie and the other nurses looked to Wil, waiting for direction.

Wil glanced at the clock on the wall. "TOD six-oh-five."

Time of death? Tori couldn't believe it. The man had been fine less than thirty minutes ago. "What happened?"

"Heart attack," Wil said, remorse evident in his eyes. "Came on out of nowhere."

While Suzie unhooked the leads, Tori did a quick visual assessment of the man's body. He was younger than she'd originally thought, maybe thirty-five tops, and in relatively good shape, judging by the muscles in his arms. The only thing seemingly wrong with him had been what looked like a relatively minor wrist injury.

Half an hour later, she was still disturbed by the man's death. Something wasn't right about the whole incident. And the argument she'd overhead between Ethan, Wil, and the now-dead man... The man had been given something in Sheridan? Something that had nearly killed him. But neither Ethan nor Wil practiced medicine outside North Metro, so what did that mean?

Tori stopped in at the nurses' station. "What was the name of the man who just died?"

"Damon Sanchez," someone said.

She came around the desk and sat in front of a computer. After entering her username and password, she pulled up Sanchez's chart. He'd come in for a deep laceration in his wrist. For someone so young, he was taking small amounts of potassium chloride. Officially, he was Ethan's patient, with Wil supervising as the ER's attending physician. Every doctor knew that potassium supplements were often prescribed to prevent or treat hypokalemia, low blood levels of potassium. If not controlled, too little or too much potassium in the blood could result in a heart attack.

She scrolled down to see what he'd been given in the ER. The portion of the record prior to going into cardiac arrest was blank. If Wil *had* been holding a syringe and used it, Ethan would have entered the injection in the man's chart.

Worry buzzed in her head like a mosquito that refused to fly away.

Tori looked up to see Wil leaving ER 2.

"If anyone needs me, I'll be grabbing coffee in the lounge," she overheard him tell the nurses. "And when you see Dr. Dexter, tell him to join me."

Tori watched him disappear down the corridor. Had Ethan made another mistake? Regardless, that wouldn't stop Sanchez's family from digging into what happened. She needed to talk to Wil when Ethan wasn't around.

She scooted back the chair and headed for the lounge. When she pushed through the door, Wil was pouring coffee into a mug. He turned abruptly, sloshing coffee onto the front of his coat.

"Shit." He jumped back. More coffee spilled from the cup, splattering the tips of his shoes. He set down the cup then yanked off his coat and began running the stained portion under cold water at the sink. "Great." Taking the dripping coat with him, he headed to the doctors' locker room.

Tori leaned against the counter, waiting for him to return. A locker slammed shut, then Wil came back, shrugging into a clean coat and refilling his cup as if nothing was wrong. As if a man hadn't just died for no explicable reason.

She crossed to the locker room, cracking open the door to verify they were alone, then returned to the kitchenette. "We should talk."

"About what?" To her astonishment, he actually looked as if he had no idea what she wanted to discuss.

"Isn't it obvious? About the man who just died."

He took a sip of coffee. "What about him?"

Wil *had* to be joking. "I just looked at his chart. There was no medical reason for him to die of a heart attack. He came in to have a laceration sewn up. That's it."

"You looked at his chart?" Her friend frowned. "He was *Ethan's* patient, not yours."

"I was concerned. I'm worried for Ethan, and I'm worried for you."

"Why?"

She still couldn't be certain she hadn't seen a syringe in his hand. "There's no record of Ethan giving him anything."

"That's because he didn't."

"Are you sure?"

"Of course I'm sure. Why would you ask such a thing? The man had a history of arrythmia. Sometimes, it just happens."

"Did *you* give him anything?" Either way, there was nothing in the chart.

"No, dammit!" His voice rose. "What is this, an inquisition?"

Arrythmias could have been why he was taking potassium chloride, but there were still too many unanswered questions. "What did he mean when he said *you* nearly killed him in Sheridan?"

"I have no idea." Wil dumped the remains of his cup into the sink. "He was getting worked up, and I think he mistook us for someone else."

"Wil." She placed her hand on his shoulder, feeling the tension in his muscles. "Is it possible Ethan missed something? The ME's office will ask questions. Given the patient's age and relatively good health, they'll send an investigator to look into his death. As Ethan's attending, you could *both* be liable. I only want to help you. You know how things like this can spiral downhill quickly."

"I do, but if you keep making noise about it, you'll only call attention to it. So let it go." He brushed past, leaving her alone in the lounge.

She stared after him, her mouth agape as she wondered what to do next. This was beyond weird. Despite his adamant statement to the contrary, she couldn't shake the feeling that something was wrong. *Accidentally or unintentionally?* Accidentally, of course. Neither Wil nor Ethan would intentionally hurt anyone. They were doctors, for chrissake.

For several seconds, she stared at the door to the locker room then blew out a breath. She couldn't believe what she was about to do.

She pushed open the door to the locker room. Just to be sure, she checked the bathroom stalls, verifying they were indeed unoccupied. Using the small wood wedge to hold the door open, she toed it between the door and the frame, just enough so that she could hear if anyone came into the lounge. Or if Wil came back.

A blue lock hung from Wil's locker, the same one that was always there. *The same one I may still have the combination to.* Unless he'd changed it.

Last year, he'd forgotten his phone in the locker and asked her to get it for him. He lived in one of the condos near Green Mountain and on her direct route home. So he'd given her the combo. She'd been doing rounds when he'd called, so she'd entered the combo into his contact page on her phone.

She rolled her eyes. *And here I am, breaking into his locker. Some friend I am.*

Tori opened up Wil's contact page. For a moment, she stared at the combination then began adjusting the numbered dials with her thumb and forefinger. She closed her eyes, biting her lip before tugging down to see if it opened. She didn't know if she wanted it to. It did, the clicking sound echoing within the narrow confines of the locker room.

Tori jerked her head to the door, peering through the crack. The lounge was still empty. She unhooked the lock and pulled open the locker. Wil's stained coat hung on a hook, still dripping coffee-tinged water onto the floor of the locker. She took the coat out, praying she was wrong about this. She looked inside the right-side pocket, the same one he'd put his hand into.

Empty.

"Thank you," she whispered to herself. Maybe she should trust Wil and just let it go. Then again, he could have tossed the syringe into the sharps container. The fact that his pocket was empty didn't necessarily mean he hadn't administered an injection.

She rehung the jacket inside the locker. Something *thunked* against the metal side. She pulled on the jacket enough to peer into the other pocket.

A medicine vial.

She reached for the tiny bottle, turning it in her hand. When she read the label, her blood went as cold as dry ice.

Potassium chloride.

The bottle was nearly empty. Only a few drops remained. If Ethan had given Sanchez too *much* potassium chloride…it could have been what killed the man. Or, as Wil said, it could have just happened. She'd been an ER doctor long enough to know unexpected things did "just happen."

She wrapped her fingers tightly around the vial. There had to be an explanation. Sanchez wasn't the only patient Ethan had seen tonight. It was possible the potassium chloride was unrelated to Sanchez, and who knew how long the vial had been in Wil's pocket? Sure, all the med vials were periodically counted and audited, but he could have forgotten it was in there.

She had to talk to Wil again. But how to do that without letting on that she'd broken into his locker? She couldn't undo what was already done.

Tori stuffed the vial into her own coat pocket then closed the door and reinserted the lock. Before stepping back into the lounge, she again peered through the crack, verifying no one else was there.

For a long moment, she stood there, thinking about the similarities between her relationships with Wil and Deck.

What she was about to do would most likely kill her friendship with Wil. After losing Deck the way she had, this hit home just as hard. There were elements of trust involved with both situations, though her problems with Deck were more complicated than that. If she was wrong about this, Wil would never trust her again. At least one day, Deck would figure out she hadn't betrayed him to a drug dealer.

She pulled the door open and headed into the lounge. She hadn't told a—

Soul, she'd been about to think to herself then froze in mid-step.

She *had* told someone.

While she probably shouldn't have, she and Wil had discussed the warrant briefly. That had been after the fact, though. But right before Deck had picked her up to go to Loveland, Wil had called. It had been such a quick call she'd completely forgotten about it. She'd told him she had to cancel their dinner plans because she was going somewhere with Deck. On a warrant. In Loveland.

No. She shook her head, refusing to go down the track her thoughts were taking.

From everything she'd seen on the news and read about, bigtime drug dealers were rich and flaunted it.

Wil drove a Nissan, a practical, inexpensive car. He didn't live in a McMansion or wear expensive watches. The only thing he talked about spending money on were his vacations, and he often joked he had to save up for those, even with his salary. Still, a patient was dead, and Wil *may* have lied to her. Whether it was about his involvement or to cover for Ethan, she didn't know. And then there was what she'd overheard outside Deck's hospital room. Someone nicknamed "the doc" had informed the Loveland dealer that the DEA was coming. This was the same person who had put the hit out on Deck.

But that didn't automatically mean that Wil was the leak. The doctor, if they even *were* one, was more likely someone who'd gotten their doctorate in chemistry or pharmacology or toxicology or any other field actually useful to creating and manufacturing designer drugs.

Neil and Max, however, certainly fit the flashy rich doctor role.

Neil in particular had been talking with Leslie Batista *before* the warrant, and Leslie had been Deck's source for information about the dealer, Jack. Neil had said they were "just chatting," but he could have been pumping Leslie for information about her drug source. He could have warned the dealer to close up shop until further notice.

But how would he have known Deck was planning on talking to Leslie in the first place? She'd never told Neil she'd been assisting the DEA. Then again, hospitals were like real-life soap operas. Within these white walls, gossip traveled at light speed. Would Wil have said anything to anyone? She didn't believe he'd do anything directly or indirectly to hurt her. He'd been a great friend to her and Suzie.

Suzie, with her expensive new ring Tori knew her friend and her fiancé couldn't afford.

Worry and uncertainty roiled in her belly to the point of nausea. These were medical professionals, all of them. They'd dedicated their lives to helping make people better, not harming them.

Paranoia crept through her, but at least she recognized it for what it was. She needed to be rational about all this. If she was totally wrong, everything would be fine. If she kept her mouth shut and didn't vent her suspicions, the results could be catastrophic. She was in no position to handle this, nor could she stomach investigating her own friends and colleagues. She had to leave it to the professionals.

She had to tell Deck.

Tori charged for the door, opening it and slamming into someone. Neil Shibowsky.

He clutched her upper arms, steadying her. She tried twisting away, but he wouldn't let her. Over his shoulder, she caught David Landry pushing a stretcher. On top of that stretcher was a sheet-covered body. Damon Sanchez. David smiled in greeting but kept going.

"Tori," Neil said cheerfully. "What a coincidence. I was looking for you. I wanted to talk to you about one of the patients you helped Wil with. Leslie Batista."

His fingers dug deeper into her arms. What interest could Neil have in Leslie Batista? Except finding out what she'd told Deck about her drug source.

"Not now," she managed. "I-I'm not feeling well. I just need some air."

"I'll go with you," he insisted. "We can talk outside."

"No." She shrugged from his grasp. "I'll be back in a few minutes. Really, I'm fine." She speed-walked down the corridor, hitting the button for the door leading to the registration desk then kept right on going outside to the parking lot. What she needed was a place to be alone and think.

She headed for her car. Some thoughtless idiot had parked too close to the driver's side for her to squeeze in. She went to the passenger side and pulled out her keys. Luckily, she kept her car key on the same ring as her hospital key chain. She hit the button to unlock the door and opened it.

Swallowing hard, she cued up Deck's number. After their last conversation, he might not take her call. Four rings later, his voicemail kicked in.

"Deck, it's Tori. I'm at work, but I need to tell you some things." Starting with how sorry she was. Two nurses walked past, waving. She waved then turned her back to the hospital doors, moving more into the shadow next to her Subaru. "I can't be sure, but I think you should look into some of the doctors on staff here at North Metro and one of the orderlies. One of them may be the drug source you're looking for. The first is Dr. Neil Shibowsky. He was the doctor talking to Leslie Batista when we walked in on them, and there was no reason he should have been there. He could have gotten information about the Loveland warrant from her."

A lump of grief formed in her throat, so big she could barely get the words out. "And something strange happened in the ER tonight. I overheard an injured patient accuse two other doctors of giving him something that nearly killed him in Sheridan. That patient died from a heart attack not half an hour later, and he shouldn't have. His name is Damon Sanchez. I think you should check it out. I hope I'm wrong, I really do. I, um…inadvertently told one of these doctors about the Loveland warrant. His name is—"

Tori's stomach clenched to the point of pain. *Am I really doing this?* She moved her hand to her abdomen when her charm bracelet caught on a corner of the open door and broke, falling to the pavement. She bent to retrieve it but stopped as something sharp pricked her neck.

"Ouch." She pressed two fingers to the sting. The Subaru wavered before her eyes. She reached out to regain her balance. "Deck…"

The phone was no longer in her hand.

She blinked and started to fall. Then the world faded to black.

CHAPTER TWENTY-SEVEN

Deck's muscles screamed as he pushed through another rep. Sweat poured off his face and down his chest, soaking his T-shirt. He'd been cleared for active duty but was supplementing his PT with late-night workouts to get his shoulder back to full strength.

T-Lo was still in the wind, and Deck was itching to put the *habeas grabbus* on the guy and lock him up for attempted murder of a federal agent. Then there was the Big D, the unidentified doctor they were really after.

Over ten thousand people in the state of Colorado could legitimately call themselves a medical doctor. Then there were the PhDs and other *non*-medical doctors. This person might not be a doctor of any kind. It could be nothing more than a nickname.

Deck racked the barbell then looked at the clock on the wall. Ten o'clock. He grabbed a towel then wiped his face, wondering what Tori was doing right now. Was she working or getting ready for bed?

Thinking of her in bed brought back memories of being there with her, buried deeply inside her body as he—

"Dammit." He whipped the towel across the room, where it hit the wall and slid to the floor.

Thor snorted, turning his head left and right as he searched the room for threats.

"Sorry, Thor." His dog had been asleep, in REM cycle, judging by the way his eyes had been flicking back and forth beneath his lids. "Go back to sleep." With an annoyed groan, Thor lowered his head between his paws.

Deck knew what his problem was. Not only had he made a train wreck of his relationship with Tori, he was in love. *That* was the problem, one of them, anyway. He couldn't force her to accept who and what he was. That was a decision she had to make on her own, and she'd already made it. His behavior that night in the park had only exacerbated her fears.

He grabbed a set of dumbbells and sat on the edge of the weight bench. If the situation had been reversed and she'd been the one in the kind of pain he'd been in, not to mention potentially doing more damage to herself, he'd have done anything to ease her misery. Anything.

And yet he'd been a complete dick when she'd tried to do the same.

Curling his fingers tightly around the weight, he lifted it, isolating his biceps.

Since the day Marianne died, he'd programmed himself into a rigid, unmovable robot where opioids—hell, *any* drugs—were concerned, and he'd done it to the point of irrationality. To the point where he'd lost the best thing that had ever happened to him. *Tori.*

Looked like he really did have a comfort zone after all, and loving her was *way* outside that zone.

Unable to concentrate on more reps, he racked the dumbbell and picked up his phone. He had to talk with her, to tell her what a colossal bonehead he was and convince her to give him another chance. Groveling would probably be necessary. A *lot* of groveling.

In time, he felt confident he could help her work

through whatever remained of her DEA animosity. Getting past the dangerous-job thing was a whole other animal. That was something she'd have to come to grips with, and she'd made it clear it was a game-stopper. But he was a federal agent. He could convince anyone to—

No. He couldn't do that to her. Manipulating her wasn't fair. She had to want to be with him of her own free will. Enough to not only step outside her comfort zone but to smash it into smithereens.

The phone was still on vibrate, and he'd missed a call. When he saw who the caller was, he froze, staring at the screen in disbelief. Tori had called about twenty minutes ago and left a message. His face was so covered in sweat, he cued it up and put it on speaker. Hearing her voice in his house made him smile. As he listened to the rest of the message, his smile vanished.

Dr. Neil Shibowsky? He remembered the guy. Shibowsky *had* seemed like he was in a hurry to get out of Leslie Batista's room that day.

He hit redial. A thousand questions pounded the inside of his skull, including why Tori had been cut off in mid-sentence and hadn't called him back. "Tori, it's Deck," he said when his call went right to voicemail. "I got your message. Call me back, no matter what time it is."

He raced to his bedroom, stripping off his workout clothes along the way. After cuing up Sammie at the Task Force desk, he wedged his phone between his chin and shoulder, flinging open the closet door.

Sammie answered after two rings. "What's up, Deck?"

"Sorry about the late hour." He yanked a shirt from a hanger. "I need you to run a complete background for me

on Dr. Neil Shibowsky. Works at North Metro Hospital."
As he described the man he'd met, he realized something
else. That was the same description he'd gotten from
Alonzo Jones, the dealer whose daughter Tori had saved.

"Sure thing," Sammie said. "When do you need this?"

"Yesterday."

CHAPTER TWENTY-EIGHT

Jostling woke Tori. She tried opening her eyes, but they felt crusted shut. "Where am I?" she mumbled.

"In your car," someone said. A man's voice. She couldn't tell whose. Her head felt as if it weighed a hundred pounds, and his voice sounded as if he were speaking to her from under water.

"How did I get in my car?" The last thing she remembered was standing *beside* her car, not being in it. In fact, she couldn't remember why she'd been outside in the first place. Shouldn't she be at work? Her brain was still so cloudy, she couldn't make sense of anything.

"You fainted, so I put you in the passenger seat," the man said.

She still couldn't focus her eyes, and her muscles felt about as firm as jelly, but the events in the ER that night came crashing back. The suspicions she'd had about Neil, Ethan, and Wil. About David Landry and his brother. Even Suzie and her fiancé, Hector. And Neil—he'd stopped her from leaving, grabbed her, and insisted on following her outside if she wouldn't speak to him. His grip had been tight. *Too* tight. She'd fled.

Had he followed her anyway?

With frantic, clumsy movements, she dug her hands into her coat pockets, searching for her phone and not finding it. It had been in her hand when she'd been leaving a message for Deck. Both her pockets were empty. Her kidnapper had taken the vial of potassium chloride.

"Here we are," he said. "Home sweet home." He turned off whatever road they were on. The car lurched and dipped repeatedly, as if they were driving over rough terrain. He brought the car to a stop inside a large building of some kind. He shut off the engine then came around to her side, opened the door, and began unbuckling her seat belt.

She tried swatting his hands away but could barely lift her arms. "Don't touch me."

Despite her feeble protests, he hauled her from the seat to a standing position. Her knees began to buckle when an arm came around her back, steadying her. What was wrong with her?

The pinprick in her neck. "Did you *drug* me?"

"You gave me no choice."

"No *choice*? How dare you?" She tried clawing at his face, but she still couldn't completely control her limbs. Even if she could, he held tightly to her left arm, effectively pinning her other arm to her side with his body. "Let me go. *Please*, let me go."

"I didn't plan on bringing you here. This was all *your* fault." He propelled her forward, keeping a tight arm around her so she didn't stumble. "For sticking your nose where it didn't belong."

A wave of nausea made her vision swim worse than it had before. Her head lolled backward against his shoulder. All she wanted was to lie down and wake up to find none of this was real, that it was all an awful nightmare.

"Don't move." He leaned her up against the outside of the building.

She sucked in the cool night air, hoping some of her faculties would return. Slowly, she slid down, landing on her butt.

Metal creaked as a door closed somewhere nearby.

"Up you go." He lifted her back to a standing position, urging her forward. His arm around her waist was the only thing keeping her upright.

She couldn't say how long they walked. The ground beneath her shoes felt soft, like grass. A wisp of wind caught her ponytail, swishing it against the side of her face. They kept walking for another minute or so then stopped in front of a small building.

Through her blurred vision, she watched him insert a key into the door and pull it open. An earthy, musty smell wafted to her nose first, followed by a weird chemical smell, one that sent out a loud warning to go anywhere *but* inside that building.

Tori pushed as hard as she could, breaking free of his grip. She fell to the ground, hitting the side of her head. As if her vision wasn't messed up before, now she didn't know which was up or down. Vertigo was a bitch. She opened her mouth to scream, but the only thing that came out was the last of her dinner as she vomited.

"There's no place for you to go," he said from behind her. "Please, don't try to get away. You'll only get hurt, and I'd hate for that to happen." He hauled her to her feet then picked her up and carried her inside.

The only thing she could make out was a glaring light as he carried her down a staircase that seemed to go on forever. Like, to the center of the earth. With every step, the musty, chemical smell intensified. The light grew brighter at the bottom of the stairs. She blinked repeatedly, trying to focus her vision. The surrounding walls seemed rough, not like the inside of a finished basement. More like an underground tunnel.

As he carried her past a clear plastic curtain hanging from the rough-hewn rock ceiling, she glimpsed tables with glass bottles, vials, and small propane tanks, and the blurry images of three men behind one of the tables.

Their faces were strange, like they had cannisters sticking out from their chins. *Face masks.* This had to be the infamous laboratory where the latest iteration of gray death was being made.

They moved past the curtain, past a row of bars that reminded her of a jail cell, only the surrounding walls were more cave-like.

She felt, more than saw, her body being lowered onto something soft. Another wave of nausea hit her, forcing her to close her eyes. "You're who Deck is looking for." Whoever *you* was.

"You were never supposed to know. I really am sorry about this." He skimmed her cheek with the backs of his knuckles. "You'll feel better once the sedative wears off."

She lashed out, trying to knock his hand away, but her arm felt like a fifty-pound weight. "Deck will come looking for me."

"Perhaps. But he'll never find you."

Her vision unfuzzed just enough to see him pluck the cap off a syringe. "No!" A feeble spurt of adrenaline shot through her system but not nearly enough. She tried sitting up, but the world spun violently, forcing her to grab the edge of the cot or plow headfirst into the floor. He loomed closer then stuck the needle into her arm. The rock walls began to ripple like a dark curtain whipping back and forth in the wind.

"We'll talk more tomorrow."

The last thing Tori heard was what sounded like a gate clanging shut, locking her in.

CHAPTER TWENTY-NINE

Deck pulled into a parking space outside the entrance to the ER, one reserved for police vehicles. In the weeks since he'd been IOD—injured on duty—his K-9 SUV had been repaired, bullet holes and all.

"Back in a few, boy." He gave Thor a quick scratch under the chin when a flash of pink caught his eye. Deck leaned over and tugged out Tori's sweater. She must have left it in the SUV the night they'd been shot at by T-Lo and his boys.

Thor stretched his neck out to sniff the sweater, uttering a soft *woof*. Even his dog missed her. He dropped the sweater on the seat, gave Thor another quick scratch on the head, then went inside the hospital.

On the way over, he'd tried calling Tori back three times. She still wasn't answering. The message she'd left him said she was at work, but he hadn't seen her car in the spots reserved for ER doctors. He was a half second from calling Brett and Evan for backup to help him look for her. First, he needed more information.

The main desk was swamped with people. Deck badged his way into the restricted ER area. At the nurses' desk, he recognized Suzie Torres sitting in front of a monitor. When she caught sight of him, her eyes lit up.

"Have you seen Tori?" she asked. The skin over the bridge of her nose wrinkled in concern. "I can't find her anywhere, and she's not answering pages or her phone."

"I haven't seen her." Warning flags waved in the back of

his head. "She left me a message saying she was at work. That was about an hour ago."

"This isn't like her to disappear in the middle of a shift." Suzie pressed her lips together. "I'm worried something's wrong."

That makes two of us. "Do you know Dr. Neil Shibowsky?"

"Yes. He's a cardiac surgeon." She tipped her head to the examining room across the hall. "He's in ER 3 on a consult."

"Thanks." He looked inside ER 3 where Dr. Shibowsky was talking to a patient. While he waited, he heard Tori being paged repeatedly, along with another doctor, Wil Barnett.

It was all Deck could do to stand still and not pace. Waiting had never been his thing. Finally, Dr. Shibowsky finished with the patient and came out of the room.

"Dr. Shibowsky?" Deck caught him before he could rush off. "I'm Special Agent Decker with the DEA. Do you have a minute?"

"Uh, sure." Shibowsky's eyes narrowed to gray slits. "What's this about?"

"Do you know where Tori Sampson is?" Deck scrutinized the man's face for any signs of bullshit.

"No. They've been paging her for a while now."

He paused to give Shibowsky time to squirm. He didn't. "When was the last time you spoke with her?"

Shibowsky thought for a moment. "About an hour ago. Right before they started paging her. She was coming out of the doctors' lounge."

"What did you talk about?" he asked, still scrutinizing

Shibowsky's body language and not picking up on anything suspicious.

"Nothing, actually. I wanted to ask her about a patient, but she said she didn't have time. She was going outside to get some air." The doctor's eyes narrowed further. "What is this about? Did something happen to her?"

He hoped not. "What patient did you want to talk to her about?"

Shibowsky hesitated.

"What patient?" Deck repeated.

"Well, since you've already met her, I guess it's okay if I give you her name. Leslie Batista, the young woman you spoke to with Tori and Dr. Barnett."

Now they were getting somewhere. Tori had mentioned Leslie in her voicemail message. "Specifically, what did you want to talk to Tori about?"

Shibowsky started shaking his head. "I can't get into the specifics of Leslie's medical condition. That would be a breach of her privacy."

Something about this guy started pinging Deck's radar. "You're a cardiac surgeon. Leslie came into the hospital as an overdose. What were you and she talking about the day I saw you in her room? What were you doing in her room?"

Shibowsky let out a frustrated breath. "Fine. She's my next-door neighbor's kid. She didn't want her parents to know she'd been brought in, but I happened to see her in one of the rooms. We were just having a frank discussion about her addiction."

Deck could easily verify if Shibowsky was lying. All it would take was for Sammie to run a quick address check on Shibowsky and his next-door neighbors. Frankly, the guy hadn't exhibited any signs of lying. "Thanks, Doc."

"You're welcome." Shibowsky began walking away.

"Doctor," Deck called out, and Shibowsky turned. "What kind of car do you drive?"

"A Ferrari. Why?"

"What color?"

"I have two. One blue, one black."

A black sports car. But he still didn't think Shibowsky had lied. The man didn't know where Tori was, and he had a plausible explanation for talking with Leslie Batista. "Thanks."

As soon as the doctor had walked off, Deck texted Sammie with his address check request. Now to look into the patient Tori had mentioned. Damon Sanchez.

He caught up with Suzie Torres, who'd left the nurses' deck and was pushing a cart loaded with supplies down the hall. "Suzie, wait."

"Walk with me," she said. "We're overrun with patients tonight. We can't find Wil—Dr. Barnett—either. One doctor walking off shift is strange enough, but two at the same time? This has never happened before."

The warning flags that had been waving in Deck's head began pounding at the inside of his skull. So Barnett was AWOL, too. "Did you have a patient die tonight? Damon Sanchez?"

"Yes." She stopped pushing the cart. "How do you know about that?"

"In the message Tori left me, she said he shouldn't have died. Do you know what she meant by that?"

"No." The frown lines above her nose deepened.

"Who treated him in the ER?"

"Dr. Dexter and Dr. Barnett."

Tori's message urged him to look into two doctors at North Metro. Three had just pinged his radar. Shibowsky, Barnett, and Dexter. "Did Dexter or Barnett give Sanchez anything before he died, something that could have caused a heart attack?"

Her brows shot up as she absorbed the implication of Deck's question. "I don't know. Whatever he was given would be in his records."

"Can you check that for me?" Deck knew what he was asking Suzie to do was a violation of medical privacy laws. "Please? It's important. I'm worried about Tori." He'd gotten the feeling Tori and the nurse were close, so he'd intentionally played the friend card.

Suzie looked both ways down the hall then lowered her voice. "Okay, but you have to keep this quiet."

Deck nodded then followed her back to the nurses' station, waiting impatiently for her to pull up Sanchez's chart.

"Here it is. Damon Sanchez. Coded from a heart attack."

Deck tugged a pad and pen from his thigh pocket and jotted down Sanchez's DOB. "Seems pretty young for heart disease. Is that what he came in for?"

"He came in to get a laceration on his wrist sewn up. According to this, he wasn't given anything prior to coding. There are various drugs we use to try and regain normal sinus rhythm. That's what these are." She pointed to a long list of drugs. Epinephrine. Lidocaine… The list went on.

"Were these administered *before* or *after* he coded?"

"After."

"Who else was in the room with Sanchez?"

"Dr. Dexter and Dr. Barnett. When he coded, I was the first nurse on scene."

"Did he have an IV in him when you first saw him?"

"No. I put the IV in myself."

Deck began tapping the pen on the pad. "So, if Barnett or Dexter administered something to Sanchez, it wasn't intravenously."

"No. I would have seen it. Besides, it's not typical for a doctor to administer injections. The doctor prescribes something, then a nurse administers the meds."

"Is the body still in the hospital morgue?"

"Yes. On the lower level."

"Is Dr. Dexter still in the ER?"

"No. His shift ended, and he went home."

"Do you have Barnett and Dexter's cell phone numbers?"

"Of course." She grabbed a clipboard. "Here it is."

Deck copied down the numbers she gave him. In a perfect world, he'd get a subpoena and ping Tori, Barnett, and Dexter's phones for a location, but that would take too long. Despite Tori's cryptic message, he still had no concrete proof that she was in trouble, let alone that anyone else was involved in her disappearance, including Barnett. However, given that Barnett was *also* missing, he was at the top of Deck's suspect list.

"Tori mentioned an orderly." Deck flipped to another page of his pad. "How many of them are assigned to the ER?"

"They're not really assigned to the ER. They come and go as needed, taking patients upstairs to surgery or to their car. Things like that."

"Any of them stand out to you?"

Suzie's expression turned thoughtful. "David Landry," she answered without hesitation. "It's nothing specific, really. Just that he's been acting strangely. During one shift, he lied to Tori about being sick in the men's room when he was actually outside talking to his brother. And before you ask, I think his shift's over, too."

"Can you give me his number?"

"Sure."

After writing down the number, Deck again flipped the page in his pad and wrote down his own cell number, handing it to Suzie. "Call me if you see or hear from Tori or Barnett, or if Dexter or Landry show back up."

"I will."

"Thanks." Leaving Suzie with a bewildered expression on her face, he headed for the elevator. Along the way, he called Barnett's number. It went right to voicemail. Dexter and Landry's phones also went to voicemail. Deck also called Sammie again, requesting she run Sanchez, Shibowsky, Barnett, and Dexter for a criminal histories and whatever background she could quickly dig up on them.

The elevator door opened, and he punched the down button with his fist. Tori's message said Sanchez had been mad about something one of the doctors had given him at Sheridan. If her hunch was right, that a doctor had given Sanchez something to kill him, it begged the question: why would a doctor murder a patient right there in an emergency room? Seemed like a big risk.

When a patient died under mysterious circumstances, which this appeared to be, standard protocol dictated an autopsy be performed, followed by an investigation, if appropriate. If Damon Sanchez *was* murdered, he must have had some pretty dangerous shit on someone.

When the doors opened, Deck followed the signs to the Hospital Morgue Unit. He identified himself to the attendant, signed a form, then waited to view the body. While he waited, he sent text messages to Brett and Evan to meet him in the ER parking lot ASAP. Whatever was going down, he needed his friends' help and knew they'd be there for him. Any time, any place.

The morgue's attendant came through two swinging metal doors. "Agent Decker, he's ready."

Deck followed the guy into the walk-in cool room, the walls of which were covered with banks of refrigerated cabinets. Three rolling trolleys took up most of the floor space. Like most morgues, the temperature ran somewhere between two and four degrees Celsius. Wearing only a short-sleeve polo shirt, Deck should have been cold but wasn't. There was enough adrenaline pumping through his veins to fire up his body for a week.

The attendant went to one of the trolleys and drew back the sheet. Two rings of barbed wire tattoos encircled the body's right biceps. The letter S had been tattooed between the rings. Deck knew each of these particular rings indicated a full year in prison, and the S stood for FCI Sheridan, the federal correctional institute on the other side of town. It tracked with what Tori overheard.

Deck ran his gaze down the rest of the body. The back of his left hand had a red mark, probably from the IV needle Suzie said she inserted. A tiny red spot on his left biceps caught Deck's attention. He was no medical examiner, but that sure looked like an injection site. It also backed up what Tori had said, that Sanchez had been given something. Something *not* reflected in his chart.

"I'd like to see his personal belongings."

"Thought you might." The attendant went to a side table and handed Deck a large envelope. "His clothes are in a separate bag."

Deck emptied the envelope onto one of the empty trollies. A brown wallet, a set of keys, and a crucifix clattered onto the metal surface. After sifting through the man's ID cards and a few family photos, he stuffed the items back into the envelope. Nothing had jumped out at him as being a reason Sanchez had to die, nor was there anything obvious connecting him to the North Metro medical staff.

Whatever Sanchez died for, he needed to find out. Based on Tori's message, FCI Sheridan could be the key.

Topside in the parking lot, Deck looked for Brett and Evan's SUVs, but they hadn't arrived yet. As much as he'd prayed Tori's car had miraculously reappeared while he'd been inside, it hadn't. *I'm at work.* That's what she'd said, and she'd wanted him to call her back. So where had she gone, and why wasn't she answering his calls? The only answer that came to mind wasn't good.

She was in trouble.

He grabbed a flashlight from his SUV then leashed up Thor and let him out. Thor wasn't a trained SAR K-9 like Evan's dog, Blue, but he liked Tori. Hoping he was right about this, he snagged the sweater and held it in front of Thor's nose for the dog to sniff. "Find her, boy. Find Tori."

Thor snorted as Deck led him over to the row of

doctors' spaces. His dog put his nose to the pavement, making sniffing sounds as he searched for Tori's scent. Thor led Deck down the row of cars, circling twice then heading in a straight line to an empty spot. A silver Celica was parked to the left and a blue Nissan to the right.

Thor sniffed louder as he searched the area immediately to the left of the Nissan. When Thor lay down on the pavement, Deck shined the beam of his flashlight between Thor's paws. Something shiny glinted up at him.

Tori's charm bracelet.

He picked it up, letting the delicate piece of jewelry dangle from his fingers. She had been there. He shielded his eyes from the overhead lighting then turned slowly in a three-sixty, searching the entire parking lot and its surroundings.

His phone buzzed with an email from Sammie. Attached were most of the lookups he'd asked for. Deck opened the first file, confirming his suspicion. Damon Sanchez spent two years and three months in FCI Sheridan. No arrests since getting released fifteen months ago.

Next, he opened up the file on Shibowsky. Negative criminal history. Two Ferraris registered in his name, one blue, one black, as he'd indicated. Shibowsky lived in a pricey section of Denver, and sure enough, one of his neighbors was Charles Batista, father to nineteen-year-old Leslie.

Dexter and Landry's records were also clean. Landry's brother, however, had a number of drug arrests a few years back but nothing recent. Deck still planned on interviewing Dexter and Landry. That left Barnett.

He opened up the next few files. Barnett had no

criminal history, not even a parking ticket. Barnett lived in Lakewood, not far from the hospital and on a direct route to Tori's house in Morrison. He scrolled to the DMV lookup Sammie had run. The doctor had one vehicle registered in his name. A blue Nissan. Just like the one parked beside what he suspected was Tori's vacated space.

Deck tried all the doors of the Nissan, not really expecting them to be open. Again, he let Thor sniff Tori's sweater then led him around the car. His dog didn't hit on the Nissan. He shined his flashlight through all the windows, searching for something that might tell him where Tori was. The interior was empty.

Two SUVs rolled into the lot and parked. Brett and Evan joined him by the trunk of the Nissan.

"What do you need?" Brett asked without preamble. His friends knew him well enough to understand that he didn't send out emergency texts near midnight without a good reason.

"Tori's missing." Thinking it had been one thing. Saying it out loud sent a shot of fear through his chest. "And oh yeah, someone who works at North Metro *may* be the Big D."

"You're kidding," Evan said in a disgusted voice.

"I wish I was. Stand by." He cued up Sammie's number, tapping his foot as he waited for her to pick up.

"Deck," Sammie answered. "I'm still working on the rest of Barnett's history. I should have it in—"

"I need you to put out two BOLOs," he interrupted. "One on Victoria Sampson and one on the red Subaru registered in her name."

"You got it." Deck heard Sammie's fingers flying across

her keyboard. "You need any backup?"

"Not yet." He looked at Brett and Evan. For now, he had all the backup he needed. "One more thing. Get me a phone number for Craig Sampson in Westminster. I'll wait."

Seconds ticked by, and Deck could feel his pulse kicking up. If this was a kidnapping, something he couldn't confirm, every minute was critical. Sensing his agitation, Thor leaned his body against Deck's leg and whined.

"Here you go."

As Sammie recited the number, Deck entered it directly into his phone, creating a contact. "Thanks, Sammie." He tapped the number. "Craig," he said when the man picked up. "This is Adam Decker, Tori's friend. I—"

"I remember you. How could I forget?" Craig's voice held a grim note of humor. "What can I do for you?"

"I'm looking for Tori. Is she there?" He held his breath, hoping he was wrong about this and praying for a miracle.

"No. She *was* here but left around three thirty. Should I be worried?"

Yes. "Is there any chance she's at her sister's?"

"I doubt it. She was going straight to work. I don't think she'd go to Margo's this late at night."

"Can you call her right now and find out? It's important."

A beat of silence then, "Hold on."

Deck clamped his teeth. Every second he waited was torture.

Craig came back on the line. "She's not there. What's going on?"

What to tell him when he wasn't even 100 percent certain? *The truth.* "She left the hospital mid-shift and no one's seen her. Could be nothing." Or she could be in deep trouble, as he suspected she was. "I've put out alerts with the police just to be sure. If I hear anything, I'll call you. Do the same and call me back at this number. If she contacts you or Margo, tell her to reach out to me immediately. I don't care what time it is."

"I will," Craig said in a concerned voice.

Deck ended the call. "Brett, I need you to go to Tori's house." He recited the address. "See if her car is there. It's a red Subaru. Search the place. I don't care if you have to break in. Let me know what you find."

"You got it." Brett went back to his SUV and peeled out of the lot.

To Evan, he said, "Go to Wil Barnett's house and do the same." He pulled up Barnett's address from Sammie's lookup. "If he's there, don't do anything. Just call me."

"Will do. Where are *you* going?"

"FCI Sheridan."

"You gonna tell Rivera?" Evan asked over his shoulder as he headed back to his SUV.

"Not yet." Not until he had something concrete. Deck loaded Thor into the kennel and took off for the prison.

All the signs pointed to Barnett, but he had no real proof. Not even the totality of the circumstances was enough to make an arrest, let alone convict the man.

His guts twisted into a ball of knots. If Tori had really discovered something that could bring Barnett down…

Deck hit the highway and slammed his foot on the accelerator.

CHAPTER THIRTY

Tori had been awake for several minutes but kept her eyes closed, pretending to still be asleep.

The air was even mustier than before. Every breath she took tasted like dirt. Wherever she was, it was cold and damp. Chills took hold, and she shivered.

Voices came to her, muffled and indistinct. Last night— or was it still tonight? She'd completely lost all perception of time. For all she knew, she'd been here for days. Then again, she couldn't recall needing to use the facilities. At some point, she'd have to take care of her basic needs.

She cracked open one eye then the other. Her vision was finally clear, but what she saw sent fear winding its way into that part of her brain that housed her panic button. Rock surrounded her. Not walls, more like a carved-out semi circle with a rock ceiling. The room she was in really *was* a cave.

Easing to her other side, she took in the rest of her surroundings. The only way in and out of the cave was a gate that looked sturdy and heavy enough to be in a bank vault.

She swallowed the scream racing up her throat then pushed to an upright position, intending to see if the gate truly was locked, but the room began to spin. Her head felt as if it were a buoy, bobbing helplessly in the ocean. She lay back down for a few minutes to let the effects of the drug wear off more. When she was ready, she gave it another go and sat up, slower this time.

Her mouth was dry, and when she ran her tongue over her teeth, they felt like cardboard. The musty scent was exactly like the air in Kartchner Caverns, a five hundred fifty–foot deep limestone cave she'd once visited in Southern Arizona.

Oh shit. The implications of her analogy smacked her in the face. She'd been kidnapped and imprisoned some-where deep underground. By whom, she still didn't know for certain.

No one knew where she was. She'd been leaving a message for Deck, but she'd been standing by her car outside the ER at the time. There was no way he could find her. Even *she* didn't know where she was.

Carefully, she pushed from the cot and stood. This time, the walls didn't move quite as much. She took a step toward the gate, nearly stumbling over a rock and reaching out for the only other piece of furniture—an old metal desk chair. After regaining her balance, she went to the gate and wrapped her hands around the bars.

Outside the gate and about ten feet to the right was an opening, possibly another room or another tunnel. Lighting was dim, coming only from two sets of fluorescent light fixtures hanging by chains in the rock ceiling. To the left of the gate was a three-foot-wide opening in the floor. An old wooden ladder stuck out from the top. Dead ahead was the room they'd passed when she'd been carried down here.

Four men wearing protective masks and gloves worked behind the thick plastic sheeting. Pressing her face closer, she tried getting a better look at what they were doing.

On one of the tables was a burner, set over which was a large frying pan. Beakers and glass measuring cups lined a shelf. The other table contained a stack of clear plastic briquettes filled with gray material. *Gray death*. No wonder the men wore PPE and the lab was protected by sheeting. If it were aerosolized, anyone inhaling it could easily take in a lethal dose.

Footsteps came to her ears, as if someone were coming down a set of stairs. A man she didn't recognize stopped outside the plastic curtain. He wore overalls, and she wondered if this was the infamous T-Lo. She'd only seen his mugshot from a distance. Another man, also wearing overalls and a mask, came from the lab. He whipped off the mask but kept his back to her.

The one she suspected was T-Lo shot her a disapproving glare. "You shouldn't have brought her here," he growled.

"Not your call to make," the man with his back to Tori said. "Just get to work."

At hearing the achingly familiar voice, nausea rolled through her.

Wil.

The other man strapped on a protective mask hanging on a hook in the wall. After grabbing a set of gloves from his pocket, he pushed through a cut in the plastic and went into the lab.

Bile rose in her throat as Wil turned to her, dangling a silver Thermos from his fingers. Even after finding the vial, her heart had refused to truly accept the possibility that Wil—her friend and confidante, a man she trusted implicitly—could have been the bad guy.

As he casually strolled toward her, as if her world hadn't

been thoroughly rocked, she forced herself to see it. To see *him*—a man she thought she knew but didn't. A man who'd consoled her during the darkest losses and celebrated her biggest saves. A man with whom she'd shared meals and laughs and stories as one of her closest friends.

But he *wasn't* her friend. No, the man approaching was the devil—the blood of all his victims on his hands, who'd killed Aidan, tried to kill Deck, and nearly killed *her*.

How could I have been so fooled?

She gripped the bars tighter, the cold metal digging into her palms and grounding Tori in her roiling anger. *Sonofabitch*. A few steps closer and she could wrap her hands around the bastard's neck.

"I'm glad you're awake."

When he smiled at her, she held back a slew of unholy words. "Don't you *dare* smile at me."

"We need to talk," he said, ignoring her outburst and holding out the Thermos. "I brought you some water. The air is pretty dusty down here. You probably want to rinse your mouth out. It's something we've all gotten used to."

"*Water*? You're holding me prisoner in an underground drug lab. Do you think I give a shit about *water* right now?"

He watched her a moment longer, as if he didn't know what to say. "I was hoping this moment would never come. Now that it has, you need to calm down and give me a chance to explain."

She let out an acidic laugh. "There's nothing to explain. You're a criminal who's killed God knows how many people—some of whom you and I tried to *save*—and you're holding me against my will. Let. Me. Go." She tried shaking the bars, but she could no sooner have moved a tractor trailer.

He shook his head. "Not until you hear me out."

"How can you possibly talk your way out of this?" Tori bit back the insults she wanted to hurl at him. Now that she knew who and what he was, how could he possibly let her go? Her only means of escape was through him. Inside, she was seething with enough molten rage to fuel a volcano, but she managed a measured, "Fine. Tell me."

"Back up, please," he said, "and sit on the cot."

When she did as he ordered, he pulled a large antique-looking key from the pocket of his overalls and inserted it into the lock. He opened the gate, then came in, keeping an eye on her over his shoulder as he relocked it. To keep from lunging at him, she sat on her hands.

He stopped a few feet from her, close enough so that she had to look up at him yet not quite close enough for her to kick him in the family jewels. *Too bad.* She was itching to give him exactly what he deserved.

Wil let out a heavy sigh then dragged the metal chair farther away from her. He swung it around, straddling it and resting his forearms on the top of the backrest.

"Where am I? What *is* this place?" She darted her eyes around the cave.

"My family used to own a big agricultural and mining co-op outside Fort Collins. We used to sell everything. Tools, fertilizer, seed, mining supplies. Explosives. After the big supply warehouses took over and the bunny-hugging environmentalists enacted so many restrictions on mining and farming, my family had to shut down the business. They couldn't even find a buyer for the place, and now most of the buildings above ground are falling down. We're in what's left of the underground explosives bunker. We used to lock everything up in this cave." He gave a quick nod to the gate.

The one she'd have to get through to escape.

"Now," he continued, brightening and proudly waving his hand in the air, "it's my personal laboratory."

"But why, Wil? Why are you doing this?" No matter which angle she considered any of this from, there was no justification he could come up with. "You're a doctor, but instead of helping people, you're hurting them. The drugs you're making in this lab are *killing* people."

Instead of answering her question directly, he looked around the cave as if he were searching for something that wasn't there. "I used to work here after school. I hated every second of it. My family was hoping I'd take it over one day, but this wasn't the life I was made for. Filling orders for farmers. Hauling sacks of manure." His lips twisted with disgust. "I wanted to make something of myself, make some *real* money, and have people look up to me, revere me. That's what I was born for."

"*Revere* you?" Tori snorted, having a hard time believing what she was hearing. "You're the head of emergency medicine at a respected hospital. How much more *revered* do you need to be?"

"It's not enough. Never was, never could be." He leveled her with an understanding gaze so familiar, it hurt. "We're more alike than you think, Tori."

Her eyes went wide. "We're nothing alike. How could you even say that?"

"Because like you, I had to work my way through college and med school. While all the other kids were out partying, I was bussing tables at a cheesesteak restaurant every night until midnight. Eventually, I hit a wall, started falling asleep in class. My grades started slipping, and I nearly flunked out. Then a miracle happened." He smiled broadly. "I met another student going through the same thing. He turned me on to speed to keep me awake, then pot so I could get to sleep. I realized there was a huge college market to be tapped, so I started a business. I could work a fraction of the time and make tons more money selling drugs than I ever could have bussing tables.

"After med school and finishing my residency," he continued, "I applied to all the major hospitals, but it seemed there was a glut of new doctors at the time. The only job I could get was at a prison, looking down inmates' throats and handing out aspirin." He made a derisive sound. "For years, I watched other people far less qualified than I was zoom up the ranks in all the prestigious hospitals around the country. Do you know how hard that was?"

Feeling as if he expected it, she shook her head.

"But," he added, raising his hand to point a finger in the air, "I had something they didn't. An affinity for chemistry and an inherent understanding of how drugs affect the human body."

When she couldn't contain her huff, he raised an eyebrow. "For the record, I *did* try helping people," he said. "The two years I worked at that prison, I created a drug that would have cut an opioid addict's rehab from months down to weeks. Big Pharma refused to take me on and let me test my drug on animals, let alone humans. I needed their financial backing, access to their testing facilities, and their name to back me up before the FDA would even look at my drug. Big Pharma refused to involve themselves in a treatment that would have saved countless lives, and you want to know why?"

A sick feeling crept through her. She knew where this was going, and worse, she understood that helpless feeling. Of wanting to help, but not being allowed to because of bureaucratic red tape. She'd seen it, watched her dad live with it.

"Because I was a threat to their bottom line." He stood and began pacing angrily around the cave. "These companies are making money on both ends, selling the addictive opioids *and* the naloxone to counter the inevitable overdoses. Of *course* they didn't want a drug out there that would make rehab easier and decrease the number of addicts. Hell no. Hypocritical assholes, all of them."

On that, she had to agree with him.

When he'd worked off his frustration, he sat again on the chair, staring at her with such an eerie calm it sent goose bumps racing up her back. "When God closes a door, He opens a window." The grin he made was more of a sneer. "I created a new drug, an opioid cocktail that far surpassed anything available by prescription. Working in a prison also provided great opportunities. A small lab. Test subjects."

Tori gaped. "You tested your drug on *inmates*?" In her head, she could hear Damon Sanchez's angry accusation. But Wil hadn't worked at Sheridan. Of that she was certain.

He shrugged. "They were more than willing."

"It was you they were after in Pennsylvania, wasn't it?"

He nodded. "I had a good thing going there. Unfortunately, the first generation of my drug was a bit too strong and left more than a few bodies in its wake. That's what caught the Feds' attention. Gray death has been around for years, but I made it better. This version is *my* creation. The best high money can buy." To her horror, his chest puffed up with pride.

Tori could only stare, dumfounded. The way he talked so nonchalantly about people dying from taking his drug...

"I had to close up shop. I moved back to Colorado, landed a job with a small hospital, and eventually at North Metro. Before starting things up again here, I had to tweak my formula so it didn't catch quite as much attention. In a way, maybe I should thank the Feds. They forced me to change. After all, if all my buyers overdosed, there'd be no repeat customers. It's a delicate balance, really, creating a drug that gives the most addictively amazing high without killing the recipient."

Tori shoved both hands into her hair, trying desperately to reconcile the monster in front of her with the intelligent, responsible, *ethical* doctor she thought she knew. "This doesn't make any sense."

"It *does*." He looked at her as if it were her that was crazy. "Those idiots, Maynard and Shibowsky, get to play God every day, and they don't have half the intelligence you or I do. They only *think* they're at the top of the food chain. They flaunt their fancy cars and shove their Rolexes in everyone's faces. What they don't know is that *I've* got better watches than they do. Did you know I own three Rolexes, two Tags, and a Patek Phillipe? Those morons don't even know what a Patek Phillipe is. It's worth more than all their watches combined. And their cars and big houses? I've got condos in Europe and the Caribbean. I've got garages crammed with better sports cars than they'll *ever* have the privilege of owning."

Tori couldn't believe her ears. Whatever insidious creature her friend had turned into was on a roll. It was a confession, of sorts. One that would take him straight to Hell. "What good is all that if no one knows you have them?"

He pointed to his chest. "*I* know. It's like buying a stolen Rembrandt and hiding it away in a special vault. No one will ever see it, but the person who has it knows, and that's what matters. Besides, when I'm out of the country, nobody knows me. It would be stupid to flaunt all that here with the DEA sniffing around. Only incompetent drug lords call attention to themselves."

Drug lord. That's how he really thought of himself—as the lord of everything and everyone around him. A superior one, no less. This went beyond greed and far surpassed the need to be better than anyone else. Wil was a sociopath, and sociopaths didn't care who they hurt on their path to success.

Sociopaths killed.

She narrowed her eyes. "You tried to kill Deck."

"Not at first."

"But you encouraged me to date him."

He shrugged. "Of course I did. What better way to keep tabs on the same fed who was investigating me? Your information about that warrant in Loveland was priceless."

"So you *did* tell the dealer that we were coming."

"I did." His expression softened like it had hundreds of times over the course of their friendship, and he leaned in just close enough to place a hand on her arm. She fought the urge to recoil. "Your relationship with Deck was incredibly useful to me, but I'm sorry you were hurt. You weren't supposed to be with him those nights. The first time T-Lo tried to kill Decker, I actually went to your house to check on you, but he was there. I waited for him to leave. I stuck around for a while." He grinned slyly. "Then I heard you screaming with what had to be one heck of an orgasm, so I figured you were okay."

"It was *you* outside my window." The person Deck had chased in the woods that night. She covered her mouth with her hand, so repulsed she wanted to throw up. And he'd known that she and Deck had been intimate before she'd even told him.

Again, he chuckled. He withdrew his hand and leaned back. "Yeah, sorry about that. Didn't mean to go all Peeping Tom on you, but it confirmed what I'd been hoping for. That you two were getting closer and if I was subtle enough I could keep getting more details from you about the DEA's investigation. Their investigation into *me*."

From the way his eyes glittered, it was obvious that having an entire federal agency after him hadn't scared him off. It had only served to stroke his ego. "You're crazy if you think you'll get away with this."

"Crazy?" He raised an eyebrow. "I'm anything but. This has become a highly successful business. A tax-free one, with the kind of income I *deserve*."

Deserve? Maybe Wil's complete and total lack of compassion over Damon Sanchez's death was just one of the signs she now realized she'd unwittingly missed.

"Damon Sanchez didn't die of a heart attack, did he?" She knew the answer to her question, had held the vial in her hands, but needed to hear him say it.

"No."

Horror dawned. "You've been working at the prison here, too?"

A smile spread across his face. "Do you remember those times I said I was going skiing with an old med school buddy?"

She *did* remember. It was last year, in early spring. Another of Wil's vacations.

"I was actually filling in for that friend at the prison. When I moved back, I left my distribution network behind. I knew I'd find what I needed here in prison."

"T-Lo."

"Yes, T-Lo. And I needed to test my new formula. That's probably where Sanchez and I met." Wil chuckled. "I didn't even remember him. The version he received was probably one I tested early on. That one was...stronger than I intended."

She gaped at him. How could he find any of this amusing? How was this the same man who used to make her laugh at his jokes or who'd held her hand when Mike had moved away? All she saw was an evil, mad scientist, and it made her stomach roll with disgust. "How were you able to experiment on prisoners and get away with it?"

"Generally speaking, prison inmates are a population that nobody cares about. Even the warden. A few bucks under the table was all it took to buy the man's silence." He reached into his pocket and tugged out a small cylindrical glass bottle filled with gray powder. "This is the last of my first-gen cocktail. I keep this little baby for posterity, so I can remember how it all got started." He held up the bottle, grinning as if he'd been inventing a cure for cancer, not creating an illicit drug that killed people.

Tori jerked back, not wanting to be anywhere near the stuff. This was worse than any nightmare. "Deck will figure this out. I left him a message, telling him what happened in the ER tonight and to look into Sanchez's death. He'll find me." Even as she said the words, she didn't know exactly *how* he'd find her, but she had to have faith.

He stuffed the bottle back into the pocket of his coveralls, looking thoughtful. "You know, I've always liked you, Tori. If I was ever going to get married, it would be to someone like you. But I could never let anyone get that close, and you're too smart. There was only one person who ever suspected anything, and that was a complete fluke. Mike."

"Mike?" As in, the doctor she'd dated?

Wil nodded. "He saw me one night in Fort Collins talking to T-Lo. Just a coincidence, but I had to get rid of him. I thought about killing him, but that's messy, too close to home. It was easier and cleaner to get him booted from North Metro."

"What? How?" She'd always thought Mike was just a victim of North Metro's ruthless administrators.

"I altered a few records then dropped a little bug in the hospital board's ears. Being the head of the ER, they listened. Two days later, Mike resigned in lieu of being fired."

She stared, wide-eyed. Yet another clue she'd missed.

"Things are getting too hot again. Soon, I'll have to leave Denver." Abruptly, he stood then knelt before her, taking her limp hands surprisingly gently in his. "Come with me.

We can start over somewhere else."

She jerked her hands away. He must be out of his mind if he thought she could ever excuse all the heinous crimes he'd committed. It took everything she had to swallow the vile words threatening to escape. The last thing she needed was to piss him off.

"Think about it." Without another word, he stood and went to the gate, unlocking it then turning around. "You're a good person. Good people wear their hearts on their sleeves. Whatever you decide, if you're lying…I'll know it. I know *you*, Tori."

The gate clanged shut behind him, and he turned the key, leaving her to digest her horrible reality. While she'd been in the dark about his true character, Wil *did* know her. Convincing him she'd consider his offer would never work. He was right. The only possible way out of this was to stall long enough for Deck to find her.

Otherwise, Wil would have no alternative but to kill her.

CHAPTER THIRTY-ONE

Deck placed his weapon in the secure lock box and pocketed the key. As usual, Thor wasn't too happy at being left in the SUV again. Given that Deck had been on medical leave for nearly two months and technically still was, his dog hadn't been working, either, and was bouncing off the walls of his kennel. This time, Thor had actually growled his frustration.

A Federal Bureau of Prisons guard led him down a gray corridor to meet the physician on call, Dr. Shuren. The walk seemed to take forever.

FCI Sheridan was a low-security federal correctional institution with a satellite prison camp and housed nearly two thousand male inmates. At each locked gate, Deck waited while the guard unlocked it then re-secured it after they'd gone through. Finally, they stopped at a door with a sign on it that read Health Services.

The guard knocked, and a moment later, the door opened. A tall man of about forty, with blond hair and wearing a white doctor's coat, stood on the other side. Dr. Shuren, he presumed.

"Special Agent Decker?" the doctor asked.

"Yes."

"Come in."

"I'll wait here for you," the guard said, following prison protocol by leaving no visitor—even a federal agent—unescorted.

Deck followed the doctor through a small reception area and into an office.

"Have a seat." Dr. Shuren indicated a metal chair then sat in a fancy leather rolling one on the other side of the desk. "I printed out Damon Sanchez's medical file for you." He handed a manila folder to Deck.

As he reached for the folder with his right hand, a twinge of pain shot to his shoulder. He began flipping through the pages in the folder, trying to make sense of all the medical jargon. "Sanchez was only thirty-five, but he had heart arrhythmia." Confirming what was in Sanchez's records Suzie had pulled up for him back at North Metro.

"Yes," Shuren said. "We get so many inmates passing through here, I can't remember all of them, but I reviewed the folder before you arrived. He was diagnosed with arrhythmia, but it never gave him any problems, at least not while he was incarcerated here. Sanchez was young and in good health."

Yet the man was dead. "Did he ever come to you for anything else?"

Dr. Shuren shook his head and pointed to his computer screen. "I didn't administer them, but his records show he came in for allergy shots during the height of pollen season."

"When was his last one?"

Shuren looked back at the screen. "About fifteen months ago, right before he was released."

Deck felt he was on the brink of figuring this out but still missing an important piece of the puzzle and didn't know which line of questioning would help him find it.

"You said you didn't administer allergy shots to Sanchez. Who did?"

"There are two other doctors on staff here. Drs. Medici and Stollen. We each work an eight-hour shift, but I wasn't on call that day."

Deck continued flipping through the pages. Sanchez's last allergy shot was administered by—

He had to read the name twice to be sure.

Dr. W. Barnett.

In her message, Tori said she overheard Sanchez accuse two doctors of giving him something that nearly killed him in Sheridan. This could be the missing piece he was looking for.

"Why is there a different doctor listed as having given Sanchez his last allergy shot?" When Shuren raised his brows in question, Deck added, "It says here the shot was given to him by Dr. W. Barnett. Not by Medici or Stollen."

"Oh, I forgot." Relief washed over his face. "If one of us takes a vacation and we can't get coverage from either of the other two physicians for some reason, we all have qualified prison fill-in doctors we can count on."

"Who did Dr. Barnett fill in for that day?"

"Me. During the timeframe we're talking about, I went up to Copper Mountain for a long weekend ski trip."

Maybe he was missing something, but an ER position seemed like a prestigious gig. Filling in at a prison every now and then seemed like a step down. "How did Dr. Barnett find out about these fill-in opportunities?"

"Wil Barnett and I went to med school together at U Penn. One of his first jobs was at a prison outside Philadelphia. He worked there for years." Shuren shook his head and laughed. "I never understood why, but even after he landed the ER position at North Metro, Wil still made a point of saying that he was always available to fill in. He'd even send me occasional emails as a reminder."

So Barnett had a history in Pennsylvania where the DEA had been investigating an opioid dealer who'd vanished. Interesting, but circumstantial. Sounded like Barnett had an ulterior motive for wanting to fill in at the prison. *Like experimenting on prisoners?* It sounded farfetched, but it was a possibility he had to consider. Whatever he'd injected Sanchez with, it sounded as if the guy either hadn't consented or hadn't known what it would do to him.

Again, he thought back to Tori's voicemail. "Has anyone ever had an adverse reaction to an allergy shot?" he asked.

"I suppose it's possible, but I'm not aware of an inmate here having had such a reaction."

"If Sanchez had a bad reaction to a vaccination, would it be here in his records?"

"Of course. We document everything. There are no secrets here."

Deck couldn't stop from arching a brow. Prisons held as many secrets as the Pentagon. He returned his attention to the last few pages in the folder and reread the last line twice.

Sanchez may not have had a bad reaction to an allergy shot, but on the same day as that last shot, he overdosed. An *opioid* overdose.

He tapped the record he was looking at. "It says here that Sanchez was treated for an opioid overdose right after he received his last allergy shot." But the man's criminal record indicated he'd been imprisoned for car theft and burglary. There was no history of drug use or distribution.

Shuren nodded. "There was a time last year when we experienced an unusual number of overdose cases."

"How many?"

"Oh," he said, waving his hand in a dismissive gesture, "just a few." The doctor's Adam's apple bobbed as he swallowed repeatedly.

He's hiding something. Deck was sure of it.

What if Sanchez was one of Barnett's first test subjects, but Sanchez's reaction was so severe that Barnett realized he couldn't disguise his cocktail as an allergy shot and keep getting away with it?

They wouldn't know until the autopsy what Barnett had injected into Sanchez at North Metro. As for what he gave Sanchez here in the prison, Deck would bet his left nut it was gray death. Or something like it.

"Can you pull up a record of all the inmates Barnett saw here?"

Shuren frowned. "I thought the problem was with Sanchez, not Dr. Barnett."

"It is." A half truth. "And if you're worried about violating HIPAA law, may I remind you that the law allows correctional facilities to disseminate protected health information to a law enforcement officer for the purpose of preventing a serious and imminent threat to the health and safety of the public which, I'm telling you, this is."

Shuren hesitated a moment longer then started clicking away on his keyboard. "Here's the list. It's broken down by inmate, date, reason for examination, diagnosis, and treatment, if any." He swiveled the monitor so Deck could look at it.

Over the last sixteen months, Barnett saw nearly fifty patients for a multitude of reasons running the gamut from headaches, allergy shots, and diarrhea, to broken bones and knife wounds. And four of the inmates seen by Barnett were deceased, cause of death: opioid overdose.

Deck took a minute to compare all the death dates to the dates that Barnett was on call at the prison. Two died on the same day they'd come in to see Barnett. The other two had overdosed on days Barnett wasn't even there. If Barnett really was using the prison as his own personal test laboratory, he'd be smart enough not to leave an obvious trail of bread crumbs.

Now to uncover the hidden trail.

"You said there was a time last year that Sheridan experienced an unusual number of overdoses." Deck knew that would get Shuren riled up, and it did. The doctor began squirming in his chair like a kid who knew he's in trouble and was about to get reamed out. "How many were there, exactly?"

"Uh." Shuren cleared his throat. "Nine."

"And four of them died," Deck reminded. "Isn't that a lot of deaths and overdoses for one prison in a year?"

Shuren sat back and crossed his arms. "Well, yes. But you know as well as I do that inmates have their own economy inside a prison, just like on the outside world. No matter how efficient our security, all kinds of goods, including drugs, are smuggled in here all the time. Whatever it was must have been extremely potent."

"Did you report all these overdoses and deaths?" Deck already knew he hadn't. When nine inmates in a federal prison OD'd, the DEA should have been notified and an external investigation would have kicked off. Deck wasn't aware of that having happened. Whenever an inmate died for any reason, a death review was initiated.

"No." Shuren scoffed. "As I said, drugs get smuggled in here all the time. We can't stop it. We figure a bad batch made its way inside, something stronger than heroin. The average user isn't accustomed to such potency, so they take more than they need to get the high they're used to."

"I know how it works, Doc." He fisted his hand, crumpling a corner of the manila folder in his lap.

"Scroll to the next page," he ordered Shuren.

The doctor made a disgruntled sound. "Agent Decker, I think we're at the point where I need DEA authorization in writing for this inquiry."

"Think again, Dr. Shuren." He leaned forward, smacking the folder on the desk and taking pleasure in seeing the man flinch. "This prison is within federal jurisdiction. These ODs and deaths should have been reported, and you know it. I suggest you tell me everything I want to know. There'll be an internal *and* external investigation. You may not survive it." Fear emanated from the man's eyes, and Deck knew he had him. "Keep scrolling. I want to see the *entire* list of inmates Barnett treated."

He didn't know exactly what he was looking for at this point, but all the circumstantial evidence in the world wouldn't get him an arrest warrant. If there was something else in the records he could actually use, he couldn't leave any stone unturned.

Shuren took a deep breath then loosened his tie. Deck sensed the man was about to crap his pants. He used the mouse to keep scrolling. More inmate names populated the page.

"Stop!" Deck stared at one of the names that had popped up.

Timothy Lomax aka T-Lo had not only been incarcerated at FCI Sheridan, but he'd been treated by Dr. W. Barnett on multiple occasions. Allergy shots, headaches, a stubbed toe. *Stubbed toe my ass.*

Deck counted all the entries. In all, T-Lo had been to the health unit more than fifteen times over a twelve-month period and only on days when Barnett was there.

Working quickly in his head, Deck ran backward through the timeline.

The first date T-Lo had seen Barnett had been only a few days after Barnett gave Sanchez the suspect allergy shot. Each of the nine inmates who overdosed did so only after T-Lo began coming into the health unit.

More pieces of the puzzle fell into place, but it was still only circumstantial.

Barnett could have struck a deal with T-Lo to distribute gray death to inmates who were only too happy to receive the free high that came with it. That way, the source of the drug could never be traced directly back to Barnett, but he'd still be close by to monitor the drug's effects and perfect his dosage as needed.

Deck already knew T-Lo had been released from prison four months ago, plenty of time to reactivate his outside distribution network.

"Print that." He pointed to the screen, and as soon as the page spewed from the printer on Shuren's desk, Deck shoved it in the manila folder and was out the door. "I'm done," he said to the guard.

After retrieving his weapon from the lock box, he ran to his SUV and unlocked the door. Thor stuck his head through the kennel window, watching Deck slide onto the seat then staring at the manila folder, as if he knew it contained something critical.

Deck's phone had been on vibrate while he'd been inside the prison, so he would have felt any incoming messages, voice, text, or otherwise. Regardless, he checked the screen, still hoping for a message from Tori. Nothing. He cued up her number and hit the call button. It went right to voicemail. "Shit."

The second he dropped his phone into the console, it rang.

Brett's name lit the screen, and he hesitated before answering. What if Brett was calling with bad news? That he'd found Tori's body. Taking an unsteady breath, he answered the call. "Brett, anything?"

"Nada. I found a way inside Tori's house. It's empty, and there's no car in her driveway or garage. Neighbors haven't seen her."

Deck breathed a little easier. It wasn't confirmation that she was alive, but for now, he'd take it. His phone vibrated with another incoming call from Evan. "Hold on," he said. "I'm conferencing in Evan." He tapped the screen to get the conference call going. "Go ahead, Evan. Brett's here, too. She's not at her house."

"She's not at Barnett's, either," Evan said. "No one is. The house is empty, and so is the garage."

"Wherever he took her, they might have taken Tori's car." The key word being *wherever*. There'd been no response to any of his BOLOs.

"Find out anything at the prison?" Brett asked.

"Yeah. Barnett did some work here on the side filling in for prison doctors on vacation. I think he was using inmates as lab rats, experimenting on them to perfect his recipe. Last year, nine inmates OD'd and four died."

Brett whistled. "I never heard about that in the news."

"That's because the prison kept it quiet. But here's the interesting thing. T-Lo was incarcerated at FCI Sheridan while this was all happening. He came to see Barnett at least fifteen times in the med unit."

"That can't be a coincidence," Evan said.

"Exactly. Being a doctor, Barnett might have the skills to whip up a super-potent opioid cocktail like the one we're chasing, but he wouldn't have the network to sell it. He'd need a distributor, someone who has contacts on the street."

"Like T-Lo," Brett stated the obvious.

"T-Lo went to prison for distribution of heroin and cocaine. He's got the connections, the street smarts, and knows all the other dealers."

"And being Barnett's assassin," Evan added, reminding them all of just how deadly this partnership really was.

"Probably not enough for a warrant," Brett stated what Deck already knew.

"True that. Even if it was, we don't know where the sonofabitch is."

Deck's phone buzzed again, this time with an email and a text from Sammie.

Finished the background checks you asked for. Emailed you the reports. Standing by if you need anything else.

"Stand by," he said to his friends and opened up the email.

Attached were a series of files on Ethan Dexter, Neil Shibowsky, David Landry, and Barnett. With what he'd just learned at FCI Sheridan, Deck went right to Barnett's supplemental database lookups. Barnett's medical credentials confirmed that he did his undergrad and med school at U Penn.

The next two files contained personal and family history. William Barnett, age thirty-eight, born in St. Joseph's Hospital in Denver. One older sister, Elizabeth, living in California. This was getting him nowhere and no closer to finding Tori. He was about to tap the file closed when the last paragraph of the printout caught his eye. *Properties Owned*. In addition to his condo in Lakewood, Barnett was co-owner with his sister of Barnett's Ag & Mining Co-op, located on Poudre Canyon Road in Fort Collins. The place closed down over twenty years ago. Fort Collins was over an hour—

North.

He stared a moment longer at the screen. How many times had he heard the Big D aka "the doc" came from somewhere *up north*?

Deck didn't have a search warrant and wasn't about to wait for one. "Brett, Evan, meet me in Fort Collins." He recited the address. "It's an old co-op. Wait on the street and we'll go in together."

"Are you calling in for more backup?" Brett asked.

Deck fisted his hand on the wheel. Not even the mile-high stack of circumstantial evidence in his back pocket would get him a warrant.

"Not yet." He hit the gas, the SUV's tires squealing as he turned onto the main road. "I still don't have probable cause, and Rivera will only tell us to stand down." That was something Deck could never do, not with Tori's life at stake. If that fucker hurt her, he'd administer his own personal brand of tough justice and smash him head first into the ground.

As soon as he merged onto I-25, he hit the strobes and punched it, speeding north toward Fort Collins. If he had to bust in there like John Wayne, so help him God, he'd do it.

CHAPTER THIRTY-TWO

Wil came back into the cave, locking the gate after him and stuffing the old key in his pocket. Stalling for time was the plan. It was all she could hope for.

He stared at her for a moment then sighed. Shockingly, he actually appeared sad. "I knew you wouldn't go for it. You *are* too good a person. Too moral and ethical. We could have been a good team."

A team. Never a loving couple. "So this is why you've never been in a relationship the entire time I've known you and why you never talked about getting married. You don't have it in you to love anyone but yourself. *You're* the center of your own universe. There's no room for anyone else."

"You're probably right," he agreed, nodding. "Although with you I would have at least tried."

Was that supposed to be a compliment?

A burst of rage welled up inside her, but she held it in. "Well, doesn't that make me feel special? A drug dealer wants me to run away with him and pretend that he hasn't killed people, hasn't created an awful drug just to fill his wallet and feed his God complex."

Instead of getting angry with her deliberately hurtful words, he merely shoved his hands into his pockets. "It's too bad you had to find out. There's nothing I can do to change that now." He pulled the key from his coveralls. "We're shutting down this base of operations and taking this show out of state." He unlocked the gate and stepped outside.

"Wait!" She rushed the gate, getting there just as he locked it. "What about me?"

"Well," he began, stroking his chin, "despite the homicidal tendencies you accuse me of having, I've never actually killed anyone. Not directly, that is, and as heartless as you may think I am, I don't have it in me to kill you. Again, not directly. I imagine you can keep going for a while without food or water. Eventually, you'll die."

Was this really happening? She stared at him in disbelief, her limbs going so numb that she sank to her knees on the dirt floor.

She watched Wil turn his back on her and walk away, continuing to stare as he parted the plastic curtain and joined T-Lo and the other men in the lab.

He really was abandoning her to die.

There had to be a way out of this mess. *Think*. First and foremost, she had to stay alive as long as possible. Deck would eventually figure out Wil was the target he'd been hunting all this time. But would it be in time to save her?

She stood and began searching the floor for something she could use as a weapon, a rock or an old nail, but there was nothing. Quietly, she stepped to the gate. Through the bars, she saw Wil, T-Lo, and the other men filling bags in the lab, heard their muffled voices. She went back to the cot and flipped over the mattress, shaking it. The bed was old, held together by filthy, rusty springs.

Her pulse raced as she tugged at the end of one of the coiled wire springs. Despite being old, the metal was still strong. She gave a strong tug until one of the coils broke with a loud snap. She held her breath, hoping no one had heard the noise. After ten seconds, no one came.

The spring in her hand was sharp at one end. Glancing over her shoulder to reverify no one was there, she pocketed the spring then went back to the gate. Gouging Wil's eyes out sounded gross, but if it got her that key…

The voices grew louder now. One of the men behind the curtain used aggressive hand gestures. They pushed through the plastic curtain, the first man gesturing for the other to follow. When the curtain closed behind them, they tore off their masks.

The man she thought was T-Lo advanced on Wil until they were almost nose to nose. "By bringing her here, you made her a witness. Now, you have to kill her."

"What I do with her is not your business. In fact, you'd do well to remember just whose business this is. Mine. *You* work for *me*."

"If you don't kill her, I will."

"Touch her, and you'll die." Wil's voice sounded deadly, and she believed him.

"What's the difference if you're going to leave her here, anyway?"

Wil's hands clenched into fists. "Get back in the lab and keep packing up."

The two other men stopped what they were doing then came through the plastic to stand on either side of T-Lo. This was a power play, and it was obvious that the two other men had allegiance to T-Lo, not Wil. Wil might be running the show, but it was three against one.

For a moment, Tori wasn't sure who was about to punch whose lights out. T-Lo's lip curled back like a feral dog's, but he turned and put his mask back on, pushing through the plastic curtain and indicating the others should follow.

When Wil began walking back toward the cave, hope blossomed in her heart. Had he changed his mind about leaving her here? But the cold, dispassionate look on his face told a different story.

Over his shoulder, she glimpsed the plastic curtain ripple as T-Lo and the other two men slipped from the lab to follow Wil.

"I'm sorry," he said. "I guess this is good b—"

T-Lo raised a metal pipe high over his shoulder.

"Wil, look out!"

Wil spun and held up his hands, but he wasn't fast enough. The metal bar crashed down on the side of Wil's head. He staggered a few feet from the gate, then crumpled to the dirt, landing face down next to the ladder sticking up from the hole. Blood seeped from a gash on the side of his head. He didn't move.

Tori jerked on the bars, knowing her efforts were useless. The old metal gate had to be made of solid wrought iron and would probably remain intact for the next two hundred years.

T-Lo rushed the gate, and she jumped back. The look he sent her was so ugly, so filled with malevolence it made her stomach lurch.

"Aren't you going to kill her?" one of T-Lo's buddies asked as he came up behind him.

"Oh, yeah." He turned and sneered at the other men. "We'll burn this place out. She won't last five minutes."

Laughing, all three of them returned to the lab.

Tori's heart leaped into her throat. If they set everything on fire, the oxygen would be eaten up within minutes.

On a scale of one to ten, one being the worst, her situation had just plummeted into negative numbers.

She backed away from the gate until her legs hit the cot. The springs squeaked as she all but fell onto the mattress. She tugged the edges of her coat as tightly around her body as possible, as if it could actually keep her safe.

Outside the gate, Wil remained motionless. Despite everything he'd done, the doctor in her wanted to help him and tend to his injuries. The woman in her wanted to bash his head in again. It was because of him that she was in this mess in the first place. She never imagined her life would end this way, but she had to face facts.

She was going to die down here.

All the mistakes she'd ever made in her life came rushing back in a useless tidal wave of regret. Starting and ending with Deck.

If he were standing in front of her right now…if this was her final chance to tell him how she really felt, she wouldn't hesitate.

I'd tell him I love him.

She lay down on the cot, hugging her knees to her chest. Tears slid down her cheeks. She'd never get the chance to say it to his face, so she might as well say it now. Before it was too late.

Knowing he would never hear the words, she whispered them anyway. "Deck, I love you."

CHAPTER THIRTY-THREE

"Cut your lights," Deck said into the mic.

Three sets of headlights went dark as they turned off Poudre Canyon Road into the abandoned co-op property. Deck led the way, with Brett and Evan's SUVs not far behind. The only illumination came from what was left of the quarter moon glowing in the sky overhead.

Dark shadows loomed in front of them, the skeletons of old outbuildings and sheds, most of which had either collapsed or looked about to any second. During the drive north, Sammie had researched the place for Deck. The co-op was comprised of over thirty acres, with many of the structures along the furthest edges of the property.

Long before Deck braked to a stop, Thor was prancing agitatedly in the kennel. His dog had already picked up on something. Drugs, most likely, considering that was his expertise. He parked and got out, meeting Brett and Evan at the hood of his SUV.

"There's something in the air here." Brett pointed to his ATF vehicle. "Blaze is going nuts back there." The truck rocked as Brett's big Chesapeake Bay Retriever stalked back and forth in his kennel. "You said this was an old ag-mining co-op, right? Could be explosive residue. Nitro, maybe."

"Great," Deck muttered. As if deadly opioids weren't enough. "Grab your dogs, respirators, and long guns."

"Do you have anything of Tori's for Blue to catch a scent

from?" Evan asked.

He nodded. Evan's German shepherd was one of the top SAR dogs in the state. "Thor knows her scent, too. If she's here, they'll find her."

He unlocked his shotgun from the carrier between the seats then leashed up Thor. After hooking a flashlight and a respirator on his belt, he racked the slide on the shotgun, charging the weapon and making it battle-ready.

Deck held Tori's sweater out for Thor and Blue to sniff, then they moved out.

Neither dog seemed to be on a track, so they headed for the largest building still standing and that had probably been the main storefront at one time. They circled the building, with neither Blue nor Thor hitting on anything.

Deck lifted his chin toward the next building, a small shed off to the side. As they neared the door, neither dog scented a track. He dropped Thor's leash and they all raised the muzzles of their shotguns. Deck pulled on the handle. The door opened with a rusty squeal. He shined his flashlight inside, but the shed was empty, save for some rotting bags of grain and a few mice that scurried away and disappeared through a hole in the rotting floor.

"Let's hit the next one," he whispered, picking up Thor's leash and indicating a large aluminum building twenty feet away, one that looked like a garage.

They hadn't gone five feet when both Thor and Blue began pulling hard on their leashes. Both dogs were on a hot track. Since Blue wasn't a drug dog, chances were they were scenting a human. *Tori.*

Deck followed his dog. As before, Brett and Evan covered him as he pulled on the handle, sliding the door open along its metal track. He released Thor and aimed the shotgun inside. The first car he recognized was Tori's Subaru. To the right of the Subaru was a black Maserati, to the left a Dodge Durango. Thor and Blue each went to a different side of the Subaru, rising on their hind legs and pawing at the windows.

"Light it up." With the shotgun aimed in, Deck waited for his friends to shine their flashlights into Tori's car. He yanked open the driver's side door. Thor nudged his head past Deck's leg, sniffing the front seat. On the seat was a cell phone. Beside the phone was a battery.

While Brett and Evan shined their flashlights into the other vehicles, Deck slung the shotgun strap over his shoulder and inserted the battery back into the phone on the seat. After it booted back up, he cued up Tori's number on his own phone. Seconds later, the phone lit up and rang. He ended the call then searched the interior of the car, finding nothing.

"The Maserati's empty," Evan confirmed, tightening his grip on Blue.

"Nothing in this one," Brett said, shutting the door of the rusty Durango, "except beer cans and a few cigarette stubs. No registration papers."

"Trunk." Deck indicated the Subaru and waited for his friends to cover the trunk. He pulled the lever beneath the steering wheel and heard a *click*. Evan flipped up the trunk then gave a quick shake of his head.

Deck looked inside. The only things in there were a cardboard box containing windshield wiper fluid, a snow scraper, and Tori's black medical bag. Quietly, he eased the trunk closed.

Thor dragged Deck back to the passenger side of the Subaru. He opened the door, and his dog sat, indicating this was the strongest scent and most likely where Tori had been last. In the passenger seat, not the driver's seat.

Next, he went to the Durango. It had been a pickup truck that had run him down in Commons Park. After T-Lo had shot at him and Tori that night on Alameda Avenue, Lakewood PD did a full background on the guy. Lomax owned a Durango. Deck shined his flashlight on the front of the truck. Someone had removed the tags, but a sizeable dent graced the right front bumper, possibly made by his shoulder, which was aching again like a mother.

Beside Brett, Blaze whined and stomped his front feet. "I'm telling you, Deck, Blaze is picking up something else here."

Deck understood Brett's warning. Somewhere in their vicinity were either fire residue, explosives, or both. But Thor hadn't picked up a drug scent. Yet.

"Stand by," he said then called Sammie.

"Whatdya need, Deck?"

"Two vehicle lookups." He recited the tag number on the Maserati, then shined his flashlight on the Durango's VIN, giving Sammie that number, as well.

Quick tapping came through the phone. "The Maserati is registered to Barnett's Ag & Mining Co-op."

"And the Durango?"

More tapping. "The Durango is registered to Timothy Lomax."

Gotcha, motherfucker. "Is the registration current?"

"Ten-four."

"Copy that. Thanks." He ended the call. "This is T-Lo's truck."

"PC?" Evan raised his brows.

Damn right, it gave them probable cause. He worked through the evidence at light speed. "There's an outstanding arrest warrant for him, and his vehicle is parked—*hidden*—on this property. It doesn't give us PC to search the place for Barnett or evidence of drugs, but it *does* give us PC to search for a wanted felon." One who'd tried to murder Deck.

First, Deck called ASAC Rivera, leaving a message when it went to voicemail. Next, he called the local PD, requesting immediate backup to search for a wanted homicide suspect. Given what they might be walking into, he also requested an ambulance.

"So what are we waiting for?" Brett asked when Deck had hung up.

"Not a damn thing." He charged from the garage, letting Thor and Blue lead the way.

Both dogs immediately picked up a hot track, leading them directly to another building ten feet behind the garage. This one was small, not even a building, really. Thor sat, a classic sign that he'd just hit on narcotics. Deck shined his flashlight on the door, which was slightly ajar and looked to be made of iron.

Blaze growled then sat just as Deck reached for the handle.

"Wait!" Brett whispered harshly, grabbing his arm. "This isn't a building."

"Then what is it?" Right now, he didn't care. The only thing that mattered was that Tori was here, and she didn't come of her own free will.

"It's the entry to an old underground explosives bunker," Brett said, still keeping his voice low. "Back in the day, this was where mining companies and co-ops that sold explosives had to store dynamite, TNT, and det cord. Blaze is hitting like crazy on something. Could be remnants, could be live material. Just saying we need to keep that in mind."

"Noted." Deck gave his friend a quick nod, thankful for his expertise. Again, he reached for the handle.

Footsteps filtered through the crack in the door.

"Get back," he whispered.

Not wanting them to get caught in a barrage of bullets, they quickly downed their dogs, who flattened their bodies to the ground.

Three shotguns leveled at the door as it slowly swung open.

CHAPTER THIRTY-FOUR

Voices cut through Tori's misery. She rolled off the cot and went to the gate. Wil still lay motionless next to the open hole in the dirt floor. His chest rose and fell. Most likely, he had a concussion, possibly a fractured skull.

T-Lo and another man were talking outside the lab. The other guy headed around a corner, slinging a backpack over his shoulder before disappearing from her view. They were packing up.

She pressed her forehead against the bars and shut her eyes. Soon, they'd leave, but not before setting fire to the place.

"Deck, please," she whispered. *Find me*. But how could he?

Still gripping the wrought-iron bars, she sank to her knees, staring at the dirt floor. A whisper of sound caught her attention.

Wil's leg twitched.

Tori straightened, flicking her eyes to the lab to see T-Lo and the other man go back through the plastic curtain.

"Wil," she whispered, reaching through the bars to grab the tip of his boot, shaking it. "Wil, wake up!" Given that T-Lo planned to let Wil die down here with her, maybe if he woke up, he'd change his mind and help them *both* escape. She doubted it, but it was her only shot of getting out of this alive.

She shook him again. He didn't budge, but her efforts had shifted his leg to reveal something half buried in the dirt beside his left hip.

The key.

It must have slipped from his pocket.

Keeping one eye on the lab, she stretched her arm through the bars, straining to reach it, but it was too far away. Taking a deep breath, she all but rammed her shoulder through the bars, shimmying to extend her reach enough to grab the key.

When the other man came from the lab, she yanked back her arm, hoping he hadn't seen what she was trying to do. After he'd disappeared in the direction of the first guy, she took an even deeper breath and closed her eyes as she shoved her arm even farther through the bars.

"Nice try." T-Lo slammed his boot on top of her hand.

She winced, trying to yank her hand back, but he ground his boot down harder on her fingers. She gritted her teeth, refusing to give him the satisfaction of crying out.

T-Lo picked up the key then lifted his boot from her hand. As she sat there, cradling her crushed fingers, he smiled, revealing uneven, yellowing teeth. "Enjoy your stay in Hotel Gray Death." He held his arm over the opening in the floor.

"No!" she cried then watched helplessly as he dropped the key into the hole.

Another man came over and grabbed T-Lo's shoulder. "We gotta go. *Now*. Once we light the fuse and it hits the gas tanks, we need to be somewhere else. Know what I'm saying?"

They were going to blow the place up. *With me in it*.

"Wait!" She rushed to the cell door, grabbing the bars.

"Sorry, sweetheart. But don't worry. As soon as the tanks blow, you won't feel a thing." He winked, then he and the other man disappeared around the corner.

"No, wait!" Tori shouted. "Take me with you!" Anything was preferable to being blown to bits. "Wil!" She grabbed a handful of dirt and threw it at his face. "Wake up! You got me into this, you asshole, so you damn well better get me out of it!"

Wil didn't move. Flames flickered behind the plastic curtain then began spreading across the tables, slowly at first, then shooting with more speed toward a small gas tank, the kind used for barbeque grills.

She watched helplessly as the entire tabletop quickly became engulfed in flames. Smoke billowed behind the curtain. It wouldn't take long before the lab was fully engulfed. Tori had no idea how much time she had left before the flames hit the gas tank.

One side of the plastic melted away, allowing smoke to billow out into the tunnel. She slipped off her coat, using it to cover her mouth and nose. At this rate, the smoke would probably kill her before the fire burned her alive. Or the explosion would, as T-Lo said, suck out all the oxygen, asphyxiating her within seconds.

"Nooo, please." She sank to her knees in front of the gate. *It can't end this way. Deck…*

Tori let her head fall back, opened her mouth…and screamed.

• • •

When Evan cuffed the guy and rolled him onto his back, Deck got in the guy's face. "How many others are down there? Is there a woman down there?"

The guy didn't answer, just stared up at him in a stupidly defiant gesture. *Yeah, we'll see about that.* Deck shouldered his shotgun then grabbed the man's hair in one hand and his Glock in the other. He yanked the guy's head back and shoved the gun's muzzle in his face. Even in the dim moonlight, the man's eyes went wider than silver dollars. "Again," Deck growled, "is there a woman down there?" He nodded. "How many others?"

"Three."

"Is T-Lo one of them?"

"Yeah."

"And the doc?" Another nod. Deck released the man's hair, holstering his weapon and unslinging his shotgun. "I'm heading in. Brett, you're with me. Evan, call it in."

"You got it." Brett handed Blaze's leash to Evan. "Watch him for me, will ya?"

Evan took the leash then pulled out his cell phone.

Deck put on Thor's mask then donned his own. In a perfect world, they'd all have on head-to-toe protective gear, but there was no time to go back to the vehicles and get suited up. "Let's go."

As a unit, he and Thor went through the door first. Smoke billowed up the stairs, obscuring whatever was below. Thor bounded past Deck just as a woman screamed. *Tori.* For a split second, he froze.

"What the fuck?" a man shouted. "Get it off! Get it *off*!"

Thor had found his mark.

Leading with the shotgun, Deck pounded down the

stairs. Brett's boots echoed closely behind him. At the bottom of the stairs were two tunnels. Following Thor's growls, he turned left into the first tunnel where the smoke was thicker. With his mask on, Thor was unable to bite but had T-Lo pinned to a wall. The other man hammered at Thor's head with a backpack.

"Fucking dog." T-Lo raised his arm, about to plunge a knife in Thor's neck.

Aiming high so he didn't hit his dog, Deck pulled the trigger. The side of T-Lo's face exploded in a mass of bloody tissue.

Ignoring the painful kick from the shotgun blast against his bad shoulder, Deck swung the muzzle to the other man, who dropped the backpack and threw up his hands.

"I give up, don't shoot! Don't shoot!"

"Brett!" Deck yelled over his shoulder, his voice muffled by the mask. "Get him out of here. I'm going after Tori."

"Make it quick," Brett shouted as he cuffed the guy. "This place is filling up fast."

"Take Thor with you." He didn't want his dog breathing in smoke or whatever else might be down here.

"Thor, come!" Brett called out, waving his arm at Thor, but the dog wouldn't leave Deck's side.

"Thor, go!" Deck pointed to the stairs. Thor sat, freezing like a canine statue as he looked up at Deck. His partner was taking a stand, refusing to leave his side.

So be it.

Deck raced farther into the tunnel, past the burning lab, with Thor on his heels. Ahead of them was a heavy iron gate, at the base of which was—*Tori*. Lying on his back near a hole in the floor was that asshole, Barnett, dead or unconscious. Deck didn't care which.

Keeping a wary eye on Barnett, he rushed to the gate, trying to open it, but it didn't move, didn't even jiggle. He dropped to his knees. "Tori!" Her body was slumped against the bars, unmoving, and she hadn't responded to his call. Was she dead? *Jesus, no.* "Tori!"

He set the shotgun on the ground. Through the bars, he cradled her head, tilting up her face. Tears streaked her cheeks. He didn't see any blood but couldn't tell if she was breathing. He touched two fingers to her neck, desperately feeling for a pulse at her carotid.

Thor stuck his muzzle through the bars, trying to lick her face even though his mask was still firmly strapped on.

Her eyelids fluttered then opened. "Deck?"

Though they were underground in a smoke-filled tunnel, his heart swelled with so much emotion he thought it would burst. "Yeah, honey. It's me. I need to get you out of here." She coughed, and he tugged the edge of her once-white doctor's coat up to cover her mouth. "Where's the key to this gate?" He looked around, searching the surrounding walls for a hook with a key on it.

"In the hole," he could swear she murmured.

Deck looked behind him at the hole with the ladder sticking out through the top. He clicked on his flashlight, shining the beam into the hole. It was at least twenty feet down.

Something popped in the lab, bursting from the flames. He had to try and put the fire out before more smoke filled the tunnels. Assuming it was a typical drug lab, there'd be gas tanks. If the fire got to the tanks, he didn't know which would kill them first, the smoke or the explosion.

Damn, but he didn't want to do this.

Working quickly, he unstrapped Thor's mask then pointed to the ladder. "Thor, get the key."

Without hesitation, Thor angled his body and began shimmying down the ladder backward.

Deck jumped to his feet, about to rush back to the lab for a fire extinguisher, water, or anything else he could use to put out the fire.

"Deck!" Tori shrieked, pointing behind him.

He turned but not in time. A hand locked on to his ankle. *Barnett*. Deck tried taking a step but started to fall face first. He reached out to cushion the fall. When his right hand hit the ground, splintering pain shot to his injured shoulder.

He gritted his teeth, pushing through it. Barnett landed on Deck's chest, straddling him. Before he could stop him, Barnett tore off Deck's respirator and began pounding on Deck's face with his fists.

He blocked the next blow with his forearms, his shoulder taking the brunt. More pain speared directly to the injury. He took a deep, smoke-filled breath, coughing as he shoved at Barnett's chest with his left arm. All those workouts in the gym paid off.

Barnett flew back, landing on his ass in the dirt. A look of undiluted rage contorted the man's features. Deck reached for the Glock in his holster and—

And nothing. He couldn't move his arm. It had gone completely numb.

While Deck scrambled to his feet, so did Barnett. Deck reached across his body with his left hand, trying to unholster his Glock. Before he could reach it, Barnett lunged, pinning Deck's arm to the bars of the gate.

"No!" Tori reached through the bars and grabbed one of Barnett's hands.

The three of them stood there struggling, Tori clinging to Barnett and Barnett pressing Deck back against the gate with his body.

As Barnett tugged something from one of his pockets, Tori jabbed a piece of metal into his neck, drawing blood.

"Dammit!" Using his thumb, Barnett popped the cap off a small bottle.

"Deck, watch out!" Before he could toss the contents in Deck's face, Tori grabbed it from Barnett's hand.

With what little strength he had left, Deck broke free of the grip Barnett had on his good arm and shoved him to the ground. He reached for his Glock, this time managing to get it unholstered.

Barnett pushed up from the dirt, his face twisted with rage. Deck hooked his left index finger around the trigger and squeezed off three rounds, triple-tapping Barnett dead center in the chest.

For two seconds, Barnett stood as if frozen in time before falling to his knees. He lowered his head as he looked down at his chest. The rage that had been on his face only moments ago was quickly replaced by shock. Then in slow motion, he face-planted in the dirt.

While they'd been fighting, the smoke had intensified. Deck shoved his gun into his belt, coughing more now. He turned to see Tori with the bottle still in her hand, her eyes wide. She dropped the bottle then stumbled back from the gate.

Deck couldn't see any gray powder on her face, but *oh God*.

He yanked his shirt up and over his head. "Tori, wipe it off! *Wipe it off!*" He stretched his arm through the bars, but she'd staggered too far from the gate for him to reach her. If that powder was what he thought it was, she didn't have much time.

Her eyes rolled back, and she fell to the ground.

"No!"

"Deck!" Brett rushed toward him, shotgun raised. "You okay? I got the fire under control, but those gas tanks are buckling and could still blow any second. We gotta— Oh, fuck." He lowered the gun.

The ladder rattled, telling Deck that Thor was on the way back up. "Help me get him up." He and Brett reached into the hole to help Thor up the rest of the way. Some feeling had returned to his right arm. Deck prayed the key was really down there and that Thor had found it.

His dog's ears appeared first. When the top of his head cleared the rim, he and Brett reached beneath Thor's front legs and pulled him up the rest of the way. "Thor?"

Thor coughed, opening his mouth and spitting out a large black key.

The relief at seeing the key was so great, it actually made his knees go weak. Deck grabbed the key and shoved it into the lock. He whipped open the gate and fell at Tori's side. Using his shirt, he wiped her face, concentrating on her nose and mouth first then her neck and chest. She was still breathing. Barely.

The sound of metal bending under pressure was like a gunshot.

"Deck, we gotta go," Brett warned again. "That tank's about to blow us to Kingdom Come."

Deck picked Tori up in his arms. "Get that medical bag from the trunk of her car," he shouted. "It's loaded with naloxone. And bring all the water you can find. I'll meet you up there." Again, he prayed. This was bad. *Really* bad. Dan Prince had nearly died from a minute exposure on his clothes. Tori may have gotten it directly in the face.

Brett took off running.

"Stay with me, Tori. Thor, let's go!"

Thor bounded ahead, turning back to make sure Deck was following.

He carried Tori through the tunnel, coughing and barely able to see through the smoky haze. Thor barked, and he followed the sound, racing past what was left of the lab. The propane tank on the back table creaked as it began to buckle. If he didn't get them out of there before that tank blew, Kingdom Come would have two new residents, three counting Thor.

Deck's heart jackhammered as he raced up the stairs. Tori's head lolled over the side of his arm. He couldn't tell if she was still breathing. Getting naloxone into her was the only thing that could save her.

By the time he got to the top step, he was coughing and breathing hard. Evan had relocated the two cuffed men a hundred yards from the entry to the bunker.

Deck took off running. Thor bounded ahead of him, leading the way.

Sirens wailed. Red-and-blue lights flashed as a wagon train of emergency vehicles turned off Poudre Canyon Road.

An explosion rocked the ground, powerful enough to make him stagger. Gently, he laid Tori on the ground. It was too dark to verify if she was breathing, so he rested his hand between her breasts, waiting to feel the rise and fall of her chest. He didn't.

Brett was there with Tori's bag and two gallon jugs of water. He set them down then opened the bag and shined a light inside.

"She's not breathing." Deck checked for a pulse at her carotid, relieved when he felt one. He tore the cap of one of the jugs of water then sloshed some on Tori's face, hands, and torso. After positioning her neck, he pinched her nose closed then began administering mouth-to-mouth. Beside him, Brett was already tearing the wrapper off an auto-injector. "Get more ready," Deck gasped between breaths, knowing one dose would never be enough.

Brett removed the safety clip then stuck the auto-injector into Tori's thigh.

Deck kept administering rescue breaths, praying she'd start breathing on her own. "Give her another," he ordered.

"You got it." Brett pushed the second dose into Tori's thigh.

Headlights illuminated the field as patrol cars and an ambulance rolled up. Seconds later, paramedics rushed over and started opening up cases.

"We'll take it from here." One of them placed a bag-valve mask over Tori's face and began squeezing the bag. "What was she exposed to?"

"Gray death." Deck watched as Tori's chest rose and fell, but not on her own.

The other medic nodded to the wrappers and Tori's

open bag. "Naloxone?"

"Yeah." Deck watched helplessly as the medics began an IV.

"Bring it with us," the first medic said. "We might need more than what we've got in the ambulance."

"Let's go," Deck vaguely heard someone say. His brain had gone numb with fear.

Like Dan had been, Tori was dying in front of him, and there wasn't a damned thing he could do about it.

CHAPTER THIRTY-FIVE

Tori woke to sunlight streaming through the window. She blinked, cringing and not quite ready for the overwhelming brightness.

"There's my girl." Someone squeezed her hand. *Dad.*

On the other side of the bed, Margo held her other hand. "You scared us." Margo swiped at a tear running down her cheek. "We thought…I thought…"

"So did I." She'd woken once, briefly, in the middle of the night with a pounding headache, nausea, and vomiting. The fingers of her right hand were achy and bruised. Now, she was just plain exhausted.

She tried remembering everything that had happened down in the tunnels. T-Lo. The fire. Wil. She didn't even know if he'd been arrested. Or killed. Despite everything, it was still difficult to process the havoc he'd wreaked. All those overdoses. *All those deaths.*

The last thing she remembered was getting gray death thrown in her face. After that, her memory was a blank slate. Except for Deck. *He came for me.*

She looked around the room, worried that he wasn't there. Had he or Thor been exposed? Were they okay?

Her dad's brows rose. "Looking for anyone in particular?"

"No," she lied. "I just—" Stupidly hoped Deck might come to see her. "Never mind."

"He was here," Margo said, sporting an impish smile.

"Deck, I mean."

Her heart gave a little flutter that reflected on the heart rate monitor visible just over Margo's shoulder. But she shouldn't get excited just because he'd shown up in her hospital room. "He probably just wanted to take a statement from me, to find out what happened with Wil before he got there." It didn't mean anything else between them had changed.

Margo gave her the same look she'd always given her when they were kids, the one that said her sister thought she was clueless. "Tori, get real."

"No, you don't understand." Her dad probably hadn't filled Margo in. "Deck and I aren't together."

Her sister made a scoffing sound. "You could have fooled *me*."

Her dad swallowed hard. "When they brought you in here, you weren't breathing." He took a deep breath, steadying himself. "Deck never left your side. Not once. Even when the nurses threatened to call security on him."

"You should have seen him." Margo laughed. "First, he told the guards to back off, then he told them to *fuck* off."

"Margo!" Her dad threw Margo a stern look of disapproval.

"Well, he did." Margo crossed her arms.

This time, it was her dad who laughed. "That, he did."

Again, Tori glanced at the monitor. The blips and numbers indicated her pathetic heart was back to a sad and steady rhythm. "It still doesn't mean anything."

Her dad's eyes locked with hers, conveying everything she couldn't verbalize. "Do you want it to?"

Yes. God, yes. But it wasn't meant to be, and she had to

accept that. There was no sense getting all worked up about something that would never happen.

"You know," her dad began, "your mother and I didn't see eye to eye on everything. No two people ever do. Right up until the end, we were as different as night and day. There were four things that kept us together. Love, respect, compromise, and acceptance." He leaned his forearms on the bedrail, giving her a pointed look. "From what I've seen and heard, you and Deck have the first two down. Just not the third or the fourth. Not yet, anyway. Those are the hardest ones to get right, but if you want something — or *someone* — badly enough, you'll walk through a firestorm to get it."

He let his words sink in. He'd always given her and Margo sage advice, but this...

"I don't know if I have the courage it takes to walk through that storm." A lump formed in the back of her throat. Margo squeezed her hand in a show of sisterly support. "I don't think I could handle losing Deck."

"Can you handle living *without* him?" he asked.

That was the question, one she couldn't answer.

Liar.

"Don't forget, sis," Margo said. "*He* almost lost *you*. After last night, I think he has a pretty good idea of what you're going through."

She hadn't considered that. Then again, she didn't even know how he felt about her. He'd never said he loved her.

Another long moment of silence followed before her dad spoke again. "I've always told you girls it's your life to live as you choose. I know you'll choose wisely. I'd just hate to see you miss out on a good thing. Even if he is a DEA agent." He patted her hand. "Consider this food for thought from your dad who loves you very, very much."

Tori sniffled. "Thanks, Dad." She turned to her sister. "Thanks, Margo."

"For what?" Margo asked. "I don't have any sage advice."

"For *being* here. You guys are my family, my rock. You've never failed me."

"Stop." Margo swiped at another tear rolling down her cheek. "And speaking of family, Zach and the kids were here waiting for you to wake up. They went home to make you cookies."

"Chocolate chip?" she asked hopefully.

"Naturally."

Her stomach took that moment to growl, making them all laugh and easing some of the tension.

"Uh, Dad has something else to tell you. Tell her, Dad." Margo nodded.

"Tell me what?"

"Deck brought me something. Something very unexpected." He began stroking his chin, and his eyes took on a faraway look.

Tori waited for him to tell her what Deck had brought him. The suspense was killing her. "What was it?"

"My pharmaceutical license. He got it back for me."

She looked from her dad to her sister, knowing she ought to say something, but no words came to mind. "That was a very thoughtful gesture," was all she could think to say.

"Thoughtful?" Another *duh* look from Margo. "It's an *amazing* gesture, and you know it."

She *did* know it but didn't dare acknowledge any

possible hidden meaning behind what Deck had done for her dad. "Dad," Tori said, watching him still pensively stroking his chin. "Do you *want* it back?"

"I don't think so. I'm happy teaching my music class. Deck must have pulled a lot of strings, but I did appreciate the gesture. Retirement's been good to me, and I don't think I want to come out of it. Besides, I've just started seeing a student in one of my classes. She wanted to meet you, so she's stopping by later."

Wait. Her dad was dating?

She looked at Margo, who shrugged, telling her she already knew. Tori clapped a hand to her mouth, not certain she could handle any more revelations in such a short period of time. And he'd said "student." Hopefully, he hadn't hooked up with a young twenty-something who, one day, might be hers and Margo's stepmother.

Suzie breezed into the room, carrying a fresh bag of what Tori assumed was fluids to keep her hydrated. "Good morning, sunshine." Her friend leaned down and kissed Tori's cheek, hesitating a moment before pulling away. Her eyes were glossy as she sniffled. "You really scared us. You scared *me*."

Again, Tori's throat clogged with emotion. *I'm lucky to be alive*.

Suzie hooked the bag of fluids on the IV pole. "Doctors and nurses have been asking about you all night, and there's a crowd of people in the waiting room to see you." Oddly, Suzie didn't mention Wil, so she assumed her friend already knew he wasn't coming back.

"Is Deck waiting to see me?" she asked, holding her breath.

"Deck?" Suzie waived her hand in the air. "No. That man would never waste time standing in line. If he was here, he'd barrel through like a steam roller and mow down anyone who got in his way. Did they tell you he almost punched out the hospital's entire security team?"

Margo and her dad nodded.

"We told her," Margo said.

Heavy, booted footsteps echoed outside the room. A moment later, Brett and Evan came in. Brett carried a glass vase of pink tulips. Evan held out a potted bromeliad.

"There she is." Brett set the vase on the rolling cart. "You scared the sh— Er, I mean, you scared us all to death. Especially, Deck," he added with a grin.

Evan put the plant on the window ledge. "Glad to see you're back in the land of the living, Doc Tori."

"Thanks. And how did you know I like bromeliads?" she asked, thinking it was a strange gift but loving it just the same.

Evan shrugged. "Deck said you'd like it."

"*Deck* said that?" Most men couldn't remember the color of a woman's eyes, let alone something as obscure to the male species as a woman's preference for air plants.

Her sister pursed her lips, shooting Tori yet another *duh* look. "Are you going to introduce us?"

"Oh, right. Sorry." She made quick introductions, then Brett and Evan exchanged looks, saying nothing but looking as if they wanted to.

Her father stood, yawning. "It's been a long night. Would everyone like some coffee? I'm buying."

"Sure, that'd be great." Evan nodded emphatically.

"C'mon, Margo." Her dad motioned for her sister to go

with him, a sign that he knew Brett and Evan wanted to discuss something privately with Tori.

"Are you here to arrest me?" she asked as soon as her family had left.

"About that," Brett said. "We never really thought you were the rat."

"Neither did Deck," Evan added, sitting in one of the chairs.

"How is he?" She hoped she didn't sound as desperate for information about him as she felt. "I mean, how is his shoulder and his ribs?"

"Better." Brett nodded. "Although he took a beating down in the tunnels."

"A beating?" She didn't remember that.

"Before he took out Barnett," Evan said, leaving her wondering what exactly "took out" meant, "the two of them had a real wrestling match. At one point, his shoulder got wrenched and went totally numb. He saved your life, by the way."

Tori sat up straighter, instantly regretting it as her head spun. "Is he okay? His dislocation was bad to begin with. Any additional stress on the joint could have lasting implications."

"He's fine," Brett reassured her. "But you can ask him yourself. He's on his way over."

"He is?" Again, she sat up, this time ignoring her spinning senses as hope flared in her chest then slowly began to die. "Aside from the investigation, I'm not really sure he wants to talk to me about anything."

"I don't think you have to worry about that," Brett said. "If he didn't have an interview this morning, he'd be here right now."

"Interview?"

"Deck's boss, ASAC Rivera," Brett continued, "is retiring. Deck applied for the ASAC position. It'll take him out of the field and put him behind a desk. It's a *safe* job."

Tori's eyes widened at the implication. *A safe job.*

"He's doing this for *you*." Evan sat in the other chair. "When a man switches jobs for a woman…well, you do the math."

"Oh, my." Her dad's words came roaring back to her. *Compromise. Acceptance.* Loving and respecting Deck also meant she had to compromise and accept him for who and what he was. He didn't want a desk job. She knew that. He really was doing this for *her*.

"Seriously." Brett shook his head. "Never thought I'd see the day."

Her chest tightened with a mixture of joy *and* misery. "I can't let him do this. It's not what he wants."

"I think *you're* what he wants," Evan said quietly.

Wanting him, being with him would mean accepting *everything* about him. Including the risk that came with his job.

"Hi."

Deck stood in the doorway, holding a giant potted orchid brimming with magenta flowers. His face was covered with light bruises. Beside him, Thor wagged his tail, his long tongue hanging from the side of his mouth.

A warm, soothing calm surrounded her, and in that instant, she knew. Living without Deck wouldn't be living at all. If things went the way she hoped they would, she was staring at her future.

• • •

"Gotta go." Brett stood and headed for the door. "Those fires are really kicking up again in the Springs."

"Yeah, me, too." Evan took Brett's cue. "I gotta go do… something. Later, Tori."

Both men smacked Deck affectionately on his good shoulder on their way out the door. They were the best friends a guy could ask for. Good friends knew when to get lost.

He searched Tori's face, taking in her weary eyes. Her hair draped past her shoulders, glinting dark red in the sunlight. She'd been through hell but was still the most beautiful woman he'd ever seen.

There were so many things to be said. Too bad his tongue was tied in knots. One look at her, and the heartfelt speech he'd prepared went right out the window.

"Are you just going to stand there and stare at me all day?" she asked.

I could easily do just that.

He set the orchid next to the plant he'd instructed Brett to pick up then realized his mistake. Now, he had nothing to do with his hands. *A tactical blunder.* Leading a team of federal agents into an op with armed bad guys was a piece of cake, but this… He shoved his hands in his pockets.

"Hi, Thor." She held out her hand to scratch his ears but couldn't quite reach them over the bed rail.

Deck found the release lever on the bed. "Up," he said to Thor, who rose gracefully on his hind legs, resting his paws gently on the bed then landing wet kisses on Tori's cheek. Deck was jealous because *he* wanted to be the one to kiss her cheeks. Dogs had it easy. Unconditional love was their thing. If only human relationships were that straightforward.

She nuzzled the side of Thor's face, laughing as he continued licking her chin. "I missed you, too, Thor." The sound of her laughter did all kinds of mushy things to his heart.

"How are you feeling?" In reality, he already knew her complete medical condition and prognosis. Since the moment she'd been rolled into the ER, he'd been tracking her treatment, meds, and recovery, much to the annoyance of the hospital staff.

"Better. Thanks to you, I'm told."

He shrugged. "If it weren't for Thor, I never would have gotten you out of that cell in time. He went into that hole and found the key."

"You're kidding?"

"Nope. Ladders are his thing."

"In that case"—she kissed the top of Thor's head—"thank you, too."

Thor *woofed*.

"How's your shoulder?" Her expression had turned to one of worry. "I heard you got it banged up. Along with your face."

"Good." When he tugged the small plastic bottle of ibuprofen from his pocket, her brows rose. "I don't go anywhere without these. At least, not for a while. Go figure."

"Go figure." She smiled. At least they were talking.

He stuffed the bottle back into his pocket. "I guess this

is a compromise."

"Compromise can be good." She bit her lower lip. "Don't you think?"

He nodded, sensing the undercurrent of the conversation. They weren't really talking about pills anymore. "I'll admit that with proper oversight and due caution, even opioids have an important place in medicine." When her jaw dropped, he held up his hand. "Bet you never thought you'd hear me say that."

Her eyes glimmered with amusement before sobering. "And I have to admit that some doctors are too liberal in prescribing them, especially without adequate follow-up."

For a long moment, they looked at each other, absorbing the implication of their admissions. Deck hadn't thought it possible for them to find a way back to each other, but this was a solid step in the right direction. It *was* a compromise, each of them admitting that the other was right *and* wrong.

As much as he wanted to rush in and cut to what he really wanted to say—*I love you*—they weren't there yet. "I, uh, wanted to be here when you woke up, but I had a lot of things to get done this morning." First and foremost, another bath for Thor to make sure he didn't have any residual gray death on his coat, followed by the most important interview of Deck's life. "C'mon, Thor. Down."

His dog lay down next to the bed and sighed.

"I understand." Tori averted his gaze. "I'm sure there was a lot of follow-up work to do after what happened. Reports to write, bosses to update."

"About that." Deck took the chair closest to the bed. "Wil is dead."

Tori momentarily shut her eyes. "I figured that might be the case. I still can't believe it. I had no idea. If only I'd—"

"Hey." He reached for her hand, entwining their fingers. "Don't beat yourself up over it. He was smart, kept a low profile. Turns out he spent all his drug money abroad. Investigating people like him is what I do, but *I* didn't see it, either." Until it was almost too late.

For what seemed like the hundredth time in the last twelve hours, his stomach hardened at the absolute fear he'd experienced not knowing if Tori would live or die. It was a feeling he never wanted to go through again.

She looked at their joined hands, and her expression turned wistful. Thinking she was uncomfortable with the contact, he released her, sitting back in the chair. "T-Lo is dead, too. We took his goons into custody, and they're singing like birds about the entire operation. The warden and half the medical staff at FCI Sheridan have been suspended pending termination for not reporting a number of deaths and overdoses. We also got a search warrant for the co-op property and Wil's house. The underground lab is destroyed. It'll take a hazmat team a month to clean it up. So far, there's over a million dollars in cash inside Wil's condo, and that's probably just the start. We're checking for offshore accounts and getting warrants for his properties abroad."

"What will happen to all that money?" She shifted, obviously trying to find a more comfortable position.

"Let me." He stood and adjusted the pillows behind her back and head, inadvertently grazing his fingers along her collarbone. She shivered, and he couldn't tell if it was a good sign or a bad one. "Better?"

She nodded. "Thanks."

"Some of seized drug money goes into the DOJ's asset forfeiture fund and stays there. Most will come back to the DEA to fund various agency programs. Eventually, all his seized assets will be sold. It'll take some doing, but I'm going to do everything I can to give 100 percent of it to teen rehab centers around Denver."

"That's a wonderful idea." She rested her hand on his.

Her touch sent another surge of hope through his veins. When she began pulling away, he again interlaced their fingers. *Now or never.* "I'm sorry I lashed out at you that night in the park. You were trying to do what you thought was best for me. Until last night, I didn't understand what it was like for you. Watching you nearly die and there was nothing I could do to stop it."

His throat constricted with so much emotion he could barely choke out his next words. "I've seen overdoses before," he continued, "but I've never watched someone I'm in love with go through it."

Tori's eyes glistened. When she rolled her lips inward then looked away, his heart sank like an elevator hitting the basement floor. This wasn't going well at all. He was about to lose her all over again, and he'd only just gotten started on what little of his practiced speech he could remember.

"Deck," she began, "I—"

"Wait," he interrupted, determined to tell her everything before she kicked him out of her room and out of her life for good. "One of the reasons I wasn't here when you woke up was because I was being interviewed for a new position."

"Deck—"

He held up his hand. "It's an ASAC position, a desk job. I won't know for a couple more days, but I think I have a real shot at it. I won't be working with Thor, though."

Thor lifted his head and uttered a mournful whine that made Deck feel as if he were betraying his best friend.

Tori's forehead creased. "What will happen to him?"

"Like any human partner, he's a DEA asset. He'll be paired up with another agent." Before making his decision, Deck had thought long and hard about it. It would kill him to lose Thor, but Tori was right. He *had* been living in the past. Taking a promotion would be a giant step forward. "I don't want to lose you. If that means taking a desk job, I'll—"

"Don't take it." She shook her head adamantly. "You love being in the field and working with Thor. I can't imagine you without him or him without you. I don't want you to do this for me. If we're going to make this work, we have to accept each other for who and what we are. Good, bad, or dangerous."

Make this work? "What are you saying?" he whispered, thinking he'd misheard her and praying he hadn't.

"I'm saying I love you. *All* of you, and I don't want you to change a thing. Including your job. That's who you are. It's *what* you are." She laid her hand on the side of his face, gazing at him with so much love he felt as if he could leap a twenty-story building. "Just promise me something."

"Anything." He meant it. For her, he'd walk right into a tornado.

"Please do your best not to get shot at again or jump in front of any more pickup trucks."

He laughed, his heart brimming with more love than he

thought possible. He stood then leaned over and kissed her, wanting to brand her so deeply with his love that she'd always be his, every minute, every hour, and every day for the rest of their lives.

"Woops."

"Should we come back later?"

He broke the kiss to find Tori's dad and Deck's mom coming through the door. "Mom? What are you doing here?" That's when he noticed Craig Sampson's hand resting affectionately at his mother's back.

"Deck?" Surprise showed on his mother's face. "What are *you* doing here?"

"Susan." Craig's gray brows bunched. "You never told me your son was a DEA agent. And your last name's not Decker."

His mother's equally gray brows rose. "It's my maiden name, and today is only our second date. Eventually, I would have gotten around to it."

Deck looked at Tori, seeing the surprise and shock he was experiencing clearly mirrored on her face.

Their parents burst out laughing.

"Tori, this is Susan Albright." Craig clasped Deck's mother's hand and tugged her toward the bed. "This is my daughter, Tori."

"So nice to meet you, dear," his mother said. "I'm so glad you're feeling better. And you"—she pointed an admonishing finger at Deck—"you've been keeping secrets from your mother again. Like the fact that you *do* have a girlfriend."

When he caught Tori struggling not to laugh, Deck dragged a hand down his face, not bothering to suppress a loud groan.

Thor stood and panted, smiling and wagging his tail furiously, as if wanting to be part of the action.

"Craig," his mom said, hooking her hand in the crook of Craig's arm. "We should leave our kids alone. I think we interrupted some serious canoodling."

"I have to agree with you." He patted her arm. "Let's let them get back to it. Tori, Deck…we'll check in later."

Deck watched his mother and Craig walk from the room. He blinked at Tori, still in disbelief. "What just happened?"

Tori burst into laughter. "You really should close your mouth before your jaw hits the floor." She crooked her finger at him. "Then you should come over here and *canoodle* with me."

"That I can do." He sat on the edge of the bed and kissed Tori more deeply than before, leaving them both breathless and gasping for air. "I could canoodle with you all day."

"Promise?" she asked.

"Promise." He reached into the thigh pocket of his cargo pants and pulled out a small packet of purple tissue paper tied with a gold ribbon. "I have something for you."

"It's not my birthday." She unwrapped the package, slowly peeling off the ribbon and parting the tissue paper. "My charm bracelet!" The smile she gave him had enough wattage to light up the city of Denver. "I completely forgot about it. Where did you find it?"

"In the hospital parking lot." He took it from her and hooked it onto her wrist. "I hope you don't mind. I added a couple of new charms. A dog, that was Thor's idea. And a heart. So no matter where you go, you'll never be without my love."

She pulled him down to her, whispering, "And you'll never be without mine."

The kiss she gave him told Deck everything he needed to know. He was happier than he'd ever been in his life, and he planned on spending the rest of his days this way.

In the arms of the woman he loved.

ACKNOWLEDGMENTS

New York City Rescue Paramedic John Pike, for your candid and spot-on insight into the treatment of opioid overdoses. Dr. Jamil Rizqalla, Associate Director of Emergency Medicine, Montefiore Nyack Hospital, for your assistance with the treatment of ODs in the ER. Dr. Rebecca Pappalardo, for all things medical and all those gin and tonics that kept me going! Lane Fire Authority Engineer/Paramedic Jeremy Howland, for sharing your field experience. My friends at the DEA, for your invaluable assistance with agency procedure and protocol. Rachel Meintz, Director of Security Investigations, UCHealth Aurora, for setting me straight on Colorado hospital lingo. Kayla Gray, hands down the best critique partner on the planet. My Street Team, for getting the word out. Last, but by no means least, my extremely patient editor, Heather Howland, for the many emails we sent back and forth to get this one just right!

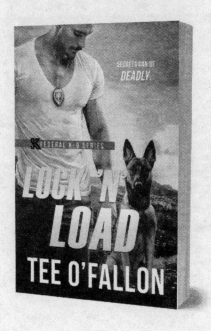